# THE AMULET OF FORTUNE

*Susannah Broome*

# THE AMULET
## of
# FORTUNE

*Doubleday & Company, Inc.*
*Garden City, New York*
*1978*

Library of Congress Cataloging in Publication Data

Broome, Susannah.
The amulet of fortune.

I. Title.
PZ4.B8734Am    1978    [PR6052.R5828]    823′.9′14
ISBN: 0-385-13317-0
Library of Congress Catalog Card Number 77–83934

THE AMULET OF FORTUNE

*Part 1*

# PENVARRION

# 1

I WAS BORN within sight and sound of the sea so, as a child, I was never afraid of it. Only after I went to live at Tregedon did it seem to me that the waves dashing themselves against the great cliffs of Tregedon Head held a menace in their thunderous roar.

I would lie awake in the raftered bedroom and feel the old house shake under the battering winds which swept in from the Atlantic to spend themselves upon that exposed length of Cornish coast, and I would shiver, dreading that yet another ship might founder in such a storm. Always after these gales and monumental seas some wreck would be found below the headland, and at times, as I lay listening, it seemed to me that my own life was a shipwreck too. But all that was long after I left Penvarrion.

At Penvarrion the sea was only a distant murmur for the house lay in a hollow between two headlands and was sheltered from the worst winds. Tall trees, rare enough on that part of the coast, surrounded it and gave shelter to the house and grounds. The walled garden was a peaceful place, filled with roses and herbs and peaches and nectarines growing espalier fashion against sun-warmed stone. Looking back now, I think that the morning in early June when we were together in the garden was the last time I was truly happy at Penvarrion.

There were seven of us. Miss Pringle, my governess—though I was nearly eighteen and had left the schoolroom behind, because I had been motherless since I was six Miss Pringle remained as my companion chaperone. Esmond's sister, Laura, was there too, with her husband, Paul. They had not long been married and had recently re-

3

turned from a visit to the Great Exhibition in Hyde Park, and this morning they had driven over to see us, eager to tell us all they had seen. Esmond had ridden over with them and now he stood beside me, tall and fair, handsomer than ever in his dark blue riding coat and white buckskins. When he turned and smiled a shiver of happiness ran through me for I was overwhelmingly in love with him, and sometimes I dared to hope that he loved me in return. Two other callers were present, the Reverend Charles Barlow, our newly appointed vicar and his unmarried sister, Miss Gertrude Barlow. The Reverend Charles was young and good looking and had recently been appointed by my father, for the living of Penvarrion was in the gift of his family.

"It was a sight I will never forget," Laura was saying. "We were into this great glass palace very early, you must know. By nine A.M., wasn't it, Paul?" and she glanced at her pleasant-faced young husband for confirmation.

"Yes, Laura, we were fortunate enough to be among those allowed in for the opening ceremony. There were only twenty-five thousand invited guests and ticket holders, and we were there to await the arrival of Her Majesty the Queen. Prince Edward and the Princess Royal accompanied her. The Prince Consort and the Queen's ministers and the foreign ambassadors and the executive committee and all the officials to do with the Exhibition were waiting there too, to receive Her Majesty."

"Oh, Kate, such a flourish of trumpets sounded," Laura broke in to say, "and a glorious fountain played in the center and the throne was under a magnificent blue-and-silver canopy. After the report and the speeches and the prayers from the Archbishop, the massed choirs sang. You cannot imagine what the sound of it was like. The choirs of the Chapel Royal Westminster Abbey, St. Paul's and Windsor Chapel, accompanied by members of the Royal Academy of Music and with a great organ of over four thousand pipes performed Handel's 'Halleluiah Chorus.'" Laura sighed. "It was so thrilling it forced me to tears."

I sighed too.

"I wish I could have been there to see it with you. But Papa has promised to take me to London as soon as ever he returns from his voyage to the West Indies. And then we shall visit the Crystal Palace together."

"When do you expect Mr. Carew home again?" the vicar enquired.

"Within a matter of a few days. I understand he left Barbados over two weeks ago, so his arrival at Falmouth should be expected soon." I gave another sigh. "I shall be so glad to see him."

"I am sure you will," Miss Barlow said. She was by no means as handsome as her brother, for her face was long and large-featured and her hair mousey fair. But her eyes were kind and thoughtful and her manner so pleasant, one could not help but like her. "This is a big house in which to be alone."

I smiled, thinking of our many servants, and of Miss Pringle and the frequent visitors who came to stay or just to call upon us. I caught Esmond's glance and saw the trace of a smile about his thin sensitive mouth and I guessed what he was thinking.

"Oh, I am never lonely," I said. And nor was I, although I was my father's only child and he had been widowed twelve years. During those years we had grown very close, and he had loved and indulged me in every possible way. Perhaps too much. Sometimes I felt I could scarcely bear to leave him even to marry Esmond, and yet I knew that when the day came that Esmond should ask my father for my hand in marriage the joy of going to him would outweigh the sadness at leaving my adored father for I could imagine no future without Esmond.

The door in the wall clicked and the figure of Borlase, the butler, appeared within the opening. He walked slowly and ponderously, as was his habit along the graveled path to where we sat in the shade of the acacia tree. On the salver in his hand was a letter and almost before I had taken it from Borlase I knew that it was from my father. Borlase nodded as if to say, "Yes, I know who has sent this," and with a little bow turned back up the path and left me gazing in happy expectancy at the envelope.

"Will you please excuse me," I said and moved away down the garden. As I slit the envelope the sun shone warm on my back and the scent of Rosa Mundi with its drooping heads of red and white

5

filled the air. A thrush was calling from a tree somewhere nearby. The murmur of voices, Laura's light laugh and the deeper one of Esmond's mingled and then everything around me faded from sight and sound as I read, and in a daze of bewilderment, reread my father's letter.

It was dated mid-May and was written from the great plantation in Barbados which had come to him upon my mother's death.

"My dearest little Kitty," it said. "By the time you receive this letter I shall be on my way home to Penvarrion and shortly reunited with my own dear daughter. If I could have written to break this news earlier to you, I would have done so, for I know that what I have to tell you will come with something of a shock. That was not possible so, now I hasten to give you the news that yesterday I was married to Mrs. Lambert, the widow of my old friend, Edgar Lambert, who owned the plantation next to Belle Tout. Mrs. Lambert and I have at all times retained a sincere friendship and respect for one another, and this has now grown into a deep affection. She, like myself, has known loss and loneliness, and so, with this mutual sympathy between us we have decided to marry. She has a daughter, Amy, the same age as yourself and a son a few years younger. I feel that our association can only be of benefit to you, my dear Kitty, for you will gain a stepsister and stepbrother, as well as a kind and loving stepmother. Because we made our final decision quickly before I returned to England I could not tell you this news before. I know that you will wish your new stepmama and myself the happiness we both hope to share with you, and with Amy and Oliver. Until we are reunited, dear daughter, I remain,

Your affectionate father,
Gilbert Carew.

I was too stunned to move. I could only stand staring down at the letter in my hand, while slowly, the full meaning of everything penetrated my mind.

My father had married again.

But why should he not? I was glad for him. How could it be other-

6

wise, if I loved him and wanted only that he should be happy? I had heard him speak often of Mrs. Lambert, and I remembered that she had two children. Indeed, I had a faint memory of Mr. Lambert, who had stayed with us a few years ago when on a visit to England. A kind quiet man, dark-haired and sallow-faced.

Then why should I feel so shattered, so lost, as if suddenly my familiar world was gone. As if the letter I held in my hand contained ominous news, rather than joyful tidings?

A new stepmother; a stranger in the house who would hope to take my mother's place. And a stepsister, someone with whom I would share my life, my home, my possessions.

Determinedly I checked such thoughts. My father was happy; he had found a life companion after the long sad years since my mother's death. Should I not be glad that this was so for I would be leaving him alone if Esmond should declare his love for me, as I longed for him to do. If my father had married again, it was surely all for the best.

I turned and saw that Esmond had come to stand beside me. He said anxiously,

"Katy? Is all well with Mr. Carew? You looked so strange standing here, staring into space. And you are dreadfully pale. I hope you have not received bad news of any kind."

Esmond had called me Katy since we were children together and now the kind note in his voice brought me to the verge of tears.

"It is only good news. My father has remarried and returns home with—with Mrs. Lambert, my new stepmother and her two children."

I heard Esmond's swift intake of breath and felt the clasp of his hand tighten on my own. It was a moment before he spoke.

"My dear Katy—I am as surprised as you must be. You have had no inkling of this? I am sure the news must come as a great shock to you." He hesitated, frowning down at me. "You are happy about it?"

I looked away from the eyes that were the same dark shade of blue as my father's. Sometimes I thought I loved Esmond especially because he resembled Papa for they were both tall and fair-haired, although my father's hair was graying now. In disposition they were not alike for Esmond had an altogether livelier nature than my father,

7

who was quiet and reserved, and whereas Esmond was gay in company, Papa was apt to be withdrawn.

"I am happy if my father is happy," I answered slowly. "I am sure he will be. Mrs. Lambert sounds a kind and understanding person, for, as my father has written, she too has known a sad loss and more recently than he." I paused before adding, "It will seem strange to have a stepsister. She is of the same age as myself. I hope that we shall be friends."

Esmond released my hand, his blue eyes reassuring as he smiled down at me.

"She will love you. Who could help doing so?"

I felt the warm glow that always came when Esmond said something nice to me or paid me a compliment.

"Thank you."

"Does your father write to say when he will arrive home?"

"No. Only that he would be at sea by the time I received this letter. There will be a great deal to do before he comes. I must speak to Mrs. Borlase for as housekeeper it will be her place to see to the preparations." I glanced toward the acacia tree. "I must tell everyone the news."

It was like looking at a painting or one of the new daguerreotypes. Laura was wearing her crinoline dress of emerald-green plaid with a narrow frill at the neck. On her dark hair was a tiny hat with a flat crown and narrow brim. Paul gazed down admiringly at her, while Miss Barlow, somewhat drab in a brown dress with a round flat collar of ecru muslin leaned forward to listen to Laura speaking. Miss Pringle, tall and slight in a dress of gray patterned wool sat with folded hands, a faint smile on her mouth, while the vicar sat very upright and handsome beside her, nodding as if in agreement to all that was said.

As I stared at them I had the strangest feeling. I seemed to be looking at some past scene, a moment caught and held in time that would never come again. A sense of unbearable sadness came over me, and I wanted to turn and cling to Esmond, as if, with his arm about me I would feel safe.

Safe from what? No danger threatened here, on this perfect morn-

8

ing of early summer. It was only fear of the unknown, of the changes that were to come with the arrival of strangers that gave me such a sense of nervous apprehension.

The news of my father's remarriage caused considerable excitement and comment to my visitors, but as we knew so little about Mrs. Lambert speculation was soon exhausted, and after a short space of time the vicar and his sister said good-by. Soon afterward Laura declared that she and Paul must also leave and would not stay to luncheon, as I pressed them to do.

"You will have plenty to do when we have gone," she said, as she kissed me good-by. "I hope all will turn out well, Katy. Things are bound to be different for you, but it's not to say they won't be just as pleasant. Come and see Paul and me soon. The garden is all being replanned and should look very well this summer."

She and Paul had only been married a year and their new home and its gardens were a constant thrill to them both.

"I shall look forward to it," I said. "Good-by, Laura."

I waved from the steps and watched the carriage move away up the curving drive. The approach to Penvarrion was from the road that ran along the top of the hill, and the house, lying in the hollow, was completely out of sight of it. The church and the village were a mile or so along the road.

Esmond was the last to leave, and I walked with him to the stables where he had left his horse. Sorrel, my beautiful mare, pushed her head over the door and whinnied at the sight of me, and we went down to stroke her satin-brown neck while Harry Martin, the groom, saw after Esmond's chestnut. Horses were my great love, as they had been my mother's. As a child I had trotted alongside her tall horse on my first small pony, but when I was six my beautiful brave reckless mother had been killed, breaking her neck at one of the cruel Cornish walls that starred the moors. It had been the greatest tragedy of my father's life and, in a lesser more childish way, mine. Life was never the same for either of us after that radiantly happy presence had gone from Penvarrion.

I tried not to think that now my father was to be consoled. I must not feel resentful that someone was coming to take my mother's place. No one could ever do that. I knew my father too surely to feel there could be comparisons. My mother had been dead these many years, and he deserved to find other happiness and affection in life.

"You are pensive," Esmond said. "Understandably. I wish I could have stayed to luncheon but my father expects me home—some business matter I must attend to." He took my hand in his. "It will be your birthday next month, Katy. I shall come and speak to your father then. You can guess upon what matter."

I colored under his intent gaze.

"I am not sure."

He smiled.

"I think you are. But it was your father's wish that I should say nothing to you until his return." He broke off as Martin came forward with Duke, Esmond's horse. Martin stood respectfully aside while Esmond took his leave and then, he sprang up into the saddle and with a coin to the groom and a wave of his riding crop he was gone, clattering over the stones and out of sight up the back drive.

At the house Miss Pringle was waiting for me, her thin face anxious.

"When will you break the news to the servants?" she enquired as we walked toward the dining room. Once she had seemed so tall and upright, now she stooped. Or was it that I had grown tall myself? I was above average height for a girl and strongly made, with more curves than I cared about. My mother had been tall, too, and dark as I was, but my eyes were not sparkling brown, as hers had been, but of a gray so dark that sometimes they were almost an olive-green shade.

"I will tell Borlase and Mrs. Borlase after luncheon, and they can inform the rest of the staff. I must tell Hester myself."

Hester was my old nurse and she had cared for me all my life, as she had cared for my mother too, when she was a girl. Now Hester was very old, but she kept busy helping to mend the linen and despite her failing eyesight, knitting endless fleecy shawls for us all and warm woolen gloves.

Miss Pringle shook her head.

"I hope the news of your father's remarriage will not upset the

10

staff. Servants do not always take kindly to strangers coming into a household. Oh dear, it has given me quite a turn myself. So *very* unexpected, though of course, I can only wish your dear father every happiness in his choice."

Perhaps because we were both more disturbed than we cared to admit to one another the meal was unduly silent. Borlase, waiting upon us, sent doubtful glances in our direction as if wondering to himself what could have caused so thoughtful an atmosphere.

A week went past, a week in which the entire household seemed to seethe in the excitement of my father's remarriage. There were endless questions to which I had no answer, demands for instructions which I could not give. All I could do was to ask Mrs. Borlase to arrange matters as she thought fit, preparing the best bedroom in the west wing for my stepmother with its adjacent dressing room for my father and a pretty guest room near my own for my new stepsister and another room for Amy's brother. We were all on edge, awaiting news from Falmouth, and at last a message came to my father's steward, Harry Trembath, that the ship had docked and he was to arrange for the carriage to be sent to fetch my father and his party home the next day.

Now none of us could rest. The house bloomed with flowers sent up by Sam Pleydell, the gardener and lodgekeeper while Barney, his son, scurried to and fro with pots and plants from the greenhouses. Mrs. Pleydell arrived as extra help to Mrs. Hubbard, the cook, and Violet and Bertha, the maids, went around dusting where there was no dust and polishing where everything already shone.

And I? I was excited too and on edge as everyone else and nervous and more fearful than perhaps any of them. It was this feeling of being unable to sit or even to stand still that drove me out into the garden and then beyond the grounds, passing through the wicket gate that led to the steep path used by the members of the household when they walked to the church.

It was a fine morning and warm for it was the beginning of June. When I reached the top of the hill I glimpsed the sea, gently blue, under a summer haze. I walked slowly into the churchyard and along the flagged path toward my mother's grave, and when I reached it I

11

stood looking down at the gray headstone and the inscription carved upon it.

"In Memory of Isabella Carew, dearly beloved wife of Gilbert Carew"
it said, and then the date
"Born 1810—died 1840."

I felt a pricking of tears behind my eyelids, thinking of my beautiful mother and how brief her life had been. I wondered why I had come here like this on such a morning. Not to be morbid or sad or to repine. To pay tribute, perhaps. To hope that somewhere my mother's loving spirit held guardianship over me? Guardianship against what, I thought, and felt a curious chill come over me; as if beyond the honeysuckle and dog roses twining along the low stone wall, danger lurked.

I turned sharply at a sound and saw the figure of a man tall and immobile, standing a few paces beyond me. He was so still, so silent that for a moment I could only stare at him while my beating heart raced in sudden alarm. Then he took a step forward removing his hat as he did so, and with a slight inclination of his head said, in a deep toned voice,

"Miss Kate? Do you not remember me?"

He was a stranger and yet familiar. I gazed up into the strong dark face, with the strange eyes that were so at variance with the jet-black hair and bar of black eyebrows, for they were the curious light gold color of an animal's—a wolf or a leopard, perhaps. I hesitated, and then saw, superimposed upon this man, powerfully built yet lithe, upon the well-cut high-buttoned coat and soft cravat tied in a large knot under the jutting chin, the shabby ill-dressed boy whom I had first met upon the moors and who had been nicknamed "The Gypsy."

I said slowly,

"*Bryce*. Mr. Dawnay. I am sorry—I did not recognize you. It has been several years since we met." I put my hand out and he took it in a firm clasp.

"Four years. I have been out of this country during that time." He looked down at me and I was held by his compelling look, the eyes that held so bright a glint in their tawny depth. "You haven't changed from the little girl I knew, only to grow into a beautiful woman."

I was embarrassed at such outspoken admiration and I pulled my hand free and said politely, almost primly,

"Have you been living abroad?"

"Living and working in Australia. They have need for miners there, and I found much opportunity. But now I have returned to live at Tregedon."

I said on a note of surprise,

"Tregedon?" for I remembered once seeing a tumble-down old house on the cliffs, built of gray stone and granite surrounded by ruined outbuildings and crumbling walls and being told that it was all that remained of Tregedon Manor.

"I intend to restore it." His face and voice were expressionless, and it brought back to mind the strangely impassive manner he had sometimes assumed as a boy. I recalled our meetings, rare but never forgotten, from the first time, when as a child of nine riding onto the moor without a groom my pony had run away with me. Out of the bracken had sprung a wild ragged figure who raced after me, to hurl itself at the pony's reins and halt him, before both the pony and I tumbled among the stones and fallen poles of the disused mine shaft in our path. He was such a dirty, ragged boy that I think I would have been frightened of him if I had not been even more terrified of crashing to the ground. But as he lifted me from the pony's back his grimy hands were gentle, and the grin he gave me was as reassuring as it was mischievous.

I had been puzzled. He looked rough and yet his voice, despite the light burr, was not a country boy's voice. Nor was his manner and the quiet self-possession with which he spoke to me.

We had parted at the top of the drive down to Penvarrion and I had not seen him to speak to for several months. Once or twice I caught a distant glimpse of him for he appeared to travel the top road that led between Penvarrion village and the coast. But I did not speak to him, for after I had related my adventure to my father and then to Hester my nurse, I was cautioned to avoid him and forbidden to go riding without a groom in attendance. My father had frowned and said,

"I know the boy you mean. He comes from an old but unfortunate family. Some trouble long ago split them up and his grandfather lost his inheritance. He went to work in one of the mines, as did his son —the boy's father. Yet, if things had gone otherwise, the boy would have been one of the big landowners of this county. The Dawnays were here long before the Carews, and one branch of the family have remained respected members of the community." He shook his head. "I am sorry for the lad, but he is not of our circle now."

Hester had not been so kindly.

"Nay, Miss Kate," she said, "the boy be no better'n a gypsy. His grandmother be that, and surely he be 'avin' the same bad blood in his veins. Best you'd not be botherin' with such wild folk."

I was more intrigued than dismayed.

"A gypsy, Hester? A real gypsy like we see on the roads, in caravans, with pots and pans and baskets hanging about it?"

"How should I know who never as much as spoke a word to her nor set eyes upon her but once. It all happened more years gone by then I cares to reckon. Oh, my dear life, 'tes best forgotten."

But I couldn't forget the ragged boy with his strange eyes set in on a slant, gleaming light in his dark face. Once I saw him standing under the shadow of some trees watching us as we drove along the road to Newquay. I glanced over my shoulder when I thought Miss Pringle wasn't looking. I saw his dark face smile and a hand lifted in salute, and on impulse, I waved back.

We met soon after on the moors. I was ten then and riding a sturdy cob for I had outgrown the small pony. When I saw him I reined in Foxfire and he came up to me. He had grown very tall; he must have been about seventeen. He was painfully thin, as if he didn't get enough to eat and not very warmly dressed. It was a winter day and he wore only a woolen shirt and a leather waistcoat and breeches tucked into high boots. He was hatless and his hair thick and jet-black, curled into the back of his neck, and I remembered how Hester had said he had gypsy blood. That was what he looked like, a gypsy. Still thinking of Hester, for a moment I was almost

14

afraid of him, then he smiled, the thin hard face lighting up in an extraordinary way and suddenly I felt as if I knew him very well.

"Good day, Miss Carew," he said. "Miss Katherine Carew, I believe."

I was surprised he should know so much about me.

"Yes. What's your name?"

"Bryce Dawnay. You may call me Bryce."

"Thank you."

"Shall I call you 'Kate'? I'd like to."

I tilted my chin slightly to show my superiority. I felt he should call me Miss Carew, and yet I was aware of being only a small girl and he seemed now very adult.

"If you wish."

"May I ride with you? My horse is over there."

I glanced around and saw a string of moorland ponies grazing the tufty grass.

"Which one?"

He smiled.

"Whichever one you wish me to ride."

I stared. "But they are wild ponies."

"It makes no matter. Horses are my friends. Which one? The black or the roan. Or the skewbald?"

I took him at his dare.

"The skewbald."

He walked away, lithe and erect, his thin body making so little movement, he seemed to skim across the grass. The ponies lifted their heads and tossing their manes, half-turned as if to race away. I heard his voice, heard words and a low whistling. The skewbald hesitated and then stood still and docile, and the next moment he was astride its bare back. I saw his hands knot into the long mane and the pony turned and came trotting toward Foxfire. Bryce said,

"Come on," and we were away, cantering over the moor, with Foxfire hard put to keep up with the skewbald, when, finally, we broke into a gallop.

The cold wind whistled past my ears, I glanced sideways and saw Bryce almost lying across the pony's neck, and I wondered how he

15

could retain his seat on such a rough ride. We came to where the moor sloped down to the cliff edge and here Bryce pulled the pony up to a standstill but how I couldn't conjecture. He looked around at me.

"You ride well."

"Thank you. But I cannot ride half as well as you do."

He shrugged.

"It is something I learned as a child. I am not rich enough to own a horse of my own, so I take the pick of the wild ones." He gestured toward the sea, gray under the gray sky, the waves racing in to shore. "That is Tregedon Head over there."

I stared into the distance and saw the great hammer headland thrusting its bulk into the angry sea. Even from so far away I could see the fountains of white spray dash against the granite cliffs, and I thought it looked a bleak and dangerous place. Not a place I should ever want to visit.

Perhaps he was aware of my thoughts for he lifted his chin and said in a proud-sounding voice,

"One day I shall live there. It belonged to the Dawnays for hundreds of years and will do so again."

I said wonderingly, "Is there a house then?"

"Yes. Tregedon Manor. You cannot see it from here—it is farther along the cliff out of sight."

I could not imagine anyone wishing to live in such a wild spot so I remained silent, and after a moment we turned and rode back, more slowly than we had come.

It was the beginning of our real friendship. Although I knew my father would not approve, I could not resist meeting Bryce from time to time. It was he who taught me to ride bareback, almost as swiftly and as surely as himself. He showed me where the fox's earth was to be found; sometimes in an old badger set or in an enlarged system of rabbit holes. Once we watched a dog and vixen return to their earth and once we saw fox cubs at play.

It was Bryce who took me one evening to a quiet stretch of river and pointed out freshly made otter tracks in the mud; five toes and the print of webbing between the toes. In the May twilight we saw

16

the badger emerge from his set and on a wild March day we watched the hares go mad, jumping and leaping and fighting. It was on that day that Bryce quoted a poem to me which I loved:

> The hare is running races in her mirth;
> And with her feet she from the plashy earth.
> Raises a mist; that glittering in the sun
> Runs with her all the way, wherever she doth run.

Weasels and stoats, hedgehogs and moles, squirrels and mice, Bryce was familiar with all their ways. Birds too. Sandpipers and plovers, snipe, bittern, cormorant, puffins, petrel, shag and gannet, he could distinguish them at first sight. The heron fishing in the mud, the magpie, the plover, the owl swooping through the evening shadows, he knew them all. With Bryce I entered a secret world other people scarcely knew existed, and in it I was at once beguiled and content.

◆

Now as I looked at the tall man before me the memory of those past meetings came back to me, and I remembered Tregedon Head and the uninhabitable place it had seemed to me that day.

"I hope you will be successful," I said slowly, in answer to his last remark.

"I hope so too." He looked down at the headstone and said, "You came to visit your mother's grave I think? Sometimes I visit my father's. He died while I was away. He lies buried in Tregedon churchyard, with my mother and the baby sister who died in childbirth with her."

"I am sorry," I said.

"I hardly knew her. I was three when she died. It is my father I shall miss. He was a grim man and sad, but there was a bond between us."

For a moment we were silent and then, as if by common consent we turned away and walked toward the wicket gate.

"You are alone? May I walk a little of the way with you?"

I hesitated.

"I think it is better you should not. I—I have to hurry. My father

17

has been abroad and is expected back this afternoon and there is a great deal to do to be in readiness for him." I paused and then added, feeling I must give some explanation for my abrupt leave-taking, "He has recently remarried and returns with my new stepmother. And her two children."

For a moment he stared at me.

"Indeed. Then I will not detain you."

"Thank you. Good-by, Mr. Dawnay."

He lifted a black eyebrow.

"Why so formal? It was Bryce once."

"That seems a long time ago."

"Not so long that our friendship is forgotten I hope. For we were friends, were we not, Kate?"

He said my name so gently it was like the murmur of a bell; the reverberations from it seemed to pass through me in waves of emotion, and because I was already unnerved and on edge on account of my father's homecoming, tears blurred my eyes. For a moment I could not speak. Finally I said in a low voice,

"Perhaps we were. Good-by, Bryce"; and turning I hurried away down the path leading to Penvarrion.

# 2

IT WAS LATE afternoon when my father arrived home. We had long been awaiting the sound of the carriage, and at last Barney came running down the drive from the Lodge to pant out the news that the horses were coming along the road.

I was waiting on the steps, Miss Pringle standing close to me and my feelings were a mixture of joy and of apprehension. What would my new stepmother be like, and my stepsister and brother?

My father jumped from the carriage and looked up to see me standing there. He smiled and his arms opened to receive my headlong flight down the steps into his embrace.

"My little Kitty."

"Papa! Dearest Papa. I'm so happy to see you again." I pressed my head into his shoulder so as to hide the tears, and when after a quick hug, he released me, my cheek was dry and I was calm again.

He turned to hand someone out of the carriage and I saw my stepmother for the first time. She stood beside the carriage, smiling at me in a charming way, and then she put a hand out and her voice was softly caressing as she said,

"My dear Katherine—this is such a happy moment for me. I have heard so much about you from your father, and I hope with all my heart that we shall be friends and love one another." Drawing me gently toward her she kissed me on the cheek and then stood back.

I wondered why I should ever have been in dread of her. She was beautiful. Not overly tall but with a regal carriage and a graceful figure. She wore a deep violet dress of thin wool printed in a woven tartan pattern. It was fringed with violet silk, and the bonnet on her russet hair was of violet silk to match. Her skin was creamy smooth and her eyes were a lighter russet-brown shade than her hair.

I said, shyly,

"I am glad to make you welcome."

She turned, to the small figure whom my father was already helping down from the carriage.

"This is my daughter, Amy. And Oliver, my son."

Amy was as beguiling as her mother, but smaller, daintier and exquisitely pretty. Her hair was shining red-gold and her eyes a clear sea-green against her pale complexion. She was tiny, her figure set off by a dress of cream silk with a spot pattern of brown and pink, trimmed with golden brown fringe.

She said in a low voice,

"Katherine," and put up a rose petal cheek to be kissed. I bent down toward her feeling overly tall and clumsy beside such delicate perfection.

"I am very happy to meet you."

Oliver was thin and sandy-haired and about fifteen years of age. He glanced away from me as we shook hands, and I sensed his painful shyness and smiled more easily than I had done at either his mother or his sister.

My father put his arm around my waist and around that of my stepmother.

"Come—let us go into the house," and followed by Amy and her brother the three of us walked up the steps to the front door.

There was much excitement during the next few hours. The servants were introduced to the new mistress of the household, for it was obvious that I should now step down. Not that I had ever really held the reins of Penvarrion in my hands for I was scarcely old enough to do that. But of late I had been more frequently consulted on this matter or that, and gradually it had been assumed that even Mrs. Borlase would defer to me.

My stepmother was so charming and gracious to everyone that any prejudice there might be against the second Mrs. Carew could not persist. She expressed appreciation of all the effort that had been made on her behalf and admired everything that she was shown.

This admiration extended to myself for, after the elaborate home-coming dinner prepared by Mrs. Hubbard, my stepmother beckoned me to sit beside her and said,

"I had no idea you were such a beautiful girl, Katherine. Your father's descriptions did not do you justice. I expect you have many admirers."

I felt self-conscious before her kind but somehow appraising gaze.

"Not—not really."

She smiled.

"There is someone for whom you have a special regard I think. At least, so I have gathered from your father." At my silence, for I could not bring myself to discuss Esmond in any way, she lifted a delicate hand and said, "Forgive me. I have embarrassed you. Perhaps, when we have grown to know one another you will honor me with your confidences. Sometimes a young girl needs guidance. It is very sad that you should lose your mother so young."

Once again I did not know in what way to reply. I felt awkward and ill at ease, and yet I was sure she was only trying to be helpful to me. My father came into the room at that moment so further discussion was avoided, and when he sat down beside her I moved away to the piano where Amy was turning over some sheets of music.

"Do you play the piano?" she asked.

"Not very well. Do you?"

"I am considered competent."

"Won't you please play something now. I am sure my father would enjoy to hear you."

"Oh, he has heard me often enough. I accompany my mother on the occasions she sings for him. My mother has a beautiful voice. But if you wish, I will play this," and she picked up one of the pieces of music. It was, "Believe Me If All Those Endearing Young Charms."

I was amazed when I heard her. Amy's little hands which looked as if they could scarcely span the octaves rippled across the keys in a most accomplished manner, and her small pointed fingers revealed a mastery I would not have expected.

"That was beautiful," I said when she had finished and my father clapped his hands in approval and said, "Well done, Amy." Then he turned and said, "Will you not sing for us, Blanche, my dear? I am sure it would give Kitty great pleasure and round off this very special first evening together."

"If it will please you, Gilbert." She smiled and as my father smiled back at her I thought I had never seen him look so well, or so young and happy in appearance. I tried to suppress the pang of something that could almost have been jealousy. I had never shared my father's affections with anyone since my mother's death, and despite all my best intentions I could not help feeling that I must now stand aside in his regard.

The notes of the rich contralto voice that stole across the room startled me out of my introspection. I had not expected such a superior performance, for like Amy's playing, it had an almost professional stamp. The words were sentimental, the intonation caressing, and I saw my father lean back with half-closed eyes as if lost in a dream of pleasure.

> Thou woulds't still be adored,
> as this moment thou art,
> Let thy loveliness fade as it will.

Toward the end of the song he opened his eyes and joined in the last phrases, his voice wavering but melodious enough. I was the only non-participator for, alas, I was tone deaf, and could not sing a note in tune.

"That was delightful," my father said. "Thank you, my dear. And thank you too, Amy, for without your accompaniment we could not have enjoyed so refreshing an entertainment. We must have many such musical occasions in the future. Do you not agree, Kitty?"

"Yes," I forced myself to say. "It has been most pleasant."

Oliver had been sitting some little way apart from us. I went over to speak to him and found that the large volume he was holding in his hands was a history of Cornwall, well illustrated.

"Is the sea far from this house?" he asked, when I had made some comment on the dangerous coastline.

"No way at all. Beyond the grounds is a track that leads past the

Home Farm where Mr. Trembath, the steward, lives, and this ends in Penvarrion Cove. It is a beautiful sheltered spot lying between the headlands. We must walk there one day."

"I should like that." He looked at me out of eyes that were a light gray-green rather than the clean translucent color of his sister's. "I intend to be a sailor. Mr. Carew—your father," he added stammeringly, "has said that I may attend a naval college."

"That would be a great thing to do. Cornwall is famous for its sailors."

He smiled shyly and I felt that we were going to be friends.

The first few days were difficult, for we were getting to know one another. Or rather, I was getting to know my new family for they and my father were already well acquainted. It made me feel a stranger at times at their many allusions to places and people which were unknown to me. My stepmother was at all times amiable and agreeable to me, and Amy I found easy to like. She was pretty and lively and chattered incessantly, but she was amusing, too, and one could not help but laugh at her as she rattled away in light-hearted fashion.

Esmond liked her too. He rode over with an invitation from his mother to dine at Borleigh Hall. When I introduced him to Amy she stared up at Esmond, her green eyes widening, her cupid's-bow mouth parted above the tiny pointed teeth which truly were as white as pearls. She put out her small hand and he took it and smiled down at her and said,

"I am happy to meet you, Miss Lambert," and I could see he was greatly taken with her, and I was glad, for I wished us all to be friends. At that moment Oliver came into the room and I introduced him to Esmond. After a few moments as if by common consent the four of us went through the casement door into the garden where the sun shone with all the brilliance of a June morning. The day before Amy, Oliver and myself had been playing croquet and now at the sight of the curved hoops on the stretch of smooth green lawn before us, Amy clapped her hands and cried,

"Oh, do let us have a game. It was such fun yesterday and now there are four of us to play." She hesitated, her green eyes raised demurely. "That is if Mr. Lambert would care to join in."

Esmond smiled down at her.

"I should be delighted to. And please call me Esmond. I know Katy so well it is impossible for me to be on formal terms with her stepsister."

Amy blushed and said, "You must call me Amy."

Matters were arranged that Esmond should partner Amy as she was the least skilled of us and Oliver and I would play together. We spent a most agreeable hour or so and if there was more laughter than stern competition between us this fact only added to our enjoyment. When Miss Pringle walked out to inform us that it would soon be lunchtime we were astonished at the way the time had passed so quickly.

I turned to Esmond.

"You will stay and have some luncheon with us?"

He hesitated, glancing at his gold hunter watch and then he shook his head.

"I only wish that I could, but I promised my father to be home by midday for he has someone coming to see us on a matter of business. I fear I am late as it is, so please forgive me, Katy, and invite me another time."

"Yes, of course." I put my hand out. "We must not delay you, Esmond. Give my love to your parents and tell them how much we are looking forward to coming to dinner with you all next week."

He took my hand in his.

"I look forward to that too." He turned to Amy. "Good-by, Amy. It has been a great pleasure to make your acquaintance. Oliver, too."

As they shook hands Oliver said shyly,

"Next time I shall hope to beat you at croquet."

Esmond smiled.

"No doubt you will succeed," and lifting a hand in salute he turned and walked away toward the stables and out of sight.

For a moment Amy stared after him, and then she sighed contentedly.

"How enjoyable a morning we have spent. I cannot imagine anything pleasanter. Can you, Kate?"

I shook my head.

"No—I cannot," thinking that all the hours I spent in Esmond's company were the happiest I knew.

———◆———

Borleigh Hall lay some miles from Penvarrion in the direction of Wadebridge. It was inland and stood in a fine park, with moorland rising behind it. Sir Ralph Borleigh, Esmond's father, greeted us in his usual boisterous fashion. He was a big burly man with a red face, which someone said came from the amount of port he drank. He was a great sportsman and spent most of his time hunting and shooting and fishing, perhaps to the neglect of his estate for I had heard my father say that Borleighs was not maintained in the fashion of Sir Ralph's father.

Lady Borleigh was thin and fair and delicate looking. Once she must have been a beautiful woman and it was apparent from whom Esmond had inherited his handsome looks. But now her complexion was faded and her fair hair was a tired frizzled gray, and she sighed often as though she had many cares of which she could not speak.

Laura and Paul came to dinner that night also, and Esmond's elder sister, Miriam, with her husband, so twelve of us sat down to dine. There was much jesting and toasting by Sir Ralph of my father and his new wife, and he was complimented several times on his good fortune. My father was used to Sir Ralph's outspoken manner and smiled quietly but good-naturedly while my stepmother sat as cool and composed as if she were in her own drawing room. I could not help but admire her, and yet I had a feeling that I should never really know her.

Because it was a large party and there was much general conversation I spoke no more than a few words in private to Esmond, but once he leaned over the back of my chair and said,

"I am glad you are so fortunate, Kate. Your stepmother is a charming woman and seems already to have grown fond of you, and you could not have a more delightful stepsister than Amy."

"No, I could not."

"When do you go to London? Your father says you are all to visit the Great Exhibition."

"Yes. I don't know when, but soon. It is to be my birthday treat." And a treat for my stepmother and Amy, too, I might have added. I waited, hoping that Esmond would refer again to his proposed talk with my father. He said nothing and perhaps this was hardly the time and place. But I was made happy when he added, after a moment's pause,

"I may come to London myself for a few days while you are staying there and offer myself as escort to you and your stepsister. I have had a glimpse of the Exhibition, but I did not see nearly enough."

"Oh, Esmond, I would so enjoy that. Please arrange to come while we are there."

He smiled down at me, superbly handsome in his dark dinner suit and frilled shirt.

"It is a promise."

Amy came tripping forward, her crinoline swaying like a bell.

"I hope I do not interrupt too precious a tête-à-tête, but your mother has expressed a wish to hear Mama sing. As I must accompany her, I wonder if one of you would be kind enough to turn the music for me?" She glanced first at me and then at Esmond and added with a pretty hesitancy. "Perhaps, Esmond—"

"Of course. I shall be happy to. Come and sit nearer, Katy, while I do my duty by Amy and her mother."

Amy pouted.

"Do not make it sound too onerous a task."

"I am sorry, I did not intend to speak so."

My stepmother sang several songs and was much applauded for her voice was truly beautiful. Everyone sat enraptured. Sir Ralph lay back in his big chair, his flushed face beaming a sleepy approval while Lady Phoebe leaned forward with eager attention, sometimes murmuring appreciatively to my father who sat beside her.

I sat with Oliver, watching Amy's small competent fingers ripple over the keyboard. From time to time she would lift her head and her green eyes would flash upward at Esmond in indication of the page of music to be turned.

When the impromptu concert was ended the Borleigh's butler appeared through the double doors of the drawing room ushering in two black-clad parlor maids bearing trays laden with glasses of Madeira wine and thin rice biscuits.

Esmond escorted Amy across the room and found her a chair beside me. Standing between us he said,

"I am sure when we are in London and I escort you and Amy to some concert or other we shall not hear any prima donna sing more delightfully than Mrs. Carew has just done."

Amy glanced up in animation,

"*You* are to be in London with us, Esmond? Oh, how very agreeable."

He gave a small inclination of his head.

"Thank you. I shall only be with you for a few days during Mr. Carew's stay, but I am looking forward to being with you all and to visiting the Great Exhibition."

"And there is my birthday ball," I broke in to say. "Aunt Serena will send you an invitation if she knows you are to be in London, so you must be sure to coincide your visit with that date."

Amy's green eyes sparkled with excitement.

"A birthday ball? What fun that will be. When is your birthday, Kate?"

"July fourteenth," I said. "I shall be eighteen." I could not prevent my glance straying to Esmond, and I felt a tremor when I found his gaze fixed steadily upon me, his dark blue eyes seeming to say all the words he could not yet express. He said slowly,

"Yes, you will be eighteen, Kate. A memorable age."

Amy frowned.

"Why is to be eighteen memorable? I am eighteen now and I cannot remember that attaining that age made the slightest difference to me."

Neither Esmond nor I could find words to answer her, but fortunately we were interrupted by Laura and Paul who had come across to speak to us.

27

It was after midnight when the carriage was called to the door to take us back to Penvarrion. We were all drowsy as the horses trotted along the winding moonlit roads and not sorry when at last we arrived home. As Amy walked ahead of me up the wide staircase she said over her shoulder,

"You are so lucky, Kate. I envy you."

"Do you? In what manner?"

"Why, because of Esmond of course. To have so handsome a beau. Is he wealthy also?"

"I do not know. And it is of little consequence."

Amy yawned delicately, one tiny hand at her pink mouth.

"I don't agree with you, Kate. When *I* marry it will be to someone as charming as Esmond but rich into the bargain."

"You will be very fortunate," I said dryly as I paused outside my bedroom door. "Good night, Amy. Sleep well."

"You too." She reached up and brushed my cheek with her soft lips. "Good night Kate."

———◆———

I had much to look forward to. The visit to the Great Exhibition and Esmond's company while we were there. Amy was as excited as myself at the idea of seeing London. You would have thought the treat had been expressly planned for her enjoyment for she smiled up at my father and said,

"Oh, you are so good to us. I have longed to visit London for I have heard and read so much about it. And we will have time to visit all the wonderful shops, won't we? Mama and I are sadly in need of new dresses."

That was true. I had been surprised by the sparseness of their wardrobes. Apart from the two ensembles in which they had arrived and which had obviously been bought new for the occasion, my stepmother and Amy wore simple unfashionable clothes, although both were so pretty and graceful that anything they wore looked well on them.

Amy confided in me, saying,

"Of latter years Mama has had to exist on very straitened means and this has made things hard on the three of us. After my father died the plantation was not managed at all well and suddenly there seemed very little money. I think this was because the man who ran it for Mama was not an honest person and in some way he stole from her. When your father came to see us he dismissed this man and put in a new manager from his own estate, and now of course Mama is married to your papa so he is able to take care of everything." She waved a piece of paper in the air and said, "Do you know, he has given me this sum of money, and I intend to spend it all on new dresses and a fur-trimmed cloak—I have longed to possess such a garment, and some bonnets and oh! all manner of things."

I could not help but wonder how much my father had given her, but it was not my place to ask and, of course, it was probably Amy's own money, paid in from the plantation. She was like a child in her eagerness and frivolity, and I was forced to smile as she danced about the room, bowing and curtseying to imaginary guests at an imaginary ball, the check fluttering in her tiny fingers.

There was only one incident that marred the time before we journeyed to London.

It happened a few days before we were due to depart. We had been talking in the sitting room and my father smiled in answer to some query regarding the proposed visit.

"You must ask Kitty here," he said. "She has been to London before."

A slight frown creased my stepmother's smooth forehead.

*"Kitty!"* she echoed. "Why do you call her by such a childish name? It is not suitable, Gilbert. She is too big a girl now for such a babyish appellation. She should be called Katherine. Or Kate, if you prefer it." Her sherry-brown eyes surveyed me almost critically. "Do you not agree, my dear?"

For a moment I could not find the words with which to answer her. When I had been a little girl my father had called me "Kitty Puss." Then as I grew older it was shortened to Kitty. He was the only one who had ever called me by that name, and I loved and treasured it. So that now I felt my cheeks crimsoning in anger, and the hot temper which had been a part of me since childhood rushed

29

to the surface. How often in the past old Hester my nurse had cautioned me, saying, "Dear life, your temper'ull be your undoing, Miss Kate. You do be as willful and tempt'utus as your mama was when ur was such an age as yours. I remember how ur would fly into a tantrum and kick and dance about when I do be combin' out the tangles o' her hair. Same as you now, Miss Kate. So mind on it and keep a watch on yourself. 'Twas the death of my dear Miss Isabella when she druv ur hoss at the wall because ur was in a temper and would not be beat, and temper'll be the death o' 'ee too if 'ee act the same way."

So I had learned some self-control but always the danger of a sudden flare-up lay beneath the surface of my nature and now anger burned through me. Anger and perhaps a marked jealousy and resentment of my stepmother.

I said in a choked voice,

"It is my father's name for me."

She stared coldly at me and I stared back. Then she shrugged slim shoulders and at the same time my father touched my arm and said,

"Your stepmama is right. Katherine is a beautiful name and we use it all too seldom."

I felt the angry tears burning behind my eyelids. Why did my father not defend the use of the name that was also his endearment to me? Without another word I rushed from the room and raced up the three flights of stairs to the top of the house where the old schoolroom stood. Here I could be alone, here no one would think to find me. Here I could shed the few tears of release while my thumping heart calmed to a steadier beat.

I was not alone. Beyond the schoolroom with its shabby furniture and forgotten toys, in the empty bedroom sat Hester, quietly knitting as she rocked herself in the old chair. She glanced up at me over the rim of her gold-rimmed spectacles and said,

"Tes you, Miss Kate. You be in a tarrible hurry to come up here. But not to see me I be thinkin'."

"Oh, Hester." I flung myself at her feet and she lifted a veined hand to stroke my hair back from my hot forehead.

"What be wrong, m'dear? You'm be as upset as a li'l child."

30

"Oh, Hester, I wish—I wish my father had not married again."

She shook her head, returning to her knitting.

"Nay, Miss Kate, 'ee can't wish your father not be findin' a partner to comfort and solace him. Tes ony natural like for a man to need ur."

"I wish he had chosen someone else. Someone more—more—" I paused, wondering what it was I wanted and knowing it was to be alone with my father.

Hester shook her head again,

"No matter who 'ee chosen tes all the same. You not be wantin' to share him and nor be ur. 'Twill make for troubles, but when you marry and go to your own man, Miss Kate, then 'ee'll not need to share 'ee. Tes a wist ole job of it, but tes natur'."

I thought of Esmond and how the days were flying by to my birthday and I felt comforted. I leaned up to hug Hester and kissed her wrinkled cheek.

"Dear Hester—you are such a wise person and you understand everything."

She kissed my forehead and said,

"When 'ee 'ave lived as long as me, reckon 'ee'll see things a mite different."

I left her and after I had washed my face and brushed my hair I returned downstairs and in my stepmother's company I was polite and good-mannered.

But my father never called me Kitty again when others were present.

The next morning Amy, Oliver and myself were just setting off for a ride when Esmond arrived in the new gig he had recently bought. It was an exceedingly smart affair and he had great pleasure in showing it off to us.

"I have only room for one passenger so shall you come with me, Katy, and Amy and Oliver can ride after us with the horses."

Before I could answer Amy ran up to Esmond and said,

"Oh, please, Esmond. *Please* take me. You know I am not fond of riding horseback. And I would adore to go with you in your beautiful new carriage." She put her two little hands together in the pret-

31

tiest of gestures and added, "Do say yes. Kate will not mind, will you Kate?" and she glanced over her shoulder at me. "Kate would rather ride her horse than do almost anything."

Esmond hesitated, staring down into Amy's smiling upturned face framed in a green-velvet riding hat that echoed the color of her eyes. He said slowly,

"Well, if Katy will give you preference?"

I would dearly have loved to have driven away in Esmond's spanking new gig, just the two of us, but I could go later. And it was true, Amy was not fond of riding and had only been persuaded to come with Oliver and myself this morning because it was such a beautiful day, and she did not want to be left in the garden on her own.

"Of course Amy must go with you," I said. "We will follow."

"Could we not give the horses a canter over the fields first?" Oliver put in. "They are very fresh to take along the hard road. In which direction will you drive?" he asked Esmond.

"Along the Wadebridge turnpike. We will wait for you at the Gallow crossroad, then you'll have time to let the horses have a good run."

"Splendid," Oliver said. Esmond flicked the long whip and the gig set off up the drive at a smart pace, with Amy turning back to smile and wave to us.

I mounted Sorrel and would have moved after them but Oliver said,

"Let's ride down to the cove first. We can then go up the track to the headland and across the fields to the Wadebridge road."

I did not mind which way we went. I only wanted to be sitting beside Esmond in his new gig, driving along the road together.

The cove was Oliver's favorite place. It was only a quarter of a mile from the house along the track that led to the Home Farm. From there the road ran beside a stream that opened farther along into the sea, and here a tiny beach lay between tall curving cliffs. A solitary stone cottage was the only habitation and before it, pulled up on the shale, was a small boat. An old fisherman named Reuben Gilbard lived in the cottage, and the boat belonged to him and to his son who worked on the farm.

Oliver reined in and stood watching the waves sweeping in on either side of the cove. They were smooth lulling waves this morning for the sea was calm, though sometimes it came in swift and strong against the cliffs. But there was usually shelter here, by comparison with farther up the coast.

"We had better get on," I said, for I knew that Oliver would stay by the sea indefinitely. Turning the horses' heads we walked them slowly up the winding track that led from the cove to the headland. It was steep but not too precipitous and the horses were used to it. Gradually the land leveled out, and when we reached the top it was open and flat.

We set off at a brisk canter, leaving the sea at our backs and riding inland across sheep-filled fields toward the main road. Once we halted, and while the horses puffed and snorted I lifted my riding crop to point out the tall chimneys of Penvarrion, far below us in the valley. Only from here could one see the house, for it was completely hidden from the road. Beyond the tall trees surrounding it were the neat squares of walled gardens and the clock tower and weather vane of the stables.

"It's like an enclosed world," Oliver said. "All on its own. I like it."

"Do you? I'm glad. I always think there is nowhere as beautiful as Penvarrion. I shouldn't like to live anywhere else. Though I suppose I—I may one day."

"You mean if you get married. Are you going to marry Esmond?" Oliver asked.

I blushed at the unexpectedness of his question and said,

"You are being too curious. We must hurry or the others will be tired waiting for us," and lifting Sorrel's reins I set off at a quick trot, followed after a moment, by Oliver.

We came out onto the Wadebridge road some miles north of Penvarrion Church and set off in the direction of the Gallows crossroad, where, years ago, it was said two robbers had been hung. The gig had not yet arrived but as we waited, walking the sweating horses slowly around I heard the clatter of hooves and behind me turned to see, not the gig, but a tall man on horseback.

It was Bryce Dawnay.

He lifted his beaver hat from his black head and said gravely,

"Good morning, Miss Kate."

"Good morning. Oliver, this is Mr. Dawnay—my stepbrother, Oliver Lambert."

The golden eyes, set in at a slight angle, surveyed us both.

"I'm happy to make your acquaintance," and then to me, "I hope I find you well, Miss Kate."

"Very well, thank you."

"Are you delayed in some manner? I saw you were waiting here."

"We are waiting for a friend—Mr. Borleigh, and for my stepsister, Miss Lambert, who have arranged to meet us here. Something must have held them up."

"May I have the pleasure of waiting with you?"

I wondered at his fine manners and yet, I remembered that as a rough-looking boy he had always shown me an immense courtesy, and remembering again our friendship I smiled warmly,

"Please do." Oliver stared at him and at his horse which was a truly fine animal standing every inch of seventeen hands and with gleaming black coat and long black mane and tail. I thought of the wild ponies Bryce had once ridden because he possessed no horse of his own and I said, on impulse,

"Do you remember the skewbald?"

He stared frowningly.

"The skewbald?" and then the dark face lightened. "Oh, very well. He was an excellent mount. I am glad you have not forgot him. You rode him bareback."

"I rode others in that fashion. You taught me."

We smiled at one another, linked by our memories of the past. Oliver gazed at us in turn, puzzled by the enigma of our conversation, but before we could explain the joke the gig came rattling down the road and with a great flourish halted before us.

"I am sorry we were not here to meet you," Esmond began and then he stopped, abruptly, his blue eyes narrowing to take in my companion. I said quickly,

"This is Mr. Dawnay. But perhaps you have already made his acquaintance. He lives no great distance from here."

Esmond gave a brief jerk of the head.

"We have met on some occasion or other. I forget where. Shall we ride on, Kate. Good day to you, Dawnay."

His manner was so curt that I blushed for his rudeness. Amy was gazing wide-eyed first at Bryce and then back to Esmond, who had not even troubled to introduce Bryce to her. Something forced me to say,

"There is no hurry, surely."

"I think there is. We must return to Penvarrion, and not gather about the crossroads like tinkers. Or gypsies," he added and with a twitch of the reins and a crack of the whip he swung the gig about and galloped off down the road.

I could only stare after him, my cheeks crimson with shame for his manner and his words.

"I am sorry," I began but Bryce, with a tightening of his set lips and a strangely masked expression that hid all indication of his true feelings, lifted his hat and said,

"I am sorry too. To have caused you embarrassment, Kate. I will delay you no longer but take leave of you. Good-by." He nodded toward Oliver. "Good day, Mr. Lambert," and tall and erect on the tall black horse he rode swiftly away.

Oliver was frowning as we followed after Esmond but made no attempt to catch him up.

"Why was Esmond so angry?" he asked. "Has Mr. Dawnay offended him in some way? I liked him."

"It is Esmond who has given offense," I said and then wondered why I should defend Bryce. Perhaps there was some good reason for Esmond's incivility.

But there was not. When on return to Penvarrion I remonstrated with him and enquired why he should have acted in so discourteous a fashion, he merely shrugged and said,

"It is not I who am in the wrong, but you, Katy. You should choose your acquaintances better. The fellow is little better than a gypsy. That is what people call him, you know. 'The Gypsy.' "

"If people call him so, it is wrong. He comes of a good family who once owned Tregedon Manor."

Esmond laughed.

"If they did, they do so no longer. It has fallen into ruin. And the good family consists of the gypsy grandmother who is still alive and lives in a tumble-down cottage nearby. She is a rag bag of an old dame often to be seen gathering weeds in the hedgerows or kindling from the woods. You are in error, Katy, to even acknowledge Dawnay, let alone pursue an acquaintance with him. I cannot think how it came about except that I know you met him as a child. But you are a grown woman now."

I wanted to say more but the high color on Esmond's cheeks and the look in his hot angry blue eyes stayed me. Of all people he was the last one with whom I should ever wish to quarrel. I loved him. And Bryce Dawnay meant nothing to me, so I subdued myself and said in a quieter tone,

"Let us forget this unfortunate incident."

"As you wish." He turned away and for the rest of his visit devoted himself to Amy, who chattered happily about her excursion in the gig and expressed her admiration of it and of Esmond's expert driving several times over, and if her ingratiating manner did not please *me,* at least it succeeded in restoring Esmond to a more equable frame of mind.

# 3

It was decided that Miss Pringle should accompany us on our visit to London though at first my stepmother objected.

"It seems an unnecessary expense. After all, Gilbert, she is only the governess."

"Miss Pringle is rather more than that," my father replied, gently. "She is like a friend of the family. In any case, my dear, it should be a satisfactory arrangement for it means Katherine and Amy will have someone to accompany them on excursions to art galleries and museums and we shall then be free to go out together."

My stepmother smiled, the heavy lids coming down over her sherry-brown eyes.

"Of course, Gilbert. I shall so enjoy that."

When we arrived in London it was to find a city sparkling in the sunshine and *en fête* for the season. The Great Exhibition had set its seal on the country and from every part of the land people were coming to visit. I shall never forget my first sight of the palace towering above the blossom and foliage of Hyde Park, its glass walls glittering in the sun. And inside were to be seen more marvels than one could possibly imagine. There was an impressive section of Raw Materials and Produce, and one of many kinds of Machinery. A third section was given over to various Manufactures and the fourth was the Fine Arts, which was of absorbing interest to me.

It was as well Miss Pringle had come to act as our chaperone for the three of us were left much together. Oliver came with us, but as the only male of the party he was apt to trail behind us on various excursions and keep to himself. After one visit to the Great Exhibition my father and stepmother did not come again. She much preferred to go shopping, and I was amazed to think of my father patiently escorting her from one store to another while she chose dresses and mantles and bonnets and rolls of expensive silk to be made up later into the fashionable crinolines.

We were to stay in London for a month altogether. Rooms had been taken in a quiet hotel for it was too much to expect my Aunt Selina's hospitality to extend to the seven of us, three of whom were strangers to her.

Aunt Selina was the sister of my dead mother, and my godmother, and she lived in a tall handsome house in Lancaster Gate. She was a widow with one daughter, Rosamund, with whom I was great friends, and two sons: Gordon, who practiced in Harley Street, and Bertram who was a few years older than myself and studying to become a lawyer. We were entertained on several occasions at my aunt's house and met many young people of our own age, and my kind aunt also planned a supper and ball for the night of my eighteenth birthday.

Esmond arranged his visit to London for that week and we looked forward to his arrival, myself most of all, for I longed to see him and I lived in a happy dream of how he would tell me he loved me and, after he had spoken to my father, would ask me to marry him.

He arrived, and our excursions became more varied and exciting. A trip to Hampton Court was planned, and on this occasion my father and my stepmother came too, accompanied by Rosamund and Bertram. A private launch was engaged, and in this we sailed upon the smooth blue waters of the Thames, viewing the great houses that lined the banks at Chiswick and Richmond and admiring the sweep of the tree-lined river and the variety of craft moving up and down it. The splendors of the Court thrilled us all, and after our explorations we sat down to a delicious picnic lunch of cold chicken and salmon mayonnaise and salad, followed by strawberries and cream, with chilled wine to drink. After this we were revived enough to enjoy the fun and diversion of the Maze, leaving my father and his new wife to rest quietly for a while.

In the Maze I lost Esmond. One moment we were together and the next he was lost behind the dense green hedge. I ran up and down and encountered Bertram who took me under his guidance, but without much success at finding our way out. I sat down on a seat to rest while my cousin wandered off in search of a fresh opening, promising to return and find me.

As I sat there, feeling warm and sleepy in the sheltered spot, I heard Amy's voice from somewhere behind me. I turned, about to call her name and then she laughed, softly, teasingly and, to my surprise, I heard Esmond's voice in reply.

"Come along, Amy. We must try and find our way out of here."

"Must we? I should like to stay here always. We could build a little house under this hedge and I declare we should stay both warm and dry."

"That might do for you, for you are such a tiny creature, but it would not suit me at all," Esmond answered. "My legs are much too long."

"Yes. You are very tall. Tall and handsome. The handsomest man I have ever met." Amy's voice was low and very sweet.

"Then you cannot have met many," Esmond said abruptly. "I will try this way." His voice faded as he moved away and I heard Amy cry,

"Please wait for me. I am coming," and then there was silence.

I sat there without moving, feeling as if I had been listening to actors in a play. How softly beguiling Amy's voice had sounded. Perhaps I should not have listened but called out at once. But there had scarcely been time. A few words, a sentence or two and they were gone.

I wondered at the sense of unease with which I was left. Why should it matter that Amy should pay Esmond a compliment? It was obvious that she admired him.

And Esmond? Did he admire Amy?

Surely I was not jealous of Amy? I got up and started to walk along the pathway and to my relief Bertram came around the corner of the hedge. He shook his head,

"It's another dead end in that direction. Let us go this way," and taking my arm he turned me around to go in the opposite direction.

We found our way out at last and eventually the party was reunited. Amy arrived pink and breathless, her eyes shining green and bright.

"Oh, it has been the greatest fun. I have never enjoyed an outing more."

I glanced at Esmond, only to find him smiling indulgently down at her, and I wished I could have said the same.

The next day was July fourteenth, my birthday. The morning was filled with the excitement of opening my presents. My father gave me a most beautiful pearl-and-amethyst necklace, and I was overwhelmed when I opened the package and saw it.

"Oh, Papa, it is exquisite. I shall wear it tonight with my new dress. Thank you, thank you, darling Papa," and I threw my arms about his neck.

He kissed me lovingly in return.

"Pearls are your favorite gems, are they not? I think you told me so once."

"Yes. And the amethyst has become another of my favorite stones. This deep violet color is so rich," I turned to display the gift to my stepmother and Amy. "Is it not lovely?"

"Pearls mean tears," Amy said and then clapped a hand to her rosebud mouth. "Oh, I am sorry! I should not have said that. It is only a silly superstition."

For once my stepmother remonstrated with her.

"Of course it is. What a foolish remark, Amy. I am surprised at you." She smiled composedly at me. "Katherine is fortunately far too sensible to pay any attention to you. The necklace is indeed beautiful and perfect to wear with your white dress."

"Thank you." But for some reason my voice was not quite steady.

"Open your other presents," my father said. "You seem to have a great many."

My stepmother had given me a charming gold comb to wear in my hair, and Amy's gift was a pair of kid gloves, very fine and soft. Miss Pringle gave me a book, as did Esmond. There were other presents; a muff of soft brown fur from my aunt, silk mittens from Rosamund, a silver photograph frame from Bertram, flowers, and bon bons and a pair of silk evening slippers. I was overwhelmed by so much kindness. I began to put notes and cards which had arrived with them aside, when Carrie, who had traveled to London with us to attend to Amy and myself, came into the sitting room and handed me a small square packet wrapped in mauve-and-white-striped paper.

"This has just arrived for you, Miss Kate," she said. "A messenger boy left it."

The packet was surprisingly light, and when I opened it, it was to find a nosegay of white roses set in a mossy bed. I had never seen anything so charming or breathed a sweeter perfume when I lifted the flowers gently out of the box. They were old-fashioned roses, the white damask, Madame Hardy, and an Alba, the Jacobite rose, a white moss rose, and a sweetly scented musk the name of which I did not know, and one other, small and delicate, its translucent petals paper thin but guarded by fierce thorns. I thought it must be the bridal rose, Niphetos, but I was not sure. All I could do was to hold the nosegay near my face and breathe in the exquisite perfume while I wondered who could have sent me so unusual and delightful a gift.

I could find no indication of the sender with the box.

"They are from an unknown admirer," Amy said gaily. "I wonder who it can be? Do you think they are from Sir Godfrey Tallin, who paid you so much attention at your aunt's the other evening. Or perhaps it was the dark man who sat next to you at dinner at the Bellamy's."

I shook my head, feeling that neither of those mundane characters could have chosen so tender-meaning a gift. Esmond, I thought. Can it be Esmond who has sent these anonymously as an expression of the love he has yet not spoken of? I longed to think so, and when later on I arranged the nosegay in a cut glass vase on my bedside table I was convinced it could be no one else.

The new dress for the ball was of white muslin with a skirt composed entirely of frills from hem to waist. The bodice was boned and had tiny puff sleeves, and the dropped shoulder line set off the pearl-and-amethyst necklace to perfection while the gold setting of the jewels shone richly against my bare skin. At the last moment I tucked one of the white roses into my hair, and as Carrie finished adjusting the skirt over the steel-hooped crinoline she sat back on her heels to say admiringly,

"I ain't never seen you look more handsome, Miss Katherine. You do be belle o' the ball tonight and no mistake. Doan 'ee agree, Miss Amy?"

Amy smiled absently.

"Yes, indeed, you look beautiful, Kate." She glanced at my reflection in the long mirror. "And Carrie has pulled your waist in well so as to make it look smaller." Her gaze moved to herself and she turned this way and that, very aware that her own dainty measurements presented no problem and needed no tight lacing whatsoever to produce an eighteen inch waist.

I felt a little dashed and, as usual, tall and heavy-seeming by comparison with Amy. But I was comforted to see that my brown hair shone glossy from Carrie's brushing and fell into becoming curls from the top-knot on my head, and that at least the long black eyelashes fringing my gray eyes were an improvement on Amy's light sandy ones, which was some compensation. So I smiled and said,

"Thank you. You look perfectly beautiful yourself, Amy," which was true.

My aunt's house was ablaze with lights when we drove up to it and a red carpet and striped red-and-white awning was spread before the wide steps. Footmen in pale blue stood waiting to escort us through the big double doors into the brightly lit hall beyond.

A small crowd of onlookers were gathered on the pavement and beyond and I heard several admiring comments on our dresses and appearance as we walked from the carriage to the steps. A woman's voice, hoarse and husky shouted out admiringly,

"Look at 'er, the tall 'un, walkin' like a queen. She's rare an' bonny."

I turned my head and saw a stout figure, red-faced and beshawled, smiling at me and involuntarily I smiled back, but as I glanced away I saw, beyond the cluster of bystanders a tall black-clad figure, the figure of a man. Incredibly I thought I recognized Bryce Dawnay standing there. But the straight stovepipe hat hid his eyes and cast a shadow over the dark features, and the next second the figure had melted away in the crowd and I was being urged on by my father.

My aunt, resplendent in black lace and hung about with jet and diamonds was waiting with Rosamund to greet us. Esmond was there too, tall and distinguished looking in a black tail coat with silk-faced revers and tight black trousers with instep strap. A single-breasted waistcoat of white satin and a white stock set off his fair hair and long fair side whiskers, which were becoming fashionable.

If we were all looking our best, my stepmother excelled herself in beauty and elegance. She wore a dress of rose-colored silk edged with finest lace and worn over a wide crinoline. Her waist was as slim as Amy's and at her long white throat she wore a necklace of gleaming topaz, while topaz earrings shone at her ears, seeming to reflect the lights in her russet hair. My father could scarcely take his eyes from her and I felt a queer pang when I saw that his were the eyes of a man in love.

But there was no time for introspection for all was movement and gaiety from then on. Because the ball was in my honor I had more than my choice of partners and was soon being whirled from one dance into another. Why had I imagined myself dancing with Esmond for most of the evening? It was not possible, and though we were together once or twice, for the most part I was being importuned by admiring strangers.

Once, as I danced with Esmond I said carefully,

"The roses I received were quite beautiful."

He gave me a puzzled glance.

"The roses?"

"I had a gift of white roses—old-fashioned ones that smelled sweeter than any I have known. There was no indication to say who had sent them."

"And you thought I might have?" He smiled. "I wish I had thought of it, Katy, but my only present to you today was the book of poems you had expressed an admiration of."

"Oh yes, and I treasure it indeed. I think Mr. Browning one of the greatest poets in the world. Thank you again for such a charming gift."

"You thanked me earlier on." He frowned. "Who can this admirer be who sends you flowers but no card with his name?"

"I cannot begin to guess."

"Because you have so many who would court you? That isn't surprising, my beautiful Katy."

"I hope you are a little jealous?"

"But of course."

We were flirting with one another. It was the mood of the evening. But I wanted more than pretty compliments from Esmond. I had received my share of those from other partners.

He said no more and the dance ended. I did not dance again with him. Yet the spiral of the evening went on ascending with dizzying momentum so that I never seemed to stop talking or laughing or spinning around, first with one young man and then another. And as I did so I began to experience a curious feeling. As if this was a very special night and I would never enjoy anything in the same way again. I felt as someone might have felt who danced at the ball in Brussels on the eve of Waterloo. With danger threatening and somewhere far off the distant guns sounding, bringing with them the threat of chaos and death.

It was an extraordinary sensation. Perhaps I had drunk too much champagne. I only know that my gaiety, like the diamond-bright evening, held a flaw in its sparkling depth.

Two days later we returned to Penvarrion.

Everything was the same as we had left it and yet, not the same. There was a change of air, a shift of the wind to another direction. And as the weeks of late summer passed into misty autumn I began to realize my stepmother's influence accounted for this difference.

The changes began in the house. The furniture was moved around or placed in different rooms. Fresh curtains were made and hung at the long windows, chairs were re-covered, ornaments removed or replaced by other ones. Where there had been a comfortable shabbiness, a new and unfamiliar elegance appeared.

I did not like it. However much the house might seem improved to critical eyes, it was no longer my beloved Penvarrion. And then, crowning offense, my mother's portrait was removed from the drawing room where it had hung since I could remember and was placed elsewhere. The morning I came downstairs and discovered it gone from its old place stunned me in a way I cannot easily forget. I realized then that my former way of life had gone forever.

I rushed to find someone and demand where the portrait had been taken to.

I encountered Borlase coming from the kitchen quarters to the breakfast room. In answer he inclined his head stiffly and said,

"The portrait of Mrs. Carew has been hung in the master's study. It was on the mistress's instructions."

"But—but my father—he will surely object to that!"

"I understand it was done with the master's approval."

I flung away from him and ran to the study to find the painting of my mother hanging over the fireplace in the dark paneled room. It looked well enough, for the light from the window shone gently onto it. Against the dark wood my mother's face, smiling, beautiful, gazed down at me. She was in the long riding habit I remembered her wearing, and tall and graceful, she leaned against a tree, her head half turned to look over her shoulder. She carried her tall riding hat in one hand and her brown hair blew in tendrils around her vivid face.

Tears filled my eyes and I whispered,

"Mama! Oh, Mama. I wish you had not gone away from us."

I don't know how long I stood there, but at a step behind me I swung around to find my father standing in the doorway.

"Papa! *Why* have you had this portrait placed in here? It was always hung in the drawing room."

He came toward me, shaking his head.

"Don't upset yourself, Kitty. This is the best place for your mama's portrait. It is in keeping with the room. See, the painting of your grandfather hangs over there. And I think, as the circumstances are now, it is better here."

"Is my stepmother jealous of Mama then—because you loved her so dearly?" I cried.

He frowned.

45

"Kitty, your tongue runs away with you and you say foolish heedless things. Your stepmama understands perfectly the love I had for your mother, just as I respect her devotion to her first husband. But we are now united to one another, and so I agreed to the suggestion that, as I spend so much time in this room the portrait belongs here rather than in its former place." He put a hand on my shoulder. "Try and understand, child."

I turned to rest my cheek against his fingers, but for a moment I was too full to speak. I blinked the unshed tears and stared across the room to where the portrait of my maternal grandfather hung. He was a splendid vigorous-looking man in his wide skirted blue coat and flowered waistcoat and high white cravat. His dark hair was powdered, he had a high Roman nose and a massive chin and his black eyes seemed to glitter with life as he stared back at me from within the carved gilt frame. He had been a great adventurer and had made much wealth for himself in the sugar isles of the West Indies. This fortune, my mother, his only child, had brought my father on her marriage. Now their likenesses hung either end of the quiet book-lined room. I sighed and in the sigh was acceptance of things as they were, rather than as they had been, but my heart was heavy as I said,

"I will try, Papa."

# 4

THE CHANGES CONTINUED. My stepmother wished to return the hospitality that she had received from friends and neighbors in the district and so now a constant stream of visitors came to the house and Mrs. Hubbard was put to it to devise fresh menus to please her new mistress. Borlase spent much time in his pantry, polishing up stored away silver that had not seen the light of day for years, and I often heard him grumbling to himself at the extra work.

Yet, despite the many callers to Penvarrion it seemed to me that I saw less of Esmond than formerly. Or perhaps it was that I so seldom saw him alone but only at a lunch or dinner or supper party. One morning I looked at the calendar and saw to my amazement that it was November. My birthday had come and gone and still Esmond had not spoken for me.

I knew he was preoccupied with home affairs. His father was ill with gout and for several weeks he had been unable to put his foot to the ground, and so Esmond had much work to do on the estate and also in conjunction with the tin mine that belonged to the Borleigh family. I tried to comfort myself with the thought that he was not free at present to make plans and I thought to myself, "Perhaps at Christmas things will be different."

There was to be a big ball at the Assembly Rooms in Truro, and my stepmother decided that we should attend.

"We must think of our girls," she told my father. "It is important for them to meet new people." She smiled serenely. "Especially if we are to find husbands for them."

47

"What a disagreeable thought," I said, without thinking. "Should we not choose our own?"

She frowned in the way she sometimes did when I spoke too impulsively.

"At eighteen neither you nor Amy are fit to decide for yourselves."

"Perhaps we have already done so."

She shrugged.

"Oh, young people have their fancies, but these usually pass away."

Amy glanced at me.

"I believe Kate has a secret fancy. Have you Kate? Tell us his name."

"Perhaps you have one yourself," I countered. "You are always daydreaming."

"I am daydreaming of my future husband. Perhaps he will be at the ball. Perhaps he will fall madly in love with me."

Her mother stood up.

"I have never heard such silly talk. Have you nothing better to do? Here comes Miss Barlow across the lawn. I hope she will have some useful mission to suggest to you."

"I wish it was *Mr*. Barlow," Amy said. "He is so good looking. Do you not think he would make an excellent husband for one of us, Mama? Kate, most probably. He admires Kate very much. I can tell by the way he looks at her."

Now I was the one to say,

"Amy, *you* are silly," and we giggled and then, hurriedly, composed our expressions as the door opened.

Miss Barlow was announced. As usual she had a request to make. She worked hard in the parish, teaching in the Sunday school and visiting poor or sick parishioners. My father supplied most of the flowers for the church, and I usually took them and helped to arrange them.

After she had spoken to us of the affairs in her mind my stepmother rang for some refreshment and when Miss Barlow left, I walked with her to the wicket gate and stood talking to her for a little while for we had become friendly, although she was several years older than myself.

Now she fixed her melancholy brown eyes upon me and said, after a moment's hesitation,

"I have a request to make of you, Katherine. Would you care to help me with the Sunday school? You have such a charming speaking voice, deep yet clear. I feel you would read the Bible stories to perfection."

I hesitated, just as Miss Barlow had done, and after a moment she added,

"My brother has so much work to do in the Parish and I help him all I can. Your assistance would greatly relieve me and I know the children would love and heed you." She smiled wistfully. "Children, like men, are attracted to the beautiful and are repelled by the mean or the ugly."

I looked at her, standing there in the brown alpaca dress, that only deepened the sallowness of her complexion, her limp hair looped back from her long plain face, and for the first time I had an inkling of what it might be like to be born of unprepossessing appearance. In a society where few women had respected employment and marriage was necessarily the most important factor of one's life, I realized that from the beginning the cards must be stacked against someone like Miss Barlow. Often they were doomed to become old maids.

And yet, she was so *good*. So kind and considerate to everyone, making few demands on other people. She was clever too, her mind informed and cultured. Indeed, in Gertrude Barlow's company I often felt woefully ignorant.

I put my hand out to her in a gesture of sympathy rather than acquiescence.

"Of course I will come and help with the Sunday school. I should like to." As her face lit up with pleasure I added in the fullness of my enthusiasm. "It will be of—of great interest to me."

"How kind you are. Thank you, Katherine. I knew I should not call upon you in vain. Charles will be as delighted as I am to hear you are to help us."

49

We spoke a little longer together, settling various small matters and then Miss Barlow said good-by to me and walked through the wicket gate and up the path leading to the Vicarage. I watched her go, a drab and angular figure, her straw bonnet slightly awry as usual, and I felt a little heartache as I turned away.

---

Truro was a matter of eighteen miles from Penvarrion, no great distance for the horses and it was arranged Bartlemay would drive the four of us there, with Harry Martin, the groom, in attendance. To my delight Esmond had subscribed to the ball which was in aid of a charity. He had taken tickets for Laura and Paul, and for David his cousin, and they planned to travel together in the Borleigh carriage.

It was the first week in December. The moon was full and bright and the weather clear so the drive was accomplished without difficulty and soon we arrived at the Assembly Rooms and divested ourselves of the cloaks and wraps and shawls with which we had bundled ourselves up against the frosty night.

I was wearing my white muslin dress again, and Amy was wearing the same white tarlatan dress with the rosebud trimming and ruched overskirt that she had worn for my birthday dance. Esmond, with Laura and Paul and David had already arrived, and after the necessary introductions were made to my stepmother and Amy, who had not met David Borleigh, I found myself standing a little apart with Esmond.

He smiled down at me and my heart turned over in the old familiar way.

"You look well, Katy. That is a remarkably pretty dress."

I colored with pleasure.

"Thank you. How is Sir Ralph? I hope he is better of the gout."

"I am pleased to say he is tolerably improved in health, if not in temper. He regrets, as does my mother, that he is unable to be with us tonight, but we are all hoping that he will be out again soon. I have been pretty well occupied carrying out his affairs for him, not always to his satisfaction."

"I realize you have had much extra responsibility." I hesitated then added, "We have missed your visits to us at Penvarrion."

"Yes. I too have missed seeing you all." He glanced away. "Laura has been looking forward to this occasion. After Christmas is over she will be curtailing her social activities. But she had better tell you of that herself."

"Oh, do you mean?" I blushed and checked myself. The violins started up and couples began moving onto the floor to form sets for dancing. Esmond smiled and bowed.

"May I have the pleasure, Katy?"

"Thank you." I put my hand into his with joyfully beating heart and skimmed across the sanded and polished boards to take my place opposite Laura and Paul who came smilingly to join us.

I danced with Esmond and with my father and with Esmond's cousin David and with Esmond again, when my stepmother beckoned to me. I went over to where she was seated and she waved her fan in the direction of the man standing beside her and said,

"I think you are already acquainted with Mr. Rossiter, Kate. He would like very much to dance with you."

I acknowledged Mr. Rossiter's bow.

"Good evening."

"Miss Carew. What a pleasure it is to meet you again. I hope you will honor me with this next dance."

I remembered Mr. Rossiter now and his fulsome manner. He was several years older than myself and had a high-colored face and long black side whiskers and a black mustache over a full and fleshy mouth. We had met at my aunt's house in London, and I did not care for him over much. It was with the greatest reluctance that I put my hand in his and allowed myself to be led forward into the next set. As we danced up and down and around and across, he panted out some compliments to which I smiled vaguely in answer. Dancing up the aisle we ducked our heads under the archway of hands and danced down again to exchange partners.

A firm hand took mine. A voice said,

"Miss Kate," and I glanced up in astonishment to see Bryce Dawnay.

51

"Bryce!" Smiling gravely down at me, my hand clasped in his, we circled the center of the set, our feet skipping to the music before moving back opposite to one another. The next couple took our place and then it was clasped hands again and more dancing up the aisle.

"I did not expect to see you here," he murmured in my ear as we bent our heads together under uplifted hands.

"Nor I you."

"May I claim a dance from you later?"

"If you wish."

He released my fingers, swung away and went dancing around the back of the set to claim his next partner. Mr. Rossiter's sharp eyes watched me from farther up the set. A small fair man with gold-rimmed spectacles sprang forward and took my hand in his and we danced away to meet the couple facing us.

When the dance was over Mr. Rossiter was at my side again to escort me back to my stepmother and the rest of the party. I looked around for Bryce and saw him some way farther down the long room. Tall and black-haired he towered above the rest of the company, the snowy stock beneath his chin throwing up the darkness of his complexion and the jet-blackness of brow above the curiously light eyes. He bent his head to speak to someone, and I saw that his companion was an extremely pretty girl with fair curls caught up in a band of roses to match the pink roses on her sprigged muslin dress.

Mr. Rossiter was saying something to me but I scarcely heeded him. I was too surprised and intrigued by the advent of Bryce Dawnay. What was he doing here, this man people called "The Gypsy"? And how different he appeared tonight from the ragamuffin of a boy I had known. A single glance at him was sufficient to show that he was the most distinguished-looking man in the room, not for reason of good looks, for his features were too rugged for handsomeness, but for the aura of strength and what other quality was it? Power, magnetism, some aura that set him apart from other people.

He was with a party; the pretty fair girl and a middle-aged man and woman and two or three other people, all well dressed and agreeable looking.

My stepmother's voice interrupted me.

"Mr. Rossiter would like to call upon us at Penvarrion. He has gone to speak to your father."

I opened my mouth to say, "I do not care for Mr. Rossiter," when Laura appeared at my side, smiling and reaching forward to brush my cheek.

"Kate dear, how lovely to see you. Shall we sit down here. I have so much to tell you."

We sat side by side on a velvet covered couch and I smiled as I touched her hand.

"You look—blooming, Laura. What is the secret?"

She gave me a radiantly happy glance and said in a low voice,

"Have you already guessed? Or has Esmond said something to you? I am to have a child in the spring."

"Oh Laura." Our clasped fingers tightened together. "Laura, I am so happy for you. Esmond did not say anything—well, not specifically. It would not be fitting. But he gave me a hint. How thrilled and proud Paul must be—your parents too."

"Yes. But it is still a secret, Kate. Until after New Year when I fear it will be no secret to anyone," she added ruefully. She looked up and said, "Who is that your father is speaking to?"

"His name is Mr. Rossiter," I began, when, my glance following hers, I saw that while Mr. Rossiter hovered in the vicinity of my father, my father was speaking to Bryce Dawnay. My father was smiling and nodding his head as if in agreement with something Bryce had said. Another man joined them; the older man whom Bryce had been with earlier. He put his hand out and my father shook it and the three of them stood talking in friendly fashion.

"The man my father was speaking to is Bryce Dawnay," I said slowly. "And I think he is approaching us at this moment."

He came up to where Laura and I sat and, with a slight bow said,

"I have renewed my acquaintance with your father and he has permitted me to ask you for a dance."

I smiled.

"I thought you had already done that. Laura, may I present Mr. Dawnay. Mr. Dawnay—Mrs. Garvin."

53

We exchanged a few politenesses until the violins began playing one of the late Mr. Strauss's waltzes. Bryce bowed again.

"May I, Miss Kate?"

Out of the corner of my eye I saw Mr. Rossiter coming toward us, and I could not put my hand fast enough into Bryce's outstretched one. The next moment we were moving slowly around the floor.

There was something intimate, almost daring about the waltz; to have a man's arm circling one's waist throughout the dance, his hand holding one's own all the time.

For a few moments neither of us spoke but gave ourselves up to the music, to the dreamy lilt that seemed to enmesh us in its fascinating sway.

I glanced up at Bryce and saw his face, dark and aloof, almost stern. If I had not known the boy in the man, I could almost have been afraid of him. He looked down and his eyes met mine. To cover my embarrassment at having been caught staring at him I said,

"I did not imagine your liking to dance. You dance well."

"I was taught by an expert."

"Here—in Truro?" I heard the note of surprise in my own voice.

His mouth twisted in sardonic fashion.

"In Valparaiso. That's South America, as you probably know. A long way from here."

"It is a long way from Australia, too, is it not? I think you said you had been working there."

"Yes. From there I went to California. It was the time of the gold rush when every man was seeking to make his fortune."

"And did you make yours?"

"Not quite. Shall we say I returned more prosperous than when I went away." He shrugged. "That wasn't hard to do as I left England a pauper."

We fell into silence again, myself because I was puzzled by his complex character and Bryce perhaps because he was thinking of those past times.

After circling the room again I said tentatively,

"Are you staying in Truro?"

"At the Britannia Inn. But, in fact, I have relatives here and it is with their party I have come tonight. The fair girl over there in the pink dress is a connection of mine. Her father was my father's cousin."

I looked across to the girl with her long fair ringlets and smiling blue eyes.

"She is very pretty."

"Yes, and as charming as she is pretty. She is the youngest of four sisters. The others are now married. Her parents have been kind to me and made me welcome to their home."

"I am glad for you."

"Thank you. It has made a difference to me, being made welcome by my family connections." He smiled and I thought, as I had thought before, how brilliantly the dark face lit up. "You see, Kate, I am beginning to feel half-civilized."

I smiled back at him.

"Only half? Yes, I believe that. The other half still goes climbing the high cliffs in search of a raven's nest, or fishing after shark. Am I right?"

He shook his head, still smiling.

"I am too busy. Trying to make my fortune."

"Do you have to do that?"

His expression changed,

"Yes. I have a most particular reason."

"May I know what it is?"

"Not now." He stared down at me. "Perhaps one day you will learn what it is."

"You have made me very curious," I began, and then something in his gaze, a peculiar intentness, silenced me and before I could speak again, the dance ended. Bryce bowed and said,

"Thank you, Kate. That was a great pleasure," and with my hand on his arm he escorted me back to where my stepmother sat. I would have introduced Bryce but Esmond was beside her and looking so cold and frowning that I hesitated to do so. Bryce after a second and shorter bow turned and walked away.

"I am surprised Dawnay should have the impertinence to ask you to dance with him," Esmond said in a low voice when he was out of earshot. "And equally surprised that you should do so."

"Papa gave his permission to ask me. I have known him a long time, Esmond. We—we are friends."

Esmond gave a scornful ejaculation.

"How can you say that? You do not mix in the same circles, you have no mutual acquaintances. He is not accepted among the people we know, and I have told you the reason why."

I bit my lip, confused and unhappy by Esmond's censure.

"Papa allowed me to dance with him. He would not have done that surely if Bryce were unworthy. What has he done wrong that you should condemn him so?"

"It is not what he has done. It is what he is. You have no judgment of character, Katy. But this is neither the time or place for an argument. Will you excuse me, please," and with an angry jerk of his head he bowed and moved away and the next moment he was beside Amy and asking her to dance.

I stared after them, tears of mortification in my eyes and a deepening regret that I should ever have danced with Bryce in the first place and so made Esmond displeased with me.

Esmond did not dance with me again and for the most part remained at Amy's side. If it was done to provoke me, he certainly succeeded, and the rest of the evening was marred by Esmond's coolness and Mr. Rossiter's assiduous attentions. I was thankful when the ball was over, and after hot soup had been served, the carriages were brought around for us to set off on the long drive back to Penvarrion.

I slept ill that night and felt listless and depressed for the next few days. Perhaps it was on account of this that I fell into a fresh argument with my stepmother.

Amy had gone out to visit one of the old ladies in the village. Because she was not fond of horse riding my father had bought her a small pony carriage and in this she drove about the district. Lately she had taken to helping Miss Barlow in various ways and was often gone on her own on some helpful mission or duty call.

56

I was in the morning room when my stepmother came to me and said,

"Katherine, Mr. Rossiter is calling upon us today. I think you should change your dress before he comes."

I glanced up from the letter I was attempting to write though my thoughts were very much elsewhere.

"There is no need for me to be present. Amy will be back shortly."

She said stiffly,

"It is not Amy Mr. Rossiter wishes to see but *you,* Katherine. He has asked your father's permission to address you."

I stared in astonishment at her.

"Address me?"

"He wishes to marry you."

I sprang up from the table, all but upsetting the inkwell.

"Well, *I* do not wish to marry him, and you may tell him so. Please spare me the embarrassment of listening to his proposal."

My stepmother's pale skin darkened with anger, her brown eyes narrowed to regard me.

"Mr. Rossiter is a wealthy and well-established man. His background is impeccable, his character admirable in every way. Your father approves of him, as I do, and in the circumstances you should give consideration to his offer."

"I do not like him," I said.

"How can you say that? You do not know him."

"I know I do not wish to marry him."

"You are headstrong and foolish to a degree, Katherine. We, your father and I, wish to find a suitable husband for you. You do not want to remain a spinster all your life, do you?"

I said airily,

"It is unlikely I shall do so. But if I do not marry the man I love, I shall not marry at all."

She said coldly,

"You prefer to remain a burden upon your father? If you do not marry he will have to keep you for the rest of your life."

The temper rose in me and my voice was as sharp as my stepmother's as I retorted.

"I shall never be a burden to my father or to anyone else. When I am twenty-one I come into my inheritance, and then I shall be independent."

She stared blankly at me as if she were taking in the gist of my words. She said slowly,

"Your inheritance? What do you mean?"

"Did you not know that the plantation in Barbados was once owned by my grandfather? After he died it came to my mother and is in trust to me until I am twenty-one. Belle Tout will be mine then. So you see you need not concern yourself trying to marry me off. Select a husband for Amy if you wish—it is your privilege. But when the time comes I will choose my own or die an old maid," and with those words I turned and rushed from the room.

I was trembling as I went upstairs. Why did my stepmother always provoke me to anger? Or was it that I provoked her. Whatever the reason, the fact remained that we were always at variance and there was constant tension between us.

*Mr. Rossiter,* I thought. Of all people. I could scarcely bear the sight of him, much less consider him as a possible husband. But I could never consider anyone as that except Esmond. Esmond whom I loved so dearly and whom at the moment I was estranged from. That fact had caused me to fly into such a temper, and already I was beginning to regret my outspokenness.

Even so, I was not going to be confronted by Mr. Rossiter and picking up my bonnet and cloak I went down the back staircase to find Carrie.

"Please tell Mrs. Carew or my father, if he should ask for me, that I have gone to the village to call upon someone. I shall be back in time for luncheon."

The day was clear and cold, which was fortunate, for Cornish winters were notoriously damp ones. I walked up the path to the church and turned right along the road toward the village. I had gone but a quarter of a mile when I saw someone approaching in the opposite direction and recognized the vicar, Mr. Barlow. As we drew level he raised his black hat and smiled, and after we had exchanged greetings glanced down at the basket in my hand to say,

"I think you are going on such a mission as I have just returned from."

"Yes, I am taking eggs, and some of Mrs. Hubbard's pasties to old Mr. Hargreaves."

"He will welcome them, poor old fellow. And not least your company, Miss Carew. I have been myself to call on Mrs. Newman. She is very low, since she lost her good man."

I glanced up at him, thinking how well the black vestments set off his clean-cut features and curly brown hair.

"You would meet my stepsister for she went to call on Mrs. Newman I think?"

He shook his head.

"No, she was not there. Nor has been lately, I think, for Mrs. Newman was bemoaning her lack of visitors, which caused me to feel extremely guilty."

"Oh." I frowned, feeling sure that Amy's parting remark as she left in the pony carriage was that "old Mrs. Newman would be waiting for her." "I must have made a mistake and it was some other person she intended to call upon. I know she visits various people from time to time."

He gave me a quick glance.

"You surprise me. I am not aware that Miss Lambert was in the habit of calling upon the village folk."

It was my turn to be surprised.

"But she does so very often. At least—" I stopped, aware that the words 'at least so she tells me' would sound curious to say the least. "She drives frequently to the village, I know. I was under the impression it was to undertake the same acts of charity as Miss Barlow and yourself."

"Perhaps she has some protégé of her own we are not acquainted with."

"Yes, perhaps so." I half turned. "I must be on my way, Mr. Barlow. Good morning."

He raised his hat again.

"Good morning, Miss Carew," and as I walked away I was aware that he stood staring after me.

I reached the village still puzzling over Amy's jaunts in the pony cart and wondering for what purpose they had been made. Then all thoughts were put aside as I sat in old Mr. Hargreaves' cottage where a wood fire crackled merrily up the chimney piece and Mr. Hargreaves himself, crouched like a Cornish quilkin in his high-backed chair, a shawl over his bent shoulders, his trembling old hands clasped one over another on his stick.

He watched me unpack the basket and exclaimed gratefully at the sight of Mrs. Hubbard's pasties.

"They be nathin' so tasty as a licky pasty, less it is one of turnip an' bacon. My old Martha ur was a fair 'and with pasty makin'. An' saffern cake—never did taste anythin' like them ole saffern cakes ur do be makin' of a Friday night. Sit 'ee down, Miss Kate. Do mine ol' een a power o' good to see a maid as bonny as 'ee. Put me in mind o' Miss Isabella, your poor mother, for she wor' the beautifulest 'ooman ur ever saw from 'ere to Land's End. And beyond, very like."

I sat down on a corner of the black horsehair sofa pushed against the wall by the fireplace.

"Do you remember her well?"

"Aye, purty well." He lifted up the empty pipe from the table beside him and stared mournfully at it and I pushed the small packet I had brought within his reach.

"Please light up, Mr. Hargreaves. Here is some tobacco sent by my father." This was a slight exaggeration, as I had taken an ounce or two from his tin-lined box in the study.

"Thank 'ee. Mr. Carew he be a good gentleman and an upright one. I hope he be well and happy in his second choice."

"Yes, he is very happy, I think."

The old man nodded, puffing noisily at his smoke-stained clay pipe.

"Ur be a pretty l'il thing as is the dawter. I zeen 'un goin' down along jes' now and young Mr. Borleigh ridin' after 'un." He coughed and wheezed in what was intended to be laughter.

I leaned forward to say slowly,

"Do you mean Miss Lambert went down the road here?"

"Aar. I say so. Drivin' that l'il gray pony she wur, an' 'im followin' arter like I zeen 'em afore."

I leaned back against the sofa and for a moment closed my eyes as if closing them against some fact I did not want to face. Amy and Esmond? And then—but old Mr. Hargreaves must be mistaken. His eyesight was bad, his mind apt to wander.

I opened my eyes to look at Mr. Hargreaves where he sat puffing away in the chimney corner, his filmed blue eyes blinking into the firelight, and before I could check myself I said,

"Are you sure it was my stepsister, Miss Lambert, with—with Mr. Borleigh?"

He glanced sharply around at me.

"I got eyes in me 'ead, un't I? Beggin' your pardon, Miss Kate, to speak sudden like. But folks do be thinkin' when folks be old they be simple as a week-old babe and blind as an airy mouse."

"I'm sorry. I know you are a wonderful old gentleman, and I hope you will keep as well and alert as you appear to be now for a long time."

He bowed his head.

"Amen to that and I thank the Lord for his many blessings. I be an old chap, but I do be 'avin' good friends, includin' yourself, Miss Kate."

"Yes." I stood up. "Good-by, Mr. Hargreaves. I will call again very soon."

"Aye, 'ee do that. And thank 'ee. Good day, Miss Kate."

I let myself out of the low door which opened onto the street. After the overly hot room the wind seemed doubly chill. I shivered under its sharpness, but I knew it was not the winter day alone that caused me to feel so cold and unhappy.

# 5

I RETURNED HOME to face my father's displeasure.

"I am surprised at your conduct, Katherine. You have behaved badly. Not only to your stepmother, for she had told me of your impoliteness to her, but to Mr. Rossiter who called here expressly to see you. And then to go running off to the village, as you did. It was uncalled for behavior."

I could only stand before him with crimsoning cheeks and down bent head.

"I am sorry, Papa. I—I did not wish to be at home when Mr. Rossiter called. Stepmother told me the reason for his visit, and I wanted to spare both Mr. Rossiter and myself embarrassment."

"You did not succeed for he was naturally vexed by your absence and we had difficulty of explaining this to him. And what distresses me even more, Katherine, is your manner toward your stepmother, who only has your best interests at heart."

The hot tears rushed to my eyes and I had to think hard to keep them at bay. I said again,

"I am sorry—truly sorry. It is just that—I do not want—I do not even *like* Mr. Rossiter and I think I—I should have been consulted on the—the likelihood of his visit and the reason for it before it was arranged."

"Katherine"—today there was no question of his calling me by my pet name—"you are eighteen years old. Of marriageable age, certainly, but in matters like this it is a parent's *duty* to give a young girl guidance, even perhaps select a suitable partner for her."

Only a short time ago I would have spoken of Esmond and asked my father to encourage him to the house, but after the incidents of the past few days I had no longer the confidence to do so. I stared down at the patterned rug at my feet and at last summoned up courage to say,

"You have never spoken to me in this way before, Papa. Please forgive me and please do not try and find a husband for me just yet."

He frowned and I saw that, under his stern manner, he too was upset. He said more gently, "It is your stepmother's wish that you should be married happily and soon. She tells me it is best for a young girl to be settled in a secure way of life while she is young. I rely on her wisdom as a woman, and a mother, and I am grateful to her for her advice, as you should be too, Katherine."

I could not tell him that for some unaccountable reason I distrusted my stepmother; that I felt my best interests were not necessarily hers and that she wished to make an early marriage because she wanted me out of the way. So I merely said,

"Yes, Papa."

He patted my shoulder in a gesture of forgiveness.

"Go and apologize to your stepmama and we will forget all about it." He smiled slightly. "And not hurry to find you a suitor." He paused then added, "Is it Esmond you are thinking of? I thought at one time he wished to address you, but he has not spoken on this subject since my return."

I said in a low voice,

"I am very fond of Esmond but—but I do not know what is in his mind or in his heart. I will go and find stepmama and tell her I am sorry for my rudeness."

"That's a good girl," my father said fondly and turned away.

In the hall I met Amy hurrying toward the stairs. She halted when she saw me and smiled as she untied the strings of her bonnet.

"Oh—Kate. Have you been out? I have just returned from the village. I—I have been calling upon old Mrs. Newman."

I looked directly at her.

"Do not say any more, Amy. I met Mr. Barlow on the road and he had been himself to visit Mrs. Newman. He told me she had had no visitors lately."

Amy's green eyes widened, small teeth caught her underlip.

"I—I do not understand. You must mean another Mrs. Newman —there are so many of the same name in the village."

"Perhaps so. But only one elderly widow living alone." I added, "Did you see anyone else while you were out?"

For a moment she stared at me then, glancing away, she said quickly,

"I met Esmond. He was taking his horse to the farriers. We—we exchanged greetings, naturally."

"Naturally." I did not wish to form an inquisition, so I turned away saying, "It is not important," and went in search of my stepmother.

But after I had made my stilted apologies and returned to my room I thought about Amy. If her meeting with Esmond was only by chance, why should she lie about her visit to old Mrs. Newman? And why had Mr. Hargreaves said he had seen Amy driving the pony cart and Esmond riding after her on former occasions?

It puzzled but most of all it grieved me. I could not help but feel that Amy and Esmond had formed some sort of secret friendship. I was deeply distressed by the idea. I had loved him all my life and dreamed that he would love me in return.

Soon after this incident I heard a chance remark that gave me further unease. I entered the drawing room one evening after dinner to hear my stepmother saying, in her smooth soft voice,

"I think it would best be done after Christmas, Gilbert. Shall I tell her or will you?"

Hesitating in the doorway I heard my father answer, "Perhaps it would be best that I do it, Blanche. I know her much better than you."

They turned their heads as I came forward looking first at one and then the other. I wanted to ask of whom they referred? But I could not bring myself to put the question and when my stepmother said,

"Come and sit down, Katherine. Amy is coming to play the piano for us—we must practice the Christmas carols," and smiled so pleasantly I could not think her remarks had anything to do with me.

Christmas was upon us before we had realized. Oliver came home from Naval College and we were delighted to see him. He had grown and he had filled out too and looked altogether more manly. There was much excitement over hiding presents from one another, and Amy and I designed and painted Christmas cards to send to our various friends and relations.

"Oh, I pray it may snow at Christmas," Amy said putting her two hands together in supplication. "I have never seen snow the whole of my life."

My father shook his head.

"It is doubtful if you will see it here, my dear. We do not get much snow in Cornwall—wind and rain are our winter hazards."

As it proved, the weather was mild but damp over the few days of Christmas. We attended church on Christmas morning and Mr. Barlow preached a stirring sermon to a crowded congregation. He was a splendid speaker and his voice, deeply musical, held us in a way old Mr. Pennington, the former vicar, had seldom succeeded in doing. Afterward we gathered in the small green churchyard to exchange Christmas greetings with our neighbors. As I stood beside Miss Barlow who was speaking to Oliver I looked over the headstones to where my mother's grave lay. I had placed flowers and a holly wreath on it the day before and recalling this I remembered the day I had met Bryce Dawnay in the churchyard. That had been the day of my stepmother's arrival, and I had been full of apprehension at the thought of meeting her.

And now? What did I feel now, I thought, as I glanced back to where she stood with my father, talking to Dr. Fullbright? She was wearing a fitted blue-velvet coat with a short basque and a bell-shaped skirt without the crinoline. The jacket was fastened by flowers of darker blue velvet and had a flat round collar of blue velvet edged with a narrow frill. As usual she looked beautiful. Her clothes were elegant to a degree. Sometimes I marveled how much attention both she and Amy paid to their dresses. And of the two, it was my stepmother who was the more extravagant. I supposed it was because in Barbados she and Amy had been poor and deprived of the luxuries that now meant so much to them both.

It was not that I did not enjoy pretty clothes myself, for I did, and my father had always been most generous to me in that respect. But I could not give to fashion the attention that my stepmother did.

Dr. Fullbright gazed admiringly at her, and my father's expression held the same look of admiration and a sort of basking pride. He at any rate was happy with my stepmother and could find no fault in her.

Then why should I always feel at variance with her? Was my antagonism a form of jealousy and the scarcely expressed criticism I sensed from my stepmother the same of me? We were both rivals for my father's love and so could never love one another as we should.

I checked myself. These were not proper thoughts for Christmas morning when all should be peace on earth and good will toward men. If my father was made happy, that was all that mattered, and I determined to start afresh and do all I could to win my stepmother's affection.

But when the Christmas festivities were over and the New Year came, my resolutions were threatened.

Miss Pringle was not well. I had never seen her look so pale and ill and her thin form seemed more attenuated than ever. She ate little at meals and sometimes I would hear her sigh or see her kind brown eyes fill with tears. I could not understand it, and one morning, finding her standing staring out of the window at the rain-sodden garden with so melancholy a look on her dear face, I put my arm about her waist and said, using my old nickname for her,

"What is it, Pringhy? What is the matter? Are you feeling ill?"

She turned her head and looked at me and I saw that she had been crying.

"Oh, Katherine. Katherine, my dear child, I scarcely know how to tell you. I have been bracing myself to do so this past week, but I have not had the courage."

I clutched at her hand with my free one.

"What is it—what must you tell me? Pringhy, darling, whatever it is we can help you—we can put it right. Just tell me what is the matter."

She shook her head, holding my hand tightly in her own.

"I am leaving you, dear. I am leaving Penvarrion."

66

For a moment I could not speak, only try to take in the words I had just heard.

"*Leaving Penvarrion?* But—but you cannot do that. You belong here. Why should you want to go away from us?"

She dabbed at her eyes with a ball of wet handkerchief.

"I do not *want* to go, dear, but I must. There is no longer a place for me here. You are a grown woman and no longer need me. As your father has explained, your stepmother will guide and counsel you in the future. It is only natural. I am leaving next week to take up another post."

I stared at her with dismay and a sense of terrible loss.

"But I *do* need you, Pringhy—I shall always need you. You've been part of my life since—since I was a little girl. I will tell my father you must stay. You will see—he will change his mind and everything will stay the same."

"Dear child—if only that could be so. But life changes for everyone. I had thought—I had hoped, perhaps, that I should remain with you until you had a home of your own. But it is not to be. Do not reproach your father—he has ever been good and generous to me, and your stepmother has arranged for this new post for me so that I shall suffer no financial hardship. And I do realize that to be retained just as your companion is an unnecessary expense in the circumstances."

I thought of the new dresses and the new furnishings and Amy's pony carriage and the many other extravagances my father had lavished on his new family, and I was wild with indignation on behalf of Miss Pringle. An unnecessary expense indeed! I knew full well who had brought up *that* excuse, and it was not my generous-hearted father. I wanted to fly in search of the instigator of Miss Pringle's departure and pour out my protests, but my dear governess must have seen the flush of temper on my face for she put her hand out to me and said,

"Do not distress yourself, Katherine. And do not make trouble on my account." She smiled sadly. "I would have had to leave you sometime if you had not left me. So say no more but accept the decision, as I have. I am not going far away. To Lostwithel only, so we

67

shall not lose touch. We will write to one another and remain good friends always."

I wept then for there was something so final in her manner. I realized then how much I had come to rely on my governess's teaching and good sense. I knew how empty the house would seem to me when she had gone.

I tried not to be selfish, thinking only of my own loss. Miss Pringle must feel even more upset for she had to go to live among strangers and make a new way of life for herself, after all the years she had been with us at Penvarrion. So after a while I dried my tears and tried to put on a more cheerful face so as not to make things harder for my beloved friend.

But it was a sad week for us both, and when finally the carriage came to take Miss Pringle and her luggage on the long drive to Lostwithiel I had all I could do not to burst into tears all over again.

When she had gone I did what I always did in times of distress. I had the little mare saddled and went riding up to the moors, dissipating grief in action, and letting my melancholy thoughts be blown away on the winds that racked the wild and empty land.

◆

Sir Ralph Borleigh was much recovered and he and Lady Borleigh came to dinner with us, along with Esmond and also Laura and Paul. Mr. Barlow and his sister came too and brought their brother who was staying with them. He was a naval officer and as handsome as Mr. Barlow with curly brown hair and a fresh open face tanned from the sea voyages. Esmond sat next to me at dinner and we spoke much to one another both during dinner and afterward, so I was happy again.

Once he looked over to where Laurence Barlow leaned over the piano where Amy performed for us.

"Amy has found a new admirer," he said.

"Yes." I glanced up at him but he was smiling and it seemed to me that my fears of his liking Amy especially were unfounded. "She— she is very pretty," I added, as if to test myself. Or was it Esmond?

"She is delightful." He looked down at me and added in a low voice, "But you are beautiful, Kate."

I could not speak for the pleasure that his compliment gave me. I could only stare down at the embroidered panel of my skirt. Then, at last, to break the silence, I said,

"Do you not miss Miss Pringle?"

He looked around as if surprised.

"I hadn't realized she was not here. She was such a quiet and self-effacing person. How long has she been gone?"

"A month now. She left during the middle of January. Penvarrion does not seem the same without her."

"Come, Katy. You are old enough now to do without a governess."

"She was no longer my governess. She was my friend and companion."

"You have other friends." He leaned down to me. "Of which I am one, I hope."

"Indeed you are, Esmond. You know that. One of my—my closest friends."

He smiled at me and my heart seemed to turn over. His blue eyes were so warm and affectionate as they met mine, that I felt sure that if we had been alone together he would have spoken to me of more than friendship.

"I like to think so," he said softly.

Amy finished her piece with a ripple of arpeggios and standing up, moved away from the piano.

"That is the end of the recital for this evening," she announced gaily, as she came to where I sat, with Esmond standing beside my chair. "And what have you two been in conference about? I saw such nods and smiles from across the room I felt sure you had settled the affairs of the nation."

The spell was broken. Esmond brought forward a chair for Amy, and the conversation became general. But though soon afterward the evening broke up I went to bed happier than I had been for many weeks. It seemed to me as I lay in the darkness remembering Es-

69

mond's smile and the things he had said to me that all was as it had always been between us.

"You are beautiful, Kate," he had said and I hugged the words to myself. I wanted to be beautiful for Esmond; I wanted to be everything that he desired in a woman.

A week or two later I went to call upon Laura, who had not been feeling well and so had been confined to the house with orders to rest. The baby was due in April and it was natural that we should be anxious on her account.

It was a fine February day with watery sunshine and a feeling of spring in the air. Laura and Paul lived outside St. Columb Major in a charming old gray-stone house, and it was arranged that I should leave Penvarrion after breakfast and have lunch with them, returning in the early afternoon so as to be home before dark.

"Take the pony carriage," Amy suggested. "I have no need of it. I am not going out today. I—I woke with the headache."

"Oh, I am sorry, Amy. I hope it is not bad."

When I glanced at her I thought she looked surprisingly well, but she put a small white hand to her forehead and sighed.

"I shall lie down I think. Then it will pass."

"Yes, do that. I hope you will feel better by the time I return."

I put some gifts for Laura in the pony cart and set off at a trot, the bells on Punch's harness jingling merrily in time with his brisk little hooves.

It was a matter of five miles to Greystokes, Laura's home, and Punch soon covered the distance. On arrival Punch was led away to the stables to be watered and fed while I was taken up to Laura's bedroom.

"I am well enough," she said in answer to my greeting and anxious enquiries, "but Dr. Fullbright has ordered me to rest here for a few days." She smiled. "I will gladly remain here a month so that the babe will arrive whole and strong."

I touched her fingers.

"Of course. Is it to be a girl or a boy?"

"I wish I could determine that. Paul longs for a son, I know. But perhaps if it is a girl, he will love her just as well."

70

We spent a happy hour or two together and then I had lunch with Paul while Laura rested, after her tray meal. Then I returned to sit with her for a little while before I said good-by and Paul escorted me to the pony carriage waiting by the front door.

"Let me send one of the grooms to ride with you," he suggested. "Or I will ride myself."

"Please do not trouble yourself. It is only a matter of a few miles and Punch is a quiet and careful fellow." I smiled at him. "I ride for miles on my own at times and come home from hunting very often by moonlight."

"I know that, Kate. I know what an independent young lady you are. But I should be happier to send Carter to escort you."

"I would not hear of it. Good-by, Paul. I will come again and see Laura, but I am sure she will soon be up and about again." I lifted the reins and turned Punch's head and as Paul called, "Good-by. Take care," we set off down the drive.

It was not yet half of three o'clock—I should be home at Penvarrion long before sunset. Punch, refreshed by his long rest and a handful of oats with his dinner seemed to think so too and needed no urging to maintain a smart pace.

We had covered half the journey when, as I steadied Punch's pace to descend the hill that led down into the Vale of Penvarrion, I saw a horseman cantering up it toward me. It needed no second glance to recognize Bryce Dawnay though, as we drew level, he appeared to be in doubt as to my identity. Then as he reined in his horse and lifted his hat, he said,

"Good afternoon, Miss Kate. I recognized the gray pony, but thought to see your stepsister driving him. Are you on your way home?"

I looked up at him, startled, as I always was at first meeting, by his height and the breadth of his shoulders and the blackness of hair and brows above the carelessly tied cravat.

"Yes. I have been to call on Mrs. Garvin at St. Columb."

He frowned, his brows a black bar above the narrowed eyes.

"You should not be alone on the roads at this time. It will soon be dark."

71

"I shall as soon be home."

He turned his horse's head.

"I will ride with you as far as Penvarrion."

I said, as I had said to Paul a little while ago,

"Please do not trouble yourself. I am taking you out of your way for you were riding in the opposite direction."

"It is of no matter. I am only going to Crantock, a few miles farther on. I could not continue my journey with an easy mind if I thought of you alone like this."

With some exasperation I let Punch's head go, and we went slowly down the hill with Bryce Dawnay riding alongside me. For a short while we traveled in silence then he said,

"I have not seen you since the ball at Truro."

"No. That was some weeks ago."

"It seems a long while to me. I hope you keep well, Kate." He had lapsed into the more familiar appellation. "And—and your family."

"Thank you, yes. And you? Have you been again to visit your relatives in Truro since then?"

"I saw them at Christmas for a day. Now my Aunt Mary, who is not really an aunt but I call her so, is staying at Crantock with her daughter, Miss Dawnay, whom I think you saw at the ball."

"And you were going to call upon them and will be delayed on my account."

"There is no hurry. I shall be there in ample time."

I glanced up at the stern dark face and I wondered if he had formed some attachment to Miss Dawnay. I remembered how pretty she had looked on the night of the ball, and the fact that he had been to Truro at Christmas and was on his way to visit Mrs. Dawnay and her daughter while they stayed at Crantock indicated surely some special interest?

I urged Punch into a trot and Bryce quickened the pace of the big black horse and in a little while we had come to the road above Penvarrion. The sun was setting behind the trees in the churchyard, and on the horizon the distant sea reflected a pearly glow on its gray waves.

I reined Punch in and said,

"Thank you for your kindness in bringing me home. It was not necessary, but I appreciate your courtesy, Bryce."

An owl swept out of the shadows and as it soared past us on wide silent wings Bryce gestured toward it with his riding crop,

"You are home in time, but barely. Good night, Kate."

"Good night."

He was gone, leaving Punch and me to drive down to Penvarrion through the winter dusk.

Leaving the pony and carriage with Martin, I went into the house by the side door. The hall was in semi-darkness—the lamps as yet unlit. The door of the study opened and someone came out. I expected to see my father, but to my surprise it was Esmond who appeared.

He did not see me but stood very straight and still outside the door he had closed behind him. His very immobility arrested my own movement. I could not think why he should stand there, and in so deep contemplation.

Then, the sudden thought struck me. Was it possible, dare I hope that Esmond's conference with my father concerned myself? Surely this was why Esmond was here. He had been speaking to my father privately, and now he would be able to tell me that he loved me.

I was about to call his name when a shaft of light moved along the passageway and Violet, the parlormaid, came into view, carrying a candelabra in one hand. The flickering light shone on Esmond's pale and thoughtful face and then moved to the carved chest upon which a large oil lamp stood. Bending forward Violet lit the wick and after adjusting the flame, went on toward the drawing room, unaware of my presence and ignoring Esmond's.

When she had gone I stepped forward and said softly,

"Esmond."

He swung around in such startlement that I halted abruptly.

"Kate! Katy—what are you doing here?" He sounded as if I was the last person in the world he expected to see.

"I have just returned from visiting Laura. Did you not know that I had gone to Greystokes?"

"No. Yes—yes, I think someone told me." He broke off, to stare at me in such a strange way that I put a hand out to him and said, "Is something the matter?"

"No—I—that is—" He put a hand to his forehead in an uncertain way. "I have been with your father."

"Yes—I saw you come from the study a moment ago." I paused, looking up at him and he stared back in a silence that bewildered me. Then he said slowly and with difficulty,

"I hardly know how to tell you this, Kate. I have asked Amy to become my wife."

# 6

I THOUGHT I could not have heard aright. I thought such a thing could not possibly be true. There was a ringing in my ears, and for a moment the hall and the glowing oil lamp and Esmond's pale anxious face spun madly around in dizzying succession. Then the world righted itself and I found myself standing quiet and ice-cold looking at the stranger who was Esmond. From far away I heard my own voice saying, shakily,

"You are to marry Amy?"

"Yes. It—it was settled today. Amy has consented and Mrs. Lambert and—and your father have agreed to our engagement."

No words would come. I could not speak or move, I was too numbed with shock. Esmond said in a low voice,

"I am sorry, Kate. Forgive me," and turning on his heel he walked quickly away.

How long I stood there I cannot say, but suddenly, at the sound of a door opening from somewhere behind me, I came back to reality and on an impulse to hide from other people I swung around and ran up the wide staircase and did not stop until I was in my room. I sank down onto the bed, my hand against my throbbing head, seeming to hear over and over again the words, "I have asked Amy to become my wife."

But *how—why—when?* How could it have happened like this? To have reached such a point in their relationship that now they were engaged to be married? I could not believe it. Little more than a week ago Esmond had seemed his old self with me—and I had thought that he loved me, as I loved him.

It was true then. They had been meeting in secret, just as old Mr. Hargreaves had hinted. And today—when Amy had pleaded a headache and suggested I take the pony carriage to Greystokes—had she known then that Esmond was calling to see her?

I felt betrayed. Yet common sense told me that Esmond had made no promises to me, no pledges of love. Perhaps I had taken too much for granted and read into his kind manner and affectionate ways an attachment that didn't exist. But we had been close all our lives. For me there never had been and never would be, anyone but Esmond.

A terrible void lay before me; a darkness, and emptiness. All that I had dreamed, hoped for and desired had vanished. Sitting on the edge of the bed with my head in my hands I was heartbroken and bereft.

I sprang up at the sound of a tap on the door and turned my head away as Carrie entered,

"Good evening, Miss. Did you want me to help you dress for dinner?"

I shook my head.

"No—I—I—later, perhaps."

She hesitated and I could feel her staring at my averted face.

"Be you all right, Miss Katherine?"

I clutched at the excuse.

"I am feeling a little chilled. It was cold driving home. I think I will lie down for a while. Please tell my father I shall not be in to dinner."

She came forward.

"Best let me help you out of your dress, Miss, and unfasten your stays. Then you be comfortable to lie down in your wrapper." I felt her quick fingers unbutton the back of my dress and unfasten the stiff petticoats I wore, in place of a crinoline. She unlaced my stays and dropped a clean nightdress over my head and placed a silken wrap over my shoulders, for I was shivering unaccountably.

"You have caught a chill an' no mistake, Miss. Best get into bed and I be bringin' you some hot soup. Cook's got some nice fish on—would you like a taste of it."

I shook my head as I lay back on the pillow.

76

"No, thank you. Just a cup of soup. And please don't worry about me, Carrie. Or trouble anyone else. I—I shall be perfectly all right in the morning."

When she had gone I lay staring up at the ceiling across which the flames from the recently lit fire cast moving shadows. I was thankful not to have to go down and face Amy so soon after hearing the news of her engagement to Esmond. Tomorrow I would have to do so; tomorrow I must offer my good wishes for her future happiness and join in the excitement of wedding plans. But tonight I could lie here in the dark like a wounded animal, hiding myself from the world.

Once during the evening the door of the bedroom opened and I heard the rustle of silken skirts and guessed that it was my stepmother come to enquire after me. I kept my eyes tight closed, feigning the sleep I longed to fall into but could not. I heard her voice say softly,

"Katherine? Are you awake, Katherine." I made no answer and after a few moments I heard her move away and the door close gently after her.

From time to time I wept, silently, secretly, and toward morning I fell into exhausted sleep.

How I got through the next few days I shall never know. Somehow I presented a calm face to my father and stepmother and, above all, to Amy. If I looked pale and tired that was put down to my recent indisposition and the fact that I was quieter than usual was scarcely noticed in the flurry of excitement which had overtaken everyone else, for there was much coming and going between Penvarrion and Borleigh Hall.

When I murmured my good wishes to Amy she thanked me sweetly and then said, in her pretty beseeching way,

"And—and you do not mind, Kate?"

I swallowed, in an attempt to steady my voice and answered as calmly as I could.

"Why should I mind, Amy? I am happy for you."

To congratulate Esmond was a more bitter undertaking.

If I could not meet his glance, neither did he look directly at me when I gave him my good wishes. We were both stiff with embar-

77

rassment, and in my own case, with the unhappiness that overwhelmed me, but somehow I got through the ordeal and retired from the room soon afterward.

My stepmother was in her element, planning an engagement party to which half the neighborhood were invited and then going on to make elaborate wedding arrangements although the date fixed was not until June. Sir Ralph had lent Esmond the Dower House known as Borleigh Grange in which he and Amy were to live, and it seemed as if every week my stepmother and Amy drove over to take fresh measurements for curtains or carpets or meet the carpenter regarding shelves or fixtures or the glazier or the gardener, while almost every other day parcels or packages arrived in connection with the wedding.

I was expected to enter into all these preparations with the same zest as everyone else, but I found this difficult to do, and the frequent visits of Esmond to Penvarrion were even harder to bear. I avoided him as much as I could and as the weeks went by I began to absent myself from the house more and more. Miss Barlow was my escape route. I went often to the Vicarage to assist her in her parish duties, take Sunday school, visit sick parishioners or help her sew clothes for the poor. Not that I was good at any of these things for I was too impatient and active by nature, but I tried the best I could and was grateful for the chance to forget my own problems in helping other people.

It was inevitable that I saw much of Mr. Barlow and the friendship between us strengthened. I liked him immensely and his courtesy and kindness and scarcely concealed admiration were a balm to someone who felt as hurt and rejected as I did. But I was careful not to encourage him in any way. I knew that I should never love any other man but Esmond.

It was April. As the days lengthened and the soft Cornish spring with its days of shimmering haze and pearly seas advanced, the heartache within me seemed to intensify rather than lessen. The scent of violets on the west wind, the primroses spilling in cream and gold profusion in the hedgerows, the bird song flutingly sweet among the tall trees of Penvarrion brought pain instead of joy. A strange restlessness consumed me, and when I was not busy helping Gertrude Barlow I would ride Sorrel along the cliff tops or over the moors until I had tired myself out and in exhaustion found a temporary peace.

Because I was unhappy and spent so much time away from the house, I failed to realize that Hester had fallen ill. But one day, calling in to see her I found her lying in bed, so thin and frail looking that I was shocked into a new awareness of her.

"Hester, dear Hester, what is the matter? Why has no one told me that you were not well?"

She moved her head on the pillow, her thin white hair plaited neatly on either side of her worn face.

"'Tis naught for 'ee to take on about, Miss Kate," she whispered in so low a voice I had to bend down to hear her words. "I be jes' mortal tired that be all."

I held her thin hand in both of mine.

"We must call the doctor in to see you—Dr. Fullbright shall come and attend to you and you will soon be better."

She shook her head.

"I not be wantin' any doctorin'. Nor to be a trouble to folk. Mrs. Borlase—she come along an' see me after Bertha fetched her, but ain't nothin' ur can do as I tell ur." She coughed, a dry rasping cough which shook her thin frame, and when she lay back on the pillow I touched her forehead and felt the fever there.

I said firmly,

"Dr. Fullbright must come and see you, Hester dear. He will give you something to ease your cough and bring down the fever. I think you have the bronchitis."

She clutched at my hand, her filmed half-blind eyes staring up at me.

"Doan' be sending me away, Miss Kate. Ur said if I fell sick best place 'ud be th' infirmary, and I couldn't abear that."

Whom did she mean by "ur"? Was it Mrs. Borlase Hester referred to?

I said as reassuringly as I could,

"You will not be sent away anywhere. Your home is here, dearest

Hester, and we will all help to look after you. But the doctor must be called in to prescribe the best medicine for you."

"Nay—ur said I mun go along o' the infirmary. Them were the words Madam said. 'Be you ill, Hester,' she say, 'tes th' infirmary will be best place for you at your time o' life'."

For a moment I could not speak for the indignation that filled me. And a sense of remorse too. In being selfishly concerned with my own unhappiness I had neglected Hester to whom I owed so much.

I kissed her gently.

"Don't worry any more. We shall take care of you and you will soon be well. I will send Carrie to sit with you, but I will return soon. Try and sleep," and I hurried out of the room.

Downstairs in the hall I met Borlase and I gave him instructions to send Barney on the pony with a message to Dr. Fullbright to call at the house as soon as it was convenient. I had just done so when my stepmother came out of the morning room. After Borlase had gone through the green baize door to the kitchen quarters I followed her to say,

"I have fetched the doctor to Hester. I did not know she was so ill. She is very worried about being sent away, but I have assured her there is no question of our doing so."

A pucker creased my stepmother's calm and lovely brow.

"Wasn't that rather unwise? It would be a burden to us all if Hester were ill here for a long time. She is very old, and old people can become a great care."

"Hester has lived with us nearly all her life and served us devotedly. She has no family, no friends. It is our responsibility to look after her."

My stepmother shrugged.

"You take a very high-handed attitude at times, Katherine. These decisions are really not for you to make, but I will speak to your father concerning Hester."

"I will speak to him myself," I said sharply. "He loves Hester and will want to do the best for her, I know."

"We all want to do that," my stepmother replied smoothly. "But we cannot have the house turned upside down for a sick old woman."

I could not answer her, only turn on my heel and rush away in search of my father before his new wife could use her influence upon him.

He was kind and sympathetic as I knew he would be and assured me that Hester would not be sent away, but he made the proviso that we must see what Dr. Fullbright said first before he could give me his promise.

Carrie was sitting with Hester, when I returned to her. We spoke together outside the bedroom, and she told me that Hester had been terribly worried that my stepmother would discover how ill she was and had made the other maids promise to say nothing of her condition to anyone.

Later in the day Dr. Fullbright arrived and after examining Hester declared that she had severe congestion of the lungs. He left pills and linctus and gave instructions as to how we could best care for her.

"The danger is if it should develop into pneumonia," he warned Mrs. Borlase and myself. "She is elderly and her heart is weak. I will call again tomorrow."

For four days we nursed Hester and there seemed little change in her condition, she was neither worse nor better. On the fifth day I went into the garden for a brief walk in the sweet spring air for I had been all afternoon in the sick room and now Hester was sleeping. As I walked along the graveled path, a shawl lightly around my shoulders for the day was warm, I saw Esmond and Amy come out of the house and go in the direction of the stables. Amy's hand was on Esmond's arm, he turned to smile down at her and I felt a terrible pain go through me. So little time ago he had smiled at me like that. I moved into the shrubbery so as not to be seen, though there was small likelihood of that. They were engrossed in one another. They moved out of sight and I continued on my way, my head downcast, my heart heavy with pain and longing.

In a little while I returned to the house and to Hester. To my surprise I met my stepmother coming down the narrow flight of stairs which led to the attic room where Hester slept. The stairway was dark, I could not see her face properly and for a moment we stood staring at one another in silence. Then she said slowly,

"I have been to see Hester. She is very ill."

"Yes. But—but there is every hope of recovery Dr. Fullbright says. It is just that her heart is not strong and she is—is elderly."

"I agree to the latter but am doubtful as to the former. However— we shall see."

I stood aside as she brushed past me in a rustle of silk and a drift of delicate flower perfume. I said quickly,

"She is not to be taken away."

"I am sure there will be no need for that," was the quiet answer and she was gone along the corridor leading to the main landing.

I found Hester awake, with two patches of bright color in her wrinkled cheeks. She sighed when she saw me and put her hand in mine.

"Ah, Miss Kate, tes you."

"Yes, dear Hester. Are you feeling better?"

"As well as I ever be now. You bin a good child—wi' wild ways but allus a loving heart. When I be gone look to 'eeself—your dear father 'ee be different man along o' ur, and Miss Amy, she be pretty as a pictcher but sharp as a ferret in her ways. Ol' Hester know she near broke your heart, but 'twill all come right in time." She sighed and closed her eyes tiredly,

"Oh, Hester." I laid my forehead against the hand on the counterpane. "Oh Hester, no one understands but you." For a moment or two I remained so, then I lifted my head to say, "But you are not to grieve or upset yourself. You will soon be better and able to help and advise me."

Without opening her eyes she said slowly,

"Nay child. I've lived o' Penvarrion these sixty years and I aim to die here. I pray to the good Lord that time be cummin zune for 'twould break my heart to lie in a strange place at the last."

I opened my mouth to protest but she looked so ill lying there that I was frightened to weary her by talking further, so I stayed kneeling by the bed for a little while. When I sensed she had fallen asleep I crept quietly away. Her words stayed with me throughout the evening and I wondered, living so remote from the main part of the house that she should seem to know so much about its inmates. "Amy sharp as a ferret." Was that true of her? I did not want to think so. I wanted to think of her as the charming childlike creature she appeared to be, and yet I knew in my heart that she was sly, for events had proved that to me.

Hester died that night. Ill as she was, we were taken by surprise. There was not time even to call Dr. Fullbright. At two in the morning, Carrie, who had been taking her turn to sit with Hester, came tapping on my bedroom door to say, with tears streaming down her round cheeks,

"It be Hester, Miss. She be going fast."

I dragged on a robe and ran down the passageway and up the servants' stairs ahead of Carrie to find Hester sunk into the coma from which she never emerged. She died as quietly as she had lived and with the least trouble to anyone, and by the time Borlase had brought my father to the bedside she was gone.

A few days later we buried her in the churchyard not far from my mother's grave, for my mother had been her best beloved and I only the legacy Hester had cherished from her.

I was sad at heart knowing that I had lost a dear friend. I puzzled that Hester should die so suddenly, almost as if she had lost the will to live, and I could not help but feel that the dread of being moved had brought this about. At times I wondered if my stepmother had said anything to her when she had visited Hester upon the last day she was alive. But doubts and recriminations helped no one, and so I pushed the dark thoughts aside and thought only that Hester was at peace.

The day after the funeral, wanting to escape the house and its melancholy associations, I went for a ride on Sorrel. The spring afternoon held a hint of rain on the wind but a sharp canter along the cliff tops helped to raise my low spirits, and I felt more myself by the time I returned to the house.

Going upstairs to change out of my riding habit I passed the open doorway of Amy's bedroom and to my surprise I heard the chatter of voices coming from it mingled with much laughter. I could not help but pause to look in and there saw Amy, dressed in white from head to foot, staring at herself in the mirror while Miss Blake, the dressmaker from St. Columb, knelt to pin up the hem of the dress. My stepmother, seated on a chair near the window, watched the process in smiling approval.

Suddenly she glanced up and saw me standing there.

She beckoned,

"Come in, Katherine. Amy is having the first fitting of her wedding dress. Is it not going to be beautiful?"

I stared, hypnotized by the spectacle of the white watered-silk jacket and skirt. The wide sleeves were tacked up and frills of double net and white satin ribbon trimmed the basque and the front of the jacket. Even in its first stages the dress was indeed beautiful and Amy's heart-shaped face, radiant and smiling above the rich silk, was beautiful too. She clapped her hands at the reflection in the long glass and cried,

"Oh, I am so happy—I could not be more pleased as to the way it is turning out. It was such a problem to choose the right thing. I am sure Mama and I looked through a hundred sketches. Tell me that you approve of it, Kate?"

I went on staring at Amy in her wedding dress and a wave of burning pain and jealousy swept over me, and I could not speak. I saw the three faces smiling expectantly at me and heard again the echo of their voices and laughter. Yesterday had been Hester's funeral but today all was gaiety and happiness as though there had been no sadness in the house and never would be again.

I felt as if I were a stranger in my own house. Everything was altered. I no longer belonged at Penvarrion. I wanted to run away from the small shimmering figure before me, from my stepmother's complacent smile and the inquisitive eyes of Miss Blake who was the local gossip, as well as the local dressmaker.

I said in a choked-sounding voice,

"It—it is exquisite," and turning on my heels I fled. Not to my room as had been my intention but downstairs to the hall and out into the garden and thence, to the stables from where I had so recently come.

Barney was sweeping the yard and he looked around in surprise to see me.

"Saddle one of the horses for me, please," and at his startled glance I added quickly, "Hurry—boy. Don't stand gaping."

"Not—not the mare, Miss? She be coolin' off after her ride."

"No—no. One of the others—one of the hunters. Perseus will do. And be quick about it."

He dropped the broom and went scurrying off while I stood switching the riding crop in my hand against my riding skirt. I was impatient to be gone. I could not bear to be at Penvarrion another moment. Always I had found relief for suppressed emotion in violent activity. For weeks now I had worn a mask of patience, of acceptance of a situation that at times I could scarcely endure. But today, the sight of Amy smiling and happy in her pinned-up wedding dress, had broken the bonds of self-control and I had to take action or explode.

Barney came forward with the roan stallion which my father often rode himself. He was fresh and eager for exercise, I saw it in his lifted head and bright searching eye as he looked about him. Barney helped me into the saddle and as I took the reins up he said hesitantly,

"Mind where you do go, Miss. The rain be surely comin' and like to be heavy by looks of it. Should I be comin' with you?"

I had no time to answer him for Perseus was dancing around as if his hooves were on hot coals. I waved my crop and called, "No—I wish to ride alone," over my shoulder and we were gone at a swift canter up the drive to the road ahead.

Perseus was a strong horse and I had difficulty in holding him back, but I managed to slow him to a trot before we reached the top of the hill. Here, instead of going along the road I turned him through a gateway and in a matter of moments we were racing across open country.

I gave the horse his head. I did not care where we went or in which direction. I only wanted to escape, not merely from Penvarrion but from myself.

The wind was strong from the headland, the rain blowing with it

85

but neither Perseus nor I cared about the weather. The great roan pounded on across the rough grass and when we came to a wall or a ditch he took them in his powerful stride. My hat fell from my head, my long hair blew wild and wet about my face and mingled with the tears streaming down my cheeks. A roll of thunder sounded on the wind, startling Perseus into a fresh gallop and still I clung to the saddle, frozen into immobility.

We had left Penvarrion far behind and reached the wild moors that ran along the coast, a countryside too bleak and exposed to grow crops or shelter cattle. Above the noise of the wind I heard the roar of the sea as it thundered against the rocks below and the threat of danger was an anodyne to pain. I *wanted* to be frightened, I wanted to feel any emotion rather than the hurt of losing Esmond.

Above the screech of the wind I thought I heard a voice; someone calling, shouting, but still I kept on. If I were trespassing then I would outride my prosecutor. I did not want to see or speak to anyone in my present despairing mood.

But whoever rode after me was catching up on Perseus's now flagging speed. I looked back over my shoulder and glimpsed a horseman, low in the saddle and coming as swift as the wind that blew from the sea, to overtake me. There was only one man who rode in such fashion, only one black horse so swift and strong. It was no surprise to me when, in a matter of seconds, I felt a hand catch at the reins to drag Perseus to a halt and heard Bryce Dawnay's voice shout above the tumult of wind and waves,

"For God's sake. What do you think to do? Tumble yourself and your horse into the sea below?"

The next moment he dragged Perseus's head around and forced him into a trot alongside his own horse, to reach the shelter of a scarred and wind-withered tree.

Dismounting, he turned to lift me down and it was only then, as I stood beside him, that I realized how spent and weary I was. Involuntarily my knees trembled beneath me, and I would have sunk to the ground if Bryce's arm had not tightened about my waist so as to hold me close against him until I had recovered from the weakness of exhaustion.

He said angrily,

"You are mad. To be riding alone like this on such a day." He ran his hand over my back and shoulders. "Your riding habit is soaked through—it will be a miracle if you do not catch a dangerous chill." He looked down at me and I had never seen his eyes so fierce and bright. "And your hair." He lifted a sodden strand. "It is like wet seaweed." He broke off and said more gently, "Oh, Kate."

I could not speak, only free myself to lean back against the tree, resting my head upon the gnarled bark.

Above us a clap of thunder sounded off like cannon and as Bryce turned quickly to hold the horses steady a shaft of lightning split the rain-dark sky, revealing a bleak and empty landscape and the storm-wracked sea rolling away under a mist of spume.

I shivered and he stared down at me, seeing the tear stains on my face. He caught my hand in his.

"You are chilled to the bone and there is no shelter here. We are only a mile or so from Tregedon—it is better I should take you there than that you should ride back to Penvarrion in the state you are in." He put an arm about me. "Come, Kate. Let me help you onto your horse and we will go to my house."

# 7

I DO NOT REMEMBER the ride to Tregedon, only that it was a short one, through a rough and inhospitable countryside. The rain still fell heavily, but the storm was passing out to sea. What I do remember is the ominous moment when Bryce turned his head to say.

"There is Tregedon."

I looked in the direction to which he pointed and saw, where a moment ago there had seemed no sign of home or habitation, a house set against the hill, so scarred and gray that it could scarcely be distinguished from the granite cliffs upon which it stood. It was a little way from the head of the cliffs and the walls surrounding it, and the gray outbuildings gave it the look of a fortress, built to withstand a seige, whether from land or sea. Without those walls there would have been little shelter for few trees or bushes could live under such battering salt-laden winds. As I stared, making out a cart-rutted track leading toward it my glance was suddenly caught and held by the spectacle of a rainbow forming overhead.

Slowly the colors deepened as it arched above Tregedon, so that the house stood limned in lurid light against the gray of sea and sky. Far below the waves rolled in unbroken swell from the far land of America to dash themselves in such fury against the cliffs that the spray rose near as high as the house. I had never seen so isolated or formidable a dwelling, and as I stared at it I was afraid. I was filled with a sense of curious foreboding.

"It—it is very remote," was all I could say in answer to Bryce.

He did not speak but led my horse by the rein down the sloping track to a gateway set in the crumbling stone wall.

There was no sign of a groom or servant when we came to the courtyard, sheltered on all sides by the house and the walls of stables and barns. A ladder and scaffolding were placed against one of the chimney stacks and stones and broken rubble were strewn on the ground. It was obvious some rebuilding was taking place.

Bryce lifted me down and leaving the horses unattended, led me through a doorway set under a stone arch into a dark slate-flagged passage. From here we entered a beamed parlor where a low fire burned in an enormous stone fireplace. A rough gray hound rose from the rug before it to greet us with a deep rumble of sound.

"All right, Boris. Good fellow." The dog, a huge one and seemingly old, flicked his long tail and then, after sniffing at my outstretched hand, lay down again.

Bryce went out of the room and returned with a towel and a wrap of warm red wool which he handed to me.

"Take off your wet habit while I see after the horses," he commanded. "And rub yourself dry before putting on the robe." At my hesitating look he added abruptly,

"You will be safe from intrusion. There are no servants here. Mrs. Porrit, the stockman's wife, who cleans and cooks for me, comes only in the mornings and is now back at her cottage."

This dismayed me even more, and I stood holding the towel and wrap without moving until Bryce said, frowning impatiently,

"Do not be foolish, Kate. Unless you wish to die in some feverish decline. This is not time for polite ways or nervous Missishness."

He went out of the room, the dog at his heels, and I heard the latch drop after him. Not until I heard the outer door bang to did I turn to the fire and begin to strip off my rain-soaked riding coat and skirt.

It was sodden wet and I hesitated to hang it over a chair back, but when I looked around I was struck by the poor and shabby furnishings of the room. A worn rug lay across bare boards, a settle by the fire, and an armchair and a few hard-backed chairs were the only seats, and other than an oak gate-legged table, a carved press of dark wood and a tall grandfather clock there was no other furniture. No paintings hung on the plain walls, the ornaments consisted only of an oil lamp and some candles in holders of dulled brass, and a pile of tattered books on a stool by the window.

Draping my habit over one of the scratched wooden chairs and seeing an osier basket filled with logs I took the liberty of placing one or two on the dying fire. It sputtered into a blaze which warmed me, and pulling the thick woolen gown around myself, I huddled on the settle and waited for Bryce to return.

When he did so, he brought a brandy bottle and two glasses on a tray, and pouring out a measure into one of them he handed it to me saying,

"Drink that, Kate. It will warm you through and prevent a chill settling in your bones."

I grimaced at the taste of the strong fiery liquid and could only sip a mouthful at intervals, but it took the cold from me and sent the blood coursing through my veins again. Clutching the robe tightly about me, for I was very conscious of wearing only my chemise and drawers and a pair of stays under it, I said,

"Do you live here alone?"

He nodded. He had removed his coat and sat now in woolen shirt and check waistcoat, his black hair curling about his head as it dried in the warmth of the fire.

"Yes." He glanced about him and frowned, as if seeing it with fresh eyes. "It is not elegant, I'm afraid, but I plan to improve it. At the moment I am bent on restoring the outside, the chimney stack is to be rebuilt and part of the outer wall. Then there are the barns to be made watertight before I can start on less important things such as furnishings and furniture."

"Do you intend to live here always then? It—it must be very lonely."

He shrugged his powerful shoulders—I saw the ripple of muscle under the thin wool.

"I am not aware of that. There is too much work to do, and the days seem hardly long enough to attend to all that has to be done. The house has been empty for thirty years."

I was startled by his announcement.

*"Thirty years!* But—but on what account? Does not Tregedon be-

long to your family? Surely some members of it have lived here during that time."

He shook his head, draining the brandy glass to its dregs.

"No. More than once the house has been let with the land, but though other people have attempted to live here they have never stayed, but returned inland." His lips curled slightly as he put the glass on the table. "I have been told the place is only fit for a gypsy like myself."

I said hesitantly,

"Is it true then—you are of gypsy blood?"

"Yes. My grandmother was a Romany. They are the only true gypsies—of unmixed blood. Because Mark Dawnay, my paternal grandfather, married a gypsy he was disinherited by my great grandfather, Matthew Dawnay. Tregedon was left to his second son, Arthur, but he never wanted to farm and was not successful. The land ran down and he lost money in the bad seasons. When he died the house was left empty and the land let out to other farmers. That is the way it has been. When I returned from Australia, having been fortunate enough to make a little money I bought it back for myself. I am determined, as I told you once before, to restore the fortunes of Tregedon. It will take time and hard work, but somehow I shall do it."

"Is your grandmother still alive? Does she not live with you?"

"No. She lives a few miles away in a cottage that my great-uncle Arthur bought and gave to her. She will not live with anyone although she is now very old. As a boy I spent much time with her for she more or less brought me up, my mother dying when I was a small child and my father working in the mining business and traveling much about." He added, "My grandmother is a most wonderful woman—I love her dearly."

"She—she has never gone back to her gypsy family?"

He shook his head.

"That would be impossible. When a Romany man or woman marries a non-Romany, from that moment her or she is excluded from the Romany community forever. He or she has no longer the right to call themselves a Romany, and the children and descendants of such a marriage are also excluded and have no right to call themselves such. This is known as the penalty of 'exclusion,' and to a true Romany is regarded as worse than death."

"Yet your grandmother loved your grandfather enough to accept that cruel ruling? I hope they were happy together."

"Yes, I am sure they were, but both paid a high price for their love. They knew it and they accepted it because, more than all the trouble and loss that came through their association, they wanted to be together."

I was silent, thinking of the passionate bitter-sweet love that had linked these two people despite all the hazards that beset them. I sighed, remembering Esmond.

"They each made a sacrifice," I said at last. "Your grandmother gave up her people, your grandfather his inheritance."

He nodded.

"I don't know which was the greater hardship. My grandmother to be abandoned by her race, my grandfather to be ostracized by his family and friends. Perhaps it fell hardest on Zena."

"Zena?"

He smiled, and in the slanting golden eyes and jet-black hair and smooth brown skin I saw his gypsy heritage.

"That is my grandmother's name. Sometimes I call her by it. The gypsy law is strong—they call it the 'Kriss'—and none may dare go against it. Gypsies are a race of wanderers—they have left behind them no buildings, no monuments, not even graves. Their language has never been written and their traditions and laws have been handed down by word of mouth only from generation to generation. And yet the true Romanies have remained undiluted in blood because of the power of the Kriss." He shook his head. "I could talk to you of it all day—there is much I have heard and learned from my grandmother."

"And I could listen. I am fascinated by it all. But"—I glanced at the riding skirt steaming in the warmth—"I must return to Penvarrion as soon as my clothes are fit to put on."

He reached a hand out and touched the still damp cloth.

"That will not be for a little while yet. And the rain has not stopped. Will you take some more brandy?"

"Thank you, but I have not drunk this."

"I can offer you little other refreshment. Beer or wine—a glass of milk? Some bread and cheese or cold meat?"

"Thank you, I require nothing and I am sure you have been more than hospitable—a fire by which to dry my wet things and"—I felt my cheeks color up—"something to wear while they do so."

"It becomes you very well—the color I mean. The red sets off your dark hair." He smiled. "It is as long as a mermaid's."

My cheeks warmed even more. I became aware that as my wet hair had dried it fanned loose over my shoulders and down my back.

"I lost my hat," was all I could say in explanation.

"I'm not surprised—not if you had ridden far at so dangerous a pace." He leaned forward, his face sobering. "You were distressed, Kate. May I ask the reason?"

I could not tell him the whole truth, and I did not want to discuss my feelings for Esmond. I looked away from his intent gaze as I answered.

"My dear old nurse died—she was only buried yesterday."

"I am sorry indeed. Were you very attached to her?"

"Yes. She had lived in the family for many years. In fact, she was my mother's nurse when she was a child. She was so wise and good —I shall miss her more than I can tell."

He said again,

"I am sorry. It is reason enough for your grief." He was silent, staring at me with an intentness which was disconcerting. Then he said slowly, "I believe your stepsister is to be married to Esmond Borleigh."

I looked away, seeing the simply furnished room. I did not want to discuss the matter, and especially with someone like Bryce Dawnay.

"Yes. In midsummer." Holding the dressing gown carefully about me, I stood up. "It is time to go. I will dress, if you will be kind enough to leave me."

"Of course." He rose and tall as I was he towered above me. Again there was a probing glance before he turned away saying,

"Take your time—I have the horses to saddle, for I will ride back with you."

"There is no need," I began but he frowned and said almost sharply,

"There is every need. I am surprised you should have no groom or companion with you today—it is not wise to ride alone in such lonely country."

"The stable boy wished to accompany me but I would not allow it."

"You will allow me, for I shall insist," he answered and went through the doorway, leaving me alone.

I was fortunate in not coming to harm after my drenching through and this was undoubtedly due in some measure to my taking shelter at Bryce Dawnay's. Returning home late that afternoon I encountered only Harry Martin, who took my mud-plastered horse from me and said, with a frown,

"You caught it nicely, by the looks of things, Miss Kate. I hope you came to no harm in the storm."

I assured him I had found shelter and hurried into the house anxious to avoid meeting anyone else. In my bedroom I rang for Carrie and after hearing her exclamations of surprise and dismay at the sight of the mud-stained habit and hair pinned up askew on top of my head, I told her to prepare a hot bath at once. I also cautioned her not to discuss what had happened with the other servants in case my father should hear of the mishap and be worried.

I was late down to dinner that night but no one commented upon it, save to say that I had been foolish to go out riding in such uncertain weather. I felt sad when I met my father's sympathetic smile for I knew that if we had been alone as in the old days, I would have told him all that had occurred. I felt guilty, too, for I knew I had been unwise in going to Bryce Dawnay's house and being alone with him there. At the time I had thought nothing of it for I was as unconventional in my ways, as Bryce appeared to be, and it had seemed the easiest and most practical thing to do. But with my stepmother's cool poised glance upon me and Amy vivaciously recounting the plans she and Esmond had made that day, I could not bring myself to speak of my adventure. I thought how the changed atmosphere of Penvarrion—its tensions and conflicts—was forcing me to be as deceitful as I guessed my stepsister to be.

Yet, oddly enough, that night I felt calmer and somehow detached from the events around me. This might have been due to physical exhaustion or the fact that in visiting Bryce's strange and lonely home and listening to his account of his Romany grandmother I had been taken out of myself. That night I fell asleep quickly for the first time in many weeks and did not wake until morning.

Some days later we heard that Laura had been safely delivered of a child, a baby girl. Esmond himself rode over to tell us the news. I was in the sitting room with Amy and her mother when he walked in, tall and smiling and so very dear to me that after his brief acknowledgment of me I had to turn away and look out of the window to hide my emotion.

I heard his voice, I heard my stepmother speak and Amy's voice, light and sweet as a bird's, answer him, and then my stepmother spoke.

"A daughter," she said. "How proud and happy your sister and her husband must be."

I swung around, forgetting all else in my happiness for Laura.

"Laura has had her baby?" I cried. "Oh, that is wonderful news. How is she, Esmond? Is all well with her? At what hour did the infant arrive?"

"Four o'clock yesterday afternoon. I took my mother to Greystokes this morning and visited Laura for a moment. She looked radiant and I understand that everything has gone as it should do. Paul is proud as Punch, as you can imagine, and declares the baby is the prettiest one ever to be born. Laura sent her fond love to you, Katy, and hopes you will call upon her within a few days."

"Indeed I will. I am so happy for her, and for Paul and all of you. Your father and mother will be delighted. Tell me, have they settled upon a name as yet?"

"She is to be called Phoebe Katherine. But perhaps I should leave Laura to tell you this."

"*Oh!* Oh, my name is to be linked with your mother's. That is kind and gracious of Laura." I felt tears come to my eyes and as Esmond smiled at me something flashed between us, and the stiffness and constraint that had affected all our recent encounters were dissolved. We were not as we had always been, that was impossible now, but we were linked once again in affection and friendship.

I became aware that Amy was watching us, her bright green glance going first to Esmond and then to myself and then back to Esmond. The rosebud mouth pouted reproachfully.

"It is unkind to address all your remarks to Kate, Esmond. I am just as anxious to hear news of Laura as Kate is likely to be, for soon we shall be as sisters."

"My dearest, I apologize for any discourtesy, but as you know Kate and I are old family friends."

She tossed her red-gold curls.

"Oh, I am aware of that."

I said gently,

"I have known Laura all my life. We shared the same schoolroom under Miss Pringle. It is natural I should be eager to have news of her."

Amy ignored me and slipped a hand through Esmond's arm, to turn him away from the window where I stood.

"I will write a letter to dear Laura at once and tell her that you will bring me over to visit her as soon as is convenient."

Esmond put his hand over her small one.

"Of course. I will take you and Kate together, for Laura expects to see her also."

I did not mind Amy's angry glance in my direction. I was happy and sad at the same time. Happy that now Esmond and I would no longer meet as strangers and sad because I still loved him so dearly and there could be no hope for me now.

# 8

TIME SPED BY to Amy's wedding. It dawned a perfect day with heat mist rolling early off the lawns of Penvarrion and a blue sky without a cloud. Surely no one ever woke to such a summer morning I thought, as I went to the window and saw the garden, radiant with the roses growing in scented profusion within its sheltered walls.

For a long time I stood there, wondering how I should be able to smile and seem happy throughout the long day. Downstairs I knew the household was already waking to activity. Everyone was excited at the thought of the wedding, and the servants, as well as the guests, hoped to celebrate later with a dance of their own.

The house was full of guests, and the distraction of their presence helped to banish introspective thoughts for there was much to do in seeing after their comfort and helping to entertain them. My aunt was staying with us and also my cousins Rosamund and Bertram. Some relatives on Amy's side were also guests in the house; an elderly aunt and uncle from Norfolk and my stepmother's brother from the West Indies and his son, who was in his late twenties and as dark visaged as his father.

Later in the morning Carrie came to help me dress, for I was to be one of the bridesmaids, in company with David Borleigh's sisters, Jane and Caroline. The dress was of white muslin embroidered with small bows in pale blue silk, as were those of the other two bridesmaids. When Carrie stood back and said on a sigh of pleasure,

"You do look proper handsome, Miss Kate," I scarcely bothered to glance at my own reflection for I had little interest in how I looked. All I wanted was for the day to pass and be over and done with and Amy gone from the house.

I remember little of the actual ceremony, which was performed by Charles Barlow, assisted by a neighboring curate. I seemed to see and hear everything as from a great distance. I remember the sudden blur of tears that swam before my eyes when Amy, a diminutive figure in shimmering white, came slowly up the aisle on my father's arm. Perhaps it was the sight of him, tall and distinguished looking in his dark waisted coat and high white cravat that filled me with such emotion, and I thought with a pang of bitterness that once I had imagined I should be brought to church by him and given to Esmond in marriage.

I had to fight hard for command of myself in that moment, and when we fell to our knees to pray the prayer book in my hand was wet with tears. There were tears again when I saw the beamed sunlight falling onto Esmond's fair head as he knelt with Amy at the altar, and I bowed my own head to pray that he would be happy for always.

Then it was over and the congregation were coming out of the little church and I was caught up in movement and chatter and laughing cries of good wishes after the bride and groom, as they ran to the waiting carriage.

The reception was a daze of people. Amy, her heart-shaped face framed in the fragile lace veil caught up in a band of pink roses, smiled radiantly at everyone in turn. I bent to kiss her, to murmur my good wishes, then my hand was in Esmond's brief clasp and his lips touched my cheek in an impersonal greeting as I wished him happiness. The press of guests behind impelled me forward. I saw my father standing beside my stepmother, almost as beautiful as the bride in her new dress of shot silk lavender and worn with a silk bonnet made of velvet pansies and pale mauve ribbons, and then I moved on again.

At the wedding breakfast I was seated next to David Borleigh. He was as attentive as ever and paid me several compliments which I scarcely bothered to acknowledge. On my other side sat Vincent DeBurgh, Amy's cousin, and with him I exchanged remarks about

Barbados and life on the plantations there. He told me of Belle Tout and said that it was the most beautiful as well as one of the most flourishing plantations on the island.

To tell the truth I did not care with whom I talked or on what topic, I only wished for time to pass.

After a succession of speeches and toasts it was time for Amy and Esmond to leave. They were to spend that night at their new home Borleigh Grange and then travel to Bath where they would stay two weeks in an apartment lent to them by a relative of Lady Borleigh's.

When they had gone, in a flurry of excitement and confetti, the hired fiddlers started up and the dancers took the floor. Outside the golden light began to fade and shadows fell across the grass as the quiet sky deepened in color to reflect the rose of the sunset.

I danced until I could dance no more, spinning endlessly like a humming top before it crashes to the ground. I could not be still, tired as I was, and when I ceased to dance I laughed and chattered without pause as if I had never been so happy.

"You must come and visit Belle Tout," Vincent DeBurgh urged, "then we shall meet again," and I smiled and said nothing would please me better.

David Borleigh appeared at my side and offered to fetch some refreshment. We walked together onto the terrace, hung as was the garden with lights, and Borlase brought us glasses of wine but I scarcely touched mine, only sat smiling at David and watching the other guests walking upon the brightly lit grass.

"May I call and see you tomorrow?" David asked and I shrugged and said,

"Oh, tomorrow I shall be in no mood for visitors. We shall all be sleeping until midday."

"The day after, then?" but I grew suddenly impatient, knowing I had little interest in him and realizing that it would be unkind to encourage him beyond the mood of the evening. I stood up and made an excuse to return indoors.

The evening ended and as the last carriage drove away down the drive, my stepmother sighed and said,

"This has been one of the happiest days of my life. Thank you, Gilbert, for giving Amy, and all of us, such a memorable occasion."

"My dear." My father put his hand on hers. "Your happiness is mine—you know that."

She smiled at him, her heavy lids lifting languorously to regard him.

"Dear Gilbert." She turned her head and caught sight of me talking to Rosamund who was standing near her. Her expression changed in some indefinable way and she said, "Here is Katherine. It will be your turn next my dear, for it seems to be that David Borleigh admires you considerably."

I said with the weary indifference I was feeling,

"If he does, it is of little consequence to me. I am not interested in him."

"You are very hard to please. First you reject Mr. Rossiter's attentions and now you are not prepared to consider someone even more admirable." Her voice suddenly changed. "He is Esmond's cousin; that should bring him favor in your eyes."

The edge in her voice, the glance from under the heavy lids made me aware that she must have guessed something of my feelings for Esmond.

I summoned up every effort of self-control and said as calmly as I could,

"I am attached to all the Borleigh family and David is included in my esteem. That does not mean I wish to regard him as a possible huband."

My father said, kindly,

"One wedding is sufficient for the moment. We shall miss Amy enough as it is and do not want to lose Katherine yet awhile. I am glad that she is not set upon marrying anyone at the moment."

"Thank you, Papa." I turned to Rosamund. "I am sure you are as ready for bed as I am. Shall we go up together?"

Rosamund smiled as she hid a yawn.

"I am half-asleep standing here. But it has been a wonderful day for us all. Thank you, Uncle Gilbert."

We said our good nights and left them. Aunt Selina and the elderly pair from Norfolk had already retired. Vincent stayed below to smoke a last cigar with my father, and the servants, who had cleared away, were gone to enjoy their own celebrations.

As Carrie was not available Rosamund helped undo my stays and I did the same for her, then we said good night to one another and she went to her room. I was exhausted and yet as wide awake as ever. I lay down on the bed and closed my eyes, willing sleep to come.

I had never felt more unhappy, or more uncertain. My step-mother's manner forced me to consider what life would be like now Amy was married. I should be even more alone without the company of my stepsister. Miss Pringle for whom I had felt a great affection and with whom I had found much companionship had gone; sent away by my stepmother, I felt sure. Hester, dear and devoted to us, was dead. With every day that passed my father was growing away from me and falling more and more under the influence of his new wife.

I sensed the implacability in her nature. Her manner was charming, her ways smooth. She seldom raised her voice and always appeared cool and composed, but already she ruled Penvarrion and my father, and she would brook no interference with her plans.

Penvarrion was no longer home to me. It was changed in every way; even my mother's portrait no longer hung in its familiar place. Yet, if I went away, where could I go to? The only prospect for any girl was marriage and the idea of that was something I could not contemplate loving Esmond as I did.

It was long past midnight. The sounds of the house quietened to a deep stillness. From somewhere far away a dog barked and then all was silence again.

I slid off the bed and pulling on a robe went to the window to stare out. The garden, which I had seen in the pearly light of dawn, was now bathed in moonlight, every tree and flower and shrub etched with silver. Shadows lay black across the lawn, the scent of stocks and heliotrope filled the air. It looked the same and yet different, touched with magic, the enchantment of Midsummer Night.

The beauty of it all made my heart ache the more and I tried not to think that somewhere, a few miles across the sleeping countryside, Amy lay in Esmond's arms.

It was more than I could bear. To forget what might-have-been, I pulled the wrap more tightly about myself and opening the bedroom door stole out into the corridor. All was quiet as I went down the wide staircase. The ancient wood creaked under my step but not loud enough to disturb anyone.

I unfastened the side door and went into the garden and walked slowly along the path. I did not know nor care where I was going. I had come out of the house simply as a means of escape from my own unhappiness.

The path wound upward, and involuntarily I found myself following it toward the high pastures. A bird flapped warning wings from out of a hedge, something small and brown and furry slipped away under my feet. I heard other noises, rustlings and squeaks, the secret animal sounds of the night.

I walked on. I thought I would climb to the top and catch a glimpse of the moonlit sea before going back. The path opened up and I was on the headland where I so often rode Sorrel. It was as bright as day and beyond the silvered fields lay the sea, calm and smooth and sparkling with light. I had never seen anything so beautiful. For a long moment I stood there and then I turned and began to retrace my steps.

Penvarrion lay hidden, save for its trees and tall chimneys. I looked over my shoulder toward the little church, where today we had gathered together. No, that was yesterday. The wedding was already in the past.

As I looked I gave a start of fear. Someone was coming toward me across the space of ground between the lych gate and the path upon which I stood. Who could be walking up here at this time of night? A poacher or a tramp? I went cold with terror, standing there alone, clutching my flimsy night attire about me. I turned to run but a voice called out to me,

"Kate! Don't go. Don't be afraid. It's only me, Bryce."

*"Bryce."* I stared in astonishment at the tall figure approaching me. "What are you doing here, at this hour?"

102

I saw his mouth twist in a smile,

"I might ask the same of you. I wasn't sure if I was seeing a ghost or a sleepwalker when I saw a figure in white walking across the fields in front of me."

"I couldn't sleep. It was so—so hot. And the moonlight was so bright." I looked up at him. "But you are miles from Tregedon."

He shrugged.

"I had business at Newquay this afternoon and stayed late with my associates. Someone gave me a ride as far as Tregurrian, and I decided to walk back by the coast. When I passed here earlier in the day Esmond Borleigh was being married. I paused, to catch a glimpse of you, Kate."

"I did not see you."

"No, I was one of the onlookers." He paused and added slowly, "So it is all over."

I looked away from him.

"Yes, it is over."

"You had a great regard from him, I think."

I sensed the probing tensity in his voice but I would not betray myself.

"We have known each other all our lives." I held the wrap close against my throat. "I must go back to the house. I should not have walked so far in the first place. It was unwise."

"A little. But when were you ever wise, Kate? As a child you ran as wild as one of the moor ponies."

"Sometimes. When I could. But I was always scolded for it when I was found out."

"Do you remember the badgers?"

"The badgers?" I frowned for a moment. "Oh, yes. You took me to where there was a badger's hole and we saw the cubs come out and play. It was wonderful. I had never seen anything like it before." I shook my head at the memory. "I have never seen anything like it since."

"I could show you it all again now. There is a set not far from here, and this is a perfect night in which to see them. They come above ground to romp in the moonlight." He added slowly, "Will you come?"

I hesitated but not for long. I did not want to return to the house, to the restless melancholy that beset me there. I knew I should not go with Bryce, that it was indiscreet dressed as I was, and at such a time of night. But as he had just said, when was I ever wise?

"If it is not too far," I began and he shook his head and said,

"The place is over there—in that woodland. But we must go quietly and keep on the leeside of the badgers." He reached a hand out to mine. "I will guide you."

I put my hand in his firm strong clasp and the years fell away from me and I felt like a child again, sharing some rare adventure with Bryce, as I had done long ago.

The dew soaked through my thin slippers as we walked quietly across the field to where the trees thickened into a small wood. Moonlight filtered through the heavy foliage, giving alternate light and shade. I had noticed before how noiselessly Bryce walked, his swift lithe steps making no sound, but as we came within sight of a small clearing among the trees the tightening clasp of his fingers checked me to a standstill.

He did not speak, only stood so close against me that I could feel the warmth of his shoulder and side pressing through my thin robe.

Moonlight shone onto a sloping bank and as we gazed, out of the hollow came a splatter of turf and then a glimpse of a blunt striped muzzle shaking itself to lift, in a grin of pleasure. After a moment came the young cubs, tumbling over themselves, giving small squeaks and yelps as they rushed about one after another, going in and out of the bushes in a game of hide and seek.

The mother, too, came into sight and for a moment sat watching the young at play before turning to sharpen her claws on the bark of a nearby tree.

I do not know how long we stood there watching the somehow touching sight of the unsuspecting little creatures disporting themselves, but the father must have caught a whiff of alien scent for suddenly with a grunt he turned and moved away, followed by the sow and her cubs and in a few seconds they had disappeared from sight.

104

Bryce looked down at me.

"Was it worth coming for?"

I sighed with pleasure.

"Oh, yes. It was better than before. Then it was dusk and one could not see the animals so well. But in the moonlight it was splendid. I wonder where they have gone to."

"Into one of the tunnels. The holt is honeycombed. Sometimes they are hundreds of years old. I am not exaggerating. The tunnels run back deep into the hillside."

I became aware that his hand was still clasping mine, that we were standing so close together that his breath was warm on my cheek. I tried to free my hand but his grip tightened. He said, in a deep grave voice that stirred me unaccountably,

"You are very beautiful. The most beautiful girl I have ever known."

I looked up at him in startlement. In the moonlight his eyes shone bright as jewels, holding my glance with the intensity of their gaze.

"You—you must not speak so," I began protestingly.

"Should I not? You have been my lode star, Kate. You were the reason I left England to find my fortune. It is because of you I began to restore Tregedon. I do not know what I hoped for, I had little to offer you. But you were my dream; my past, my present and my future. Because you were years younger than I, I thought I would have time to make something of myself. Then I heard you were to marry Esmond Borleigh. But it was not true, and I began to hope again."

I did not know how to answer him. I was aware of his hand holding mine, of the beat of his pulse against my own, sending strange tremors through my blood. I wanted to pull away, and yet I stayed near him, as if in his warmth and strength and professed love I should find comfort for my loneliness.

"You—you scarcely know me. We have met little more than a dozen times."

"I know you with every fiber of my being. Forgive me, my words alarm you. You are pale—or is it the moonlight that makes you look so? You are pale and lovely as a white rose."

The words echoed through my brain. I stared at him in amazement.

"A—white rose? It was you. It was you who sent the white roses on my birthday."

He nodded gravely.

"Yes. I was in London when you were, and I remembered the date and that it was your eighteenth birthday. I found out where you were staying, and I sent the flowers on an impulse. I knew you would not guess from whom they had come but perhaps conjecture upon an unknown admirer?"

"That is what I did. I was puzzled." Remembering something else I said slowly, "Did I see you outside my aunt's house in Lancaster Gate on the night of my birthday—as we were arriving for the ball?"

"Yes. You wore one of my roses in your hair and it made me happy. I have been on the fringe of your life for a long time, Kate. Watching you. Waiting for you to grow up. So that one day I might kiss you. Like this," and drawing me into his arms he bent his tall head and put his lips on mine.

Esmond had kissed me once, a light caress that I had long remembered. But I had never been kissed like this. First with gentleness and restraint so that I had no fear but succumbed to the pleasure of it, to the tenderness and ineffable sweetness. Then, with a more demanding passion so that I felt my own involuntary response.

Do we make our own Destiny? Is there a moment when we can take this path or that one and the choice is ours, or is what happens to us fated from the beginning? Looking back, it seems to me that Bryce neither forced nor persuaded me into anything that night, but that all I did I chose to do. For weeks I had worn a mask, endeavoring to appear calm and happy over Esmond's marriage while all the time a current of black misery had run under the surface of my life. I was hurt and bewildered by what had happened, for I had been so sure Esmond loved me. My father, too, had seemed to reject me, in putting someone else in my place. And so, in that moment when Bryce kissed me a dam of emotion broke within me and I went with the flood. My education and upbringing, all the taboos by which I had lived, counted for nothing. In some strange fashion I wanted to

106

punish Esmond for the pain he had caused me, but in so doing I punished only myself.

There was a moment when I could have drawn back. We sank down onto the bracken at our feet and Bryce was leaning over me, kissing my lips and my throat and my bare shoulder where the robe had slipped down. Suddenly, abruptly he lifted his head to say, in a harsh almost breathless voice,

"We must not—my dearest Kate, this is wrong. I want you utterly and completely, but I must protect you." He tried to loosen his arms from me but I tightened my clasp around his neck and closing my eyes against the dark face so near my own said over and over again,

"Please—please—*please*," and he came back to me.

From somewhere an owl called—a strange and lonely cry, then all was silence again. I felt Bryce's fingers unfasten the ribbons at my throat; I felt his hand on my breast, the warmth and weight of his body on mine as we lay together on the moonlit grass, and then I was lost in the madness of the Midsummer Night.

After it was over I lay, drained of all emotion, a hand across my eyes to shut out the aching moonlight. Bryce too, lay still beside me but when after a while I began to shiver, he put a hand out to touch mine and said,

"You are cold. I will take you home."

I jerked my hand away.

"Don't touch me." I started to rise to my feet, but as I did so a long shuddering sob racked my body and I bowed my head on my knee and wept at the enormity of what I had done. He bent over me.

"For God's sake—what is wrong? What is the, matter, Kate?" He put a hand on my shoulder, but I went on weeping. After a moment he lifted me to my feet. He would have pulled me into his arms but I turned from him in stammering protest.

"Don't—I don't want—it is wrong—"

He said gently,

"I ask you to marry me, Kate."

I turned and stared at him, the tears wet on my cheek. I thought of Tregedon, that bleak and fearsome house standing high above the

107

wild tumultous seas, I shivered at the remembrance and said, in a shaking voice,

"Marry you? I do not love you. We—we must not meet again."

He flinched as if I had struck him, the slanting eyes narrowing. There was a long moment before he spoke.

"You can't mean that. Not after—after what we have experienced together."

I couldn't explain how I felt. The sense of shame, the searing awareness that I had betrayed not only my love for Esmond, but myself. I was in revulsion from everything that had happened.

"It was a terrible mistake. I only want to forget tonight, forget everything that has happened. I did not know what I was doing—I did not intend—" I stopped unable to go on.

"But you—" Bryce began and then he too paused and I knew what he had started to say. "You wanted me to make love to you."

I pulled the robe closer around me for though the night was warm I was shaking uncontrollably.

"I must go home." I turned and walked away across the clearing and he came after me. We walked in silence over the fields, bright with moonlight, and went down the path leading to the house, still without speaking.

When we came to the door in the garden wall I lifted my hand to the latch and Bryce put his on it first.

"*Kate.* Kate, don't go like this. You belong to me."

I looked up and saw his face, pale and set in the shadows cast by the trees under which we stood.

"I shall never belong to you—or to anyone."

"I can't believe you mean what you say."

"I mean every word. Please go away. Please keep away from me from now on."

He stared at me and his hand dropped from the latch. He turned, then turned back to say slowly, and with a strange impassivity,

"If ever you need me—if ever you wish to ask anything of me I am at your service. I shall never change, but long for you till the day I die," and then, swiftly, silently, he was gone.

I went into the garden, keeping close to the hedges, dreading that someone might see me, that I should encounter my father or my stepmother, but the household slept on, undisturbed, and I reached my room in safety.

My teeth were chattering, with cold, with shock, with the aftermath of a violent emotion. I stripped off my wet robe and the long cotton nightdress I had been wearing underneath it, and found a clean dry one to put over my head. Glancing at my bedside clock I saw that it was ten to three. I had been out of the house little more than three hours.

I lay down on the bed and closed my eyes as if to shut out the unbelievable events of the evening. I did not know that what had happened in those few short hours would change my life forever.

# 9

I SEEMED TO BE two people in one. Outwardly I was the same as I had always been, going through the mechanics of everyday living; speaking, listening, smiling, but inwardly I was someone else. Someone threatened and bewildered by what had happened. I wanted to forget the shattering experience of Midsummer Night and at times I did that, pushing it to the back of my mind and refusing to think about it. But there were other times when the recollection came back to me in its full intensity and then I was consumed by guilt and shame. I felt as if everyone who looked at me could read my secret in my face. I knew that I should never be the same person again.

One thing helped. It had been arranged that I should go to my aunt and Rosamund for a few weeks' visit to London and then, with the season ending, accompany them to Aunt Selina's house in the country near Sherborne, before returning to Penvarrion. I was more thankful than I could say that this was to happen. I felt I could not bear to remain in surroundings which had become hateful to me. It was with a feeling of great relief that I said good-by to my father and stepmother and drove away with my aunt and cousins to Plymouth, where we were to catch the London train.

The carriage rolled along the dusty road; my aunt sat in one corner seat with her eyes closed, nodding in the summer heat. Rosamund sat in the other corner, gazing out at the fields filled with newly stacked hay while Bertram sat beside me, reading one of Mr. Dickens' latest novels. I thought how, little more than a year ago, I had traveled to London with my father and my new stepmother and stepsister and brother and how everything had changed since then. I closed my eyes, not to sleep as my aunt did, but against the tears that threatened to spill over.

Yet, once at the house at Lancaster Gate I felt better and life began to swing back into perspective. As usual, there was much to see and do and so my mind was distracted from its bitter introspection as I tried to forget all that had happened.

That I did not entirely succeed was proved by Rosamund saying to me one day,

"What is the matter, Kate? Sometimes you are so quiet and thoughtful. Are you not enjoying your visit with us?"

I turned quickly.

"But of course I am. More—more than I can say. London is full of interest and it is such a change from life in the country."

Rosamund smiled. She was tall and beautiful, with honey-brown hair and deep dark blue eyes.

"I am relieved to hear you say so. I thought you were moping for Penvarrion. Or else that you had fallen in love."

I looked away from her mischievous glance.

"No. No, I have not done that. I have perhaps been feeling a little tired. We have had so many outings and—and it has been very hot here in London."

"Too hot. I shall be thankful to be leaving for Dorset next week." Her smile deepened. "And not only because of the weather. I am expecting to renew a certain acquaintance when we are at Sherborne." She paused as if waiting for me to make some comment and I roused myself to say enquiringly,

"An acquaintance? Do I know him?"

She burst into laughter.

"Now why should you say him instead of her, but you are right. *He* is a friend of Bertram's and in the Navy. His parents live at Lyme Regis, and I hope he will be on leave while we are at Channings, and then you will meet him."

"Then it is *you* who has fallen in love?"

She still smiled, but the mischief had gone and there was tenderness in the curve of her mouth.

"I am not sure. I only know that I admire him very much and that

111

I enjoy his company above any other man's I know. Oh, it has been so boring here this season. Everyone, including Mama, has been expecting me to make a good match and heaven knows there has been opportunity enough, but I have had no interest in anyone except Lieutenant Henry Alton. Oh, Kate, you will love him. But, of course, not too much. You must promise me that!"

"I promise," I answered gravely.

"Good. Now I will tell you something about him," and she proceeded to do so.

I listened as sympathetically as possible. It appeared that Lieutenant Alton was twenty-six and serving on a frigate. He was tall and good looking with dark brown hair and hazel eyes. He came of a good family and had a private income of his own, but he was not a wealthy man and his prospects were dependent upon his career in the Navy.

"My mother likes him, I know, but she looks upon him only as a friend of Bertram's. I do not know how she will regard him—as my suitor."

"It has developed as far as that?"

She bit her lip.

"He has not made an offer but—but, Oh Kate, you know how it is. One somehow *knows* what is in a man's heart."

I was silent. I had thought that once; I had thought I knew how Esmond felt for me but I was wrong. He had had only a kindly affection for me. If he had truly loved me, he could never have fallen in love with Amy, however beguiling her ways.

I said slowly, aware of Rosamund's eyes on me,

"Sometimes perhaps, but not always. Be—be careful, Rosamund. Do not give your heart away before it is asked of you."

She stared, her blue eyes widening.

"But, Kate—you have not—" She broke off and I put a hand out to her, saying quickly,

"I am only warning you to be wise. But I am sure you are. I am sure Lieutenant Alton is sincere in his regard for you. I look forward very much to meeting him."

112

She stood up, her hand falling away from mine. She turned on one foot as she stretched her arms above her head.

"Oh, I cannot wait to meet him again myself. This time next week we will be at Channings. It will be your birthday a few days after. Shall we have a picnic—and invite Lieutenant Alton? Yes, we will do that."

My birthday! I had forgotten about it. Had a year come around so soon since the night of the ball? I remembered how Papa had given me the pearl-and-amethyst necklace and Amy had said, *"Pearls mean tears!"* And how I had danced and danced and known then that I should never be so happy again.

"I shall be nineteen," I said.

"I am nineteen now," Rosamund said gaily. "Oh, it is a nice age. I am glad to be nineteen. We are grown up, now, Kate, and of eminently marriageable age. Do you not think so?"

"Yes, but I do not think I want to marry. Not—not yet." I forced myself to smile. "You see, there cannot be *two* Lieutenant Alton's in the world."

"Never mind, Kate. We will try and find someone as like him as possible for you."

"Thank you." Rosamund was too happy in herself to notice how forced was my own gaiety, but my manner served to content her and we went on to talk of other things.

After the heat of London, Sherborne seemed an oasis of green and peace. Channings, my aunt's house, was old and picturesque, with two beautiful gatehouses of russet-colored stone on either side of an archway, leading to a flagged courtyard. The garden was laid out with old-fashioned flowers such as lavender and rosemary and bordered by tall yew hedges.

Within a week of our arrival Rosamund had her wish and Lieutenant Alton came to call. I liked him at first sight. He was quiet but gave an impression of latent resources, and I could imagine him as a disciplined and courageous officer in the Service. It was obvious he admired Rosamund, and I was pleased that my aunt seemed prepared to encourage his visits to Channings rather than the reverse.

My birthday was celebrated by a drive to the Sherborne Castle followed by a picnic near the ruins. It was a perfect day and the party of friends invited by Rosamund enjoyed the outing to the full. Henry Alton continued to call and then, at the end of July just before my return to Cornwall, Rosamund's engagement to him was announced.

"I'm so happy for you, Rosamund," I said as we embraced one another. "Henry is a splendid man and he loves you deeply."

"As I love him. I'm glad it all happened while you were staying with us, Kate. I feel you are part of these past wonderful weeks. I can only hope that one day you will be as happy as I am."

A few days later I left for Penvarrion, traveling by road to Yeovil. Here I would catch the train to take me via Exeter and Plymouth as far as Wadebridge, where my father had arranged to meet me with the carriage.

It was a long journey and I seemed to be traveling for most of the day, but the interest of the changing scenes and the company of two garrulous old ladies who shared the First Class "Ladies Only" carriage with me made time pass quickly. Soon we were pulling into Wadebridge station and there was my father's tall figure waiting upon the platform for me.

"Papa!"

"Kitty. My darling child." He kissed me fondly and for a moment kept his arm about my shoulder. "How are you? You look thinner in the face."

"I am well, Papa. Are you?"

"Yes, indeed. We are all well, including Amy who is home with Esmond and settled into her new home."

I felt my teeth catch at my underlip.

"Oh, that is nice." And then quickly, to cover the stiffness of my voice, "You know that Rosamund is engaged—I wrote to tell you of it?"

"Yes, we are all delighted. He sounds an admirable choice—a naval lieutenant. Your aunt is pleased about it?"

"Oh very. Henry is soon to have a captaincy."

"Splendid."

We had come out to the carriage, Masters walking ahead with the luggage he had taken from the porter. In a few moments we were driving across Breock Down, rose-tinged in the early evening sunshine. The same dear land I had always known. I loved it the more for having been away from it, and yet I was sad at heart to return. Nothing here would ever be the same to me.

My silence affected my father for he turned to look at me.

"Where is my chatterbox Kitty? It is not often you sit so quietly beside me."

It was so seldom these days he called me "Kitty." Warmed by the use of his pet name for me I rested my head against his arm for a moment.

"Oh, Papa."

"You are tired. Is that it?"

I seized upon the excuse.

"Yes. The train was wearyingly slow from Bodmin."

"We shall soon be at Penvarrion."

"Do you know I have been away six weeks? Is it just the same? Has anything been happening?"

"Nothing especially." He paused and when I glanced up saw that he was frowning. "One thing I forgot. While you were gone Bryce Dawnay called to see you. I was not aware you were on those terms of friendship, Katherine."

For a moment I could not speak, and then with a quick intake of breath to steady my voice, I said as calmly as I could,

"Oh, we have met from time to time. Since—since the evening at Truro you permitted me to dance with him, Papa."

"But that is months ago. Have you mutual acquaintances then, that you should speak of frequent encounters?"

"Not—not frequent, Papa. I have little interest in Mr. Dawnay and I cannot imagine why he should visit us."

"Then do not encourage him if he calls again. It would be as well to decline to see him."

"Yes, Papa. I will be sure to do that."

My heart was thumping against my side yet I felt cold all over. Why should Bryce Dawnay call at Penvarrion? I had told him I never wanted to see him or speak with him again. All I wanted was

115

to forget everything that had happened between us, forget the guilt and misery that our encounter on that fated Midsummer Night had brought upon me. Yet it would not do to show too obvious a resentment at the mention of his name for then my father would wonder in what way he had offended me and perhaps question me further.

I felt sick, sick with—yes, *fear,* for that was the word, and so tangible was my dread that a wave of nausea swept over me as Martin swung the horses a little faster along the road before we ran down toward Penvarrion. I was thankful indeed to see the gates and the lodge house come into view.

My stepmother's first words of greeting were in the form of commiseration at the sight of me.

"My dear Katherine, how pale you look. Has the journey overtired you or have you not been well? I thought to see you look blooming after your long holiday."

"I am very well, thank you, Stepmama, but the train journey was tiring in the summer heat."

"Of course. Come and sit down and Borlase shall bring us some refreshing tea."

The evening passed and at last I was able to retire to bed. But when Carrie had left me I could not sleep for thinking of Bryce Dawnay and dreading that he would call again at Penvarrion. I told myself that it did not matter. I would refuse to see him and that would be the end of it. He could not force himself upon me. With that thought for comfort I fell asleep.

Next morning there was a further ordeal to face for not long after breakfast Amy and Esmond arrived upon the scene. I heard their voices in the hall as I came in from the stables where I had been to visit Sorrel, to take her sugar and assure her we should soon be riding out together.

It was all I could do not to turn and run back to the yard, but I braced myself and went forward into the house and into Amy's eager embrace.

"Kate! Oh, it is lovely to see you again. I hope you had an enjoyable visit to your aunt's? It is exciting to hear of Rosamund's engagement—when is she to be married? Is he rich and handsome? But never mind all that—Esmond and I have come to invite you to our housewarming party. We delayed it until your return."

She looked radiant, her small face pink with color, her green eyes sparkling bright. She was wearing one of her trousseau dresses and it became her immensely.

Esmond came forward to take my hand. For a moment our glances met and then we both looked away. His lips brushed my cheek in a token kiss as he said, with formal politeness,

"How are you, Katy?"

"I am well, thank you."

"You look a little tired. Perhaps it was the long journey yesterday."

"I expect so."

He moved away and I heard myself let out a long sighing breath. When we sat down I glanced at Esmond when he was not looking and thought how well *he* looked, how handsome and contented, and I could have wept for all that might have been.

A week later we went over to Borleigh Grange to the housewarming party. I had visited the house once before, in company with Amy and my stepmother when they were deciding upon the new decorations. The house had been empty for some time, after the death of Sir Ralph's mother, an old lady of ninety-one. It had been filled with heavy dark furniture and a collection of valuable china and ornaments and rich Indian rugs, for the old lady's husband had held some post in the East India Company. I remember that Amy had grumbled on the way home that day wishing the house was other than it was but saying that Esmond could not afford to buy a place of his own and had no choice but to accept the loan of his father's property.

Now all was transformed. A great deal of money must have been spent, most of the dark old furniture had been relegated to the attics except for some of the more graceful pieces. The rooms looked light and charming, there were new curtains at every window and in the arrangement of everything I thought I saw the practiced hand of my stepmother.

"It is delightful," I said in sincere admiration as I was taken from

117

room to room, for we had arrived some time earlier than the other guests, at Amy's special request.

Sir Ralph and Lady Borleigh were next on the scene; Sir Ralph looked more red-faced than ever while Lady Borleigh seemed paler and more faded than usual by contrast. I did not think Sir Ralph looked well; his high color was mottled and the skin of his heavy jowl drooped like an old dog's and he walked with difficulty, as if the gout still troubled him.

Soon Laura arrived with Paul and we embraced one another in warm affection.

"It is so long since we met, Kate," Laura said, her arm about my waist.

"How is my dear little goddaughter? I long to see her. I shall find her grown again, I expect."

"Oh, yes. She is so advanced, it is unbelievable. Paul declares there has never been such a baby. She sits up quite strongly and says 'Da-Da' and 'Ma-Ma' as clearly as can be."

I smiled, happy for Laura in her love for Paul and for her little daughter.

The other guests began to arrive quickly, one after another, and soon the big drawing room was filled with laughing chattering people. Amy looked exquisite in yet another new dress, this time of rose-pink faille, and Esmond handsome in his ruffled shirt and dark evening clothes, was the most charming and attentive of hosts.

It was obvious that Amy had engaged an experienced staff. The dinner was perfectly cooked and served and the courses varied and delicious although I had little enough appetite for Globe artichokes swimming in butter, followed by fresh salmon with Dutch sauce and roast grouse or *chaud-froid* of chicken.

Seated on my right was Paul, while my other dinner partner was Charles Barlow. Between the two of them the conversation was kept at an animated level so that I had little opportunity to sink back into the mood of introspection which was becoming habitual to me. I felt as if I were acting in some play; that everything around me, the sparkling glass and shining silver, the rose-wreathed china, the great silver-gilt epergne in the center of the table filled with rainbow-hued sweet peas and delicate maidenhair fern was part of a set scene. Voices rose and fell as from a great distance; a mingling of laughter and chatter that echoed in my ears like waves upon a distant shore. Once I saw Charles Barlow glance at me in puzzled fashion but I reassured him with a smiling shake of the head, saying, "It is very warm this evening."

"Indeed, yes, despite the windows over there being open to their fullest extent." He lowered his voice discreetly. "Take comfort in the thought that we have reached the dessert stage."

"Yes, soon we shall be leaving the gentlemen to their port and find cooler conditions in the drawing room or on the terrace."

We smiled at one another and I thought fleetingly that Charles was very good looking for a clergyman, and then the thought was gone.

I managed to swallow a few mouthfuls of the syllabub that was brought to me, and a little later I caught Amy's glance as she nodded and rose from her chair at the head of the table, to lead the way through the wide double door held open by a footman.

In the drawing room, newly hung with a striking sea-green watered silk paper and furnished with graceful French Empire pieces sat my stepmother, all smiles, almost as much the hostess as Amy. On impulse I went across to the latter and complimented her on the delightful dinner.

As I might have expected she said,

"Oh, that is all due to Mama who chose the menu and instructed cook. I would not have known how to go about it. Mama says we must engage a housekeeper to attend to such matters, but Esmond says we already have more staff than we need or can afford." Her mouth pouted childishly. "Surely he does not expect me to deal with everything."

"You will learn in time," I said consolingly.

Amy tossed her head.

"I do not know that I wish to."

The gentlemen joined us after an interval and as the evening was so warm and still, some of the guests drifted out onto the terrace to sit in small groups talking together while others went down the steps to wander along the garden paths.

119

I remained on the terrace, seated beside Miss Barlow, as colorless and unobtrusive in her gray silk dress as a moth. Her brother joined us, and after a few moments Esmond, whom I had thought to be in the garden with Laura and Paul and Amy, appeared before us.

I forced myself into conversation.

"What a wonderful party, Esmond. Your house is beautiful and Amy is to be complimented on being a perfect hostess."

He inclined his head. "Thank you. I am glad that you approve. Have you seen everything—our new conservatory?" And when I shook my head he added, "Come this way, Kate. Miss Barlow too, and of course, Charles, if neither of you have as yet viewed it."

Esmond escorted us to the end of the terrace and then led the way through a double door into a domed room built entirely of glass. I had no idea what it had been like before, but now it proved to be a bower of velvety blossom and greenery. There were ferns and a date palm that looked as if it had been growing there forever, so shining green were its long arching leaves. There were hydrangeas and begonias and deep purple heliotrope, breathing a scented richness. On the tiled floor stood a wrought-iron table and some chairs painted white, while several handsome tubs of delft blue surmounted by pots of red and purple gloxinias splashed color.

Miss Barlow was staring about her in the same entranced amazement as myself.

"Why, Mr. Borleigh, you have a created a positively tropical environment—everything is so profuse."

"Amy wanted to make it a place where we could sit on winter days and enjoy the sunshine."

"What a splendid notion," Charles Barlow said. "We do not make nearly enough use of our colder seasons." He glanced about him. "Here it will always be summer."

Miss Barlow bent her head toward a tall plant that bore inverted bells of white blossom between shining broad leaves.

"I do not think I know what this is. Do you, Charles?"

Her brother moved to her side.

"It is a datura. The flower is beautifully scented."

I sensed Esmond's glance upon me.

"Do *you* like our innovation, Kate?"

I said quickly,

"Yes. It—it is fascinating—the way everything has been arranged and as if it had always been this way."

Esmond shrugged.

"Well, the vine has been here many years of course, and also the date palm. And most of the ferns. But everything else was old and dusty and neglected and had to be thrown away. I must admit it was Amy's mother who saw the full possibilities of the conservatory and advised us how to improve it."

"I can imagine." My voice was dry and he glanced at me and smiled.

A pang went through me. He was so happy. As Amy was; happy and a little smug. As my stepmother had looked a short while ago, seated in the drawing room.

I *wanted* Esmond to be happy. Of course I did. But seeing his contentment made me aware of my own loneliness, and intensified the feeling that I had put myself beyond the bounds of his and Amy's lives. So much had happened to me of which they must never know.

The heat and airlessness of the conservatory seemed suddenly to overwhelm me. I could not breathe in this claustrophobic world of green growth and the sweet almost cloying scent of the tuberose blooming on the nearby ledge made me feel faint.

I moved toward the door saying abruptly,

"I am overwarm. I will wait on the terrace if you do not mind."

I was conscious of Esmond's surprise, the expression of rebuff on his handsome face, but he did not come after me. I stood, panting slightly, grateful for the cool night air on my cheeks and a moment or two later I was joined by Charles Barlow who escorted me to a seat on the terrace. Here we encountered Dr. and Mrs. Fullbright and Esmond's sister, Miriam, and her husband. Esmond and I did not speak to one another again until it was time to say good night.

———◆———

It was a week after the housewarming that Bryce called again at Penvarrion. I was in my bedroom, a place to which I very often retreated to be on my own, when Borlase tapped at the door to tell me that a Mr. Dawnay was downstairs and wished to speak to me.

121

I felt the blood rush to my head and then ebb away, leaving me cold and frightened and for a moment, unable to speak. Turning away from Borlase's impassive gaze I said,

"Please tell Mr. Dawnay I—I am resting and unable to see him."

"Very good, Miss."

"Is—is my father in."

"No, Miss. He has gone down to speak with Mr. Trembath."

I bit my lip. In my cowardice I had wished that my father would see Bryce and ask him not to call again.

"Then—then just give Mr. Dawnay the message."

"Yes, Miss."

When he had gone I stood immovable in the center of the room, my hands against my trembling lips. Why did he persist in coming like this? I wished he would go away somewhere, far away from Tregedon, and I might never see or hear from him again. Yet some impulse forced me to the window of my room which overlooked the sweep of the front drive, and from behind the chintz curtain I waited to see Bryce Dawnay leave the house, as if to be sure he had gone.

He appeared at last, a tall figure in dark gray riding clothes. He walked away with the lithe easy stride, the upright carriage that was so characteristic of him, in the direction of the stables. He did not look back, not once, but swiftly and with noiseless footsteps, he was gone.

For a long time I remained half hidden behind the curtain, my forehead resting against the shutter until my shaking limbs would carry me over to the chair by the bed. I had escaped an encounter with Bryce this time, it was unlikely he would seek another rebuff.

I was wrong, for a few days later when I rode out on Sorrel, careful to go in the opposite direction to Tregedon Head, he appeared with startling suddenness, leaping over a wall behind me and cantering to draw level. Sorrel danced away at his approach, and I was tempted to flick the crop against her side and gallop off. I hesitated, feeling Bryce would be certain to ride after me and sure enough he leaned forward and snatched hold of the rein so that flight was impossible.

For a moment he stared down in silence at me, his light eyes narrowed. Then he said slowly,

122

"It seems you are trying to avoid me, Kate. You were too tired to see me the other day when I called at Penvarrion. At least your butler said you were 'resting.' "

"I asked you to—to keep away from me."

He jumped down from his horse and holding the reins, put out his other hand to me.

"I cannot do that. Not until we have spoken together. Please stay a few moments with me."

Reluctantly I slid to the ground and stood, my arm linked through Sorrel's rein.

"What is it you wish to say to me?"

He said gently,

"So much, and so little. That we belong to one another. We are linked together indissolubly."

I bit my lip, looking away from his intent gaze.

"I have told you. I do not love you and I never can."

He shook his head.

"I will not believe that. We have meant too much to one another. All my life I have held the thought of you close to my heart. I ask you again to marry me, Kate."

I clenched my hands together.

"I cannot. You do not understand. What—what occurred that night was madness—a folly I wish with every drop of blood in my body, had never happened. I want only to forget my own insanity."

He said in a low voice,

"You gave yourself to me with all the warmth and passion of your nature—do you call that insanity? It is the deepest reality you will ever know. You should count yourself fortunate that you are capable of experiencing the truth. Many die without ever having truly lived, because they cannot love."

I heard my own voice, sharp and high on the quiet air,

"To lie with a gypsy in the grass—you call that love? I am ashamed that I ever was so weak and—and reckless. For it was not *you* I loved, but someone else."

His head jerked back, the dark face froze. After a long endless moment in which we looked at one another he spoke.

"You cannot mean—Esmond Borleigh?"

I did not answer but turned Sorrel and somehow, without help, sprang back into the saddle. I glanced over my shoulder and saw him standing there tall and still, staring down at the ground, his dark face expressionless. Then he lifted his head with an abrupt jerk and said, in a harshly bitter voice,

"You may rest assured I shall not pursue you further with my unwanted attentions. I leave you to the questionable enjoyment of your unrequited love." In one swift moment he had sprung onto Caspar's back and turning the horse's black head, he set off at a gallop across the fields from which he had come and disappeared out of sight.

The relief that I felt was tempered by remorse. I had said too much. I had been more cruel than I had intended, but with a sense of being trapped by my own folly I had tried to break free of him. Now I had done so. I was sure of that. Yet I knew, deep down, that what had happened that night in the moonlit wood had been my fault as much as Bryce's.

I rode soberly home to Penvarrion, my heart curiously heavy when I remembered the look on his face, as if I had slashed my riding crop across those dark features.

The weeks went by and there were no more unwanted callers at the house. Nor did I dread that I should encounter Bryce upon my rides as I had earlier feared. It was finished. I would not see him again.

August was hot and the air felt strangely airless. Mist hung over the fields and the sea, sometimes I felt I could not breathe. Often I walked down the Penvarrion Cove and sat there, ostensibly occupied with water colors and easel, for painting was my only artistic talent. But instead of putting down on paper the scene before me I would sit staring at the sea and the sky.

September came and the fields were golden with stubble and the shadow over me deepened. I was afraid and I could not speak of my fear to anyone. And then, one day, something happened and I had to face the terror in my mind.

I had gone to visit Laura. It was sunny and we spent most of the afternoon in the garden. After little Phoebe had had her rest the nurse brought her to us and for a while she lay on my lap, gurgling and cooing at the moving shadows of the leaves overhead. She was so pretty, her small body soft and warm within the circle of my arms. I loved her, and as I bent to kiss the downy dark hair upon her rounded head I thought how wonderful it must be to have a child of one's own.

A laden tea tray appeared and Laura said,

"Let me take Baby now, Kate, and you shall pour the tea for us."

I stood up, holding Phoebe carefully in my arms. I bent down to lay her in Laura's outstretched ones and as I straightened up a strange dizziness came over me. For a moment the tea table, Laura's smiling face, the lawn and trees swam in a haze and if I had not sat quickly down again I think I should have fallen.

I breathed deeply, my head resting against the back of the cane garden chair. I heard Laura say quickly,

"What is the matter, Kate? Are you unwell?"

"It's nothing. Just the—the heat."

She stared at me, frowning, and leaving Phoebe on the rug the nurse had put across the grass she said,

"I will pour the tea. It will refresh you."

"Thank you. But I am quite recovered."

I sipped the tea gratefully. The sight of cucumber sandwiches and saffron cake increased the sense of nausea and I shook my head in refusal. I thought how yesterday morning I had been sick and had comforted myself with the notion of having eaten something unsuitable the night before. There had been other mornings lately, signs and omens that I refused to consider.

I could not believe what was happening to me.

Soon I felt better but the fear remained with me. I longed to talk to Laura, to question her, but I hesitated to do so for no one discussed such personal matters, certainly not a married woman with an unmarried girl, however close the friendship between them. And even if I had been able to do so I should have been afraid that I would reveal what had happened between myself and Bryce. Laura would not only be astounded, she would condemn me, and never understand how such a thing could possibly occur. I could hardly explain it to myself.

I felt utterly isolated and alone as I sat drinking afternoon tea as if I was without a care in the world. Sometimes it seemed to me that

125

was the hardest part of all; that I was no longer myself *to* myself, or to other people. I was someone whom nobody knew; a hypocrite and a sham.

I drove away from Greystokes at last, in the pony carriage that once belonged to Amy. She had a carriage of her own now, with two dappled grays to draw it. I made wild plans. I would go somewhere where I was not known and find a doctor. I would have to put a wedding ring on my finger, give a false name.

I shuddered from the thought of such an ordeal and yet, I knew I would have to do something. I could not go on indefinitely. Supposing it were true, supposing I learned that the thing I dreaded was a fact? It would not be long before my stepmother's sharp eyes assessed the situation, and the thought of her scorn was something I could not bear.

If dear old Hester had been alive I would have gone to her. She had nursed me from a child; she had loved and understood me; I could have trusted in her wise ways and her unchanging affection.

But Hester was dead, and there was no one.

Two days later I told my father and stepmother that I was going to meet Miss Pringle, and taking some money and the gold wedding ring that had belonged to my mother, I drove to St. Austell, a town where I felt no one would know me. It was a matter of fourteen miles or so, a long drive for Punch, but he was a sturdy pony and I would make sure he had a good rest before we made the return journey.

I found what I thought looked a suitable doctor's house. It was in a quiet road and of respectable appearance without appearing to be fashionable. The doctor was out but I was told that he would be returning shortly and that I could wait for him if I wished. I was almost too embarrassed to speak. I made some answer and, with the veil of my bonnet shielding my face took a seat in a shabby leather furnished room and there waited, with thumping heart and hands clasped tightly together to prevent their trembling, until the doctor should see me.

# 10

I SUPPOSE in my heart I had hoped for a reprieve. To be assured that the situation was normal, it was just a small aberration from the ordinary, and things would right themselves. But the doctor, a burly red-faced man who looked more like a butcher or a horse doctor than a physician, did not hesitate over his diagnosis. Instead he informed me, genially, that I was three months pregnant. He added that I appeared to be in excellent health and gave me a few instructions and a bottle of medicine to ease the morning sickness.

"You must see your own doctor when you return to Dorset, of course. I think you said you were visiting the district while your husband is away at sea?"

"Yes." I bit my lip, thinking of the tissue of lies building up about me, but what else could I do but invent some suitable background for this visit to the Surgery. My fingers clasped the ring on my left hand as if for reassurance. Luckily it fitted more than firmly, for my hands were larger than my mother's had been.

I paid the fee asked and thanked him and said good-by.

"Good-by, Mrs. Rouse. I am sure everything will go well with you, but it is as well to take these few precautions before you see your own physician."

Walking back to the inn where I had stabled Punch and where I hoped to take tea before setting off on the drive back, I thought how I had used Hester's surname as an alias. She would not have minded; she would have wanted to help me.

The inn was quiet. A maid servant brought me a tray of tea and some buttered scones and would have stayed to chatter but my stumbling answers and abstracted manner soon sent her away. I sat like someone stunned, sipping the strong bitter tea, unable to think of anything except that I was to bear Bryce's child.

What was I to do? What could I do? I would not marry him. I felt I hated him as much as I hated myself. Or perhaps I hated him *because* I hated myself? Could I go away somewhere and have the baby and no one would ever know about it? I thought of Phoebe and the sweet feel of her warm little body in my arms. A child of my own? I could never part with her or him.

As I sat in the dark little room of the inn I felt more alone and more desperate than I had ever felt in my entire life.

The sun was still shining when I reached Penvarrion for it was not yet six o'clock. Martin took Punch away and I went into the house. My stepmother was coming down the stairs as I crossed the hall.

"So you are back, Katherine. Did you enjoy your visit to Miss Pringle? I hope you found her well."

Lies and more lies.

"Yes—she is well."

"Did you have lunch with her at Edgcumb Hall? It is very good of the Ashton's to allow Miss Pringle to entertain visitors, but of course, I knew I had found her an excellent position when I recommended her there."

"Yes." I felt the monosyllable answered everything without committing myself to more falsehoods. "If you will excuse me, Stepmama, I am somewhat dirty—I had to attend to Punch," and without further delay I hurried to my room.

I ate little dinner; so little, in fact, that my stepmother commented on my lack of appetite.

"I hope you are not sickening for something. Though you look well enough for I believe you are plumper, Katherine. That blue dress pulls across the back of the waist. You must ask Carrie to let it out a little."

I could have sunk through the chair. I did not know where to look, certainly not in the direction of my stepmother's cool scrutinizing glance. I mumbled something about the dress always being a little on the small side. But that night, when Carrie came to help me at bedtime, I made an excuse and sent her away and said that I would undress later. I was terrified that she would begin to notice my thickening waist and I felt more distraught than ever.

A few days passed. Like a trapped animal I sought an escape from the pit into which I had fallen but there was none. I rode Sorrel in demonical frenzy across the moors jumping stone walls that would have daunted a Master of Hounds. Perhaps I hoped for an accident, some injury that would end my problems. And then I considered gallant little Sorrel and thought how she too might hurt herself—or worse—and checked in my own reckless folly.

One afternoon, feeling at the end of my tether I walked into the churchyard and stood by my mother's grave, as I had stood once before. That was the day Bryce had come back into my life, a day I should regret for evermore. I think I hoped for comfort, a sign. Was it true what some people said, that those we love and who have loved us, never leave us but become as guardian angels? If that were so why had I not been stayed from going into the badger's wood that Midsummer Night? Yet, as I stood staring down at the worn headstone I felt more peaceful and on impulse I turned and went into the church and sat down in one of the back pews. I tried to pray. "Help me," I whispered into the silence. "Please help me," but whether I was praying to my dead mother or to God I did not know.

When at last I stood up and walked toward the arched doorway it was to find Charles Barlow standing there. His face lit up at my approach.

"Miss Carew—Kate—I was not sure if it was you. How are you? I have not seen you except in the distance for some weeks. You have been away I think?"

"Yes. To stay with my aunt and cousin in Dorset."

"Gertrude has missed you. As I have." He smiled, his pleasant open face bent to mine. "Will you be resuming your work at Sunday school with us soon?"

I looked away from his gaze which, as ever, was warm and admiring. I wondered how he would look if I said, "I am in terrible trouble. Please tell me what to do." His friendly smile would fade, he would be shocked and horrified. He would regard me as someone who had "sinned" like the village girls who produced babies outside wedlock.

I made a murmured excuse.

"I—I am not sure. I may be going away again very shortly."

"Oh." He looked downcast. "That is our loss. I trust your absence will not be for too long."

"I am not certain of its duration."

"But you will come and see us before you go. May I tell Gertrude to expect you?"

"I—I will send a message. Please excuse me now, Charles. I must return to the house."

"Of course. Let me walk a little way back with you."

He left me half way down the track to Penvarrion, lifting the black hat from his curly brown hair and holding my hand in his a fraction longer than was necessary.

I went on alone, aware that I had come to some sort of a decision. My dead mother could not help me but my father loved me dearly I knew. I would throw myself on his mercy. Tell him what had happened and beg him to allow me to go away somewhere—abroad perhaps, where no one would know me. Such things happened—I had heard stories. Scandals might be hushed up but there were always rumors. If I had to give my baby up, then, heartbreaking as that might be it would be the price I must pay for my wrongdoing. I would beg my father to keep my secret, never to speak of it to my stepmother or Amy. Surely he would do that for me?

I went through the gate in the wall along the path and across the lawn. I must find my father at once before my courage failed me. I went into the house by the side door and there, walked into a scene of great distress.

My stepmother sat upon the high carved settle, a handkerchief to her eyes while beside her knelt Amy, holding her mother's hands wiping away her own tears. Esmond stood nearby, his face pale and frowning. In the background hovered Mrs. Borlase, her hands clasped over her ample stomach, her eyes anxious and frightened in her flushed face.

Everyone turned to look at me but no one spoke and I cried out in alarm,

"What is it? What has happened?" and then, sharply, "Where is my father?"

My stepmother shook her head from side to side without speaking and Amy started to cry. It was Esmond who came to my side to say with gentle kindness,

"Your father has met with an injury. He was kicked on the head— an accident with his horse. He is upstairs—Dr. Clarkson and Dr. Fullbright are examining him, at this moment." I gasped aloud and Esmond took my hand in his firm clasp and added, "Be brave, Katy. Your father will be all right, I am sure. He was unconscious when they brought him in and the doctors fear concussion, but he is in the best of hands."

I leaned against Esmond, thankful for his comfort and kindness. He was more dear to me than ever in that moment of shared anxiety, but as I saw Amy turn her head to glance at us I knew that I must not look to Esmond for consolation. I pulled my hand free and said,

"Forgive me—it was the shock." I moved away. "I must go to my stepmother—she is greatly distressed." As I did so Amy stood up and crossed over to Esmond's side saying,

"Oh, Esmond. Poor dear Steppapa—I hope he will recover," and I saw Esmond put his arm about her and smooth her bright hair.

My stepmother was calm, despite the tears she had shed.

"This is a dreadful thing, Katherine. Let us pray that the doctors can do something to help your dear papa." She shuddered. "When they carried him in on the gate I thought he was dead. He was so still and quiet and his face and head were covered in blood."

I did not know how to answer her, I could only put a hand on her shoulder in lieu of words and stand silent beside her. We turned in unison as Dr. Clarkson came slowly down the stairs. He inclined his head gravely,

"Madam—Mrs. Carew—may I speak in private with you," and my stepmother, whom I had helped to her feet, nodded and with a gesture led the way into the study.

I longed to go with her, I longed to hear what the doctor had to say about my father, but all I could do was stare beseechingly at the closing door and murmur a quiet prayer.

But the news was good. Well, if not good, hopeful. My father was

131

concussed from the blow he had sustained and was unconscious. Dr. Clarkson predicted that he would remain in this state for some days, if not longer. He must be kept completely quiet, and if all went well, he would slowly recover consciousness.

"It will take time," my stepmother told us when she returned from seeing my father. "Dr. Clarkson fears that his memory may be impaired for some weeks—he may scarcely know us. But with careful nursing and absolute rest he should recover. Dr. Clarkson knows a good and reliable person who has helped nurse several of his patients and he will send her to us, and of course, we will all take a share in looking after my dear Gilbert."

Later I went in to see my father. He lay quiet and still, his eyes closed. He had no awareness of my presence, when I took his hand in mine and laid my cheek against it there was no answering pressure. It lay limp in my clasp. I stayed with him for a while and then, with tears streaming down my cheeks, I left him.

For several days there was no change. He scarcely stirred in his bed. We took turns to sit with him, to administer a sip of water to his parched lips or a spoonful of the cordial prescribed by Dr. Clarkson. Mrs. Rumble, the rosy faced countrywoman who was engaged to attend to him, was a tower of strength, assuring us that every day he was improved though I could see little sign of it myself.

At first I was too concerned for my father to worry about myself, but as the days went by my fears returned and I was desperate to know what to do. I should never be able to ask my father to help me now, it was too late. Yet time was passing. If I did not act soon my secret would be guessed by someone—by Carrie or by my shrewd observant stepmother.

And so, one morning, after a sleepless night and in a mood of utter despair, Sorrel was saddled and we set off on the long ride to Tregedon.

It was the only answer. To confront Bryce with the truth of the situation and humble myself enough to ask for his help. He had offered to marry me. He had said once "If ever you need me, if ever you wish to ask anything of me, I am at your service." I must hope that he would stand by those words.

I did not stop to think how it would all come about. How, with my

132

father lying unconscious I would get permission to marry Bryce, what my stepmother and everyone would say. I *dared* not think what sort of a marriage I was committing myself, and Bryce, to. A marriage without love, at least on my part.

It was a cool windy day; the clouds were low and gray upon the headland as I came within sight of Tregedon and the wild sea tossing below the high cliffs. As before, it looked a harsh unwelcoming place with its granite walls and broken chimney stack. I reined Sorrel in, staring ahead to the house set fortresslike against the hill. It was a sight enough to daunt anyone and I shuddered at the mere idea of living there. I would have gladly turned around and galloped back to Penvarrion but I was driven on by my desperate circumstances and so, slowly and with quailing heart I rode forward again.

Everything was as it had been before except that, if anything, the surroundings of Tregedon looked more forlorn and neglected than ever. There seemed little sign of the improvements Bryce had spoken of undertaking.

I came to the gateway and, dismounting, walked Sorrel into the courtyard. Ladders and ropes still hung about the crumbling chimney stack, rubble still covered the ground. No one came forward to greet me but I heard a deep bay from the house and I guessed it was the dog, Boris.

I tied Sorrel to a ring in the wall and went to the door by which I had entered last time. I knocked but there was no reply. Boris barked again and on impulse I lifted the latch and went into the dark hall. I called,

"Is someone there?" but no one answered. The house was silent, empty. And then I heard the clatter of tin and the sound of running water from what I guessed must be the kitchen quarters. The low-beamed room, white-washed and stone-flagged was empty but the sound of running water came from a scullery beyond. I pushed open the door and halted abruptly on the threshold.

Bryce was standing by the earthenware sink pumping water into the tin bucket in his hand. He swung around, staring in amazement at the sight of me. With a clatter he dumped the bucket to the floor and said sharply,

"What the devil?"

133

"I'm sorry. I—no one answered. I heard sounds—water running —so I came this way." I stammered again. "I'm sorry."

He reached for his jacket hanging from a nearby hook. As he pushed his arms into the sleeves I looked at him and saw that his chin was dark with stubble and the tawny eyes were shadowed and bloodshot. He said abruptly,

"You must excuse my rough dress. I have been attending to the stock." For a moment he stared coolly at me. "Well—to what do I owe the honor of this visit?"

I glanced around the scullery wondering how to begin even as I longed to escape. I wanted to run away from this man who was no more than a grim-faced stranger and with whom it was impossible to think I had ever shared an emotional relationship.

"It—it is nothing. I have come at an inopportune time. I'm sorry." I turned as if to go, but a hand shot out and gripped my wrist.

"Not so fast, Kate. I hardly think you would have come all this way, alone and unattended, on an entirely unimportant errand. Especially as you were at such pains to tell me the last time we met that you wanted to have no more to do with me. Let us go into the other room where we can discuss this sudden change of heart."

He let go of my wrist and held open the scullery door and then the kitchen one and gestured for me to go ahead into the parlor. It was dark and cold, the fire a residue of gray ash. He pulled forward a chair and flicked a hand over it with an air of mock gallantry.

"Please sit down. I must apologize for the neglect. Mrs. Porritt, an inefficient housekeeper at the best of times, is away at her daughter's, and in her absence I have found the wine bottle a good companion."

I sat down, very stiff and upright. Boris subsided at my feet watching me out of filmed brown eyes. Bryce's taunting manner made me feel that he hated me and this was scarcely a good beginning to the interview. But in a way, it was a challenge. If he no longer loved me, we were equal opponents. And now I was here, I must go through with the matter, for my father's sake. Because he was gravely ill and I could not bring shame on him at such a time.

So I said coldly and clearly and without equivocation.

"I am to bear your child."

134

He had been staring down at me, one black eyebrow raised in sardonic fashion. Strangely, his expression scarcely altered. A tremor passed over his dark features, the light eyes narrowed and the hard jaw twitched. That was all. With an impassivity that astonished me he said slowly,

"Are you sure of this?"

"I have visited a doctor—he assured me of the fact."

"I see." He walked to the window and stood staring out, his arms folded across his chest. In the ensuing silence I gazed helplessly at his broad back. After what seemed an endless pause he turned and came back to me to say briefly,

"And what is it you wish me to do in the circumstances?"

I stared at him. With his stubble of beard and narrowed bloodshot eyes he looked fierce and hard, a gypsy in truth. Our glances met and held and I knew that he would give me no quarter. Once I had humbled him, now I was to be humbled in turn.

But submissiveness did not come easily to me. I said sharply,

"I would not have come today to ask favors of you but for one thing. My father has met with an accident and lies seriously ill," and I went on to recount what had occurred. "So you see," I concluded with less certainty than I had begun, "I cannot look to him for help as I might have done. I have no alternative but to—" I steadied the sudden tremble in my voice, "to say I will marry you if—if you are still of that mind."

"And being a man of honor, of course, I have an obligation to fulfill. I am sorry indeed to hear of your father's accident and I hope sincerely he will recover. Meanwhile, put your mind at rest. The Banns will be called."

He was still taunting me. There was little of love or affection in his glance. I wondered in bewilderment how he could ever have beguiled me into the passion of that Midsummer Night.

I bit my lip, hating that all the overtures must now be mine.

"It will be necessary for you to come and see my—my stepmother. To ask her permission, in lieu of my father. I—we cannot delay matters overlong. I cannot think what she will say, how she will understand that I could—that we are—" I paused, unable to go on.

"Rest assured I shall convince her of my undying passion. I shall tell her I worshipped you from afar and then, by God's good grace, was able to win your affections. Your father's illness will be the excuse for a quiet wedding. The family only, your stepsister, of course, and—*Esmond.*"

The name dropped, hard and cold as a pebble rolling along a dusty road. I met his glance; the mockery had gone and only a relentless impassivity remained. I was filled with a sudden fear. I said quickly,

"I realize this will be—a marriage of convenience only. Neither of us would wish to pretend it could be otherwise. Once my—our child is born I can leave you. You need not endure my presence longer than you wish."

He leaned toward me, his eyes holding a strange glitter in their golden depths.

"You are mistaken, Kate. If I marry you, I shall wish very much that you will always be here—at Tregedon. You—and our child. Those are the terms of the marriage. You will live here and make a home for us. At present it is a trifle neglected, but it will soon improve under a woman's care." He shrugged. "There is no lack of money for any amenities you may wish for. As for it being a marriage of convenience, I am certain there are as many of those that endure to the grave as the ones which stem from a more romantic origin."

When I made no answer, but sat like an animal hypnotized by a snake, he straightened up and added,

"I suggest now that you return to Penvarrion. I will shave off my beard and put on my best coat and ride over to your home later today. Perhaps it would be as well to warn your stepmother that your importunate suitor is on his way—then it will not be such a shock to her when I appear." He put a hand out to me. "Do you agree?"

I stood up, avoiding his outstretched hand.

"Yes." I walked to the door and he opened it for me, and when we reached the yard he untied Sorrel and before I realized what he was about to do he put his hands on my waist and swung me up as if I were light as a bird, into the saddle. For a moment he kept his hold on me, his dark head level with the reins.

136

"It is *au revoir* only, Kate."

I did not answer. He released me and the next second, without looking back, I was gone from Tregedon and riding along the cart track to the open country beyond.

So it was done. I was to marry Bryce and he would father my child. I was to live at Tregedon, that fearsome lonely house. And I was to stay there. There was little hope of escape. God help me, I thought, I had made my bed, and now I must lie on it.

*Part 2*

# TREGEDON

# 11

AFTER THAT affairs moved swiftly. It was not easy. I had to bear the brunt of my stepmother's astonishment and angry questioning. And her reproaches.

"At such a time when your father is so ill and I need your help. And Bryce Dawnay, of all people. We know little about him, except that his grandmother was a *gypsy*. You must be out of your mind, Katherine."

"He comes of a good family," I mumbled. "And a very old one. I have known him a long time."

"Not with our knowledge," she rapped back at me. "Not only are you selfish, but you have acted deceitfully in forming this association behind our backs. And now you want to be married with your father knowing nothing about it for although he has recovered consciousness, Dr. Fullbright says he is not to be worried in any fashion or be caused stress. As it is, his memory is very bad." She sighed. "Yesterday he did not know Amy when she called to see him."

"It is because Dr. Fullbright says that Papa's recovery will take weeks, perhaps months, that I thought it would be best that Bryce and I should be married quietly now. Papa will understand that he was not able to give his consent at this time."

"You should be content to wait until he is restored to good health." She stared at me, her russet eyes speculative. "You are in a great hurry, Katherine. Have you a special reason?"

I was determined not to look away, not to let my own guilt and inner confusion show. Somehow I stared calmly back at her as I said,

"No more than that I am now prepared to marry. You were al-

141

ways urging me to do so, Stepmama. If you remember, you pointed out to me the drawbacks of remaining a spinster."

A tinge of color showed on the creamy cheeks, the thin lips tightened.

"I have no more to say, and no more objections to make. You must please yourself."

"Thank you, Stepmother."

As I left the room, far from exultant at my victory, I thought that if my stepmother had been a different kind of woman I might not have rushed into marriage with Bryce. If she had been kinder, more understanding, if I had felt she truly loved me, perhaps I would have gone to her, as to my own mother.

And then I thought, but if such had been the case, I should never have gone with Bryce that night because I should not have felt so alone and unwanted. The present unhappy circumstances would not have arisen.

Useless to think if—if—if. If I had been another sort of girl, a less impetuous impulsive character. There was no end to these speculations.

Bryce had been and gone, clean and shaved beyond reproach, only the bloodshot eyes and lines about his mouth tracing a shadow of dissipation on his face. His manner and dress were unexpectedly formal; somehow he convinced my stepmother of his suitability, so that toward the end of the interview she was polite, if not gracious.

The Banns were called and arrangements made for the wedding, but of all this my father knew nothing.

I sat with him every day. Sometimes he spoke to me but the words he said were vague and hesitant. He had no recollection whatsoever of the accident, and though he had been told what had happened he forgot and seemed to think he had been ill of a fever. He always knew me, but sometimes he did not remember who Amy or Oliver were and once he called Esmond by his father's name. When Laura came to visit him he did not know her or Paul, but he remembered Sir Ralph and Lady Phoebe. It was all very confusing. Dr. Clarkson warned us this state of things might continue for a long time, until the pressure on the brain lifted.

I think I realized, then, seeing my handsome active father lying so frail and lost to himself, that he would never be the same man again. More than once I wept as I left the room.

There was little I could do to help; the brunt of the nursing was undertaken by Mrs. Rumble, though Borlase had become a tower of strength and now acted less as butler and more as valet to my father. My stepmother was in constant attendance, sitting in the sunny bay of my father's room, busy at her embroidery or tapestry. Sometimes he answered her occasional remark but often his words were completely out of context.

Amy and Esmond were told of my forthcoming marriage. Amy was amazed saying, "Bryce Dawnay! I remember you dancing with him at the Truro Ball. I did not know you were well acquainted."

Esmond was angry. He waited until he was alone with me and then he said without preamble,

"Kate, what is this folly? You are mad to marry a man like Dawnay. You will regret it for the rest of your life. He has nothing to offer you, and you are worthy of the best."

I turned away from him, hiding my distress as best I could.

"I should prefer your good wishes to your censure, Esmond. My mind is made up."

"But why? How has this all come about? You cannot be in love with him."

"Why not? As you have just said, he has little to offer but himself."

"You scarcely know one another."

I said almost to myself,

"We are better acquainted than you think."

"Katy." He put his hand on my arm and turned me toward him. "Katy, I am thinking only of your welfare. I feel you are rushing into this marriage without sufficient thought. And at a time when you are needed here, to be a comfort to your stepmother."

I looked up and met his glance for the first time. His eyes, so deep and dark a blue, looked into mine. I felt the old ache of love and tenderness for him.

143

"She has little need of me, Esmond. She never has. There is no place for me at Penvarrion. I have known that for a long time."

"So you are marrying to escape?"

"It could be one reason."

"And the others?"

"They do not concern you."

"I think they do. We are linked in a family relationship now, Katy. You are as a dear sister to me."

For a moment I could not speak. I was too overwhelmed. Not in gratitude for Esmond's words but with a sense of heavy-heartedness, almost of loss.

"It is good of you to regard me as such, but nothing you can say will change my mind. I shall marry Bryce Dawnay for better or for worse, and so you must bring yourself to regard *him* as a brother."

He let go of my arm.

"That would be impossible. There is no more to be said." He turned and then paused. "I came here—Amy and I came here today with news which we felt would cheer her mother and you, and your father too, if he can comprehend it. It is better perhaps that Amy should recount it."

"But what news? Please, Esmond, tell me now."

He looked around, the frowning expression fading from his face.

"It is wonderful news. The best in the world. Amy is *enciente.*"

I said faintly,

"With child? Amy is to bear a child?"

"Yes. You can imagine how pleased and proud I am. Her mother will be delighted. Amy is gone to tell her. I hope she will not be upset that I have revealed the secret before she has had the chance herself."

"I am very happy for you, Esmond. For you both."

"Thank you, Katy. I knew you would be. Now if you will excuse me I will go to Mrs. Carew."

"Yes, do not delay. I will come in a few moments and give Amy my good wishes."

When he had gone I stood with my hands pressed against my eyes, as if to shut out Esmond's proud smiling face. Amy was to bear his

144

child. And in circumstances of love and happiness that I could only envy. I would have given the rest of my life to have been in her place.

———◆———

One day Bryce rode over and I took him into my father's bedroom and said hesitantly,

"This is Bryce Dawnay, Papa. Do you remember him?"

My father stared frowningly up at Bryce and then he shook his head.

"Not—met—before."

"You have, Papa dear, but it was some time ago. Bryce and I are —are close friends. We—we hope to marry."

He stared in puzzlement.

"Marry? Is it Esmond? Esmond married. Remember—remember the wedding." He sighed and shook his head. "Such a beautiful day."

"Esmond married Amy, Papa," I said but he closed his eyes as if too tired to talk and after a short while, seeing he was asleep, we left him.

That was the day Bryce took me to meet his grandmother.

"She is the one person I care about," he said in the abrupt manner he used to me on the few occasions we met. Though to outward eyes we were a betrothed couple, when alone together we were as strangers. "It is important that she should meet you."

I don't know what I had expected. A bent old crone, some wild witchlike figure? I was curious to meet old Mrs. Dawnay, but I was aware of a sense of trepidation when we arrived at the small stone cottage half hidden down a narrow lane a few miles from Tregedon. Yet if the dwelling, poor and bare, did not welcome one, the garden did, for enclosed by a low wall, it was filled with a profusion of flowers and sweet-smelling herbs. The scent of them was in the air, as, after tying the horses, we walked up a narrow path set with uneven old bricks. I glanced about me, seeing lavender and thyme, purple and green sage, and mint. There was tall-growing lovage and short-stemmed savory; tarragon and fennel and origanum with its leaves of gleaming gold. A bush of blue flowering rosemary stood

145

under the casement window, patches of bright-headed marigolds around it.

Before Bryce could lift the latch the door opened and a woman stood there, grave and unsmiling, her hands folded under a black shawl.

Was she old? I knew from what Bryce had told me that she must be in her seventies and yet, standing there, enormous black eyes in an aquiline-featured face, jet-black hair with scarcely a fleck of gray in it, piled up on her head, her brown skin lined only infinitesimally, she seemed ageless.

She smiled and the change was startling, there was light and brilliancy where before had been only a calm and serious scrutiny. She inclined her head and said,

"Come in and welcome."

We went into a room, tiny and low-ceilinged, filled with plants in every kind of container, shining brass and copper, gaily painted china. There was a profusion of colored glass, green and red, deep violet and rich blue, and other glass ornaments with gleaming lusters moving in the draught of our passing. A lurcher dog, smooth-coated and bright-eyed, came toward us and Bryce patted his head and said,

"Hallo, Nezer. Grandmother, this is Katherine Carew, whom I am to marry. Kate, my grandmother."

She put a hand out to me and holding mine in a firm clasp, placed her other hand over it. She did not kiss or embrace me, but for a moment stared at me with great intentness. She said slowly,

"Yes, you are beautiful. My grandson loves you. I knew that before he even as much as spoke your name. You will love him too." Releasing my hand she gestured toward a shabby rocking chair. "Please sit down."

I did so, wondering why she had said, in that strange way, "You will love him too," instead of, "You love him too." The future rather than the present tense. But perhaps it was just the way she used words?

"I would like you to call me Zena," she said, as she poured wine from a dark green glass decanter. "It is more suitable for I am not

146

*your* grandmother." There was the inflection of a smile in her voice though her face was grave again.

"Thank you."

She lifted her glass.

"Let us drink to the joy that will come to you. Joy and sorrow are as a two-sided coin, one is the face of the other."

Again I was startled by her words, but I nodded and sipped the wine which was sharp tasting yet not unpleasant.

"Has Bryce told you I shall not attend the wedding? You must forgive me but these days I seldom leave my cottage."

"I understand."

Bryce drained his glass and stood up saying abruptly,

"I will leave you to become acquainted while I attend to Caspar—his girth requires easing."

When he had gone we sat in silence, one on either side of a circular table, covered with a brown chenille cloth. Zena had thrown the shawl back from her shoulders, revealing a blouse of brightly colored red and green. Long earrings hung from her ears, on the lap of the long black skirt her hands were clasped in calm composure.

I felt she would not speak unless I did. Not knowing how to begin a conversation I said,

"Your garden is very pretty. Bryce tells me you have lived here a long time."

"Yes." She shook her head. "I have forgotten how long. The days and the years pass so quickly I have lost track of time. When I go, the cottage will go with me."

I stared in bewilderment.

"Go? Go where?"

A slight smile touched her lips.

"That I cannot tell you. Where does one go at the end?"

I had never met anyone who spoke so strangely. I might have thought she was a little crazed if it were not for the bright intelligence in the hollowed black eyes.

Before I could answer she leaned toward me and said in her deep husky-sounding voice,

147

"You and Bryce are well-matched. The fire is in both of you. But remember—fire destroys fire."

She spoke in parables. I tried to find words with which to reply but none would come. I would have welcomed Bryce's return, and yet I was fascinated by this strange woman and drawn to her in a way I could not understand.

"Tregedon is a—a lonely place." I heard myself say as if someone else had spoken.

"Aye. Few are welcome there. The shadow of the past lies over it. But shadows cannot remain forever. No day is without the sun, or night without the moon." She broke off as the door opened and Bryce came in. He glanced at us in turn.

"I see you have been getting to know one another. I'm afraid we must go now, Grandmother, but I will bring Kate to see you again." He added shortly, "After we are married."

Zena stood up.

"That will be soon now. In a week's time?" She turned to me. "I am always here, Katherine. Come and see me whenever you wish."

"I shall be happy to. Thank you." I hesitated. She was aloof in her reserve and yet her black eyes were kind. When she took my hand and held it for a moment I leaned forward impulsively and kissed her cheek.

Bryce had gone ahead of me. I was about to follow when Zena's clasp on my hand tightened. I looked at her but she was gazing past me, her black eyes strangely fixed. She said,

"Your son will be born with the morning light. Care for him and for yourself. Danger lies across your path."

If she had wanted to frighten me, she had certainly succeeded for a tremor went through me and I stared at her in alarm. Then, before I could speak she let go of my hand and pushed me gently away from the step and the next moment the door of the cottage closed behind me.

I walked down the path to where Bryce was waiting with the horses. The trancelike state shattered immediately I reached him. I said angrily,

"You should not have told your grandmother about the baby. It was wrong to do so!"

He frowned blackly.

"I have said nothing of it to her. Why should you imagine I did?"

"Because she has just told me I shall have a son—and—and that I must take care."

He laughed unexpectedly.

"I should have warned you. There is little need to tell my grandmother of any future happenings. She sees them for herself."

"That isn't possible."

He shrugged.

"Rationally speaking, I agree with you. But events have proved otherwise. She has the gift of second sight as many another Romany." He slipped the reins over Sorrel's head. "Rest assured we shall have a son."

"And the danger?" I said slowly. "She warned me of danger."

"A necessary caution, perhaps, in pregnancy." He put his hands on my waist to lift me into the saddle. "I will take care of you, Kate. For our son's sake. I want a son for Tregedon."

If for nothing else, I thought, bitterly, as we rode away in silence.

At the crossroads we parted, Bryce to go on to Tregedon while I returned to Penvarrion. I had not been to Tregedon since the day we had agreed to marry.

"There is no time in which to put the house to your liking," Bryce had told me coldly. "Better to leave it until your coming, then you can arrange things as you wish." He added sardonically, "It will be an occupation for you."

I could not visualize life at Tregedon. Would there be servants? Bryce spoke of a man and his wife who worked for him but I had never seen them. He said there would be money for my needs. Then why was the house so bare and poorly furnished? I thought of my two visits there; the somber parlor and, that second time, the barn of a kitchen and the scullery full of unwashed pots and empty wine bottles. It did not bear thinking of.

Carrie had begged me to take her with me when I left Penvarrion but I made an excuse. It would not do. Soon my pregnancy would begin to show and how could I explain this to Carrie, so soon after my wedding day? It would be too humiliating, so I explained that

149

Mr. Dawnay already had servants in the house but that I would send for her later.

I had no trousseau to speak of, no bottom drawer to take with me to Tregedon. I was going empty-handed, but I consoled myself with the thought that in less than two years I would come into my inheritance and then I should have money of my own and be independent.

Or would my husband have control over my income? That was something I was not sure about. I could not ask my father for he was too ill to answer such questions and I had no intention of enquiring of my stepmother. I should have to wait until my father was recovered, but meanwhile the money was in trust with him, I knew, and out of it he made me an allowance. Was that to continue? I did not want to have to ask Bryce for every penny I might need. Perhaps one day I should need to consult a solicitor. There was no time to dwell on such matters now for in less than a week I would be married.

During these last few days I thought often of Zena Dawnay's words. "Your son will be born with the morning light. Care for him and for yourself. Danger lies across your path," she had said.

*A son.* I would bear a son and despite the misery of my situation I felt a strange sense of joy. Joy, Zena had said, was the other face of sorrow. How strangely she had spoken. Was it possible that she really could see into the future?

A letter came from Bryce's uncle in Truro inviting my father and stepmother and myself to visit them before the wedding. There was no question of my father being well enough to accept, but my stepmother insisted that she and I should go.

"It is only right that we should become acquainted with them for I stand in lieu of mother to you, Katherine. The whole affair is hole and corner enough without our entirely ignoring the conventions. We will go on Tuesday and stay until the Friday, as Mrs. Dawnay suggests."

———◆———

I think my stepmother was as surprised as I was by the taste and comfort of the tall house in Pydah Street. It was obvious that Bryce's

150

relatives were people of substance, and the welcome we received from Mr. and Mrs. Dawnay entirely disarmed my stepmother. Her graciousness soon became evident and it was clear that Bryce's aunt and uncle were charmed by her. They were kindness itself to me, and if they thought me somewhat quiet and reserved for a bride-to-be, they were not to know that my manner was due to the invidiousness of my position rather than any lack of affection toward them.

I could not help but be relieved when the three-day visit was over and we set off for the drive home to Penvarrion.

"Well, Katherine," my stepmother said as she leaned back against the carriage seat. "I can at least put your father's mind at rest as to the suitability of your fiancé's relations. They appear to be both acceptable and agreeable, so you may count yourself fortunate. It remains for Bryce to prove himself to be the same."

"Thank you, Stepmother," was all I answered.

My wedding day came. A quiet affair with only my stepmother, Esmond and Amy, Laura and Paul, Sir Ralph and Lady Borleigh, and Mr. and Mrs. Dawnay and their daughter, Cecilia, in attendance. My Aunt Selina was also present, but not Rosamund who had arranged to visit her fiancé's parents and could not postpone her plans at such short notice. Aunt Selina was pleased to come because she was also wanting to see my father, for she had been concerned for him since his accident. Oliver did not attend for he was away at sea.

Mr. Barlow performed the ceremony, and after it was over and I walked out on Bryce's arm I caught a glimpse of Gertrude Barlow sitting in a pew, while at the back of the church were some of the household staff and several of the villagers who had crept in uninvited because they had known me since childhood and were doubtless curious about the whole affair.

I did not care what anyone thought or said. I was in a state of numbed shock. I sat as stiffly upright as a statue throughout the wedding breakfast which we returned to Penvarrion for. After Carrie helped me change out of the simple white dress I had worn into a going-away costume of brown velvet trimmed with turquoise I went to say good-by to my father.

I had called in earlier, before leaving for the church, but he was

151

resting and when Borlase gently roused him he was too vague and drowsy to take in what was happening and where I was going to.

Now he was awake and as I tiptoed in he smiled and said,

"Kitty! How nice you look."

Tears came to my eyes.

"Thank you, Papa. It is a new dress. I called in this morning but you were sleeping."

"I do not remember." He put a hand against his forehead. "Are you going to call upon someone?"

I knelt by his bed and took his other hand in mine.

"I am going away, Papa. I am married now. I was married today."

He frowned, puzzling.

"My little Kitty married. But he is a good man, and will be kind to you. His father is kind, too, and Lady Phoebe."

"I am married to Bryce Dawnay. Do you not remember, he came to see you."

He shook his head.

"I do not know him. Why have you not married Esmond?"

"Esmond is married to Amy—have you forgotten?" At the worried anxious expression that came over his thin face I stopped abruptly, and with tears in my eyes bent to kiss him.

"Do not concern yourself, dearest Papa. It will come back to you in time. Now I must go, but I will come and see you very often. Good-by. God bless you."

He seemed not to have heard my last words—his eyes were closed, his brow still puckered in a frown. I went out of the room as quietly as I had gone in and for a moment stood in the corridor leaning against the wall in a paroxysm of tears. Then I pulled myself together and wiping my eyes, drew the veil of my velvet hat over my face and walked slowly down the wide staircase to where Bryce, tall and somber in a black coat and striped silk waistcoat above dark gray trousers stood waiting for me.

I had said the only good-by that mattered to me; the rest was a mere formality. As I stepped into the carriage that was to drive us to Tregedon I glanced over my shoulder and saw the group on the steps of the house. My stepmother in another new and elegant dress of pale green ottoman, Amy diminutive in spotted muslin, Esmond tall and handsome at her side. Sir Ralph red-faced, stouter than ever, Lady Phoebe bent and frail in unbecoming gray satin. Laura was there too, dark and pretty in blue and white, Paul at her shoulder. In the background stood Mrs. Borlase, majestic in black satin, Carrie behind her, the rest of the staff smiling and waving. The horses set off, and the curve of the drive took them out of sight. At the Lodge Mr. and Mrs. Pleydell and Barney were waiting to catch sight of us and they waved, and then we were through the gates and on the road to Tregedon.

Penvarrion and my old life were left behind forever.

# 12

WE SAT in silence—a space of cushioned seat between us. Bryce leaned back with folded arms as if he were alone in the carriage and I stared out of the window at the misty September fields. I could not believe that I was the wife of this frowning black-browed stranger. He was not the gypsy boy I remembered nor the grown man I had met that day in the churchyard and come to know and like. He was someone quite other.

I shivered.

"Are you cold?" For the first time he spoke, putting a hand to the open window to close it up.

"It is the damp."

"Yes, the fog is rolling in from the sea. It will be a bad night." He lapsed into silence again watching the drifting vapor which indeed grew more dense as we approached Tregedon.

I could scarcely see the house when we drove along the rutted track toward it. I was not sorry. The fortresslike walls and gray stone were forbidding at the best of times, and today I was full enough of fears.

Harry Martin had brought us in my father's carriage, with Barney following in the cart with my trunks and boxes and portmanteau. In the courtyard a manservant dressed in rough brown frieze came forward and Bryce introduced him as Joshua Porritt. A stout red-faced woman standing close behind him was Mrs. Porritt and a boy of about sixteen, clad as a laborer in woolen shirt and breeches was Jem Steele who looked after the stock. Lastly a young girl came forward, blushing and bobbing, who proved to be Mr. Porritt's niece, Minna.

The luggage was brought into the house, and I thanked Martin and Barney and said good-by to them. Bryce gave them a coin apiece and then they left. My last link with Penvarrion was gone.

I was surprised by the effort that had been made for my comfort. A bright fire burned in the parlor and a warm rug lay across the freshly swept and polished floor. There were curtains of new velvet drawn across the windows and on the mantelshelf the brass candlesticks twinkled and shone in the firelight. Most amazing of all, a great copper jug filled with autumn leaves and the shaggy heads of late chrysanthemums stood on the table in the corner.

Mrs. Porritt led me upstairs, and pushing open a heavy oak door said,

"Here be your room, Ma'am and the Master's. I done best I can wi' it seein' as 'ow Master said 'twas all to be refurn'led for 'ee come Christmas toime. Fire be lit for 'tis a damp ol' day wi' fog an' all. Can I get 'ee anythin', Miss—Ma'am?"

I stood on the threshold of the room, long and low-ceilinged with windows set only a foot or so above the sloping floor. A fire burned reluctantly in the iron grate, emitting puffs of smoke as if the chimney had been little used. Worn rugs lay across the oak boards, a tall-boy, some chairs and a mahogany dressing table and matching washstand was the extent of the furniture, except for a massive four-poster bed which seemed to dominate the entire chamber. It was curtained with faded red damask and a bedspread of shabby silk echoed the same color.

*The bridal bedchamber.* The thought of sharing that enormous forbidding couch with Bryce filled me with apprehension. I wanted to turn and rush down the stairs and out of the house after Martin and the returning carriage as fast as my feet would carry me.

"Be everythin' all right, Ma'am?" Mrs. Porritt's voice said anxiously, her round head with its bun loaf of gray hair tilted to one side as she stared enquiringly at me.

I pulled myself together.

"Yes. Yes, thank you."

"I'll send Minna up to unpack for 'ee."

"Thank you." After she had gone, stumping heavily down the

155

staircase, I went to one of the windows and stared out. I could see nothing but drifting gray fog. It enclosed the house, the headland, the whole of Tregedon, shutting me in like the prisoner I felt myself to be. On impulse I pushed open the casement as if, not being able to see anything, I could at least hear something. But the fog had deadened sound. I could not even hear the sea, the wild Tregedon sea that always seemed more fierce and threatening than at any other place.

The damp air made me cough. I closed the window at the same moment that Minna, pale and whey-faced, tapped on the door and came bobbing and tiptoeing in.

When at last I went downstairs it was to find Bryce standing by the fireplace, one arm resting along the high mantelshelf. At the sound of Minna opening the door for me he turned.

"I hope you found everything to your satisfaction."

"Yes, thank you."

His glance flicked over me and I felt that for the first time that day he was seeing me. Until now he had treated me as if I was as much a stranger to him as he seemed to me. I had taken off the velvet bonnet that matched my dress and my hair was drawn smoothly back from a center parting and turned over at the sides. I sat down in the chair he drew forward for me, trying to appear calmer and more composed than I was feeling.

He said slowly,

"No Dawnay every brought a more beautiful bride to Tregedon than I." His lip curled sardonically. "Albeit a reluctant one."

I didn't want compliments from him, or admiration. I wanted him to remain aloof from me, as he had done these past weeks. I thought of the great four-poster bed upstairs and I felt myself tremble.

"Will you take some wine? Mrs. Porritt will be bringing in the supper soon."

Supper time already. The day almost over and now it was evening. Perhaps wine would give me courage for what lay ahead.

"Thank you—one glass, if you wish."

He poured some from a heavily cut glass decanter. I saw that the table was laid with a surprising elegance. The silverware was heavy and beautiful, the china old and delicate. The centerpiece of late roses graced the linen damask. I was at once surprised and touched by the evidence of care taken, and I glanced sideways at Bryce, wondering if he was responsible for such effort.

"We will drink to the future and to the son who will inherit Tregedon."

I bowed my head over the glass without answering.

Supper was an elaborate meal. It was obvious that Mrs. Porritt had gone to considerable trouble to prepare something in the nature of a bridal repast. Bryce ate well and drank plentifully of the wine. Once he shrugged and said,

"You have little appetite. I hope in time you will do justice to our fare."

"I shall try."

He glanced at me from under lowered brows, the flush of wine on his lean cheeks.

"You look pale. And tired. You will be ready for bed when the time comes."

He was playing cat and mouse with me; he knew how tense and fearful I was inside, though doing my best not to reveal my feelings.

My chin tilted.

"As ready as you are."

His hand shot out and caught hold of my wrist.

"By God, you are not to be mastered easily, Kate. That light in your eyes—it is not love for me, but loathing. And yet once— once—" He broke off, dragging the decanter toward him with his free hand.

I could not refrain from a protest.

"Have you not drunk enough wine?"

His grasp tightened.

"What? Have you turned into the censorious nag already and not yet bedded? A wife, Kate, should be docile and forbearing and, above all, *willing*. Willing, and acquiescent. If you have not those virtues, you must be taught them."

He had pulled me nearer to him. With his face only a few inches from mine we stared at one another. His eyes, golden as a wolf's glittered with their curious light. I forced myself to look back at him and found an answer.

"In church today I promised to obey you."

He flung my hand away, leaving it smarting from his grip.

"Obedience. A cold stark word. As cold as your bridal embrace will be I have no doubt."

We finished the meal and Mrs. Porritt came in and cleared away. I sat in the one armchair by the fire while Bryce sprawled on the settle, staring at me from under lowered brows. In a far corner of the ill-lit room the grandfather clock ticked, slowly and menacingly, as if threatening me with passing time.

After what seemed an interminable interval in which we spoke little, Mrs. Porritt reappeared.

"I be done now, sir, so if 'ee not be wantin' ought I be goin' down along."

"Very well, Mrs. Porritt. Thank you. Good night."

She stared curiously at us, first at Bryce and then at me as if she had never seen a less nuptial-looking pair.

"Good night, zur. Good night to 'ee, Ma'am."

When the door closed behind her stout back I said, nervously,

"Does she not sleep in the house?"

"No. She and Porritt have the cottage down the lane. It is a tied one and goes with the farm. They lived in it when the land was let and stayed on when I came to Tregedon. They couldn't sleep in the house anyway as so few of the rooms are habitable. In time they will be made so and then some servants can sleep here."

"It—it is not a very convenient arrangement," I said.

He leaned toward me.

"Do you not think so? I prefer to have the house to myself. We are alone. No one will overhear us. Or interfere."

I felt myself draw back involuntarily.

"Do I alarm you?" His smile was mocking. "Surely there is little reason for that. It is not as if we are—unacquainted with one another, Kate."

I straightened myself in the chair and said coldly,

"It pleases you to taunt me."

His face hardened.

"As it pleased you to disparage me. There is no love lost between us." His eyes narrowed as he glared at me. He said softly, "And yet I think I desire you as much as any man desired a woman."

I said between gritted teeth.

"I think I hate you."

He caught hold of my hand.

"Hate is a powerful emotion. Where there is hatred there cannot be indifference."

I struggled to free my hand but his grip tightened.

"Are you indifferent to me, Kate? Or do you fight me because you are afraid of your own nature. That night in the wood when you gave yourself to me—so recklessly and so passionately—was it because you longed for Esmond? Or was it because there has ever been a bond between us? Call it love or hatred, hunger or desire, it is there, and you cannot deny it."

I turned my face away from him.

"I do deny it. Or if I admit to anything, it would be to an emotion so base I am ashamed that I was ever betrayed by it. It has been my undoing. I am to bear your child and I am trapped in a marriage that is not of my choosing and never would be."

He let go of my hand and stood up.

"You have put the situation clearly. There is little hope for either of us. Well, Madam, I will leave you to retire while I close the stables and lock up. I shall join you shortly," and he strode from the room.

I was trembling. The echo of his words *"I shall join you shortly"* hung on the air. My head turned from side to side like a hunted animal's seeking escape. But there was none. If I ran out into the yard Bryce would hear and come after me. Slowly, stiffly, I rose to my feet and after a last look round the bare room I made my way upstairs.

There were corridors and stairs leading into a shadowy darkness. An oil lamp burned on a blackened oak chest near the door which Mrs. Porritt had opened for me earlier on. I pushed it open and saw the room and the four-poster bed and my nightdress and robe lying across it. A fire burned in the grate, and on a table beside it stood a lit candelabra.

I closed the door behind me. I think I would have locked it if there had been a key, but there was only the wrought iron latch. I went to the window and drew back the curtain but could see nothing. The vaporous mist still drifted eerily about the house. Yet I thought it looked less dense.

I undressed and washed my hands and face in water from the china ewer. Then, shivering, I crept into bed and lay there, the cold sheets close under my chin.

I couldn't stop shivering but whether from the chill of the bed or the sense of apprehension that filled me I could not say. I listened for every creak of the stair, every sound of Bryce's approaching footsteps, but he did not come.

The candles burned down and went out, the fire was only a dim glow of wood ash. I had stopped shivering and now, despite my fears, the long exhausting day began to take its toll of me and from time to time my eyelids drooped and waves of sleep stole over me.

I must have drowsed off for suddenly I was wakened by sounds in the yard below. I heard hooves clattering over the cobbles and voices shouting and a thunderous banging on the back door. I sat up in alarm. What was it—what had happened?

My pendant watch was on the table by the bed, I peered at it in the darkness but could not make out the time. I slid out of bed and striking one of the matches near the candles saw that it was one A.M.

Then I had slept for over an hour. But where was Bryce? What had become of him? I dragged on my robe and went out into the corridor. All was silent again, the voices were gone. I crept downstairs and as I reached the hallway the kitchen door opened, and Mrs. Porritt, a shawl thrown about her head and ample frame appeared on the threshold.

"Eh, Missus O Ma'am—there 'ee be. I were feared to wake 'ee but 'tis for sure you heard the men acomin' and a callin'. There be wreck down along the cove—Porritt'ee be gone to 'elp bring ur in and Master be gone wi' 'un."

160

"*A wreck!* A ship, you mean? Yes, I heard the voices. I did not know anyone lived around here."

"They be from Tregedon village—miners and such. 'Tis their way to help when there be wreck or ought like." She shook her head. "Tregedon Cove be a mortal bad place for wrecks. Many's the good ship gone down off'n them cruel rocks that lie at the foot o' the cliffs."

"We must go and help too. There must be something we can do."

"Nay—not out there. Master said to get blankets and hot bottles ready for any that might be brought off. We can do no good down along the cove—'tis nigh impossible to see the hand in front o' one's face."

"I'll put warmer things on—this robe is only thin."

"Aye, do that—Ma'am, while I see to makin' up the stove."

When I came downstairs again, dressed as quickly as I could in a woolen dress over warm under clothes it was to find Mrs. Porritt bustling about the kitchen. The fire roared up the chimney and a big copper kettle and huge iron pan were heating at the side of it. Thrown over some kitchen chairs were blankets warming by the fire.

The minutes ticked by and we waited. It must have been over half an hour before we heard footsteps and voices outside. The next moment, through the scullery came Mr. Porritt and Jem, carrying a figure in what looked like a rough hammock. Water dripped from the sodden clothes, I caught a glimpse of a blue-white face and sea-wet hair.

"Put 'un down," Mr. Porritt grunted. "He be young chap but 'tis a rare pull up from the cove." He shook his head. "He's near a gone 'un."

Mrs. Porritt, without more ado, started to strip off the wet shirt and breeches before my eyes. She reached a hand out behind her.

"The blanket, Ma'am. Poor dear, he be cold as a corpse," and with rough, but gentle hands she wrapped the warmed blanket carefully around the unconscious young man.

For a moment I stood helplessly by and then I said,

"You cannot leave him here—on the stone floor. Bring him upstairs to one of the beds."

161

She stared up at me.

"Nay, Missus, there be no beds, but yourn and Master's. He can bide here unless there be more to come." She looked enquiringly at Porritt who shook his head.

"There be two dead 'un laid in the barn. That be all us could save. The rest must 'a bin swept overboard when the ship went aground in the fog and broke up."

I bit my trembling lip, appalled by the horror of his words. I said as calmly as I could,

"It would be better that he rests in a bed. Bring him to my room, Mr. Porritt. We can make the fire up, it is still alight."

In a few minutes the boy was lying in the four poster, the sheets having been stripped off and more blankets wrapped about him. Mrs. Porritt carried up two stone bottles to put at his feet while I went downstairs to find brandy and warm milk.

As I came out of the parlor with the bottle in my hand I heard Bryce's voice and pausing I went toward the kitchen from where I had come only to encounter him in the doorway.

I stepped back at the sight of him. Blood was trickling from a cut on his head, one arm hung helplessly at his side, the shoulder and sleeve of his coat gaping open as if torn by a gigantic hand.

I gasped his name.

"*Bryce!* What has happened? You are hurt."

He grimaced rather than smiled and took the brandy from my hand.

"Thank you. I can do with a drink of this," and with no more ado uncorked the flagon and lifted it to his lips. He gulped some down and rubbed the back of his hand across his mouth. "That's better."

I wiped the top of the bottle with the cloth in my hand.

"Someone needs this even more than you. The boy who is upstairs."

He frowned.

"Upstairs?"

"In my—your bed. It seemed the only place to put him."

"The deuce! He would have done well enough in the parlor. I doubt he'll live the night through."

162

"Don't say that. I must go to him." I turned and then looked back at Bryce. "What happened to your arm?"

"It is broken. I'll get Jem here to tie on a splint until Dr. Laker comes. Someone has gone to fetch him to the fellow upstairs."

For a moment I stood staring at him, and at the arm with its sliver of protruding bone.

"I'm sorry." I shivered, remembering Mr. Porritt's remark about the two drowned men in the barn. "You must have your head seen to."

The fire was crackling up in the bedroom. I lifted the candle nearer to look down at the pale pinched face lying on the pillow. It was so young a face. A boy not much older than Oliver, with rat's tails of fair hair framing thin features. I touched his hand under the blanket. It felt cold and flaccid. Fearfully I put the candle down on the bedside table and uncorking the brandy wet the half open lips with a spoonful.

He did not swallow and the brandy trickled onto the pillow. I tried again and then again and at last saw the movement of his throat as he feebly swallowed a trace of it.

The door opened and Bryce came in, his arm strapped to his side with a slat of wood. A rough bandage was wound about his black head. He came to the bedside and stood beside me, looking down at the figure lying there. He gestured toward the brandy.

"Has he taken any of that?"

"The smallest amount. I think he managed to swallow some."

Bryce frowned.

"He'll need more than a spoonful of brandy to pull him around, poor young devil." He moved away to the fireplace and sat down stiffly and awkwardly in the chair beside it. He leaned back, his eyes half closed. He looked exhausted, his mouth grimly set, two deep lines running from nose to chin.

"What happened?" I asked. "Porritt said no one else was rescued alive."

"None we could find save the boy over there. We don't know how many men there were aboard. The ship was a three-masted schooner rigged steamer. She must have been going at full speed in the fog,

163

against all the rules of navigation, and the current would have carried her northward onto the rocks below Tregedon Head. The impact ripped the bottom out—she was breaking up when we got down to her. Two men were picked up for dead, the boy was the only survivor. The other men must be lost, including the captain."

I shivered again. He sounded so matter of fact, so little disturbed by the tragedy.

"Surely you haven't given up all hope of rescue?"

He shrugged, opening his eyes to look at me.

"Some of the miners are still down at the cove, but there's a heavy ground sea. The bodies may not come up at all with such undersea currents. We are used to it. You must know, Kate, this is the most dangerous stretch of coast in the whole of England and with not a harbor, particularly after high water, in which any ship caught by gales on a lee shore can find safety. Only ten years ago nine vessels were lost in one February night. You've heard the rhyme—

> From Padstow Point to Lundy Light
> Is a sailor's grave by day and night
>                                          .

Tregedon is no exception, the black rocks that lie beyond the headland have taken many a ship to its doom." His mouth twisted grimly. "There was a time when the villagers of Tregedon helped to bring that about. In the days of the wreckers before the Coast Guard was formed."

"It is a cruel place, a cruel coast. Not like Penvarrion."

"Not in the least like Penvarrion, I can assure you of that." He stood up, his face twisting with the pain from his arm. "I had better go down and see if there is any news. I would have stayed with the men but with this arm I was useless."

"How did you injure it?"

"One of the masts came down on me as we were climbing off the schooner, breaking my arm and cracking my head. But it did not matter, we had done all we could by then." He came to the bedside. "I wouldn't mind another swig of this," and he reached for the brandy bottle. With it in his hand he looked down at the figure on

164

the bed and then he halted abruptly, and dumped the bottle back on the table.

"What's this? There's been a change." He took the boy's hand in his own and then releasing it lifted the sunken eyelids. "He's gone."

"My hand went to my throat.

*No!* Oh, no."

"I fear so. Have you a mirror—thank you." He bent over the bed and after a moment he straightened up. "He was all but dead when we brought him in. I doubted he would live." He folded the pallid hands over the thin chest and drew the cover over the white face. "God rest his soul."

"Amen," I whispered through dry lips. I was saddened to the heart. I felt as if I was living in a nightmare. This poor boy, young and unknown, his life over before it was scarce begun. Down at the cove a ship lay battered on the black rocks of Tregedon. Men had drowned in its treacherous seas.

My wedding night, I thought. And in the bridal bed a dead man lying.

# 13

It was dawn before the doctor arrived. We spent the night in the parlor, myself in the armchair, Bryce half-sitting half-lying across the settle. In the kitchen were the Porritts and Jem and another man. I heard the murmur of their voices as I dozed uneasily, starting up from time to time as if wakened by some sudden alarm.

Dr. Laker, who had ridden over from Wadebridge, examined the dead men. They would be buried in the churchyard at Tregedon, unnamed and unknown, for they were Frenchmen.

Dr. Laker was in his mid-thirties, thin and dark with shrewd dark eyes. He stared closely at me when we shook hands and for a moment I wondered if he could guess my condition by merely looking at me. Surely that was not possible at this stage? I was embarrassed and could not meet his keen glance. A bride of a day and over three months pregnant? I hoped he did not know how short a time Bryce and I had been married. But he said no more than,

"You have had a sad night of it, here at Tregedon, Ma'am. You look tired and need to rest."

"You are Dr. Laker's patient now, Kate," Bryce said lightly. "So if you need to consult him at any time, he will visit you here."

I knew what he meant. Sooner or later I should have to put myself under a doctor's care and this was the man to whom I must look.

After setting Bryce's arm in a formidable looking splint Dr. Laker took breakfast with us and then rode away, leaving Bryce to deal with the sad formalities of death.

Mrs. Porritt came bustling to where I sat, crouched over the parlor fire.

"Do 'ee come along, Ma'am, and lie down for a while. There be a couch aired and ready for 'ee in Master's dressing room. Come mi-dear." She put a hand under my arm to help me up. "You dun't look very clever to me."

She was rough but kind and I was grateful for her motherly comfort. I let her help me upstairs and into a small room next to the bedroom where I had lain for a short time the night before. I glanced at the adjoining door and said hesitantly,

"Is he—has he—?"

"He be gone, poor dear. Keepin' company wi' his friends in the barn. I laid 'em out meself, with Minna's help, all right and proper as 'twere. We'll get your bedroom to rights later, Ma'am, but for now do 'ee rest here." Her eyes, round and black as two currants in her russet-brown face gave me a quick inquisitive glance. "Just 'ee sleep and take care." Her hands pulled the rug over me in a gently smoothing motion and it seemed to me they lingered for a moment over my form. I bit my lip. Why did I think everyone could guess my secret? Mrs. Porritt was only being kind.

I lay on the ottoman staring up at the raftered ceiling. The room was narrow and bare, little more than a cell. A corner wardrobe, a small table and chair were its only furniture. Mrs. Porritt had called it "the Master's dressing room." Did he sleep here at times, or was the big four-poster his usual bed?

I was too tired to think. My eyes closed and I fell asleep.

I must have slept for a long time. I woke suddenly, as if at some sound, and found Bryce had come into the room and was gazing down at me.

I started up in alarm, but he said quietly,

"I'm sorry. I did not intend to disturb you. Would you care for something to eat? Minna will bring you a tray."

"I have slept so long?" I lay back with a sigh. "It was a dreadful night. Those poor men—and—and the boy who died without our knowing. We were talking and he was gone."

"There was nothing anyone could do. Dr. Laker told me that."

I was silent and then, after a moment I said,

"How is your arm? Is it painful?"

167

He shrugged.

"Not particularly. But it's a handicap and a nuisance. I cannot get on with what I wish to do."

We were strangers making conversation, our words stiff and stilted. I knew in my heart that Bryce's accident was a relief to me. At the moment he was *hors de combat* and that gave me a brief respite.

"I think I will get up."

He nodded.

"Good." He moved to the door and then he turned to say, over his shoulder. "Perhaps you had better sleep in here for a few nights. In a couple of days Jem can drive us over to Truro and you can choose new furnishings for the other room and for elsewhere in the house. It will help to lay the ghosts."

I knew what he meant, and I was grateful for his consideration. I had dreaded the thought of returning to that dark and gloomy bedroom. And that sad four-poster bed.

"Thank you."

———◆———

Bryce decided we should spend three nights in Truro.

"It is a long way to get there and back in comfort." His mouth twisted in a grim smile. "It will be in lieu of our honeymoon, though as things are at present I cannot vouch for the full truth of that."

Jem drove us in a high uncomfortable cart.

"I am sorry I do not run to a carriage," Bryce said offhandedly. "We may aspire to one in time."

At Truro we stayed at the Britannia Inn and to my relief Bryce had reserved two separate rooms, though with a communicating door.

"At the moment I am not a restful sleeper—this contraption on my arm gives me some discomfort." His eyes gleamed sardonically as if he sensed my secret relief. "Never fear, Kate, it is not a permanent affliction. We shall enjoy our connubial bliss on a later occasion."

I did not answer him. I was too glad to have escaped the gray fortress of Tregedon for a short time to mind his taunts.

Truro seemed full of fashionable people and the shops were smarter and more plentifully stocked than anything to be found in Wadebridge or Bodmin. Unhappy as I had been and still was, I yet found pleasure in choosing new bedcurtains and bedspread for the gloomy four-poster and a handsome flowered carpet to cover the expanse of bare boards.

Bryce did not accompany me on my expeditions, for he had business to do in the town. I was pleased to be on my own although worried about how much I should spend.

"You must tell me the amount," I protested.

"I leave it to your good sense. I have told you, Kate, I am not a poor man."

"You live like one. Like a pauper." The retort was out before I could stop myself.

"Because to date I have plowed my money back into the Tregedon land and into the mine I recently reopened. There is lead there, silver lead, but the vein has been neglected. It's now being reworked. Don't stint yourself or the house. It has been waiting all this time for you to come and put it to rights. Buy everything you wish for the child, too."

That I was glad to do. There was a nursery to be furnished, baby clothes to buy and to make, but I should have to be discreet as to their arrival. Many of the packages would not be undone for several weeks.

One evening we went to dine with Bryce's uncle and aunt. They were kind and welcoming to me and I soon felt at ease with them. Their youngest daughter was at home, the other three being married and living in towns other than Truro. Cecilia Dawnay was the fair-haired girl I had seen before with Bryce, and as he had once told me, she was as charming as she was pretty.

She was so friendly and agreeable to me that I could not believe she had been in love with Bryce as I had first thought. And yet, when her blue eyes rested on him and she smiled sweetly and yet wistfully at his remarks I sensed a deep affection.

After we had returned to the inn that evening and I was preparing for bed the communicating door, which I had not thought to lock, opened suddenly and Bryce stood on the threshold. He said with frowning abruptness,

"I am sorry, I must ask for your assistance with the unfastening of these," and he indicated the satin waistcoat he was wearing with its myriad of tiny buttons. He had taken off his dress jacket to reveal a shirt with frilled front and cuffs.

I was undressed in my petticoat and stays, my loosened hair hanging down my back. Pulling a silk wrap over my shoulders I said as calmly as I could,

"Of course," and would have gone over to him but he came farther into the room. My fingers seemed awkward and fumbling as I undid the buttons and I was very conscious of his nearness and the fact that his dark face was only a few inches above my own. "I do not know how you got them done up in the first place," I said, to break the spell of silence.

"I hailed a waiter passing in the corridor and he assisted me. It is bad enough that I have to ask you to cut up my meat at dinner without looking to you to dress me. Or undress me," he added, with a grim smile.

I eased the waistcoat over the splint.

"Is there anything else?"

"Perhaps the buttons on the shirt, then I can drop it from my shoulders."

I did as he asked and when I would have stood back his hand came out to touch my hair and hold me by one of the long tresses wound around his finger.

"Your hair was loose like this the first time you came to Tregedon, the day of the storm." When I did not answer he said, "What has happened to us since then, Kate? We were friends once."

I felt myself tremble. Standing so close to him I was aware of the same warmth and animal magnetism that had engulfed me that night in the woods. It was as if he cast a spell over me, as if the strange tawny eyes gazing into mine could mesmerize me into submission.

This time I was in command of myself and was not to be betrayed by my own weakness.

"We are enemies now," I said slowly and deliberately. "Because

170

you want something from me I cannot give. You may take but only in hostility."

The dark face hardened. His hand unloosed my hair, and moved to my throat to encircle it. I felt his fingers tighten into the flesh.

"God, Kate, but you are unforgiving. As cold as this magnolia-smooth skin under my touch. Handicapped as I am I could choke you into unconsciousness if I wished, and there would be a curious satisfaction in doing that." The grasp of his fingers slackened. He stood back. "But don't worry. As the mother of the child-to-be you are safe from any onslaught on my part. If we are at war, it is on your side only." And turning on his heel he walked through the doorway and closed it firmly behind him.

I rubbed my smarting skin, seeing in the mirror the reddened fingerprints where he had held me. My knees were trembling, and I sank down onto the edge of the bed. I could not understand how, after these few days of truce, the battle between us should have started up again.

I had nothing to give Bryce because I loved Esmond. And Bryce knew this. And so we looked at one another as through a distorting mirror, seeing only the dark and ugly side of our natures. Anger, fear and jealousy had taken the place of the innocent affection we had once shared, and now we came together as two different people. It seemed to me that there was little hope for us.

The next day we returned home. Jem drove us, for with the use of only one hand it was not easy for Bryce to take the reins over the rough roads. He sat in front with Jem while I sat with my back to them, gazing out at the empty countryside my heart sinking with every mile that took me nearer to the wind-swept Tregedon.

When we arrived back it was to find that Barney had brought Sorrel over to be stabled at Tregedon and with her, a letter from my stepmother.

"Your father is much the same," she wrote. "He has been asking after you and seems to think you have been gone for weeks. He is very fretful. Perhaps you and your husband would care to come to early dinner next Thursday. It may help to ease your father's mind."

171

I did not want to go, and yet I longed to see Papa again. Bryce was coldly indifferent when I put the proposal to him.

"Do as you wish. I would as soon stay at home, but if you go, I shall of course accompany you."

I bit my lip.

"I feel I should go now because later on it will be difficult. My—my condition will begin to show and I shall be embarrassed by their questions. It is then I, too, shall prefer to remain here."

"Then accept," and turning on his heel he walked away.

I sent an answer back with Jem and on the following Thursday dressed carefully for my visit to Penvarrion. I was four months pregnant now. Being tall, I showed little of my condition. But aware of my stepmother's critical gaze I wore my least figure-revealing dress and was grateful that the fashion of the crinoline was fortunately a concealing one.

The cart had a hood of sorts which gave some protection for the October night was cool and I was glad to sit under it and under the shawl and the thick rug Bryce had handed to me. Caspar, the tall black horse Bryce usually rode, was put between the shafts and we drove away in the silence that was becoming habitual to us.

There was no wind at Penvarrion. It lay, peacefully sheltered below the hillside, bright moonlight tipping the tall familiar chimneys with silver. I felt a lump come into my throat. *Penvarrion.* Once my dear home. But when we arrived at the foot of the steps and Martin came to lead Caspar to the stables I lifted my head and walked proudly up the steps to be greeted by Mrs. Borlase as if I were the happiest wife in Christendom.

My stepmother was all smiles and graciousness, though her beautiful hooded eyes were no less sharp in their observance.

"You look well, Katherine. But, Bryce—what is wrong with your arm? Have you met with an accident?"

He explained what had happened and she shook her head saying,

"I have heard that Tregedon Head is a dangerous place though I have never been there. Come, Katherine, your father is waiting to see you. We have managed to get him downstairs for your visit."

172

Carrie, bobbing and smiling, took my wraps and murmured a "Good evening, Miss—Ma'am" with blushing cheeks and then I hurried into the drawing room to greet my father.

"My little Kitty." The tears filled my eyes. I felt the incongruity of the endearment as I stood beside him, tall and young and strong, while he seemed an old man in his new frailty, the fair hair which had been scarcely touched with gray now almost white.

I kissed him fondly.

"Darling Papa. I am so happy that you are well enough to come downstairs," I said, hiding my distress as best I could. I held his hand tightly in my own two before turning to say, "You remember Bryce, my husband?"

He frowned, blinking a little as if in bewilderment, but Bryce took his hand and said quietly,

"Yes, of course you do. I am happy to see you so much recovered, sir," and I was momentarily touched by the kindness of his deep voice.

While we were sitting together, drinking the Madeira wine Borlase had brought us, the Reverend Charles Barlow and Miss Barlow were announced, the only other guests to dinner which tonight was at the earlier hour of six o'clock.

I was pleased to see them. They took on the burden of conversation so that Bryce and my stepmother were occupied while I sat beside my father, holding his hand in mine. From time to time we spoke together, though the vagueness of his remarks made sustained dialogue difficult. It appeared that Charles Barlow was a regular visitor to my father and often came to read a book or newspaper to him, for the injury to his head had impaired my father's eyesight.

"We had hoped that Amy and Esmond would have come tonight," my stepmother told me as we went into dinner. "But Amy has not been feeling well of late." She lowered her voice. "She has always been delicate and her present condition is burdensome to her."

"I am sorry," I said. "Please give her my love and good wishes."

"She hopes to visit you in your new home when you are settled."

I said quickly,

"I do not know when that will be for there is so much to be seen to." We were sat down at the table now and I looked across to Bryce for confirmation as I added, "Bryce will tell you we are not in a fit state to receive visitors until he has undertaken various renovations."

Bryce inclined his head stiffly.

"Kate is right, Mrs. Carew. The house has been empty for a long period of time and it cannot be quickly put in order."

My stepmother frowned.

"Would it have not been more practicable to have undertaken these matters before Katherine's marriage to you? It sounds as though living conditions there must be extremely uncomfortable."

Bryce's mouth twisted in a grim smile.

"Indeed they are. For both of us. But I was so eager to take Kate home as my bride that I did not want to wait indefinitely." He turned his head and his light eyes glinted sardonically at me. "Nor did Kate. And of course, it is better that she should be there to supervise the improvements so that all will be eventually as she wishes."

I wondered what improvements he referred to. Some new bed furnishings and a new carpet?

My father retired early, and when Borlase had helped to put him to bed I went to say good night to him.

"Come again soon, Kitty," my father urged. "I miss you and I am lonely."

"But, Papa dear, you have Stepmama, and many other people here to care for you. And does not Amy come to visit you?"

"Your stepmother is busy—she has so much to see to. She tells me so. I am left alone a great deal."

"It is so you can be quiet and rest," I reassured him and yet inwardly I was dismayed. Could it be true that my stepmother was too preoccupied to spend much time with my father now? Did she perhaps find his vagueness and forgetfulness wearisome? I had sensed an impatience in her attitude toward him, as if his weakness irritated her. But on the other hand one could not rely too much on my father's statements for he would often contradict himself on account of his bad memory.

He sighed,

"Perhaps. But Blanche is away from the house a great deal. She goes to visit Amy."

"Amy is going to have a baby." I bent nearer to him, thinking I would prepare him a little. "I hope that I too shall have a child in time, Papa. Would that make you happy?"

"Yes." His hand came out to mine. He seemed to have forgotten my words. "Come again soon, Kitty."

"I will try, Papa darling," but as I kissed him good-by I wondered how many visits I could make before I betrayed my situation.

I was quiet and sad on the drive back to Tregedon and Bryce was as silent as myself except when once he said,

"It seems we played our parts satisfactorily."

"Yes. But I hope no one will come and visit us yet. I should be—" I was going to say "ashamed" but I bit the word back.

He must have guessed my intention for he said harshly,

"I meant what I said. We are to put Tregedon to rights. You shall arrange the house, and I will see after the farm and land. One day you will be proud to invite anyone you wish to visit us."

All I could say was, "Thank you," and wonder how it was to be done.

Bryce was as good as his word. Two days later workmen arrived at Tregedon and began to paint and paper the rooms. Even the attics were cleaned out, with Mrs. Porritt and Minna scrubbing the floors and putting on the huge bonfire in the stable yard worm-eaten chairs and broken tables and suchlike.

I continued to sleep in the small dressing room, for which I was thankful. Another room was tidied for Bryce's use and the excuse for our separation was the fact that the big bedroom was being done over and partly refurnished. Bryce's arm was still in a splint. He remained restricted in his activities, but he was out and about all the day either at the mine or on the land.

One day he drove me to Wadebridge to make more purchases for the house for it was sadly depleted of furniture.

"It must have been sold or taken away during the times the house was empty. I never went inside until I came to live there, so I do not know exactly what the place contained."

"I wish I could have some of the things from Penvarrion," I said. "My father would give them to me if I asked him."

"I would prefer that you didn't."

175

I glanced sideways at the aloof dark face, the one hand holding the reins.

"When I am twenty-one I shall have money of my own," I informed him. "I shall not need to ask favors of anyone."

He looked around at me, his eyes narrowing.

"So you are an heiress? I was not aware of that fact."

"The inheritance is from my mother," and I went on to tell him of the Belle Tout Estate.

He listened intently and without comment. All he said at the end was,

"And in the event of your death, does the property come to your heirs?"

"To my heirs? Do you mean my children?"

He frowned.

"Not necessarily. It could mean the person to whom you willed your estate." His mouth twisted. "Your loving husband, for instance."

I must have looked as startled as I felt for before I could answer he went on,

"I am joking, of course. I appreciate that I should never be considered in any way. Though, of course, you must realize that unless the estate is in trust for your heirs, it would automatically come to me as your husband. That is the law."

I was still too dumbfounded to speak, turning over in my mind the implication of his words. After a while I said slowly,

"If it is not already formed into a trust, I shall make one. So that my children may inherit anything of mine."

He smiled oddly.

"As a minor, you cannot form a trust. You have not the power in law to do so. You will have to wait until you are twenty-one."

I set my lips.

"I shall consult my father. When—when he is able to deal with such matters."

"Yes, that would be advisable." He shook the reins and Caspar quickened his pace, and we did not speak again until we arrived at Wadebridge.

I had no time to think further of our conversation for I was too

176

occupied in making my purchases. It was market day and Bryce had gone to see after some cattle but when, my shopping done, I went to meet him at the hotel as arranged, I found him in conversation with Sir Ralph Borleigh.

"Katherine. This is a pleasant surprise. How are you keeping, my dear? You look blooming. It must be Bryce's care of you, eh?" and he laughed with a meaning glance first in my direction and then to Bryce. Yet, despite his hearty cheerfulness I thought he looked far from well. His sagging cheeks were a purplish gray and the pouches under his eyes were deeper than ever.

"Will you stay to take a glass of wine with me?" he asked, and though I did not wish to linger, for old time's sake and the friendship I had enjoyed with the Borleigh family I accepted.

We spoke of Lady Borleigh, of my father, and of Amy and Esmond. Then Sir Ralph glanced from under beetling brows to say,

"What's this I hear, Dawnay, about your reopening the Tregedon mine? You're a lucky devil. At some of the mines ore is running out. We're having to sink deeper and deeper at Borleigh and that costs a mint of money. From what I hear you're a man who can smell tin like a hound scents the fox. Where did ye learn such a skill?"

"I have been a miner since I was fifteen years of age, sir. My father was a miner too." Bryce smiled ironically. "We were neither of us fortunate enough to be landed proprietors."

"Oh, aye. Aye, so I recollect. Some family troubles in the past, eh?" Sir Ralph said blusteringly. "But you're back at Tregedon now, where Dawnays have lived since time back."

"Yes. And I intend to stay there."

"Good, good. Now another glass of wine? Katherine?"

We both refused and soon afterward took our leave of Sir Ralph. I felt sad as I shook hands with him and said good-bye. He seemed a caricature of the robust Squire I remembered.

For a month I went to see my father every week, riding over on Sorrel when the weather was fine. My visits seemed to cheer him, though his memory did not greatly improve. Sometimes he remembered I had been before, sometimes he reproached me for staying away. Once Amy was there and we talked together. She did not look well, for being so small she early showed her coming pregnancy. Her heart-shaped face looked peaky and she was fretful, bewailing her tiredness and the fact that she could not wear her more becoming dresses. I could not help but feel sorry for her.

It was then I decided not to go to Penvarrion again for a while. I would leave a suitable interval and then when I went back I would reveal my pregnancy and hope that, with my height and with careful dressing, matters might appear less-advanced than they were in actuality.

I made the weather the excuse. With November came a bad spell. Fierce gales and heavy rain swept the countryside. The fields were muddy, the roads waterlogged and it was no longer safe for me to ride Sorrel.

After the main bedroom had been redecorated and refurnished I dreaded that I should have to share it with Bryce. But to my relief he elected to remain in the smaller room he had chosen earlier.

"You had better tell Mrs. Porritt the reason for my marital abstinence," he said curtly one evening. "Though I have no doubt that by now she has guessed your condition."

I colored under his sweeping gaze.

"Is it so obvious? I will tell her tomorrow."

"When will the child be born?"

"Dr. Laker told me to be prepared for sometime in late March."

Bryce nodded.

"He is a good man. He will see after you." He gave me a sharp glance. "There is nothing to fear, Kate."

"I am not afraid," I stated rashly.

That wasn't true. I was afraid. I was very afraid. I was afraid of the unknown, of giving birth to the child of a man I did not love. I was afraid of Tregedon; the winds that shook the house and the boiling seas that crashed below by day and night, bringing death and destruction in their wake. The new wallpaper and the pretty fresh furnishings of the bedroom could not make me forget that a man had lain dead there.

I was afraid of the loneliness of the isolation. And sometimes, looking at his dark impassive face, meeting the watchful eyes with their strange glint I was afraid of Bryce.

178

# 14

I TOLD Mrs. Porritt about the baby. Her small shrewd eyes surveyed me; she nodded and said,

"'Tis good news, Ma'am. We'm all be glad o' a babby at Tregedon." She added cryptically, with a shake of her head. "'Tis happen afore and 'twill happen again."

I wondered what she meant by that remark.

Bryce returned one day from Wadebridge with a sturdy looking Dartmoor pony.

"It is for your use, Kate. You cannot go on riding Sorrel, and she is not used to harness. Brownie, for that is his name, will take you to Wadebridge for shopping or to Penvarrion, whenever you wish to visit your father."

It was thoughtful of him and I expressed my thanks.

"I shall go to Penvarrion tomorrow, if it is fine, and break the news of the coming child to them."

Next day I dressed carefully and drove the pony, who proved to be a quiet sensible fellow, to Penvarrion. To my surprise, I found Amy with her mother and so she was there to hear of the baby.

She seemed genuinely delighted, her small pointed face broke into smiles and she clapped her hands in the familiar gesture of pleasure.

"Oh, what fun, Kate. We shall have our babies together. When is yours expected?"

"I—I am not sure. Dr. Laker says the date of a first child is often a little uncertain. I think sometime in May."

My stepmother gave me a slow sideways glance, her russet-colored eyes surveying me from head to toe.

"I am surprised the doctor is so certain so soon. You have changed from Dr. Fullbright?"

"Yes. I—Dr. Laker is Bryce's doctor and lives at Wadebridge which is near to us."

She shrugged.

"Dr. Fullbright is at St. Breock. That is even nearer." Her eyes narrowed as she stared at me. "No doubt, you have your own reasons for consulting a new doctor."

I felt embarrassed under her close scrutiny, and I moved away to sit beside Amy and ask,

"When is your child due to be born?"

"In April, so you see there will be little difference in age between our two. They will be cousins. Well, cousins by marriage, if not by blood. Do you hope for a boy or a girl, Kate?"

"I do not care. I mean, I do not mind which it is." I thought of Bryce's lean dark face and frowning brows. "A daughter, I think. Someone who will look like my mother, perhaps."

"*I* wish for a daughter, too," Amy cried. "I shall dress her in the prettiest of clothes and she will be beautiful and with blue eyes and fair curly hair."

I found myself smiling.

"It is all decided, I see."

She pouted.

"Except that Esmond wants a son. Well, if that has to be, I hope he will be handsome like Esmond and tall and distinguished looking."

"Let us wish that they will be happy," I said slowly. "That is all that matters."

I left them and went upstairs to see my father who had been resting, and when we had embraced and kissed one another I told him my news.

I was touched by his obvious emotion. He held my hand in his and said with a sigh of happiness,

"I hope you will give me a grandson. I shall have something to look forward to now."

Since his illness my father and I had grown close again. He looked to me in a way he had not done for years. As if my presence gave him some reassurance and comfort he needed.

Because we seemed even nearer to one another that morning I ventured to speak to him of my inheritance, asking him if I should still be able to receive an allowance from it, as I had done in the past.

He frowned.

"But it has not been stopped. Your allowance is still being paid to you as usual. There has been no change. It is your right, Kitty. The money is yours. I am only the trustee for it."

I was relieved to find him so sensible, but I hesitated to worry him, for I knew how any concentrated effort of the mind brought on confusion of thought or a bad headache.

"Thank you, Papa. I hope you did not mind my asking."

He shook his head.

"No, child. But I do not deal with such matters at present. Mr. Quennell will look to it. Your stepmother consults him on my behalf, and he sees after things. He will attend to your allowance, if you ask him."

I said again,

"Thank you, Papa darling," and then sat in silence by the bedside while he lay back with his eyes closed for a little while. I decided that I would trouble him no further but enquire of Mr. Quennell, the solicitor, about the terms of my inheritance.

This I did, shortly before Christmas. I remembered Mr. Quennell, who was a short stout man with a completely bald head and wore steel-rimmed spectacles with such powerful lens that from behind them his eyes looked like glassy green marbles.

"Miss Carew. I am happy to meet you again," he said beamingly, as we shook hands.

"It is Mrs. Dawnay now, Mr. Quennell. I was lately married."

"True, true. For the moment I forgot. My clerk wrote the appointment in as Mrs. Dawnay, but when I came in just now I could only think of you as Katherine Carew. How does your father keep? I have not seen him for several weeks though I have been dealing with Mrs.

Carew, who at the moment has to deal with his affairs. Power of attorney, you know."

"So I understand. My father is improving but very slowly. It is he who advised me to see you, Mr. Quennell, over my allowance. I have not received it since I was married."

He stared at me.

"It has been paid to Mrs. Carew along with other monies, which in the ordinary way, your father received. Since his illness she has dealt with the household accounts and wages and so on. I think the allowance your father made to you out of the trust was paid in cash to you, was it not?"

"Yes. In gold sovereigns. The amount was five pounds a month."

"Your stepmother has obviously taken charge of it for you, but she may have overlooked the payments to you. If you wish, I will remind her of this."

I bit my lip, not wishing to offend my stepmother. Seeing my hesitation Mr. Quennell added,

"Perhaps you do not understand the position of the trust, Mrs. Dawnay. Your father has full use of the money from the Belle Tout Estates until you reach the age of twenty-one. Out of this, of course, he had paid for your education and so on, and made you a personal allowance, which," he smiled at me, the marbled eyes blinking behind the thick spectacles, "I feel, should be suitably increased now you are a married lady. After you are twenty-one the income will come to you."

"And—and if I should die, what happens then to the money?"

"My dear Mrs. Dawnay—you are far too young, and beautiful, if I may say so, to contemplate the thought of your demise. It is most unlikely I am sure. However, in the event of such a tragedy the terms of your late mother's will are that the estate will revert to your father if he is alive, or to such other heirs as he may name."

"And if I should leave a child?"

"In that case, if you should die over twenty-one years of age, the estate would come to him or her as your rightful heir and would not go to your father."

"I see." I was silent for a few moments and when I glanced up I saw that Mr. Quennell was closely observing me.

"Is there anything else you wish to know?" he asked.

"I don't think so."

He gave a little bow.

"I am always at your service, Mrs. Dawnay. If you have any other queries, please call and see me at any time."

"Thank you. I will do that."

We spoke for a few minutes more and then I thanked Mr. Quennell again and said good-by. As I drove Brownie over the bridge and out of the town I thought of all that Mr. Quennell had told me, and I wondered how much of the wealth of Penvarrion depended upon the money from the Belle Tout Estate. I did not know what the amount was, and I had hesitated to ask Mr. Quennell, in case he should think me mercenary. I was not. But I had begun to realize that when I was twenty-one I should be independent of Bryce. The thought gave me a new impetus.

One day I called to see Bryce's grandmother. I had thought of her often and of the lonely cottage with its beautiful little garden. I felt diffident as I walked up the path, but Zena had asked me to come and see her at any time and so I could only hope I should be welcome.

The flowers were gone now; only the rosemary and lavender bushes showed above the bare earth. A spiral of smoke issued from the low chimney. Before I could knock on the door it opened and Zena stood there, gravely smiling.

"I am glad you have come," she said in her direct way, as if she had been expecting me. She gestured for me to enter and I went into the room where Nezer rose to greet me and a black cat sat blinking beside the wood fire.

"Let me take your cape." She removed it gently from my shoulders and said, "Please sit down."

I did so, thinking how cosy the little room seemed after the winter cold outside. The colored glassware reflected the firelight in gleams of red and green and violet, the brass and copper shone with an even richer glow. The plants were bright with blooms.

183

Zena busied herself pouring two glasses of wine and then sat down in a chair opposite to me, folding her hands on the lap of her long skirt.

"You look well, Katherine. When is your child due?"

I was momentarily startled.

"Of course, Bryce has told you."

She inclined her head.

"I did not need to be told." She lifted the wine glass. "Let us drink to the safe coming of your son."

"Thank you." I took one of the waferlike biscuits she held out to me. "You seem certain it will be a boy."

"Yes. You carry well, Katherine. You are tall and strong. Your son will be the same. Bryce has chosen well."

"Thank you."

We sat in silence for a few moments. The cat rose and stretched himself and then came to sit beside me.

"Yerko favors you," Zena said. "That is a good sign."

I put a hand on the shining black head, and felt a vibrating purr under my fingers.

"Yerko. That is an odd name. I've never heard it before."

"It is Romany." She gave the smallest sigh. "I am no longer a Romany in the eyes of my people, and yet the old ways and the old names persist."

"Did it make you very sad—to give up everything? Bryce told me that is the law if a Romany marries a non-Romany."

"It was hard. What I could not do was to give up the man I loved, and so I had no choice. And though it was hard, I found a happiness in life I would never have known without my man—even though it seemed at times as if my life had been sliced in two, and one part of it had gone from me forever."

"Because you could never go back? Bryce told me something of this."

"Yes. As a boy he loved to hear me tell of my own childhood. After his father died I brought him up. He was always asking me about the people he was part descended from. Especially when he went to school and there were those who were cruel to him—taunting him and calling him 'gypsy.' That is not the name for us." Her chin lifted. "We are Romanies. I told Bryce he must never listen to the sneers of the ignorant but be proud of his inheritance, although I myself had gone against the law of my people and in doing so had wronged them."

"Why was that?" I asked after a moment's silence.

"Because only in keeping our unmixed blood can we remain true Romanies, *true* gypsies. There are others—tramps and tinkers—call themselves gypsies, but they are not of our people. In marrying a gaujo—a non-gypsy—I went against this law. We are an ancient and a nomadic race who came long ago from India. Although when we first arrived to Britain which, it is said, was at the beginning of the sixteennth century, we were known as the 'Egyptians' and from that came the title of 'gypsies.'"

I sat enthralled, wanting Zena to go on talking. And as if my fixed gaze prompted her she continued by saying,

"It is recounted that a troupe of gypsies were brought to the court of the King of Scotland to dance at Holyrood Palace. As you may know, we are famed for music and dancing and singing and for foretelling the future."

"Yes, I have heard that. You—you too have this sight?"

She nodded.

"I have seen things good and bad. And told many people what is to come to them. But this gift—it is not at one's command but comes in a sudden flash—lightening the future." She turned her intense black gaze on me. "Do not ask me what lies ahead for you, Katherine. Only take heed if ever I should tell you." Her voice changed. "Will you take more wine?"

"No thank you. It is time for me to leave. I have enjoyed so much talking to you, Zena. May I come again to see you?"

She inclined her head.

"It would make me happy." She stood up and Nezer and Yerko rose with her, standing on either side of her like sentinels. We walked to the door.

"Will you come and visit us at Christmas?" I asked.

"Perhaps. We will see what Christmas time brings. But thank you

185

for your thought." She did not kiss me but held my hand in hers for a moment. "Good-by, Katherine."

I walked down the path to where Brownie, a rug over his broad back, was tied up in the shelter of the wall.

"Good-by," I called again, and waving my whip, drove away.

That night another ship foundered on the rocks below Tregedon. The alarm was sounded and Bryce went down to the cove, with Mr. Porritt and Jem and some others and they managed to get the crew of three off to safety but the ketch, bound from Cardiff to Scilly, broke up in the heavy seas.

I thanked God that there were no deaths such as last time and was grateful that we were able to provide food and shelter for the brave men who had been rescued. And I thought, as I had thought so often, that Tregedon was a dangerous frightening place in which to live.

Two days after that we received the news that Sir Ralph Borleigh had died suddenly of a seizure. My stepmother sent a message by Barney to tell us of the sad event, and although I remembered that I had thought Sir Ralph looked ill at our last meeting in Wadebridge, nothing had prepared me for such news.

"Oh, poor Lady Phoebe. I am so sorry for her. I must write to her —and to Esmond, and Laura."

Bryce glanced sharply at me.

"You are very attached to the family."

"I have known them all my life. Laura has been as a sister to me."

"And Esmond? Was he as a brother to you?"

I looked away from his probing glance.

"We have always been good friends."

He gave a sharp ejaculation.

"Do you expect me to believe that it was friendship only you felt for him? Whatever he may have felt for you."

I turned and walked away, refusing to make any further comment upon Esmond. And later in the day Jem rode off to Borleigh Hall and to Greystokes with my letters of condolences.

A few days later, which was the week before Christmas, I drove over to visit Laura, at her special invitation. Since my marriage we had not met as frequently as before but the warmth and affection was undiminished between us as we embraced.

"Dear Laura—I have been so grieved for you. And for your mother and Esmond. How is Lady Phoebe?"

"She has been very brave although my father's sudden death was a great shock to her. And to us all." We sat down together by the bright fire. Laura looked pale and drawn in her black dress. She smiled wistfully at me as she said, "How are you, Kate? I was so pleased to hear that you are to have a child. Amy told me."

"Thank you. Yes, it will be a great event in our lives. How is my little goddaughter?"

"She is well and full of mischief. Hannah shall bring her in to see you," and rising, she pulled at the bell rope hanging beside the marble fireplace and when the parlormaid had taken the message, a rosy-cheeked country girl appeared with Phoebe Katherine in her arms.

She was growing into the dearest prettiest little girl with Laura's dark hair and Paul's blue eyes. She was at the chubby stage and her round cheeks were dimpled and her merry mischievous smile quite won my heart. She sat on my knee but only for a short while for it was her delight to crawl about the room and roll and stagger in an attempt at walking. I thought it was not easy for anyone to remain quiet and sad when so loving and happy a little creature played among us. Laura's thoughts must have echoed my own for she said,

"My mother is coming to stay with us for Christmas. It will be a hard time for all of us, but little Phoebe will be my mother's great consolation. She adores her. I am glad that Amy and Esmond are to have a child soon. That will be another comfort for my mother."

As she finished speaking the door opened and to my astonishment no other person than Esmond himself was ushered in by the maid.

Laura and I both stared, and then Laura said,

"Why, Esmond, this is a pleasant surprise. We were only talking of you, and of Amy, a moment ago."

He came forward, his fair coloring set off by the dark mourning clothes, his skin glowing from riding in the winter cold. My heart seemed to turn over, and I thought painfully that I would never cease to love him.

He took my hand in his and said, gravely,

"Thank you for your kind letter, Katy. How are you? Amy has told me your good news. I must congratulate you—and your husband."

"Thank you. I am well. I trust that Amy is the same."

He frowned.

"My father's death has distressed her, and at the moment her spirits are very low. Her constitution is a delicate one, as you are probably aware, and she is easily upset. My mother is with us at the moment, and her unhappiness has a bad effect upon Amy, in her present condition."

"I am sorry," was all I could say.

"Amy will feel better soon," Laura broke in consolingly. "I remember how ill and dreary I felt early on but it passed and I was in good health the rest of the time."

Esmond sighed.

"I hope it will be the same for Amy, but things were different with you, Laura. You had nothing to grieve you. Amy is very sensitive. The atmosphere depresses her and I do not know how to restore her to cheerfulness."

I was surprised that Amy should be so upset over Sir Ralph's death for he was only her father-in-law and not a real parent as he was to Esmond and Laura.

Phoebe came crawling and rolling toward Esmond, and he stooped to gather her up in his arms, kissing her petal soft cheek and saying, with a smile that lightened his shadowed face,

"How is my little niece today? What mischief have you been up to, eh?"

"Sit down, Esmond dear," Laura said. "I will ring for more coffee. Do you realize—we shall have three children soon between the three of us? Isn't it a lovely thought? They will grow together and be great friends."

"As we were," Esmond said. He sat down, dangling Phoebe on his knee. His blue eyes met mine and for a moment we stared at one another. Then he added slowly, "They were good times."

"Yes," was all I could say.

188

"We see too little of you these days, Katy. When are you going to invite us to Tregedon?"

I said with difficulty,

"Later on, I hope. When—when we have made something of the house. It is still in a poor state."

"But you are happy there?"

Phoebe was pulling at his cravat and so he did not see me bite my lip.

"Of—of course. It is my—our home."

Soon after that I took my leave of them for I had to drive home before dark.

"Come and see us again soon," Laura urged. "We shall be spending a quiet Christmas here with my mother, for as you know we can do no entertaining for a while. You will be at Penvarrion, with your father and stepmother, I suppose?"

"Yes, I expect so," I answered, though to date I had heard nothing of this. "Good-by, dear Laura." I kissed her and hugged my little goddaughter and last of all, shook hands with Esmond and said good-by.

On Christmas Day we went to Penvarrion to be with my father and stepmother. We had invited Zena to be with us at Tregedon, but she had declined to leave the cottage, so we drove to see her on Christmas Eve, taking food and wine and presents and shared a quiet but pleasant evening with her.

To my surprise when we arrived at Penvarrion next day Amy and Esmond were there, having arrived the previous afternoon. It appeared that Esmond would have liked to have gone to Laura's and been with his mother, but Amy wished to be with *her* mother. As my father was unable to travel to Greystokes, the two families were divided.

I felt sorry for Amy. She looked far from well and the pretty color was gone from her cheeks. She complained a great deal, turning pettishly on Esmond when he made some comment and sighing from time to time, as if the cares of the world were on her small shoulders.

It was a difficult day. Sir Ralph's recent death cast a shadow over us all, and my stepmother did not make things easier by taking me aside, soon after we had arrived, to reproach me for calling upon Mr. Quennell.

"I cannot understand why you should take such an extreme course, Katherine," she said coldly. "I was about to make arrangements for the allowance to be paid to you, but you hide yourself away so much at Tregedon that I have had little opportunity to discuss such matters. I may say, you worried your poor father unnecessarily."

"I did not intend to. He did not seem troubled when we spoke together."

"It was afterward—when he tried to remember. You know how Dr. Fullbright cautioned us not to worry your father in any way. He must have no cause to tax his mind."

"I am sorry—very sorry. I would not distress Papa for the world."

"Then in future pray come to me first. I am in charge of your father's affairs, in consultation with Mr. Quennell, of course," she added, seeing my startled look. "It is quite beyond your father to deal with business matters."

"I see."

"I hope you do." Her eyes narrowed. "I suppose Bryce has need of your money with all the talk of his restoring an old property."

"He has never as much as mentioned it. He had no idea that I had this inheritance from my mother." I felt indignant on Bryce's behalf, for whatever his faults he had always been proud and independent.

My stepmother laughed unkindly.

"You are innocent if you think that, Katherine. He has doubtless heard local gossip. He will be aware that your mother was an heiress."

"*You* did not know," I cried.

She shrugged slim black-clad shoulders.

"I came here as a stranger. How could I be expected to know anything like that?"

"Were you not aware Belle Tout had belonged to my mother?"

The heavy lids came down over the bright hazel eyes.

"Perhaps I heard a rumor—I forget." She opened a drawer, taking a packet from it, and held it out to me. "This money is in notes. Mr.

Quennell will pay the next quarter to you in a bill. Now—shall we rejoin the others," and she turned away, ignoring my stammered,

"Thank you, Stepmother."

I was not sorry when it was time for us to leave. My stepmother had originally suggested that we should stay the night because of the difficulties of winter travel, but to my relief Bryce made the excuse of seeing after the stock. He had given the Porritts the day off and with Minna they had gone to Wadebridge to spend Christmas with their married daughter who had recently had a baby. I was thankful. I dreaded that we should have been forced to share not only a room but a bed. Fortunately I was spared that embarrassment.

"You are quite the *working* farmer," my stepmother said smoothly. "It is not usual among people like ourselves."

I did not hear Bryce's answer for I had moved to take my cloak from Carrie who had brought it in. She would have helped me with it but Esmond was standing near and with a nod he took the cloak from her and placed it around my shoulders. As he did so his hand inadvertently brushed the back of my neck. The touch of his fingers seemed to immobilize me so that I stood very still and he said quietly, bending his head to me,

"You look well, Katy. Even mourning becomes you."

I was wearing a dress of black velvet skillfully cut and concealing, and I knew the richness of the material set off my skin and hair. For a moment, as I met Esmond's admiring glance, I could not help being glad that I was tall and strong and carried my child so easily.

"Thank you," I murmured, and turned away. As I did so I became aware of Bryce staring at me from across the room, and of my stepmother's watchful gaze. Only Amy, sitting with my father near the glowing fire, seemed unconscious of the little tableaux.

———◆———

Brownie, warm and well fed from the stables, set off at a brisk pace along the moonlit road and we were halfway to Tregedon before Bryce spoke.

"Well, that is over, thank God. If I do not see your family again for another six months, it will be no hardship."

"Because they are not your family. *I* enjoy to see them, Father especially."

"You mean *Esmond* especially. I saw him making sheep's eyes at you despite the presence of his pregnant bride."

I turned on him,

"That is a hateful thing to say."

"But it is true. He is still in love with you. I warn you, Kate, I'll have none of it. You are my wife now—in name if not in fact. There is to be no hankering after the past because Borleigh has made a mistake and will not be held by his wife's shallow charms."

"You are horrible—monstrous." I all but spat the words out at him, trying to make out his face in the gloom of the hood, but seeing only the dark averted profile.

I sensed him shrug, saw him lift the reins to quicken the pony's pace.

"Say what you will about me—think what you will. We have made our pact and I intend to see that you abide by it."

I was silent, trembling with anger at him, until we arrived back at the house, which stood cold and unlit, save for the moonlight on its gray walls. The sea was quieter tonight. Instead of the thunderous roar of waves it sighed against the rocks, seeming almost to "sing" in a curious haunting manner. So that even in my rage, I was arrested by the sound and sat for a moment listening to it.

Before I could jump down Bryce reached up and, against my will, lifted me to the ground. His hand on my arm, he checked me, saying,

"Do you hear that too? They call it the Doom Voice of Tregedon."

I dragged my arm free.

"Everything is doomed here—where the cruel treacherous sea brings death to so many. I wonder that you could ever have wished to live in such a place. And I wish to God that I did not have to."

I flung away from him into the house. He came after me to unlock the heavy back door with a gigantic key. The kitchen was in darkness but a shaft of moonlight through the dusty window revealed Bryce's hard unsmiling face, unusually pale.

"That is a pity, for Tregedon is your home now. As it will be the

192

home of your child. You had better learn to make the most of it. And Kate," he put a hand out and caught hold of my wrist, "remember this. I have spared you certain aspects of our life together for various reasons. The injury to my arm, your state of increasing pregnancy. But don't think I shall always be so forbearing. I am by no means celibate by nature."

He let go of my wrist and went through the doorway to the stableyard. I stood in the darkness trembling with cold and fear. Slowly, I groped my way up the stairs and into the empty echoing bedroom. Mrs. Porritt had left the fire laid and I put a match to it and as it blazed up I crouched on the floor, holding my trembling hands out to the blaze.

I was trapped. There was no escape from Bryce. "Tregedon is your home now," he had said a few moments ago. A home? It was little better than a prison.

I thought of Penvarrion, its warmth and comfort, the atmosphere of elegance, almost luxury, my stepmother had created there. Now these spartan surroundings were to be mine forever.

I rose to my feet and went to the window as if compelled by an inner urge. I pushed open the casement and leaned out and listened.

Yes, there it was. The sad sighing, the singing of the waves that was like a lament. The Doom Voice. What did it mean—whose doom did it foretell?

I was nervous, overwrought. The conflicts of the day, first with my stepmother, then with Bryce, had upset me more than I knew. As I stood by the window it seemed to me that the sighing sea murmured my name over and over again. *"Katherine—Katherine—Katherine."*

I shivered and closed the window with shaking fingers.

It was past midnight. Christmas was over and done with. I dreaded what the New Year would bring.

MY FEARS were still with me when a few days later I sat by the fire in the parlor while Mrs. Porritt bustled about the room. It was raining and as I stitched at one of the small garments I had set myself to make, I asked Mrs. Porritt the question that was in my mind.

"What is the Doom Voice, Mrs. Porritt. What does the name mean?"

She glanced up from the old oaken press she was dusting.

"Have 'ee bin a'hearing of it then? That old whisperin' that do come and go when wind and tide be a certain way. Porritt say it mean no more than a change o' the weather, but I've heard tell it is the voice o' the men in the Doom Cave. They be sighin' for Christian burial, you see, for they be all lost one night o' winter storm and ne'er a body found."

I put the sewing down on my lap and said somewhat fearfully,

"Was it another shipwreck?"

"Aye, a tarrible one of a Jan'ary night. 'Twas years gone back when the Wreckers be about—flashin' o' their lights and lurin' poor folks to their deaths. This ship were laden wi' gold by all account— 'twas a Spaniard or some such. It broke up along the rocks of Tregedon and seven men got away in two boats and were never heard of again." She shook her head. "But they wasn't drownded in the sea but died in the Doom Cave what they had sought shelter in."

I was transfixed, staring at her in dread.

"The Doom Cave?"

"Ah—'tis set in the side o' the cliff above the cove. There were never entrance to it save from a boat when the tide be high. 'Tis reckoned they reached the Cave for the wreckage of the two boats were found along of it, but that night was the time o' the tall seas and the sand was swep' in mountains over the shore and rocks, same as it will be at one time or another, changing the shape o' everythin' around. Folks here can tell you of many a village and church that lies deep under the sand, and many a body that be 'sanded.' "

"Yes, I've heard of this. But—the Doom Cave—what happened to the men who sheltered there?"

"Why—Ma'am, the mouth be blocked wi' sand, o' course. 'Twas a cruel end to escape the sea and then be suffocated where they had thought to be saved."

"How terrible. Those poor men." I was silent for a moment, thinking of them.

"Is the opening to the cave still blocked?" I asked Mrs Porritt, after a moment or two.

" 'Tis and 'tisn't—you might say. The sea have washed a mite of it away but no one knows how much do still fill the cave. Men be feared to go in and dig lest the sand shift and swamp 'em, same as it did them other poor souls. Folk say 'tis the wind and sea whistling through the rock that make the sound o' the Doom Voice." She shook her head gloomily. "But when I hears the whisperin' o' it, I bain't so sure."

"Oh, it is just superstition," I said firmly. "There is usually a practical explanation for such things."

Mrs. Porritt gave me a sideways look.

"Maybe so, Ma'am," and flicking the soiled rag in her hand over yet another piece of furniture, she ambled slowly from the room.

January was a wild wet month. It seemed as if it rained every day. And with the rain there was always the wind. At Penvarrion the rain had fallen gently in the valley, for we were sheltered from the fiercest gales. But at Tregedon there was no escape from the wind's battering onslaught, and the great seas boomed like thunder, crashing in on the rocks below as if to devour us all.

I felt more imprisoned than ever. The rain had made the rough roads almost impassable except on horseback, and when Bryce took the cart out it became stuck in the mud and he had to abandon the attempt.

We lived in a state of siege, neither giving much quarter to the other. We spoke only when necessary and then only upon topics connected with our daily lives. Conversation as such was something we never attempted. Most days Bryce was gone out of the house from dawn until dusk and I was left alone, save for Mrs. Porritt and Minna's daily visit. Often I was filled with a sense of despair, thinking about the child that was to be born, the child of a man I did not love. At times I felt very old, older than my years.

I did my best to keep myself occupied, sewing and knitting, reading over again the few books I had brought with me. If the clouds lifted for an hour I would essay a short walk, splashing through the mud in my pattens and picking my way along the tracks upon which Bryce had thrown ashes and rubble. Boris accompanied me, for of late the old dog had become my constant companion.

One afternoon in late February I took him on one of our brief outings. It had kept fine all day, which seemed a miracle to me, and wrapping a warm cloak about myself I attempted to go a little farther than usual. Behind the house a narrow track led toward the headland, and this was the way I chose.

It was rough going, but the soil was sandy here, covered in season with ling and gorse. I went slowly until I was out of sight of Tregedon and could look down at the cove below.

The cliffs were incredibly steep. I could not imagine how anyone ever clambered down them, much less rescued men from a shipwreck. Yet somewhere here I knew the villagers found their way to the shore. As I stood gazing about me I wondered where the Doom Cave was situated, and I realized then that this had been the object of my walk.

There was no sign of cleft or fissure in the great green-stone walls. Perhaps the opening was in the side of the cliff upon which I stood? I shivered with something more than the cold as I thought of the seven brave men lying in their tomb, far below. The wind rushed at me, tugging at my skirts and lifting my cloak behind me like a sail. Beyond Tregedon Head the treacherous rocks lifted their jagged heads and a trio of big black-backed gulls came crying and screaming through the clouds as if in warning. It was time to go back.

The weather had changed again; the blue already gone from the sea and a curtain of haze hid the horizon. I called to Boris and turned toward home and as I did so I saw, emerging through clouds of blurry spray, a small ship tossing from side to side in the trough of waves.

I stared, wondering why it rolled so helplessly and then, my eyes watering from the sea spray, I made out a broken mast, lying at a right angle across the deck and I knew that the ship was drifting to its doom upon the rocks.

My mouth opened—I wanted to scream a warning but they would never hear me and it was doubtful if they could even *see* me, standing high above them on the cliff.

It was horrible—terrifying, to watch the little ketch, so absolutely at the mercy of the sea. It was a nightmare scene and I could not take my eyes from it. Then, common sense returned, and realizing I could do nothing to help from where I stood, I started to run back toward Tregedon, Boris lumbering at my heels.

I could not go quickly, the coming child made me clumsy in movement and I was fearful of falling. More than once I stumbled to my knees but picked myself up and went on. By the time I was back at the house I was muddy and breathless and for a moment, could scarcely gasp out Mrs. Porritt's name as I sank down onto a bench in the kitchen.

And then I remembered. Mrs. Porritt and her husband had gone that day to Wadebridge to attend the christening of her grandson and would not be back until the morrow.

*Bryce.* Where was Bryce? He could be at the mine, or somewhere out on the farm. Jem? Jem would be with him, no doubt. That left Minna.

I staggered into the hall and called her name, hoping she might be somewhere about the house but usually at this time she was gone back to the cottage. When there was no answer I made my way across the courtyard and along the lane to where the cottage stood.

To my relief a glow of lamplight shone in a downstairs window and when I knocked on the cottage door Minna herself came to open it.

She stared, her eyes wide in her pale face.

"Why, Ma'am—what be 'ee—!" She broke off at the sight of my windblown hair under the hood and my mud spattered cloak and boots. "Do 'ee come in and sit down," and she put a hand out to steady me as I swayed toward the chair she pushed forward.

"You'm not ill, Ma'am?" she asked, bending anxiously over me. " 'Tain't the babby?"

"No—no. It—there's a ship in distress near the Headland. You must find Mr. Dawnay—*someone?* There's a chance of rescue if help can go to it in time."

She looked blankly at me, her light eyes bewildered.

"Dunnunt know where Mr. Dawnay be, Ma'am. Nor Jem. 'Tis three—four miles to the mine, if they be there."

"Then go to the village, Minna. Find some of the men—the fishermen, anyone who can take a lifeboat out. Go quickly. Don't just stand there, girl. Every minute counts. Take one of the horses—Brownie."

"Brownie be gone along o' Jem."

"Then Sorrel—Caspar—one of the others."

She shook her head.

"I dursn't ride the big 'un—nor the mare."

I stood up, impatient with her timidity.

"Then I must go—I can ride Sorrel. Come and help me saddle her."

A hand went to Minna's open mouth.

"Nay, Ma'am—'ee better not be riding way 'ee are. Ur'll come to harm."

"Nonsense. Just give me a hand with lifting on the saddle."

She protested but feebly. Soon Sorrel was saddled and stepping up the stone mounting block I slid onto the mare's back. Tucking my cloak about me I set off in the direction of the village, having first told Minna to go into the house and put water on the stove to heat, and find some blankets and rugs, in case such were necessary.

It was dark now and the wind was bitter. Sorrel would have skittered at shadows, at the few trees bending like gaunt old men under the blast, but I steadied her to calmness and she picked her way along the muddy track to the village as if she knew what a treasured burden both she and I carried.

The journey was only a matter of a few miles but in the darkness, with the stark branches of the trees tossing like giant's hands against the night sky and the wind increasing in fury at every step, the ride seemed a feat of endurance.

At last a welcome light shone through the gloom and then another and another. We had reached the scattering of cottages and a few yards farther up the narrow street stood the Compass Inn to which I was bound. Somehow I slid down from Sorrel's back and my loud knocking quickly brought the landlord to the door. In a matter of moments he had been told the reason for my visit and had gone off to sound the alarm while his wife, with upraised hands and cries of consternation, fetched me a restoring drink. Soon we heard voices and shouting from the street and thankfully I guessed help was on the way to the little ship I had seen struggling so desperately in the sea.

I was more exhausted than I knew and was glad to sit quietly, my head resting against the back of the chair while I recovered my strength. When at last I spoke of returning to Tregedon the land-lord's wife shook her head and said, hurriedly,

"Nay, Ma'am, 'twould not be wise to ride back same as you come. 'Tis begun to snow and lord knows what sort o' night 'twill turn out to be."

*"Snowing?"* I could not believe her.

"Aye—the wind shifted early on to the Nor'west and when it do that 'tis heavy the falls can be."

I stood up.

"Then I must return to Tregedon at once. It is not a long ride. Perhaps there is someone to walk with me?"

She shook her head again.

"Every able-bodied man be gone down to the cove. Best you'm stay along o' me, Ma'am, till some 'un come back."

199

"Heaven knows when that might be. I must go now. Don't worry about me—my mare is careful and sure footed."

She came after me, wringing her hands.

" 'Tis madness, Ma'am, seein' the way you are."

I would not listen but had her lead me to the stable where Sorrel, still saddled, a rug over her back, was tied up. I tightened the girth and the landlady helped me mount. With a few words of thanks and reassurance I said good-by and set off. In a few moments the lights of the village were left behind and we were riding through the night to Tregedon.

The snow fell lightly; it was more a nuisance than a danger, and I kept my head well down under the hood of the cloak and left it to Sorrel's wisdom to find the way home.

More than once I asked myself why I had not remained at the inn. I was not so enamored of Tregedon that I longed to return to its bleak walls. Yet something, some inner compulsion, seemed to force me back there, and I never doubted that I should arrive safely at my journey's end.

But I was thankful indeed to see the lights of the house looming ahead for by now the snow was falling more heavily and the wind turning to blizzard force.

Minna came running at my call and when I slid from Sorrel's back she had to put her arms about me to hold me upright for I was stiff with cold.

"Oh, Ma'am—come away in. Oh, Ma'am—thank the Lord to 'ave 'ee safely back. I was worrited half to death and wished I'd gone a'stead of 'ee." She was almost crying with relief, but I was too weary to answer.

Only when I was seated in the chair by the parlor fire, my cloak removed and a warm shawl about my shoulders, did I speak,

"I am all right. See to the mare. Give her a drink and some feed—and rub her down. Hurry, Minna—don't just stand staring."

A feeling of lassitude had come over me and I was lying back in the chair when the door burst open and Bryce, his coat and hat powdered with snow, stood on the threshold of the room. He said explosively,

"What the devil is this I hear? That you have ridden alone to the village on such a night as this and in your present condition. Do you not realize what harm you might have come to? It seems there is no end to your foolhardiness, Kate."

I looked up into his angry frowning face and then looked away.

"Do not distress yourself on my account," I answered coldly. "I am safely returned, as you see. There was no one else to go. The Porritts are at Wadebridge for the night and Jem was somewhere with you. Minna was too nervous to ride one of the horses, so I took Sorrel. I saw the ship with its broken mast from the headland and I could not bear to think no one would try to rescue the men on it." I glanced back at him. "Did you—have you heard anything?"

He came farther into the room.

"You will be relieved to hear the lifeboat took the crew of three men to safety. The ketch was left to break up on the rocks—there was no hope for it."

I gave a sigh of thankfulness.

"Then my efforts were not in vain. I thought anyone rescued might have been brought back here—Minna had everything ready."

"No. They were taken to the village. Just as well, for you are in no state to attend to half-drowned men. Where is that girl—Minna? She should be looking after you."

"She is seeing to Sorrel."

He gave an angry exclamation and left the room. In a few moments Minna returned, scarey eyed and tearful.

"Master says I'm to help 'ee to bed, Ma'am, and make 'ee some supper." She put a hand out to me. "Do 'ee come along o' me, Ma'am, or Master be rampagin' somethin' awful at me." She sniffed. " 'Ee call me a twitterin' rabbit, though 'tain't my fault. I never could abide to be near 'osses."

Together we slowly climbed the stairs and after Minna had made up the fire she helped me to undress. Soon I was lying in the wide four-poster and I had never been so thankful to be there. When she had gone I lay staring up at the firelight flickering on the beamed ceiling. I heard the wind battering at the bastion-thick walls. With the sound of the storm outside the room seemed a warm safe place in which to be.

Minna came back with a bowl of bread and milk, for I had no appetite for more hearty fare. As it was, I had to force myself to swallow any of it, and I was only halfway through when I felt a spasm of pain shoot through me.

I put the bowl on the side table and lay back on the pillow. Had I eaten my gruel-like meal too quickly? But no. Every mouthful had been a slow effort. I was tired, my digestion impaired.

The dragging pain, the heaviness came again and I felt the sweat of fear break out on my hands and forehead. I was unduly apprehensive. This could not be what I first thought, surely?

No. All was well. The pain was gone again and had been only cramp or some twinge of indigestion. It would have been better had I not forced myself to eat when I had so little appetite. I would lie here and compose myself to rest.

There. I was quite all right after all. I had been lying half an hour or so without further discomfort when the door opened and in came Bryce. He walked to the bedside and stood looking down at me.

"Are you all right?"

"Perfectly, thank you."

"You have not eaten your supper. Would you like Minna to get you something else?"

I shook my head vigorously.

"No—no thank you. I am not hungry."

"You should be—you can have had little to eat since dinner."

"Please do not trouble about me—I am feeling warm and rested." The words were hardly said when a spasm, sharper and fiercer than the first, shot through me and involuntarily I winced against it.

"Kate!" Bryce's hand came out to mine. "There is something the matter—why do you look like that? Are you not well?"

I took a deep breath and said calmly,

"I am quite well. It is nothing—a twinge of indigestion."

He sat in silence, holding my hand in his. I did not withdraw mine from his clasp—the feel of the firm strong fingers was oddly reassuring, and I was concentrating, almost counting the minutes.

202

It came again—a powerful muscular contraction that held me for a moment like a vise and then released me swiftly as it had come.

I didn't realize how tightly I had gripped Bryce's hand until it was over.

"I—I'm sorry," I said, and my voice sounded breathless in my own ears.

He said gently,

"You had better prepare yourself, Kate. Unless I am much mistaken, the child is on its way."

I said through gritted teeth,

"How is it you can claim to know more about this than I who am to have the child?"

"Perhaps because I have attended more births. Oh no, not those of human beings but the births of animals, creatures of the forest and the field."

"Thank you for comparing me to an animal, but the two states are rather different I think."

"I am not so sure about that. We are all animals, Kate. Every one of us is basically a living creature of Nature."

"You may think you are, but I—aahh—" My words tailed off in a sort of sighing gasp as I felt another sharp contraction. When it had gone I lay for a moment with sweating brow. Then without opening my eyes, I whispered,

"Please don't say it."

I sensed him bend toward me, felt his breath upon my cheek.

"Say what?"

"That if I am to have the child prematurely I have brought it upon myself. Riding Sorrel as I did—overexerting myself. Yet, what else could I do—seeing the ship there? The Coast Guard missed it—I felt I must give the alarm." I opened my eyes and met his steady gaze. "Now I am frightened."

He said brusquely,

"Nonsense, Kate. You are never afraid. Everything will be all right. It will be an eight-month child—" He stopped abruptly, and I knew what he was thinking. An eight-month child did not often live.

"If only Mrs. Porritt were here—she would be of so much help."

He stood up, releasing my hand.

"I am going for the doctor, Kate. Then you will be in safe hands. The child may not come for hours yet—a first birth is often delayed." I felt the touch of his hand on my forehead. "Rest as much as you can. I will send Minna to you." I heard the door close after him while I waited, supine, for the pain to return.

Minna tiptoed in—looking more whey-faced and frightened than ever.

"Oh, Ma'am—you done yourself a harm a'goin' ridin' in the dark and everythin'. Now the babby do be comin' and no one here but us-selves."

I struggled up into sitting position.

*"Minna!* Please do not talk so foolishly. The Master is gone for the doctor and—and you and I can manage meanwhile. I am sure you will be of help to me for you must know something about childbirth. Did you not tell me you had married sisters?"

She stared at me, her eyes widening in alarm.

"Oh, aye, Ma'am—but the elder one she do be 'avin' a tarrible time. Near dead she be afore they delivered her of a stillborn 'un, and the second sister she be torn near to pieces on account of the child being twisted all across like."

I could not answer her for the spasm that wracked me. When it was over and I had got my breath back I rose from the bed and said with more confidence than I felt,

"We—we must make some preparations. Try to think what we should do, Minna, and what things we shall need. I will find some of the baby clothes I have made. The doctor will soon be here."

Minna shook her head,

"Nay, Ma'am—I doubt Master'll ever get through the lanes wi' the snow an' all. The wind be so powerful strong 'twill be makin' driftses taller'n a man. 'Tis always the same hereabouts when the Nor'west wind be blowin'.'"

I could have screamed at her, such was my state of nervous apprehension. Somehow I controlled myself and started to move about the room, opening the drawers of the tallboy in search of the baby layette I had spent so many hours sewing. I urged Minna to make

204

.

herself useful and after staring about in her usual bewilderment she suggested putting a draw sheet on the bed and making other preparations her memory prompted her to do. In the midst of my own activities the waters suddenly broke and I was left bewildered and afraid while Minna mopped the floor and found me a clean nightdress, sighing and shaking her head the meanwhile.

"Oh, Ma'am—poor Ma'am. This be a tarrible time for 'ee. Same as it was for our Jessie. And for Leah, too, come to that." She sighed gloomily. " 'Tis be worse for you bein' as how the babby be a'comin' afore its time. 'Twill be a miracle if it lives."

I could stand no more of it and I gasped,

"Go and see if the Master has left yet. Tell him I wish to speak with him."

When Bryce came into the room I felt a tremendous relief though the sight of him wearing his hat and great coat and thick muffler filled me with alarm.

I put a beseeching hand out,

"Don't go. Please don't leave me, Bryce. I cannot stand to be left here with only Minna. She is upsetting me, and making me afraid."

In two strides he was at my side, my trembling hands in his own two.

"I must go, Kate, and at once. The snowfall is so heavy now I shall never get through to Wadebridge if I delay. Be a good brave girl and bear the pain as well as you can until I return with Dr. Laker."

I had never thought to cling to Bryce, but now in my fear I did so.

"Stay with me. *Please,* Bryce. I cannot endure what lies ahead with Minna weeping and wailing over me. She will sap all my courage. Only you can help me now." I gazed imploringly up at him. "Send Jem—Jem can go for the doctor."

He hesitated.

"He is young—and not reliable. He is more than capable of turning back for home if conditions defeat him."

"I do not care. You must chance that. Please stay with me."

Slowly he nodded.

"Very well. We must risk Jem getting through the snow storm. I

205

will go and give him his instructions. Lie back Kate, and compose yourself. You will need your strength for later. And don't worry." The trace of a smile edged his mouth. "You will be as safe with me as a prize heifer, and that is saying a great deal."

I would have smiled back at his poor joke if I could, but I had to hold onto all my self-control in that moment and when I was recovered he was gone.

# 16

I SHALL NEVER forget that night. That strange and at times, terrifying night. Outside the blizzard raged and in my quieter moments I heard the snow shuffling against the windowpanes. Inside the room, with the fire burning brightly and the oil lamps turned up high another storm took place as my child fought his way into the world. And at my side, helping and sustaining me, was Bryce. He stayed with me throughout it all.

At first the pains came at irregular intervals and though gripping, were bearable. For a time I walked about the room, encouraged by Bryce. I found it eased me to stand, leaning with both hands upon the low chest, as I gasped and panted. But after a few hours the contractions partook of a curious rhythm. I felt as if the storm which surged over the house with enormous gusts and then subsided, only to rise again, was of the same element that urged me on with such powerful force.

I was lying on the bed when I felt the change come over me. I struggled into a sitting position and Bryce's arm came about me as I pushed hard against the pain. I clung to him as to a life line, and through the cataclysmic sensations I heard his voice, deep and calm,

"Hold on to me, Kate. You are a good brave girl. All is going well. It will not be long now." I felt his free hand smooth back the hair from my sweating forehead, felt a cloth cool and damp against my lips and cheek, and then once more I was taken over by the tremendous power that seized me.

Sometimes I was very aware of all that was happening, but at other moments I seemed to be in a dream with everything remote from me. Minna had been sent away for I could not bear her staring frightened gaze upon me. She seemed like a Jonah. I did not want her in the same room with me.

Bryce's arm moved from my back and his hand pulled free of my grip.

"Now, Kate. *Now,*" and without being told I knew that the child was coming. I felt my breath catch, a supreme pressure forced me on and then, in one incredible wonderful moment that I shall remember forever I saw the tiny wet dark head in Bryce's hand. It moved and two minute shoulders appeared; I heard a feeble cry and the next second my child was lying on the bed.

I lay against the pillows. I was crying, the tears pouring down my cheeks as Bryce stooped to the bed. I heard him say, "Here is your son, Kate," and felt him place the baby in my arms.

I could not believe it. This tiny creature, the puckered mottled face, the strangely shaped head, the eyes closed and wrinkled against a world he was not yet ready for. Bryce had wrapped him in some warmed toweling. He was a shapeless bundle in my arms and yet the feel of him, so small and helpless against my breast, filled me with a passion of love such as I had never known.

I stared up at Bryce through a blur of tears.

"It is over. He is safely here. What would I have done if you had not been with me. Thank you—*thank you,* Bryce." I added hesitantly, "He—he is perfect?"

"Absolutely. You have given me a beautiful little son, Kate."

I bit my lip as I looked down again into the tiny face.

"He is premature and will need great care. It is my fault—I was reckless and unthinking. Poor baby."

"He will be very sleepy." Bryce touched my cheek with his hand. "And that is what you must be now. Go to sleep together. Dr. Laker should be here soon."

I yawned, aware of an enormous lassitude.

"What is the time?"

He went to the window and drew back the curtain.

"The sky is lightening," he answered, "it is morning."

The room was flooded with light from the snow outside and with the colors of the dawn. Small blue clouds floated on a sky of shot pink silk. As I gazed they changed and the clouds became golden hued on a sky of pale blue.

The night was gone. And with the break of day my child had been born.

I sighed.

"Please send Minna to me, and then I will sleep."

Minna sidled in, at first timid and owl-eyed, and then smiling feebly as she saw the child in my arms. She made me comfortable and then, almost before she tip-toed out of the room my little son and I were asleep.

I woke to find someone bending over me; a thin dark face, shining dark eyes and a gentle hand on mine. It was Zena.

For a moment I could only stare while she looked gravely down at me before saying,

"You have done well, Katherine. A fine son and a strong one for all he has come early into the world. May Heaven bless you both."

"How—how did you come here?"

"Bryce fetched me. He rode Caspar through the snow and then led me back on the horse. The roads are blocked to Wadebridge and the doctor has not been able to get through as yet." She laid a hand on my forehead. "I have come to look after you and your son, if you will allow me."

"Thank you. I am very glad you are here." I looked around, aware that I was alone on the bed. "Where is my baby?" I heard my voice sharp with anxiety. "Please bring him to me."

She gave me one of her rare smiles.

"He is here, sleeping in his cradle." She moved away and I saw her bend over the wooden crib that Bryce had brought home one day from Bodmin. The next moment the child was lying in my arms and the feel of his tiny body, so soft and helpless, filled me with the same inexpressible emotion that I had felt at his birth.

I said tremblingly,

"I am frightened. He is so little? Will he thrive—will I be able to nurse him?"

"Of course. Why should you not? Nature will see to that even though he is born a month too soon."

I looked up into Zena's face, beautiful and serene despite her age.

"We will call him Luke. Do you remember? You told me he would be born at morning light, and the name Luke means light."

She inclined her head.

"It is a good name." She turned away, "I am going now to prepare a drink for you. It will cleanse the system and help bring on your milk. Because the baby is premature he may seem lethargic and will need to be coaxed to the breast. But do not worry, Katherine. He is a strong child and as big as many a one that has gone the full time."

When she left me I gently unwound the woolen shawl in which he was wrapped. Zena had washed him, for the creamy substance which had marked his skin in places was gone, and a binder and a flannel vest and the shawl were substituted for the toweling. His head still seemed a queer shape to me for I was not used to newborn babies, but I thought it appeared less bumpy. I marveled at the trace of eyebrows on the small face, the sparse little eyelashes, I put my finger to one minute hand and was amazed to find it gripped and held fast for a moment. Suddenly, for the first time, I saw his eyes open. He seemed to gaze at me with a curiously searching look as if to assure himself that I was the person he knew. Then the tiny eyelids closed again, the mottled pink face fell into wrinkles of oblivion and he slept.

But the tremor of joy stayed with me, the awareness of whom he was. A new-born soul, a real and living entity. *Luke.* And the last doubt and fear that had darkened my thoughts, the dread that the child conceived by a man whom I did not love, would seem alien to me, was gone. I knew I would give my life for him.

For several days we were snowbound. Dr. Laker did not manage to get through to Tregedon until the second day, and the Porritts were unable to return until the carrier's cart brought them back two days after that. Meanwhile, under Zena's wise care I managed to bring Luke to take a little of my milk albeit slowly and infrequently.

Dr. Laker when he came was astonished that the baby had been born safely and well in such difficult circumstances.

"You have been fortunate, Mrs. Dawnay, to come through your ordeal so well and to have borne so strong and healthy a child." He frowned and for a moment his eyes narrowed to stare at me. "I can only be of the opinion that you made an error in your calculation of dates—natural enough at the birth of a first child." He shook his head. "Well, no more adventures. You must rest and take care. In fact, I should prefer that you stay in the house for the time being for if you caught cold in this weather it would be dangerous for your son. I will call and see you again in a few days."

And so I remained in my room for over a fortnight and then came downstairs to sit in the parlor with Zena for company and occasionally Bryce when he joined us at meal times, though sometimes he was gone out all day.

I felt curiously shy with him, which was extraordinary after all we had been through together. Or perhaps it was *because* of that experience? Certainly we seemed to have little to say to one another, but that was no rare thing. The only difference was that the sense of violence between us had gone. We were, if not friends, no longer enemies.

When the roads were clear, I sent Jem over to Penvarrion with a letter to my father, telling of the arrival of his grandson. Almost by return came a warm and loving message written in the handwriting that had now become shaky and almost undecipherable. My stepmother wrote, too, a note of congratulation that did not attempt to hide her surprise at the safe arrival of so premature a child. I knew that if she had come to visit me her suspicions would have been expressed more openly. Other letters followed; from Amy and Laura, my Aunt Selina, Rosamund and her husband, from Gertrude Barlow and her brother and from other friends and relations, including Bryce's cousin Cecilia Dawnay. All were full of warmth and kindness but enough remarked upon the unexpectedness of Luke's arrival to make me feel not a little self-conscious.

One of the nicest surprises of all was a visit from Oliver. Mrs. Porritt showed him into the parlor one morning, a tall figure in naval uniform, his sandy fair hair framing a sun-tanned face. He smiled at me with a trace of the old shyness before saying warmly,

"Kate. How good it is to see you again. Mama wrote to tell me the splendid news that I have a nephew, and I thought I must ride over and see you on my next leave. And so here I am."

"I am so happy you have called." We kissed one another affectionately and then he sat down on the settle opposite me. "You look well, Oliver, and very handsome in your uniform."

The color came up in his cheeks.

"Thank you. I have been away at sea, you know. It was a grand experience." He frowned slightly. "A lot seems to have happened during the months I was away. You have produced a son and Esmond has lost his father. My mother says he died a poor man, and this fact is a great worry to them all."

"I did not know that. Sir Ralph was thought to be wealthy."

Oliver shook his head.

"Apparently not. It appears he was a great gambler."

He broke off, "I am sorry—I am only repeating gossip and there are more interesting topics to discuss. Am I to have the pleasure of seeing my nephew?"

"Of course. But he is very tiny you know, and sleeps most of the time, for his arrival was premature. Would you like to come up to the bedroom?" I led the way and as I went slowly up the stairs I thought of what Oliver had just told me—that Sir Ralph had died leaving money problems behind. I was astonished. The Borleighs had lived in such style and Esmond had always seemed fortunate and happy.

Luke as usual was sleeping, a warm cocoon of wool in his cradle. He scarcely stirred when Oliver touched his hand. A breath of fair down had begun to grow upon his head, already he looked more like a baby and less like a wizened little old man. Yet to me he had been beautiful from the very first day.

We went downstairs again, and I asked Zena if she would come and take some hot chocolate with us. She was such a reserved person that she never put in an appearance if a stranger arrived. But when she met Oliver and found him, despite his smart naval uniform, young and shy, she unbent and soon we were talking happily together.

"I am sorry Bryce was not at home to meet you," I said when at last Oliver took his leave. "He has a great deal to do for he is restoring the property which has been much neglected."

"I am sorry, too, but please give your husband my kindest regards. I hope to see him another time." He kissed my cheek. "Good-by, dear sister. I am glad to find you looking so well and"—he blushed slightly—"beautiful as always."

"Thank you, Oliver. God keep you until we meet again."

I was happy to have seen him but was left anxious concerning Esmond. I wished I could go over to Penvarrion, but to date Dr. Laker had forbidden me to drive out and so I had to spend another week or two confined to the house.

I felt restless and only Zena's quiet company saved me from the boredom that threatened. We had not even made arrangements for Luke's christening as yet.

But at last, the wind shifted to the south and overnight it was spring. I was allowed to walk a little way along the lane and saw the first brave primroses in the hedgerows and the new green mint growing in the ditch, while under the shelter of the few bent trees a scatter of daffodils shone golden in the sunlight.

Zena made plans to return to her cottage, taking Nezer and the cat, Yerko, with her, for she had brought them on the night Bryce fetched her from her cottage. She had already described to me how Nezer floundered through the deep snow after them and how Yerko, mewing and protesting had been carried in a basket on the back of Caspar. "For I could not leave them to fend for themselves," she had explained.

"I am thankful that you came to be with me. Luke would never have thrived as he has done without your help and kindness," I said. "You are so wise."

She sat looking at me, her arms folded under the dark shawl she habitually wore. Gold earrings swung under the piled up black hair, the hollowed black eyes glinted with the strange light that always

213

seemed to lie in their depth. As usual, the somberness of her dress was broken by touches of bright almost gaudy colors; a red-and-yellow handkerchief at her long neck, rows of emerald-green braid edging the long brown skirt, a glimpse of green blouse under the black shawl.

"Perhaps wisdom comes with age, with judgment and reflection. Young people cannot be wise until they have made the mistakes that teach them to be prudent."

"I have made so many mistakes already that if that is true I should surely be one of the wisest people living," I said with an edge of bitterness in my voice.

"Do you think so?" She shook her head. "Perhaps what you consider an error of judgment will prove to be correct, and what you thought to be the truth will turn out to be an illusion."

I frowned.

"You often talk in riddles, Zena. I cannot understand you."

She touched my hand in a brief caress.

"You do not have to understand me but to know yourself, for our natures are our destinies. Take heed of the courage that can become rashness and the confidence that becomes imprudence."

I stared at her and then I sighed,

"You are right. I might have lost Luke through my want of caution."

"As you may lose another, equally dear to you."

Did she mean Esmond? But he was already lost to me, and not through any fault of mine.

Although Zena was so quiet the house seemed empty after she had gone, and I missed her more than I would have thought possible. Mrs. Porritt bustled about with especial zeal as if to prove that she was more in charge than ever. She doted on Luke, but I was already thinking of engaging someone younger to act as nursemaid, for Mrs. Porritt and Minna had enough to do about the house. I thought longingly of Carrie and wondered if she would still want to come to me. Perhaps she would not care for Tregedon. It was such a wild and lonely place, and although many improvements had been made it was still poor-seeming by comparison with Penvarrion.

I was now pronounced strong enough to travel, and I told Bryce I would like to go and see my father at the first opportunity and take Luke with me.

"Certainly. It is only right. Perhaps Mr. Carew will be well enough to come to the christening, whenever that it is."

"It should be within the next few weeks—we must make the arrangements." I hesitated before adding, "I thought of asking Carrie to come and work for us. She was my maid at home, but she would look after Luke if she came here. Is the idea agreeable to you?"

"Yes. I think it is a good one. You need someone other than Mrs. Porritt, and Minna is not responsible enough." He frowned before adding, "I am afraid I cannot leave the farm at present to go with you, but Jem shall drive you over whenever you wish."

I was surprised at my sense of disappointment. Then I shrugged as I answered,

"Thank you. I will send a message to Penvarrion."

It was a fine morning in early April when Jem drove me over in the pony cart, Luke warmly wrapped up and lying snug in my arms. I was happy beyond words at the thought of seeing my father again and of introducing him to his grandchild. As we drove along I gazed about me as excited as if I were on a holiday outing. The world looked bright and new to me after so long a spell indoors, and the farther we went from Tregedon with its rugged cliffs and cruel seas and the nearer we drew to Penvarrion and the sheltered green valley in which the house stood the more joyful I became.

I had forgotten how beautiful it was. How tall the trees grew, flushed with new green leaf; how smooth and sweeping the wide lawns, how colorful its shrubs and flowers. It was like returning to another world.

Borlase opened the door to me and after a few words of greeting Mrs. Borlase appeared, majestic as ever, and then Carrie, hurrying to my side, eager to lift Luke into her own arms and joyfully tearful at the sight of him.

Strangely, there was no sign of my stepmother, but I did not delay, only hurried up the stairs to my father's room, telling Carrie to follow me in a few minutes.

He was dressed and sitting in an armchair, a rug across his knees. Although the day was warm a fire was burning in the grate. His head was sunk between his shoulders and at first I thought he was asleep, but as I drew near I saw that his eyes were open and he was staring in melancholy fashion, at the burning logs. He looked pale and sad and somehow, so lonely, that I felt a sadness in my heart.

I said gently,

"Papa."

He turned his head and an expression of joy came over his thin face. A trembling hand came out to me.

"Kitty! My darling girl."

I flung myself onto my knees and put my arms about him.

"*Dearest* Papa. How good it is to see you. Are you well? Do you feel better? It is such a beautiful day I had hoped to find you downstairs and sitting in the sunshine."

For a moment he did not speak, only rested his cheek against mine.

Then he kissed me again and drew back to look down into my face.

"It is *you* I must ask after, my dear. Is all well with you? And—and the child? We—your stepmama and I have been most anxious for you."

"I am very well, Papa darling, and I have brought your grandson to meet you. Carrie is bringing him in." I was about to call to her when there came a tap on the door and Carrie entered, the baby held close in her arms. I took Luke from her and drew back the lacy shawl so that my father could see him properly. "This is Luke, Papa. Is he not beautiful?"

My father gazed down at the tiny face and at that moment Luke opened his eyes and stared unblinkingly back at him. One tiny starfish hand waved above the shawl and my father put out his finger which was instantly caught and held. I saw his eyes fill with tears, but his smile was full of a tender happiness.

"Why, Kitty, it is hard to believe. That this little creature is my grandson." He shook his head. "Indeed, he is beautiful. I never saw a more lovely child."

216

"Of course he is small, Papa. He was premature, but he has made wonderful progress, and Dr. Laker says he is a strong healthy boy."

"A *boy*." My father nodded with satisfaction. "To have a grandson is a splendid thing."

I rested my head against the arm around my shoulders.

"It will make up for the fact that I was only a girl, Papa."

He pressed a kiss on my forehead and whispered,

"I would not have had you any other. You have been the greatest joy of my life, my darling."

"Luke is to be christened soon. Do you think you will be strong enough to attend?"

He shook his head wistfully.

"I do not know. I seem to make little improvement in walking. Most of my days are spent up here, in my room."

I thought of the lonely looking figure I had glimpsed on entering the room and my heart ached,

"What does Dr. Clarkson say? I will ask my stepmother. I have not seen her as yet, Papa? Where is she?"

He frowned as if puzzling.

"Is she not at home? She is out a great deal I know. I do not always know where. Or I cannot remember." He looked across the room to where Carrie waited quietly. "Where is your mistress?"

She came forward, her face shadowed with distress.

"Oh, sir, have you forgot? The mistress was sent for yesterday. She has gone to Borleigh Hall—to Miss Amy. Lady Borleigh, that is."

*Lady Borleigh.* The name echoed strangely in my ears until I realized that of course, since Sir Ralph's death Amy had become Lady Borleigh and Esmond's mother was now the Dowager Lady Borleigh.

I said slowly,

"Is Lady Borleigh not well?"

Carrie seemed for a moment as if she could not speak. Then she said in a low sorrowful voice,

"Miss Amy was delivered of a stillborn child yesterday evening."

217

# 17

I HEARD myself gasp.

"Oh! Oh *no*."

"It be so, Miss Kate." Carrie glanced at my father as if expecting him to speak, but when he remained silent, only frowning as if he was considering her words, she went on hesitatingly, "Lady Borleigh she be poorly on an' off for some time like. Not carryin' well, they said, beggin' your pardon, Sir, Ma'am. She bein' so small and all that." Her voice trailed off as if she was diffident of being more explicit.

"I am very sorry, very grieved for Lady Borleigh. And for—for Sir Esmond." I thought of the risks I had taken over my own pregnancy, and I shivered with fear of what might have happened. I lifted Luke from the rug on my father's knee, where he had been lying with my arms about him. "Will you take the baby, Carrie. You may show him to Mrs. Borlase and the staff. Take great care of him," I added. "I will come downstairs in a little while to speak with you."

She smiled reassuringly, as she held out her arms.

"I be takin' every care of him, Ma'am. You may be sure on that. Shall you be wantin' me to tell Mrs. Borlase you be staying for dinner, Ma'am?"

"Yes. I will take it up here with my father."

When she had gone I sat down beside Papa, and held his hand in mine.

"How grieved poor Stepmother must be. It is the saddest news." I sighed. "Poor Amy. And poor Esmond."

218

"Yes." My father shook his head. "I had forgotten. Just as Carrie said, I forget everything now."

"You remembered about me, about Luke, Papa," I said consolingly.

"However bad my memory, *you* are ever in my thoughts, Kitty. How is"—he frowned—"your husband? You see at this moment I cannot even remember his name."

"It is Bryce, Papa. He is well and sent his apologies for not coming with me today, but he is so busy with the farm and with the Tregedon mine which he has reopened."

"I remember knowing something about Tregedon. I wonder what it was?" He was silent for a moment and then he said slowly, "Are you happy, child?"

I did not want anxiety for me added to his loneliness.

I said quickly,

"Yes, Papa, I am happy. I have my little son and—and Bryce is," I was going to say "good," but I was not sure if that were true, so I substituted "strong" for Bryce was certainly strong. Strong and resolute. "And *kind,*" I added, for I knew from experience that this was so.

He sighed, as if comforted. We went on to speak of other things, and I told him that I would like to ask Carrie to come and work at Tregedon and would he have any objection.

"Of course not, child. I am sure it is what Carrie would like. She very often speaks of you."

So it was settled. Later I went downstairs to discuss the matter with Carrie and with Mrs. Borlase. Arrangements were made for Carrie to come to Tregedon the following week. Then it was time to feed Luke, and after I had nursed him in the quiet sunshine of the morning room Carrie took him away to sleep in my old cot and I returned to sit with my father.

Driving home with Jem late that afternoon, my thoughts were full of Amy and her bitter loss. And of Esmond, who was now Sir Esmond Borleigh. I held Luke's warm little body closer in my arms as I prayed that they would be comforted and one day be blessed with a healthy living child.

A week later Carrie came to be with us. I saw that at first she was awed by her surroundings; by the house that stood like a bastion standing high above the raging seas, the countryside that stretched behind it in a waste of gray fields and stone walls. The simplicity of Tregedon's furnishings seemed to take her aback, too, as if she had expected something much grander, although I had warned her that we lived very simply.

"I hope you will like it here, Carrie," I said aware of her uneasy glances.

"I like to be with 'ee, Ma'am. 'Tis just that this be a terrible wild place, and seeming miles from anywheres."

"The village is but three miles down the lane," I said consolingly. "And you will have Mr. and Mrs. Porritt and Minna and Jem for company. You shall go home to your parents once a month and often to Wadebridge or Bodmin when the pony cart is going that way. But if you are not happy at Tregedon, then of course you must not stay with us."

She shook her head.

"If you be happy here, Ma'am, reckon I'll be content enough."

I showed her over the house, the narrow stairs that led up this way and that, the rambling passages that turned sharp corners as if going back the way they had come. I had made her bedroom bright and welcoming with new curtains and rugs. I could see she was pleased by it, for the attic rooms at Penvarrion were dark and furnished in sparse old-fashioned style. Leading off the bedroom was Luke's nursery.

A few days later when she was settled and acquainted with the Porritts and Minna, I left Luke with her and went to visit Amy. Bryce drove me over to Borleigh, which pleased me, for I did not want to go so far alone, or only with Jem for company.

The first person we saw was my stepmother. She was as elegantly dressed as ever in a green plaid dress, which set off her russet hair, but her face was pale and strained.

"It is kind of you to call, Katherine. Amy will be pleased to see you. I will take you up to see her in a few moments. I am afraid Esmond is away from home, Bryce, or he would be here to keep you company." She added stiffly, "I must congratulate you both on the arrival of a son. You have not brought him with you?"

"No. I—it seemed best to leave him at home."

She inclined her head.

"It would have upset Amy to see him. She is heartbroken by the loss of her child. And far from well."

"I'm so sorry," I said. "Poor little Amy."

"She would have had a son." The heavy lids lifted and she looked directly at me. "Like you."

I was startled by her glance, the malevolence that she made no attempt to hide. She had never liked me, but at that moment I realized she hated me because my child lived while Amy's was dead. I wished I had not come and yet I had felt in the circumstances I must call to see my stepsister. My heart was full of sympathy for her, and for Esmond.

When I went up to see Amy, Bryce took a walk around the grounds. My stepmother led me into the bedroom and then left us together. Amy's small face was pale and sharp-featured against the snowy pillows, her red-gold hair straggling over her shoulders. She put her limp little hand in mine and sighed, in answer to my query.

"I feel so tired. All those dreary months carrying the baby and at the end of it all, nothing. Just a feeling of being a thousand years old."

"Poor little Amy. It is a sad and bitter blow for you, and for Esmond. But you are not a thousand years old. You are young and you will feel better soon. One day you will have another child."

She withdrew her hand from mine and said pettishly,

"It is all very well for you to talk, Kate. Everything went well and easy for you, and you have your son to show for it. For my part I hope I am never pregnant again."

"Please don't say that, Amy."

She moved her head restlessly on the pillow.

"Oh, I shall be. Esmond will see to it. He is mad for a son." She shrugged. "I suppose someday I shall have to go through it all again. Though I don't know how I shall endure it. You have no idea of the pain I went through." She met my glance and added impatiently,

221

"Oh well, I suppose you have. But your sufferings could not have been anything like mine." Unexpectedly, she began to cry. "And all to no purpose."

I took her hand in both mine.

"You feel like this because you are still weak and ill. When you are stronger life will seem easier."

She rubbed her eyes with the back of her hand in a curiously childish gesture.

"I hope so. Anyway I am glad to see you, Kate. In a way, I've missed you."

"I think I have missed you too."

"When I am well again I will come and visit you at Tregedon. I hear it is a wild lonely place." She stared at me. "Are *you* lonely there?"

"Yes. Sometimes."

"But you are happy? Are you very much in love with your husband?"

"Why else would I have married him?" I said as lightly as I could, adding, "Bryce brought me over today. Would you like him to come and see you?"

She shook her head.

"No. Not like this. I look ill and ugly. Next time perhaps."

"Yes, of course. He did not expect that you would want more than one visitor at present."

I kissed her and said good-by. Downstairs in the beautifully furnished drawing room that was in such contrast to the dark paneled parlor at Tregedon, Bryce was sitting with my stepmother, making an attempt at conversation with her. He stood up with an expression of relief on his face when he saw me and after a few moments, went to the stables to bring around the pony cart.

My stepmother turned to me with a frown,

"I understand Carrie has left Penvarrion and gone to work for you. You did not consult me over the matter."

I stared at her.

"I consulted my father and he had no objection."

The look of displeasure deepened,

"Your father has nothing to do with the running of the household. I am the mistress of Penvarrion, Katherine, and it would have been common courtesy to ask my permission before engaging Carrie for your own purpose."

I was too taken aback to do more than stammer an apology.

"I'm sorry. It did not occur to me that if my father agreed you would resent Carrie coming to me."

"You must understand that your father has little say in any matter concerning Penvarrion. His mind is too confused to make a decision or, if he did, remember it twenty-four hours later. He is virtually an invalid now and, I may add, a great care and responsibility. In future, Katherine, please make any request you may have to me in the first instance."

I said stiffly,

"There will be no future requests. I apologize again. Good-by, Stepmother."

She inclined her head and stepped back. We did not attempt to kiss one another, and leaving her, I went out onto the steps of the house to await Bryce.

He must have noted my set face and flushed cheeks for he said, as we drove along the road,

"What is the matter, Kate? You look angry."

I told him what my stepmother had said and he laughed harshly,

"Poor Kate. You are always rushing in where angels fear to tread. But your stepmother takes too much upon herself. She is not only mistress of Penvarrion, if she had her way, I suspect she would be mistress of Borleigh too. I do not envy your friend Esmond his mother-in-law."

"I am sorry for Amy," I said. "She is not happy."

I sensed his sideways glance.

"Then she is in good company, for which one of us is?"

Three weeks later Luke was christened in the church at Tregedon. No other members of the family were present but ourselves. My father could not attempt the journey, my stepmother made an excuse, Amy was still confined to the house and Esmond was away in London. Only Laura and Paul and little Phoebe came, for Paul was to be

223

one of Luke's godfathers. Oliver was his other sponsor. The Porritts were there and Minna, and of course, Carrie, who held the baby for me part of the time. Afterward Laura, Paul and Phoebe came back with us for the Christening Tea. Laura was pregnant again and she was delighted at the prospect of another child.

I did not want Carrie to feel lonely and miss her family and so before she had been a month with us I arranged that she should go home for a night to her parents. As I intended to see my father at the same time I asked Bryce to drive us to Penvarrion, instead of Jem as he suggested.

"I know Papa would like to see you. He was enquiring for you on my last visit. Please come."

He said reluctantly,

"I am very busy."

He stared somberly at me from under frowning brows.

"I have to work. If I did not—" He paused and then shrugged. "Very well, I will take you to call upon your father."

It was a warm afternoon in May. Larks were singing overhead as we drove into the valley and the blue sky was without a cloud. Carrie was left at the Lodge and we stayed to exchange a few words with Mrs. Pleydell who beamed and smiled and duly admired Luke lying in my arms. It was arranged that Barney should drive her back to Tregedon the following day.

I walked into the house carrying Luke and to my surprise Esmond appeared from the direction of the library. For a moment the three of us stood staring at one another then Esmond came forward saying,

"Katy! How good to see you again. And looking so well." He nodded to Bryce as he added, "You have brought your son with you." Bending his tall fair head he looked down at Luke who gazed back at him with wide open eyes.

He said slowly,

"His eyes are blue, Katy. Like your father's."

"Yes. I think he resembles Papa. He is not like me. Or—or Bryce, though I think his hair will darken in time." I did not say what I had thought more than once. That somehow he looked a little like Esmond.

Esmond straightened and turned to Bryce.

"You are fortunate—to have such a fine boy."

Bryce said stiffly,

"Yes. We realize that."

"How is Amy?" I asked. "I hope she is feeling stronger."

"I think she is a little better. You will see her for yourself." He hesitated. "We are living here at Penvarrion for the present."

I stared at him in astonishment and saw that Bryce looked equally surprised.

"Living here?" I echoed.

He gave me an embarrassed smile.

"Yes. It is Amy's wish—to be with her mother until she is recovered in health. And Mrs. Carew desires that too. But I must not keep you standing here—shall we go and sit down?" He led the way toward the drawing room and held open the door for me to pass through. I had no sooner sat down with Luke upon my knee than my stepmother came into the room.

She greeted us with her usual composure but her face seemed to harden as she glanced at Luke.

"So this is your son. He is small for his age, is he not?"

"He was a premature child."

She sat down with a rustle of silken skirts.

"Ah yes." She frowned as if considering something. "Remarkably premature I should imagine. In which case he is quite a big child."

I saw the glint in Bryce's narrowed eyes, but neither he nor I made any comment. Esmond broke the awkward pause to say,

"Is Amy still resting, Mrs. Carew? She did not sleep well last night and went to lie down."

"She will be with us presently. Poor child—she is in low spirits at the moment, but that is not to be wondered at."

"I will take Bryce up to see my father," I said. "They have not met for a long time."

My stepmother inclined her long graceful neck.

"As you wish."

I think we were both relieved to escape from her presence. Bryce

225

carried Luke up the stairs and in a few moments we were sitting with my father.

When I saw my father was beginning to weary we left him, promising to come back and sit with him again before we returned home.

Amy put in an appearance just before tea time. She wore a white muslin crinoline which emphasized her paleness but set off the beauty of her red-gold hair and eyes, larger and greener than ever in her small face.

I was glad that Luke was fast asleep after I had nursed him. Amy did no more than peep at him and say tearfully,

"Oh, there he is—your baby. I cannot bear to look at him—it makes me too sad," before she turned away and went to sit beside her mother.

It was warm enough to take tea in the garden, and we sat under the acacia tree, just as we had so many times in the past. To outside eyes, we must have looked a happy family group and yet I thought each one of us was living in separate worlds. My stepmother, calm and smiling but ever watchful. Amy shadowed by her present unhappiness. Esmond, usually animated and gay, not much more forthcoming than Bryce, who sat silent with folded arms and dark aloof gaze. And myself? I too had my inner preoccupations. A sense of heartache for Esmond, who seemed changed. His handsome face had a heavy look, his cheeks more flushed with color. For the first time I saw in him a resemblance to his father.

Later I went up to sit with my father again.

I kissed him and took my leave and went downstairs to find the others. There was no one about, the chairs under the acacia tree were empty. I was puzzling where everyone might be when Esmond's voice said from close behind me,

"They have gone to the greenhouses." I turned, startled and he said gently, "Let us walk the other way, Katy. It is so long since we talked together."

I was startled but not unhappily, so I turned with him and as if by common consent we went slowly in the direction of the rose garden. For a few moments neither of us seemed able to break the silence that fell between us but at last I said,

226

"How is Lady Phoebe? It is a long while since we met."

"My mother is fairly well. As you know, she was never robust. She has moved to the Dower House with Miss Dobson her companion. The Hall is to be let—had you heard?"

"Yes, Laura told me." I looked up at him. "I am so sorry, Esmond to hear of your present difficulties."

"Thank you, Katy. You will understand, if anyone does, what a hardship it is to me to give up my inheritance. But I cannot afford to live there and that is all there is to the matter. The place cannot be sold because of entail, so we must find a tenant for it as soon as we can. The rent will bring in some income."

"Things have not been easy for you."

He looked down at me, his blue gaze serious on my own.

"No harder for me than for you, Katy. You gave up a great deal when you married Bryce. From what Laura has told me, you live somewhat spartanly." He added gravely, "I hope the sacrifice has been worth-while."

I looked away from him, frightened he would read the secret in my eyes.

"We are comfortable enough."

Silence fell again between us. Perhaps my dark thoughts were mirrored on my face for after a pause Esmond said gently,

"You look sad. Of what are you thinking?"

I sighed.

"I was thinking that sometimes I feel very old. As if my life is half over before it has begun."

He said slowly,

"How strange. For that is exactly how I feel at times. A fearful awareness that the best part of my life is behind me."

I turned my head and found his gaze fixed on me and for a moment I could not look away. His blue eyes, shadowed and unhappy, seemed to ask a question of me. I felt his hand reach out to mine and heard him say softly,

"Oh, Kate—I wish to God things could have been different. It is my fault—I should never have married Amy—"

My heart beat fast, I could not take my glance from his; I was very

227

aware of his hand holding mine. Then reason asserted itself and I pulled my hand free as I stammered a protest,

"Don't say that. Please don't say such things, Esmond. You cannot mean them." I forced myself to move away from him and as I did so, I saw with a start of fear Bryce's tall figure standing under the archway leading into the rose garden. He was staring at us, his face dark and forbidding, his light eyes narrowed. When he spoke it was to say curtly,

"It is time to go, Kate."

I glanced quickly at him and then as quickly away. I wondered how much he had seen or heard. But I had done nothing wrong, I assured myself. I had not encouraged Esmond to any indiscretion. Unconsciously my chin tilted and my voice was cool as I answered,

"Of course. I am ready."

In a few minutes we had said good-by to my stepmother and Amy and, lastly, Esmond. Luke, wrapped up in a shawl, was lifted up in my arms as I sat in the high cart, and with a crack of the whip we set off up the hill.

Caspar was between the shafts and he went like the wind. So much so that as the cart rocked from side to side along the narrow road I clutched Luke more closely to me and forced myself to protest.

"Need we drive at such a dangerous pace?"

He gave me a sharp sideways glance and said through gritted teeth,

"You may be reluctant to return to Tregedon, but that is where you belong. Not at Penvarrion, although I realize it holds certain attractions for you."

I did not answer him but stared straight ahead. As if to further unnerve me, he cracked the whip sharper than ever so that Caspar almost leaped into mid-air and for a moment I thought the cart would turn over. Luke woke and started to cry and I gasped a warning,

"Consider your son's safety, even if you have no thought of me or yourself."

Although he made no answer I realized thankfully that after a few moments Caspar's speed was checked and we drove the rest of the way home at a more sober pace and in silence.

228

At Tregedon he lifted me down from the cart, Luke still in my arms, and still without speaking led Caspar away to the stable.

The house was cold and gloomy despite the evening sunshine outside. Mrs. Porritt had left a supper laid and a log fire burned low in the grate. I carried Luke upstairs to the nursery and washed and changed him before giving him his feed. Tonight he was restless, and would not settle. The drive must have upset him or perhaps he was overtired. At last, sleepy and replete, I laid him in his cradle and leaving the door ajar, went to the bedroom to wash and tidy myself.

The house seemed ominously quiet. I went downstairs and into the parlor. It was empty. For a moment I stood irresolute, wondering where Bryce might be, and then at a sound behind me, I turned to see him standing in the doorway. Because he was so tall he had to stoop his head and with a hand on either side of the framework he blocked the daylight out, looking so strange and menacing that instinctively I took a step backward. When he did not speak but continued to stare at me from under lowering black brows, his mouth set in a hard line, I said uncertainly,

"Do you wish for some supper? Mrs. Porritt has left it all ready for us."

"I am not hungry."

I tried to look away but his eyes, narrowed and glittering, held mine. He said abruptly,

"What was he saying to you—back there?"

I knew he referred to Esmond.

"It—is—of no consequence."

"Of *no consequence!*" He rapped the words so sharply back at me that I took another step farther from him. "No consequence that he holds your hand as tenderly as a lover, while you—you stood there blushing and smiling in a way that sickened me to the heart. I've had enough of this play acting, Kate." He moved from the doorway and came toward me. "You are married to me, and by God, I will make sure you are aware of it."

He was so threatening in appearance that in sudden fear I retreated to the other side of the table. He gave an ejaculation that was half a laugh and half a sneer and gave the table a push so that I was

229

trapped between it and the wall behind me. The crockery rattled and knives and spoons fell to the floor and I cried out in alarm.

"Be careful."

For answer he caught hold of the cloth and with one swift movement dragged it from the supper table in a rattle of broken crockery and glass. His teeth flashed wolfishly against his brown skin as he leaned across to say,

"It is not food I want or need, Kate. It is *you*. You have tormented me long enough. I kept away from you these past months. First when you were carrying the boy, afterward while I waited for you to grow well and strong after his birth. I hoped against hope that you might turn to me at last, smile at me, welcome me home. But I find that like the bitch you are, you only want to go fawning after Esmond. But it is not Esmond you are married to. It is me, and if you are not certain of that fact, I will teach it to you."

I leaned panting against the wall, the table edge pressing against my knees.

"You are mistaken—it is not so. I have never—Esmond has not—" my voice trailed off and a grim smile twisted Bryce's mouth.

"He has not what? Not told you that he admires you, that he loves you still. That you are beautiful. As you are. And never more so than now, with your eyes shining in fear and your hair falling loose and your face white as the rose I once compared you to." He took hold of the table and with a twist of his two powerful hands overturned it and came toward me.

I had never seen such temper before in him and I was terrified. His arm came out to seize me and I bent to elude him. His hand caught the back of my dress and I heard it tear down the middle. But it freed me. I swung around in one wild movement and ran stumbling over the broken pots and plates toward the door. Bryce came after me as I went panting and gasping up the stairs. I rushed into the bedroom and flung myself against the door, but I could not hold it under his weight. He hurled it open, flinging me onto my knees. With his heel he kicked it shut and leaned against the wood, his labored breathing the only sound in the darkened room.

I straightened up and for an endless moment we stared at one another and then he moved slowly toward me, backing me remorselessly to the bed. I felt the edge of it press into my legs as I was forced against it. I struggled, pummeling at his shoulders, clawing at his face and hair, but it was useless. Slowly he overpowered me, holding each of my hands in a grasp so fierce and strong I could have cried out at the pain of it. I was filled with horror. Not at the thought of being wife to him but at being taken against my will. At being taken in bitterness and hatred.

Slowly, inexorably Bryce pinioned me down with outstretched arms upon the bed. The heavy weight of his body came down on mine, I felt his breath, fierce and hot upon my cheek. His face, no longer impassive and masklike, was that of a stranger, so contorted in lines of violence and passion. I closed my eyes against the cruelty in it and as I did so I heard his voice, harsh and deep, saying,

"Once I took you in love. I worshipped you. But you have destroyed that love. Now I take you in a different fashion."

His savage kiss silenced my whisper of protest. His hand tore my dress from the shoulders and I went down into the brutal darkness and was lost under him, consumed in a fire that held more rage than desire in its ferocity. Helpless in his imprisoning arms, I knew then that he hated me as much as ever he wanted me.

*Part 3*

# THE DOOM CAVE

# 18

WHEN HE WAS gone I lay, bruised and ravaged, on the tumbled bed where once a man had died in peace. There was no peace for me now, only a sense of stunned despair. The slow tears trickled down my cheeks as I stared into the darkness, wondering what the future held. One thing was certain. I could not stay here with Bryce. I could not endure the thought of it.

I thought dazedly, "What has happened to us? Why have our lives gone so wrong?"

Was it my fault more than Bryce's—because I had been forced into the terrible mistake of marrying him without love? But that happened to many women. Arranged marriages; marriages of convenience, marriages for money or for ambition. Did such unions unleash the same violent emotions as ours had done? I found that hard to believe.

I was exhausted both physically and emotionally, and I could not think clearly. I felt it would be impossible to sleep yet I must have done so, for a sudden sound woke me. I started up in fear, clutching the sheet about my aching body. The grayness of dawn filled the room and in its dim light I saw the door slowly open and Bryce standing there.

He did not advance into the room but stood staring at me. He was fully dressed, his unshaven face set in grim lines. As I cowered back among the pillows, unable to speak or make a protest, he said in an expressionless voice,

"I am going away, Kate. If I remain here I shall destroy myself and you. A man who violates his own wife is little better than a brute." He held a sheaf of papers in his hand. "Everything is here for you. Money, instructions to the bank and to my lawyer, Mr. Sedlescombe. He will deal with any queries you may have. Payments from my share in the Tregedon Mine will be made to you. Josh Porritt will help run the farm while I am gone."

I found my voice at last.

"Wh—where are you going?"

He shrugged, placing the papers on the tallboy near the door.

"It does not matter. Abroad most probably. Somewhere I can forget all that has happened between us. I can only hope that you may do the same. For the present we shall be better apart."

I sat up, pulling the sheet across my bare shoulders.

"I do not want to be left here alone. You may stay here and I will go. Go—go back to Penvarrion."

He turned, a darkening frown on his face.

"No, Kate. I cannot agree to that. You are to remain here. If you leave Tregedon, you will not keep the child. That I promise you. Luke is to live at Tregedon and not at Penvarrion or anywhere else. I shall be in touch with Sedlescombe and he will report matters to me."

Anger took the place of my fear of him.

"He is to spy on me, you mean?"

He inclined his head stiffly.

"If you wish to think so. Remember what I have said. This is your home and Luke's. And you are my wife. I wish you to conduct yourself as such. Good-by." The door opened and closed after him. I heard his slow footsteps going down the stairs.

I lay, tense and listening. A door banged from far below. After a while I heard the clatter of hooves over the cobbles. Then silence. He was gone.

Clutching the sheet about me I crept out of bed and went to the window. A faint luminosity from the sun rising behind the house pierced the mist rising from the milky sea. All was quiet. Only the sound of the waves washing on the rocks below broke the silence. And as I stood there shivering it seemed to me I heard again the

236

echo of my name in the whisper of the sea. The Doom Voice calling softly, *"Katherine. Katherine. Katherine."*

I turned and ran on trembling feet, along the passage to the nursery. Luke slept, rosy-faced, innocent, angelic. Lifting him gently from his cradle I carried him back to bed, where I lay, holding him close against my bruised breast.

Bryce had gone and I was alone. But I was still a prisoner at Tregedon.

During the next few days there were many explanations to be made. The Porritts were bewildered and openly curious; Carrie and Minna and Jem puzzled at the sudden departure of their master. I answered their questions as best I could, explaining that Bryce had been called away unexpectedly on business matters, some mining interests abroad which had to be attended to. It was a lie, but the best I could do to save face and at the same time, give them reassurance. The one thing I did not explain was the wreckage of the dining room. I had forgotten about it, and though Mrs. Porritt must have wondered at the chaos she found there she never spoke of the matter. At times she gave me curious sideways looks or frowned as if at some inward thought, but I was too stunned to care and soon it was behind us and a nine-days' wonder.

When I felt recovered I drove into Wadebridge and made the acquaintance of Mr. Sedlescombe, who proved to be a quiet courteous man, evincing no inquisitiveness and seeming only to have a sincere desire to be of help to me.

Slowly I settled down to a new existence, with the reins of Tregedon in my hands and a great responsibility upon my shoulders. In a way I was no more lonely than I had been before. Bryce and I had had little close contact or companionship, and since the terrible night when he had forced himself upon me with such brutality, I did not want to think about him. I wanted to forget. So I busied myself in every way I could, caring for Luke, with Carrie's help, consulting with Josh Porritt about the farm, paying the wages, the household accounts, gradually learning as much as I could about the running of Tregedon.

Not long after Bryce's departure I went to call upon Zena. I was hesitant, uncertain. I wondered what she would say when she heard that Bryce had gone away. But my carefully thought up explanations were unnecessary. She opened the door to me with her usual grave smile of welcome and said,

"Come in, child. I have been expecting you," and when I sat down in the high-backed wooden chair she said,

"So you are alone now."

I was too startled to answer and she added gently,

"Bryce came to say good-by to me that morning. He said that he had made you unhappy and that he was going away for a time. I am sorry, Katherine. For both of you. Bryce is unhappy too, you know."

I did not know what to say. I looked away from her hollowed black gaze and down at my tightly clasped hands.

"Our—our marriage was a mistake. It is my fault as much as his."

She shook her head.

"It is true what I told you. Fire destroys fire. But Bryce will never love any woman but you."

I said in a low voice,

"He does not love me now. Nor—nor I he. Things have gone very wrong between us."

She leaned toward me.

"You are mistaken. Nothing can break the bond that links you."

I wanted to say, "There is no bond to be broken," but I did not want to distress her. She loved Bryce so dearly.

As if aware of my thoughts she rose and said,

"We will say no more about it. I will make tea for us. Tell me, how is Luke?"

I spoke of him, promising to bring him with me on my next visit. We talked of the farm, of the animals and the crops. And then I said good-by to her and left.

The weeks of summer went by. I visited my father at Penvarrion. Sometimes Esmond was there but very often he was not. Amy was fully recovered but made fretful by Esmond's frequent visits to London.

"I cannot think what he does there. It is all business, but it does not seem to improve our affairs for us. Still, it is better than being gone for months, as Bryce is. When do you expect him to return?"

"Not—not for some time yet."

"Then he will not be here for your birthday? It is but two weeks away."

"My birthday!" Had another year gone by already? Soon I should be twenty. I had an aching remembrance of my eighteenth birthday and the ball my Aunt Selina had given for me and how I had felt. I had my whole life before me, a life to be shared with Esmond. Now I was like someone imprisoned with no hope of freedom and nothing to live for.

*Luke.* I had Luke, my darling little son. And I knew that even to undo the past hateful year I would not be without him. He was a part of me. I must be hopeful and work and make something of my life for his sake, I thought.

It was soon after my birthday that at his request I went to see Mr. Quennell. After we had shaken hands and exchanged courtesies he leaned forward across the polished desk and said slowly,

"I am concerned about the money that is in Trust for you, Mrs. Dawnay. The income, which as I explained to you before, was paid to your father to use at his discretion, has, since his illness, been handled by your stepmother, Mrs. Carew. This, of course, is quite in order in the circumstances, but I have become anxious as to the extent of the sums of monies which she is drawing upon. They seem extravagant in relation to the amounts your father required. You are not aware of this, of course?"

I shook my head.

"No. I receive the increased allowance that you arranged for me, and it is sufficient for my needs at present."

He frowned.

"You are entitled to much more, but your stepmother is against increasing your allowance. She says your husband will take it for his own use."

I sat up, unexpectedly indignant on Bryce's behalf.

"She is unjust to him. He has evinced no interest in my fortune."

Mr. Quennell stared down at his plump folded fingers.

239

"The fact is, Mrs. Dawnay, I have a suspicion that your step-mother is using the greater part of the income from your Trust fund to assist her family. That is, her daughter, who, I understand, is living at Penvarrion with her."

"But Amy is married. She is now Lady Borleigh."

"Precisely. And it is common knowledge that the late Sir Ralph Borleigh died a bankrupt. I feel it is my duty to put these matters before you and enquire whether you wish me to proceed further."

I stared at him, biting my lip. Then I shook my head.

"It would distress my father if you did so. He has never used the Trust fund for anything but the good of his family and—and Penvarrion. Now that he is ill and my stepmother has command of it I cannot alter things. It is only for another year—or just under. I am twenty now—soon I shall be twenty-one and the inheritance will come to me."

Mr. Quennell gazed thoughtfully at me.

"It will impoverish your father to a certain extent. You are aware of that?"

I was silent, considering.

"I did not realize. But—I suppose I could reverse the situation. And make *him* an allowance?"

"That is certainly possible. But you would not be rich enough to subsidize another family too. The Borleighs, for instance."

"I do not expect to. It will not be long before Sir—Sir Esmond recovers his fortune."

"Let us hope so," Mr. Quennell said dryly.

I went away full of thought. Yet not surprised at the way my stepmother had acted. Amy was her first and last consideration. I knew that. Well, it was of no great matter. If the use of the money would help Amy and Esmond through a difficult period, I had no objection. The inheritance would come to me in the end, and what I did with it would be my own business.

No word or letter came from Bryce. He could have vanished from the face of the earth for all I knew. Save for one thing. Mr. Sedlescombe had intermittent news of him and always, whether deliberately or by chance, passed this on to me, on my fortnightly visits to him

240

which he had suggested that I should make. On these occasions we went through various business matters together and he would advise me on any queries I might have. I was too proud to reveal that Bryce never wrote to me, and I allowed Mr. Sedlescombe to think that we were in correspondence, though from what the lawyer said, Bryce had no fixed address and was constantly moving about.

Throughout that strange lonely summer I went often to see Zena and a few times I prevailed upon her to visit me at Tregedon. But as the year turned into autumn I began to see a change in her. She grew thinner and looked more frail and tired every time I saw her, but when I enquired after her well being she assured me she felt perfectly well.

Few visitors came to Tregedon. Laura and her children, sometimes accompanied by Paul. My stepmother came with Amy, but after a critical glance around and a few derogatory remarks about the house's isolation, she did not come again. Once Esmond brought Amy, but neither of them were at ease and I became aware of a tension between them. Esmond seemed restless and Amy was quarrelsome. I felt dull and workaday, a veritable farmer's wife unable to talk about anything but the weather, and I was self-conscious with Esmond. Altogether the visit was far from a success and I was relieved when they drove away.

Luke was now eight months old and growing fast. He sat on my knee and stared about him in the liveliest fashion and his smile, with his eyes so deep and dark a blue, laughing up at me, rejoiced my heart. Some tiny white teeth were already showing, and soon he would begin to crawl, Mrs. Porritt assured me. The entire household doted on him. I thought we should have to be careful not to spoil him as he grew older.

One wild autumn day I rode over to see Zena. This time I did not take Luke for the wind was cold and he had had a touch of earache. I was glad to turn inland, and leave behind me the ceaseless roar of the sea, as it dashed in angry waves on the rocks below Tregedon.

When Zena opened the door to me I was shocked by her appearance. She looked thin and gaunt, the black shawl clutched about her stooping shoulders seemed to emphasize the pallor of her fine-boned face. She coughed once or twice as we sat down and I said quickly,

"You are not well. Will you not let me call a doctor?"

She shook her head firmly.

"I am in no need of one. It is nothing—a chill only, caught in the garden."

"Please come back to Tregedon with me. We will take care of you."

She smiled in the sweetest way at me, and I thought how beautiful she was.

"You must not concern yourself for me, Katherine. When I die, I shall die in peace and in my own way. Remember that." She held a hand up at my murmur of protest. "If I could plan it, I would wish to see you and Bryce reunited, but that may not be yet awhile." Her eyes looked past me into the flames of the fire. "Sometimes I am afraid."

I stared at her in alarm.

"Afraid? Of what? Of being ill?"

She shook her head.

"No, no. My own life is of little importance now." She turned her head to look at me. "I have two requests to make you, Katherine. One is—please take care of Yerko. He will be content with you. The second is," she paused, and stiffly, as if every movement was an effort, she got up and went to the sideboard and opened a drawer. Taking something out of it she came back to me and said,

"Wear this, child. It is an amulet and very old. It will help to guard you. If ever you are in danger, hold it between your fingers and think of the one you love."

I stared first at the talisman in my hand, a greenish stone fastened to a thin gold chain with a curiously carved branch upon its surface and then in growing alarm at Zena.

"What do you mean? *If I am in danger*. And why am I to take Yerko; what is to happen to you and to—to Nezer?"

She put a hand on my arm in a rare caress.

"I have frightened you. I am sorry. It is just that—" She broke off,

242

and after a moment added, "Promise me that you will always wear the amulet. And do not worry about Nezer. He will be with me."

"I will wear the amulet. But—but I don't understand."

She smiled gently, reassuringly.

"You will do, Katherine." She coughed again and when the paroxysm was over she said, "We will take a glass of wine together. It will do us both good."

When she had poured out the translucently golden liquid she raised her glass and said softly,

"To Bryce's return."

I could have wished for a different toast and yet, as I sipped the wine I thought that, in some strange way, I should be, if not glad, relieved to see him again. Sometimes it seemed to me I had been on my own for long enough.

When I left Zena kissed me, in an unexpected gesture and said quietly,

"Good-by, Katherine. God go with you."

I rode home, bewildered by her words and saddened at the change in her. I did not know what to do for the best, but I resolved to visit her again very soon.

The resolve was not kept for a variety of reasons. Luke was teething and suffered from a fever that kept him awake at night. Carrie caught a bad cold, and so I could not leave Luke in her care but instead had to help nurse her, with Minna's inadequate help. The month of November came in with the worst storms and gales we had experienced in years. I had never seen anything like the tremendous seas that raged below Tregedon, casting mountains of spray hundreds of feet into the air so that the very cliffs were hidden beneath the spume. The house shook beneath a thunder of sound, and sometimes when I lay alone in the big four-poster I shivered with a fear I had never known before.

There were many shipwrecks that autumn and many brave men went to their deaths in seas from which they could not hope to be rescued. But some were saved and brought up to the house and nursed back to life while others were taken to the village and given shelter by the cottagers.

243

Then one morning we woke to find that the wind had dropped and the entire household breathed a sigh of relief. Mrs. Porritt who had endured a non-stop headache for the past week smiled wanly and said,

"Thanks be to God the wind's stopped scrithin' for now my pore head be steady on my shoulders agin. 'Twas the worst storm I do ever recall."

I looked out of the window at the battered landscape and thought of Zena. Tomorrow I would ride over to see her and take some provisions.

Shortly before tea time of that same day I sat in the parlor sewing. Luke, who had started to crawl, was tumbling about on a rug at my feet, gurgling happily to himself, with an occasional look and murmur in my direction when I spoke to him. We were in the habit of holding such conversations, and I was sure that he understood much more than I realized.

The door opened suddenly and Minna stood there with face averted in her usual abashed manner,

"'Tis a gentleman called for to see 'ee, Ma'am," and without more ado she ushered in Esmond.

I started up in surprise as he came toward me, smiling and holding out his hand.

"I hope I do not disturb you, Katy. We have been anxious for you during this recent bad weather, and I decided to ride out and see how you were."

My hand in his I looked up to meet his warm blue gaze, and then glanced quickly away.

"It is good of you to call, Esmond. I am well, thank you, as we all are, though Carrie has been indisposed and Luke is just over another bout of teething. How is my father? And of course Amy and—and her mother?"

"They are well and send their love and good wishes." He smiled down at me. "I have brought mine in person, as you see."

"Yes." Gently I withdrew my hand. "Please sit down. I will ring for some refreshment."

He took the chair opposite to me.

"There is no hurry. Let us sit and talk together." He looked down at Luke who came crawling toward him. "How handsome your little boy is—and so sturdy." He shook his head putting out a hand for Luke to catch hold onto. "I envy you, Katy."

"I hope that you and Amy will have a son of your own before long."

"I hope so." He sighed. "She is not anxious to have another child at present. It is only natural, after the ordeal she went through."

"Of course. I am sorry." I was sorry for Esmond as well as Amy. I thought that despite his handsome looks his face fell quickly into lines of harassment and his eyes were heavy and red-rimmed as though he did not sleep well or had the habit of late nights.

We spoke of his mother and of Laura, whom I had not seen for several weeks. I was made happy by Esmond's presence and yet in a way I was uncomfortable. The old sense of freedom was gone, and in its place was an awareness that we had changed and were no longer the same people.

Once he said, with a thoughtful glance around,

"Your husband has been gone a long while, Katy. Are you not lonely without him?"

"Yes—I—I miss him, of course. But I have Luke—and Carrie is with me, and the other servants." Not wishing to pursue the subject I went on to enquire if he still visited London as often.

"Yes—I go up regularly. Amy is always plaguing me to take her with me. She does not understand I have business matters to attend to. I cannot be dancing attendance on her and her frivolous engagements. Besides which, it would be deuced expensive."

The room was growing dark now except for the firelight and I suggested again that I should ring for wine or tea and for the lamps to be brought in.

"As you wish. Thank you."

I reached toward the bell rope, but before I could do so, Esmond stood up and catching my hand in his own said with a strange intensity,

"You do not know what it means to me to be here with you like this. You are never out of my thoughts, Katy. To see you here, with your son, who could have been *our* son, and more beautiful than ever, breaks my heart with regret."

For a moment I could not speak, only stare up at him seeing his face in the shadowy firelight. Then I pulled my hand free of his clasp and said slowly and unhappily,

"It is too late, Esmond. We have made our choices."

"I did not make mine. Amy—Amy made it for me. She beguiled me with her prettiness and her childish ways. Oh, I know I should not say that—you think it weak and caddish of me, but it is the truth. I think I have never stopped loving you, Katy." He put a hand out toward me again. "Is it not the same with you?"

I wanted to say "Yes. Yes, it has always been the same with me," but I could not. Luke at my feet gave a little cooing cry and in one swift movement I caught him up into my arms and held him close. What I felt or did not feel for Esmond did not count. Luke was all that mattered. I must remain Bryce's wife to keep my son. And so I shook my head and said in a trembling voice,

"No, Esmond. It is not the same. And you must not think or speak in this way to me again." I pulled on the bell rope with my free hand and sat down, with Luke upon my knee. Minna came in and I told her to bring in the lamps and draw the curtain. Esmond had gone to the window to stand with his back to me, staring out.

Minna returned with one of the lamps and placing it on the table went to draw the curtains. At the same moment Esmond made a sharp ejaculation and turned to say,

"What is that burning over there? Is it a rick or some farm destruction? The sky is alight with the flames from it."

I hurried to the window, holding Luke, and saw on the horizon an orange glow flaring against the blackness of the November evening. I stared, puzzling what and where it might be and then, in sudden dread, I realized that the fire came from the direction of Zena's cottage.

I cried out sharply,

"Minna—fetch Josh! He will know in what direction the fire lies. Hurry! And tell Carrie to come for Luke."

In a matter of minutes Carrie had taken Luke, and Josh was standing before me, shaking his head in ominous fashion as he said,

"That fire surely be from one place and none other. 'Tis from the old lady's cottage—there be naught else that way to burn. No rick nor byre nor nothing. We'd best be setting along o' there to see what befalls 'ur."

"Yes." I turned to Esmond. "I must go at once. Will you ride with us?" and at his nod I sent Minna for my cloak and told Josh to have Jem saddle the horses. "Your wife must stay with Luke—Carrie can come with us, she is young and strong and may be of help. Let Jem ride the plow horse and you take Brownie, Josh. I will ride Caspar, and Carrie can ride Sorrel." Caspar has been brought back to Tregedon by the post boy of an inn a few days after Bryce's departure on the horse.

The sky grew brighter and more lurid with flame as we rode, a mixed cavalcade, across the wild countryside toward Zena's cottage or what remained of it, for as we clattered up the track and came within sight of it, I saw, in sinking horror, that the little house was all but gutted.

It was so dreadful a sight, that as I slid from Caspar's back I felt sick with fear. I heard my voice rising on a shriek of despair and ran forward crying,

"*Zena!* Oh, God, Zena! Where are you, Zena?"

I think I would have rushed into the flames had not Esmond caught hold of me, and held me fast.

"For heaven's sake, stop Katy. You can't go in there. Can't you see—no one could be in those hellish flames and stay alive."

I struggled against him calling,

"Where is she? Josh—Jem—help her. Please—oh, please. We must find Mrs. Dawnay."

The heat from the burning timbers scorched our clothes and faces. Esmond pulled me back a few paces. In a numbness of terror I saw Josh and Jem beating at the flames with their jackets while Carrie led the frightened horses away.

I felt as if I was in some awful nightmare.

247

"Is there *nothing* we can do—nothing!" I sobbed, dashing the tears away from my smoke-grimed cheeks. But I knew the answer even before Esmond spoke.

"There is nothing we can do. The fire must burn itself out."

I whispered her name,

"*Zena.*"

"Who—who is Zena!" he asked gently.

"Zena? She is Bryce's grandmother. She was old—ill. Oh, what has happened to her— It is too dreadful."

Esmond was frowning.

"The gypsy woman?"

I scarcely heard him—I was aware that other figures were arriving on the scene—villagers, farm workers. They were advancing on the flames, beating at them, with spades and brooms.

"Look!—Other people have come to help. Perhaps we shall rescue her—there may be hope still."

Esmond released his hold on me. He said hurriedly, in a low voice,

"I must go, Katy. There is nothing I can do, and with these people here, it is best that I should leave." He called to Carrie who was standing nearby, staring in horrified bewilderment at the scene before her. "Take care of your mistress," I heard him say and then he disappeared into the shadows.

I scarcely noticed his departure. My attention was on the fire. Some buckets had been found; a line of helpers formed between the burning cottage and the well. I flung myself into action. Carrie, who had tied up the horses came back to stand beside me and help. Slowly and surely, the flames were extinguished and soon there remained only black smoke and the smell of charred timbers.

I could not bring myself to watch Josh and another man clamber among the fallen beams and debris in search of Zena.

They found nothing. No person, no dog, or cat and I was weak at the knees with relief. Zena had escaped and must be sheltering somewhere. But where? There was no other house for miles. Was it possible she had attempted the long walk to Tregedon?

Some of the villagers had begun to drift away. I spoke to as many as I could and thanked them for all that they had done.

"But we have not found Mrs. Dawnay," I told people. "Please watch for any sign of her as you go home."

"Aye, us 'n do that, Missus," said one and then another voice spoke up.

"Why—there be her ol' cat. I seen it many a time afore when I be goin' down along—sittin' on the wall it'ud be. Hey Pussy! Puss—puss puss. Cat be safe enough anyway."

I swung around to see Yerko, with flattened ears and glaring yellow eyes crouched in the shelter of a smoke-blackened bush. I went quickly but quietly toward him, hand outstretched.

"Yerko! Why, Yerko, what are you doing here? Poor pussy, poor Yerko. Where is your mistress—and Nezer?"

As if he would answer me he mewed plaintively and reached his head toward my hand.

I said again,

"Where is she, Yerko?"

He stared at me with his yellow eyes, the great pupils glowing like miniature lanterns. Then he sprang up and darted away as if to hide.

I went after him calling,

"Yerko. Come back. Pussy—puss—puss."

He was gone into the darkness. I hesitated, for the ground beyond the garden was rough and uneven. And then I saw that he had stopped to stare around at me—I caught the gleam of his eyes and was about to go forward when I heard Jem say, far behind me,

"I'll help catch him for 'ee, Missus. Do I go around this ways he'll run toward 'ee for sure and then 'ee can get hold on him."

"Yes—"

He blundered off around some stunted bushes. I waited calling Yerko's name softly and coaxingly. I heard Jem cry out and then there was silence. For a moment I wondered if he had fallen over something. The long grass rustled and I sensed something come toward me. I looked for a sign of Yerko, but it was Jem who appeared out of the darkness. I couldn't see his face properly but there was something strange about the way he came and stood before me without speaking.

"What is it, Jem?"

249

He jerked his head backward.

"Ur be there—Ma'am. Ur and the ol' dog. They be lyin' in the grass—they'm both dead, I reckon."

I could only gape at him with open mouth.

"*Dead?* Where? Take me—quickly. Show me."

He led me back the way he had come and I stumbled through the wet tussocky grass after him. In the darkness I made out a clump of trees and something lying under them. With thumping heart I knelt down and found that it was Zena.

She lay still and cold, her head and hands covered by her black shawl. I could just make out the thin bony face. Her hand was stiff in mine and I felt, uselessly, for a pulse that no longer beat. I shivered and Jem whispered from behind me,

"Dog be here, Ma'am. Lyin' at her feet."

I turned my head and saw the bulk of Nezer's body outstretched on the grass and I wondered incredulously how he could have died at the same time as his mistress. Unless she had made sure that it should be so?

"Fetch Josh," I told Jem in a shaking voice. "We must take Mrs. Dawnay back to Tregedon."

When he had gone I wiped the tears from my cheeks and I said a prayer for Zena. Her last words to me had been "God go with you" and now I repeated those words. "God go with you, Zena."

I looked back at the smoking ruins of the cottage. I thought how Bryce had once told me that when a gypsy was ill he or she was taken outside to die, and how after the death, all the belongings of the deceased would be thrown away or burned. Sometimes the gypsy wagon was burned too. Had Zena at the last followed the tradition of her race and knowing she was to die, gone into the open, leaving her cottage and possessions to burn to the ground? We should never know the truth, but I felt that this was what had happened.

A few days later she was buried in Tregedon churchyard. She had died from natural causes and so was laid in her husband's grave. The day after we brought her back to Tregedon I sent a message to Mr. Sedlescombe asking him to contact Bryce as soon as possible and tell him of Mrs. Dawnay's death. To save my face I told the lawyer I was not certain of my husband's present whereabouts and hoped that he perhaps had received more recent news. But Mr. Sedlescombe wrote back that he had not heard himself from Bryce for some time and understood that he had left South America, where he had been living.

A week went by, two weeks. I thought often of Esmond's visit and the things he had said to me. Was it possible he still loved me? No, I must not think of such things. I was sure he loved Amy. It was just that at the moment things had gone wrong for them. I was aware of a sense of vague disappointment in Esmond, as if in some way he had failed me. I did not like the way he had hurried away the night of Zena's death, yet I understood his wish not to become involved in the tragedy. Zena had been no concern of his.

I had brought Yerko back to live with me, as Zena had asked me to do. He seemed to settle down well enough, but at first I did not allow him to roam far on his own.

One evening in early December I went out to the courtyard to make sure he had not gone far. At my call he came running toward me, pantherlike with his sleek black coat and shining yellow eyes and when I picked him up, he submitted reluctantly to my caress. Turning to go back into the house I heard a step on the cobbles behind me and glancing over my shoulder saw the figure of a man in a bulky greatcoat and tall hat standing in the shadows.

My heart thumped against my ribs. I called uncertainly,

"Who is it? Who is there?"

I knew, even before he moved toward me, that the man was Bryce.

# 19

A SHIVER ran through me. I spoke the first words that came into my head.

"Where have you come from? I—I did not expect that you would have heard as yet from Mr. Sedlescombe."

Frowning down at me he seemed a tall and intimidating figure. I could not see the expression in his eyes for the brim of his beaver hat cast a shadow over his face.

"Sedlescombe? I have not heard from him for over a month."

My hold tightened on Yerko and he gave a mew of protest.

"Then you do not know? About—Zena?"

"You are talking in riddles." His voice sharpened. "What should I know?"

I could not think how to tell him. Looking up at him I saw that his face was gaunt and tired, his clothes creased and travel worn. He must have traveled in a hurry from a long distance. I said slowly, choosing my words with care,

"Zena is—I am sorry, Bryce, indeed I am sorry to tell you this, but your grandmother is dead. She died two weeks ago." He stared at me in such stunned surprise that I hurried on, in an attempt to give him time in which to recover.

"Mr. Sedlescombe sent the news to you, but he thought you might have already left the address to which he wrote. We did not know when you would come home." I paused. "She is buried in Tregedon churchyard with your grandfather."

He made no answer and I stood silent before him, holding Yerko in my arms, the cold night wind blowing about us. I thought how

252

often I had dreaded the idea of Bryce's return, how I imagined my heart would be filled with fear and hate at the sight of him. Now he was here there were no such emotions, only a feeling of sadness at his evident shock and grief.

After a pause he said,

"I am grateful to you, Kate. For—for attending to everything. What happened? Was she ill for long?"

"No—I—she was—" I turned, with the cat in my arms. "Let us go into the house. I will tell you of it there."

He followed me into the house and Carrie appeared surprised and smiling, bobbing a welcome to him and after her, Minna and Jem, staring shyly. No sooner had Bryce taken off his coat and Minna gone scurrying away to prepare supper for him than Mrs. Porritt arrived panting on the scene followed by Josh and there were further cries of greeting and welcome. At last Mrs. Porritt went bustling off to the kitchen, affirming that only *she* could make a meal fit for her master.

When she had gone and Josh with her, Bryce turned to me and said,

"Before you tell me of Zena—how is my son? Does he do well?"

"Very well. He crawls everywhere and is almost able to stand. Soon he will be walking. And he is such a contented happy little boy. Let me show him to you before anything else."

Together we went up the stairs, and I thought in amazement that we might have been any happily married couple reunited after an absence. But things were not as they seemed, as well I knew. Too many resolved problems ran below the surface of our lives.

I watched Bryce's face when he bent over the cot in which Luke slept. It revealed little, the impassive mask was back. Yet as he put out a finger to the flushed rose-leaf cheek on the pillow I sensed the tenderness in the gesture. And strangely, Luke, who always slept so soundly, woke unexpectedly and stared up at him out of momentarily unfocused blue eyes. The drowsiness fell away from him and suddenly he smiled and at the impact of that smile, so innocent and sweet, I heard Bryce catch his breath. Luke's waving fingers clutched at his hand and for a moment father and son were linked in an immemorial affection.

Bryce said slowly,

"I did not know he would be so beautiful. Or so much a person. I shall always be grateful to you for Luke."

He went away to wash and refresh himself and for a few moments I nursed Luke and gave him a drink of water and then I put him in his cot and went downstairs. Bryce was sitting by the brightly burning fire, and taking a chair opposite to him I began to relate the sad details of Zena's death.

When I had finished, with scarcely an interruption, he leaned forward, his hands linked between his knees. For a long moment he stared into the flames then said, with a sigh,

"I wish I had seen her before she died. She was ever my best friend, the closest to me. More so than my father, who, as I have told you before, was little at home with me after my mother died." He frowned, "It is strange. Some weeks ago—it must have been when Zena was gravely ill and perhaps knew that she was not going to get better, I had a sudden urge to return home. I quickly settled my affairs and booked a passage on the first ship sailing back to England. If it had not been for the terrible storms we encountered at sea, I might have been back in time to be with her at the end."

Something in his voice, the note of deep regret, moved me to compassion. On impulse I put a hand out and touched his arm,

"It is sad. But perhaps she wanted to die alone."

He turned his head to look at me and for a moment there was silence between us. Then he said slowly,

"Perhaps," and after a further pause added, "You say there is nothing left of the cottage—of Zena's possessions?"

"Nothing. There is only a ruin."

"I will ride over and see it tomorrow."

His dark gaze returned to the fire, and as I stole a glance at him I found it hard to believe that this grave thoughtful man was the same one as the violent being who had used me so cruelly the last time we had been together. Had he changed, or was it the fact of Zena's death that had sobered him?

254

Mrs. Porritt had excelled herself and produced an appetizing and ample meal which Bryce did full justice to. Afterward I gave him an account of my stewardship and answered his many questions as to matters that had occurred while he was absent.

"I had not expected you to do so well," he said finally. He glanced away from me before adding stiffly, "We parted in unhappy circumstances. Is it too much to hope that you have forgiven me?"

My voice was abrupt as his when after a moment, I said,

"There were faults on both sides."

He gave me a quick glance.

"Perhaps so. And—and there is Luke."

"Yes, there is Luke." I stood up, suddenly restless. A strange tension filled me.

Bryce rose and followed me to the door.

"One moment, Kate. You had better make your mind up on this. Now I am home to stay." He stared down at me, his light eyes, narrowed yet expressionless. "Do you intend to be wife to me?"

I felt the fear of him rush back to me. He was quiet enough in manner but there was an implacability about him that daunted me. I wanted to run away but there was nowhere to run to. Swallowing on a dry throat to steady my voice I said coldly,

"It seems I have no choice. I am married to you and I cannot leave you. If I do, you threaten me with the loss of my son. So I must submit to you as many another woman has done to her husband."

He gave a sharp ejaculation.

"Submit! You are not an innocent child, Kate. You are a woman. You have known a man, in love," and his voice dropped a note, "and in lust. You have borne a child. Do not play the affronted virgin with me. I warn you—I lived here with you like a monk for months, but there is to be no more of that. If you refuse me, I shall take a mistress. Better men than I have done that—and fathered bastard children into the bargain."

I flung around on him.

"How dare you say such things to me! To talk of bastard children —with your son lying asleep upstairs. You are incredible."

255

His eyes glittered.

"Then it is agreed. Go to bed now. I will come to you later."

I could not speak for the rage and dread that choked me. I found myself shaking from head to foot. My fingers fumbled for the latch, but he was at the door to hold it open for me to pass through. With downbent head I brushed past him and hurried away up the stairs.

That night we shared the big four-poster bed. He took me, not in furious passion, as before, nor tenderly, as on that first time, but coldly, deliberately, almost indifferently. My own lack of response seemed not to matter to him, it was the act of imposing his will on mine that was important. Afterward, he slept beside me, a strangely broken sleep of out-flung arms and muttered words. Lying awake, listening to the crash of the waves on the rocks below the house, I wondered at such restlessness for he had seemed weary enough earlier on. For once I was glad to hear the booming voice of the sea. Tonight, of all times, I could not have borne to hear that other sound, the treacherous whisper that ever seemed to echo my name in warning.

The pearl-colored streaks of dawn were showing in the winter sky before I slept. And when I woke Bryce was gone from my side.

We settled down into a state of neutrality. I was a wife in letter, if not in spirit. I told myself I hated him, and yet that wasn't true. With his return Tregedon was changed. There was a life and bustle which had been lacking before. Bryce's vitality and strength, the impact of his personality, seemed to animate the rest of the household so that its inmates moved a little quicker, spoke more energetically, even smiled more often. If he had gone away again we should have missed him.

He loved Luke and Luke loved him. He would stretch out his arms toward his father, bubble with laughter when he was swung up into the air, and murmur indistinguishable words which might or might not have been "Pa Pa."

Bryce was out long days on the farm or at the mine. I knew from what he had told me that the lode deposits were found at low altitude and the Tregedon mine was sunk well over 1,200 feet underground. One day Bryce was very late returning home and when he finally arrived I could see from his tired and grimy face that there had been trouble of some kind.

"One of the pumps is broken," he said in answer to my questions, and then added "The watery mud has to be elevated up a wooden trough and this can't be done. I have been trying all day to repair it, with help from some of the men."

"I am sorry. It must be worrying for you."

He gave something between a sigh and a yawn.

"Yes. We shall fix it in the end, I suppose. But meanwhile it is holding everything up."

He went to clean himself, and I told Carrie to bring in the supper which had been keeping hot. As I served him and served myself also, he glanced across the table.

"You waited to eat with me."

"Yes. I—I kept thinking you would soon be home."

"That was kind." He smiled and the shadow of weariness lifted from his face. "I like to see you sitting there, Kate, at the head of my table."

Hesitantly, I smiled back and for a moment we were in harmony, and then I said with a briskness I was far from feeling,

"Will you take some more squab pie?"

———◆———

The week before Christmas Bryce drove home in a smart little barouche, a handsome chestnut horse between the shafts.

"It is for you, Kate," he said. "Your Christmas present, if you like. That old cart is scarcely fit for you to drive—Josh and Mrs. Porritt can have the use of it—for going to market at Wadebridge and so on and Brownie will be handy about the farm."

I was overwhelmed, and stammered my thanks which he dismissed with a shrug saying,

"Things are improving for us, Kate. The mine is flourishing and my business ventures abroad have turned out successfully."

"I am glad," I said.

"The horse is called Rufus. Would you care to take the reins and try him out along the road?"

"Oh, yes. Yes, I would."

Scarcely waiting for his hand to assist me I jumped into the driving seat and untied the reins.

"I will not take him far," I called over my shoulder as the horse swung around and we set off down the lane.

I was not sure whether Bryce had intended to accompany me, but I spent an enjoyable half hour trotting along the road to Tregedon, turning around before we reached the village, and talking to Rufus all the time, watching his ears flick forward and back as he listened to the sound of my voice.

There was no sign of Bryce when I returned to the courtyard, but Jem appeared and duly admired the horse and the equipage before leading Rufus away to the stables. I turned to go into the house and at that moment Bryce came around the corner from the barn. He saw me, and his face, already frowning, darkened still further. I thought he must be angry because I had driven off without him and I started to say, feeling somewhat guilty after his generous gesture,

"I am sorry I did not wait. I was so eager to try the horse out—" My voice broke off at the cold fury in his glance.

He said stiffly,

"You did not tell me you were in the habit of entertaining Esmond during my absence."

I stared at him, taken aback by his sudden accusation.

"I have never entertained Esmond," I protested and then I stopped, remembering that November day when he had called. The evening the cottage burned down.

"You are not liar enough to deny that Esmond was here? That he was here the night that Zena died. He even went with you to the fire. Josh told me of this."

I bit my lip.

"Yes—but it was once only he visited Tregedon. On his own, that is."

"And you expect me to believe that?"

I shrugged.

"You may do as you please. It is the truth."

His mouth twisted bitterly.

"Perhaps it is true he came here the one time, but how many times did you meet him somewhere away from Tregedon? Some secret trysting place where there was no chance of anyone seeing you. Tell me that?"

I turned away from him.

"I refuse to answer your jealous accusations. They are entirely unfounded."

He gripped me by the shoulder.

*"Why* did Esmond come here—alone? That is what I wish to know. Why should he ride out to see you, to speak with you."

"He—they—my father and stepmother were anxious for me. The weather had been stormy—I had not visited Penvarrion—so Esmond came to see how I was. And then—he—we saw the fire from the burning cottage, and we rode over—all of us—the Porritts and Jem too—to try and put it out."

"Esmond did not stay to help, from all accounts," Bryce said sardonically.

I did not answer him. I felt his hand move along my shoulder and catch on the collar of my dress. He said with a sharp ejaculation,

"What is this chain you wear?" I felt his fingers lift it, heard him say, "A damn curious looking object. Did Esmond give it to you?"

I snatched the chain from his hand and held the amulet against my throat, as if the spell of it would guard me from his anger.

"Your grandmother—it was a gift from Zena."

He stared hard at me, the glinting light eyes narrowed in scrutiny of my face.

"Yes. It is possible. I have no more to say." He half-turned and then glanced back at me. "Except that you will not be visiting Penvarrion over Christmas. I have accepted an invitation from my uncle at Truro to stay with him and my aunt. Tell Carrie she is to come with us—to see after Luke."

His offhanded arrangements left me in trembling rage. I could not bear to think of my father's disappointment at not seeing Luke and myself at Christmastime. Had Bryce truly intended all along to go to Truro or was it a last-minute decision made as a form of punishment for me, to make sure that Esmond and I did not encounter one another? I did not know. I only knew that I was once more in complete disagreement with him.

Yet, surprisingly, the week spent at Truro over Christmas was more pleasant than I had anticipated. Mr. and Mrs. Dawnay were welcoming and kind, and made much of Luke. Cecilia, Bryce's pretty cousin, now married, was there, and a gathering of relatives and friends came and went to the big comfortable house in Pydah Street. I had not realized how lonely and isolated I had been at Tregedon during the past months until I found myself in such warm and friendly company.

The night before we came away we attended a ball at the Assembly Rooms. I wore a dress of *eau de Nil* satin trimmed with ninon drapes of the same color. Carrie dressed my dark hair in ringlets high upon my head, held there with a diamond studded comb that had belonged to my mother. I knew I looked well. I did not need Bryce's intent glance upon me or Mr. Dawnay's courtly compliments or the heads which turned to look after me to assure me of that.

As we took the floor in a square dance I was reminded of that other night I had danced here. I had danced with Esmond and been happy and with the odious Mr. Rossiter and been miserable. And it was here I had encountered Bryce and I had been surprisingly pleased to meet him again.

Now I was married to him. We danced up and down, now meeting, now parting, our hands touching briefly before we separated once more.

Our lives were like this dance, I thought. Meetings and partings, gestures that meant little, at times coming together yet ever separate in ourselves.

He was near Cecilia now, his grave dark face softened in a smile, as taking her hand he twirled her around. Cecilia smiled back and I thought that, although she was married now to her good-looking young doctor, once she had been a little in love with Bryce. Perhaps he should have married her in the first place? They were better suited to one another than Bryce and I could ever be.

I had to admit he was still the most impressive-looking man in the room with his height and his somber looks and the air of something vital and strong held in leash. When, suddenly, as if aware of my gaze upon him he turned his head to meet my eyes, I glanced quickly away lest he read the thoughts there.

Later we danced together. Not in a waltz, as once before, but in the mazurka. We scarcely spoke throughout the dance and yet I was very aware of Bryce, of his arm about my waist, his breath on my cheek when once he bent his head to make a brief apology for a mistaken step. I was aware of him as a *man,* and I thought how strange it was that one could be at utter variance with someone and yet be drawn to him even against one's will.

Perhaps it was the effect of the music and the wine, the stimulation of lively company and the escape from the past months of loneliness and of Zena's tragic death. But afterward when Bryce came to me in the softly lit guest bedroom at the Dawnay home, I felt, for the first time since that night of Midsummer two years ago, the stirrings of response toward him. I struggled against it, telling myself that I did not love him, nor did he love me, that this was only part of the strange magnetism that he had always held for me. His lips were against my throat, I heard him murmur something and for a moment I thought I heard the words "love" and "dearest" before I succumbed to the sensation of delight that overwhelmed me as I lay close within his arms.

Afterward we were assuaged. Bryce fell asleep quickly and peaceably. For a short time I lay awake thinking that in two days' time it would be New Year. Perhaps for us, too, it would be a new beginning? And then I, too, slept.

The first thing I planned to do upon my return to Tregedon was to visit my father. I had not seen him for several weeks and I was anxious about him. Being unable to write letters, the only news I had of him was from my stepmother and she was an unsatisfactory correspondent. So a few days after New Year I made arrangements to ride over to Penvarrion. When I told Bryce of this he frowned and said,

"Why do you not take the barouche? I bought it for your use."

"Sorrel had had little exercise this past week and I thought Rufus would be better for a rest after the long drive from Truro. Besides, it will be quicker to ride over the fields than go by the road."

"I should prefer that you use the barouche. It will do Rufus no harm. You can then take Luke with you, if you so wish."

I hesitated.

"Luke is tired after his visit to Truro and all the excitement of Christmas. He was fractious yesterday and will be better to stay quietly at home with Carrie."

"Then go by yourself but go by road. I will harness Rufus and have him ready for you."

I made no further demur and when eventually I drove away in the smart new equipage I was rather pleased than otherwise to show off Bryce's present to my stepmother.

The day was unexpectedly fine and mild for January and for once there was little wind. I did not force Rufus's pace but allowed him to take his time, alternately walking and trotting him along the road to Penvarrion. The stable clock was striking midday as we came down the drive, and it was with something of a flourish that I took him smartly up the approach to the house. Barney appeared quickly from the stables and was full of admiration for both horse and carriage. Glancing up, I saw my stepmother standing in the bay window gazing out at us, and I lifted my hand in a wave of greeting before leaving Barney to lead Rufus away.

"Well, Katherine, you are quite a stranger," was her cool greeting to me when Bertha showed me into the drawing room.

"Yes, I am sorry. I would have come before, but as I wrote and told you, we went to Bryce's uncle and aunt at Truro for the week of Christmas. How are you, Stepmother? And—my father? I hope he is well."

"As well as we can expect, in the circumstances." She sighed. "He is a great care."

"Poor Papa." I added, "Is Amy well?"

"Yes, she is herself again, I am pleased to say. But—she has a worrying time at present. Esmond's affairs are far from settled." She paused, biting her lip, and as I glanced at her I realized that she was changed. Two small vertical lines marred the formally smooth brow, her mouth had a pinched look, she looked every day of her age. I was unexpectedly sorry for her knowing that my father, a sick man,

262

must be a heavy responsibility, and in addition there was Amy and Esmond with their financial difficulties. But my sympathy was short-lived, for as her sharp glance met mine she said abruptly,

"So Bryce has returned to you. I hear he has improved his prospects abroad. Your new carriage is evidence of that."

"I think he has prospered," I answered calmly.

She gave me a long considering look.

"If he had not, it would be of little consequence. Is it not this year you come into your inheritance?"

I was surprised by the directness of her remark.

"Yes, I shall be twenty-one in July."

"You are fortunate. You could afford to marry a poor man. Not like—" she broke off and her brown eyes closed but not before I had caught the look in them, an expression so strange that I was taken aback. I realized afresh her envy and dislike of me. Yet I had done her no harm and had made no objection to the fact that she had full use of the Trust monies for her own and Amy's benefit.

I could not bear to be in her presence when she liked me so little. I turned away saying,

"I will go and see Papa."

My father was much the same. Gentle, forgetful, loving. He seemed unaware that Christmas had come and gone. I told him of Bryce's return and promised that he would accompany me on my next visit.

When I returned downstairs Amy was waiting to greet me. She was wearing a green-velvet dress trimmed with fur which set off her red-gold hair and green eyes. She kissed me in friendly enough fashion and said,

"How nice to see you, Kate. I was feeling so dull. Esmond has gone to London again. I hear that Bryce is home—why did he not come with you today? Did you enjoy your Christmas at Truro?"

She prattled on, scarcely waiting for an answer. She looked well and pretty, but her eyes had a restless darting look.

"Mama says you drove here in a smart new carriage." She laughed prettily. "Well, anything would be better than that old pony cart. I

263

would have *died* to have driven around in such a countrified-looking thing."

"But we are country people," I said gently. "After all Tregedon is a farm."

She shrugged.

"I suppose so. And it cannot be much duller there than it is here, with Esmond away so often and very little money for doing anything that is enjoyable. I never thought it would be like this. I imagined myself, as Lady Borleigh, entertaining my friends and giving parties and dinners and balls." She shook her head. "Why does life never turn out the way one wants it to?"

"That is something I have often wondered myself," I said, wryly.

Luncheon was served late for my stepmother had gone for one of her rare walks in the garden.

"I felt I needed some fresh air," she explained when at last she put in an appearance. "I spend so much time indoors with your father," she added with a meaningful glance in my direction.

Perhaps she was tired, for she contributed little to the conversation between myself and Amy, and when the meal was over she said,

"I am going to rest for a while, so I will say good-by to you now, Katherine."

"Good-by, Stepmama. If Papa is not asleep, I will sit with him again before leaving for home."

"Yes, do that. He seems to appreciate your visits."

It was shortly after two o'clock when I said good-by to Amy who had come to the front steps to see me off and to duly admire Rufus and the new barouche, which Barney had brought from the stables.

Rufus, refreshed after his rest, set off at a good pace and we soon left Penvarrion behind and were on the road to Tregedon.

We must have driven more than halfway home when Rufus, after walking decorously for a mile or two, quickened his pace and took the last hill at a gallop. We topped the rise and I tugged at the reins to check him so that he would walk down the slope on the other side. But instead of slowing at my pull he continued on at a headlong pace, the barouche rocking unsteadily from side to side as it careered downhill.

Desperately I heaved at the reins but there seemed no tautness in them. And then, suddenly, without warning, one of the traces snapped. The shaft of the vehicle tilted dangerously and Rufus, freed on one side and startled by the imbalance of the weight, plunged and reared before galloping on faster than ever.

The barouche was now out of control and the horse, maddened with fear, kicked and dragged at the reins in his efforts to pull away. Suddenly he broke free of the other trace and raced away down the hill while the carriage, rattling on for a few seconds under its own momentum, careered across the road rocking and rolling at a dangerous angle. I had remained, half-crouched, half-standing, holding on to the side of the seat with both hands, but some warning of the peril ahead galvanized me into action and as the barouche crashed forward into the high bank ahead I jumped clear of it and fell headlong into the ditch at the side of the road, and then I remembered no more.

# 20

I DO NOT know how long I lay unconscious on the roadside. When I came to it was to find someone bending over me, a dimly recognized voice saying,

"Mrs. Dawnay—Katherine, my dear child—what is this? No, do not try to get up for a moment. Lean against me. There are no bones broken—I have made sure of that."

It was Dr. Fullbright. I gazed dizzily up at him and gave a sigh of thankfulness that my rescuer was someone so kindly and so familiar. With a hand against my bruised forehead I said shakily,

"I do not know what happened. I was driving down the lane and —and Rufus seemed to slip and he broke free of the harness. The carriage went over—that is all I remember."

"My groom has gone after the horse—we passed him along the road. I was coming from St. Merryn where I had been to call upon a patient. Can you stand if I help you? That's better. You may feel a little giddiness, but it will pass. Ah, here comes Mundy with your horse. We will tie him up to the back of my gig and take him back with you to Tregedon. Your barouche will have to be seen to later."

With the assistance of the groom Dr. Fullbright lifted me up into the gig while Mundy took the reins. The kindly doctor kept an arm about me to stop me from falling over for I felt unaccountably dizzy, and in a little while we arrived back at Tregedon.

Bryce was out, but Mrs. Porritt came hurrying to help me down and into the house.

"See your mistress into bed," Dr. Fullbright commanded, "and then I will come up and make a thorough examination of her before

I leave. You will have to rest quietly for a day or two," he added, with a look in my direction.

When he had gone, pronouncing me free from any serious injury and leaving a sleeping draught and some ointment for my cuts and bruises, I was glad to rest. I woke to find the room darkened by the drawn curtains, and lay for a few moments trying to recollect what had happened. It seemed to be extraordinary that so dangerous a mishap should have occurred while driving the new barouche.

The door opened and Bryce came into the room. Approaching the bedside he said quietly,

"You are awake. I looked in earlier but did not wish to disturb you. Mrs. Porritt warned me the doctor had said you must rest. She does not seem to know what happened—only that you met with an accident driving Rufus, and that Dr. Fullbright brought you back here."

"Yes. The—the barouche overturned—Rufus broke free of it." I tried to explain as best I could what had happened.

Bryce stared somberly down at me.

"You might have been killed." He shook his head. "I cannot understand how the accident came about. The harness could not have been properly secured. I will question Jem about it at once."

I could not see his face properly in the dimness of the room.

"But was it not you who put Rufus between the traces? I thought you went to do so." I sensed rather than saw him frown.

"Did I? Yes, I had the handling of him, but Jem was there, he saw after him too. There must have been some carelessness on his part." He released my hand and stood up. "I will go and speak with him and we must see about rescuing the broken barouche. Try and sleep again, Kate."

"Yes. Thank you, Bryce."

But when he had gone I did not sleep again. Instead I lay puzzling over his words. Someone had certainly been careless, but was it Jem?

Or Bryce? I had no way of knowing. But one thing I was certain of. I had had a narrow escape from what could have been a very dangerous accident.

In a few days I was up and about again. The incident faded from

267

my mind. Bryce did not mention it again, and I did not question him further. I was busy with various matters, and I did not go driving again for the barouche was badly broken and had to be repaired. I had almost forgotten the mishap until one day I took Luke to visit the stables. There was nothing he loved more than to stroke Brownie's patient head or gaze timidly but admiringly at Caspar or, laying his tiny hand on mine, allow Sorrel to gently nuzzle a slice of carrot from the palm of it.

As we made our tour, Jem came in sight, carrying a bucket in either hand. He put one to the ground and touched his forehead. Luke waved in answer and called out some unintelligible words of greeting for Jem was a great favorite of his.

Jem came over to us.

"Reckon he'll be a proper horseman when he do grow big, Ma'am," he said.

"I hope so. He loves horses best of all and is not a scrap afraid. Except perhaps of Caspar," I added with a smile, for tall Caspar was tossing his black head above the stable door and knocking his hoof against the wood, which behavior somewhat awed small Luke.

"Ah, well, Caspar be a bit mettlesome. Rufus now, he's a young 'un but quiet like." Jem gave me a sideways glance. "That were a nasty accident you had along o' him, though, Ma'am. You was lucky not to have been worse hurt, seein' as 'ow the trace were snapped right off."

I stared at him.

"Was that what happened? But did you not notice some sign of weakness when you harnessed the horse up that day?"

He shook his head.

"The Master seen after him, not me, Ma'am. 'Tis a mystery to me how it come about, same as it would be to the Master for he must a' found, as I did arterwards, that the trace be cut plain through."

*"Cut?"* I said slowly. "You mean—cut with an instrument—a knife or something?"

He shrugged.

"Somethin' like that— Somethin' with a terrible sharp edge for it cut through new leather."

I could only stare in bewilderment.

"But how could it—I mean—it must have been tampered with."

A slow flush came up under his brown skin, he looked away almost sullenly.

"I doan't know nothin' about that. 'Tis not anything of my doin', I give 'ee my word, Ma'am. And Master, he told me not to speak on it in case it frittened 'ee."

"I understand, Jem. I should not have questioned you. Do not worry. It is over and done with. But be sure to take extra care in future."

"Aye, Ma'am. You may be sure o' that. We doan't want no more such like accidents." He touched his forehead again and picking up the buckets, walked slowly away.

Luke was jumping up and down in his impatience and so I took his hand and led him away to Sorrel's box. I resolved not to think any more about the accident. The trace must have been faulty in the first place, I told myself, and where it had snapped off it had looked as if it were cut. Because *why* would anyone cut the trace. And whom?

I did not speak of the matter to Bryce for I did not want to get Jem into trouble. As I had told the boy, it was over and done with.

But in some way I was frightened.

———◆———

I had not seen Esmond since the night of Zena's death, and then an invitation came for us to go to dinner at Penvarrion as it was my father's birthday. It was arranged that we should stay the night there and return the afternoon of the next day. Bryce, as usual, was reluctant to accompany me, but he had no alternative but to accept the invitation for he had been but once to visit my father since his return to England.

Carrie accompanied us so as to see after Luke. To travel, I wore a wool tartan jacket in rich dark green with a short basque over a plain dress of the same color. The jacket had wide turned-back cuffs, and with it I wore a tiny tartan bonnet trimmed with feathers. Since Bryce had been home he had been generous to me and insisted that I should buy some new clothes for I had had little since my limited

269

trousseau. Now, as he helped me into the barouche he said, with a swift glance,

"You look well, Kate. Green becomes you. It deepens the color of your eyes."

"Thank you. Some people say the shade is unlucky, but I have never found it so."

We drove away, Luke sitting upon my knee, while Jem followed in the pony cart with Carrie and the luggage. It was a bright April day and the steep banks were thick with primroses, the hedgerows flushed with the first green of spring.

I was surprised by my stepmother's unexpected gesture of hospitality toward us. Hitherto she had not been particularly welcoming, and I always felt that my presence was a duty rather than a pleasure to her. But I was so happy to be visiting my old home and to be seeing my father for more than a few hours that I was determined to be as agreeable as possible to everyone—in particular, to my stepmother.

She must have been of the same resolution, for I marveled at the warmth of her greeting, and if her smile was not reflected in the hooded watchful eyes, that was not unexpected.

Amy seemed happy too and was almost her old effervescent self as she kissed me and whispered,

"I have such news for you. Wait until later."

My father had been brought downstairs, and frail but smiling was waiting in the drawing room to embrace me. Altogether, it was the most pleasant occasion at Penvarrion that I could remember for a very long time.

Only Esmond was out of spirits. His handsome face wore an introspective look, he frowned from time to time, and the high color of his cheeks seemed unhealthily bright.

When he took my hand in his for a moment his gaze held mine and then he glanced away, saying,

"Are you well, Katy? You look—very beautiful."

I said stiffly, aware of Amy standing nearby,

"Thank you—I am well," and turned abruptly away.

Luke was made much of, even by my stepmother, who usually begrudged him any caress. My father doted on his little grandson and did not want Luke to leave his side. While everyone was occupied Amy drew me into the wide bay window and said in a conspiratorial voice,

"You are the first to know, after Esmond and Mama. I am to bear a child again."

"Oh, Amy." I touched her hand. "I am very happy for you. And for Esmond. When is the baby due?"

"In August sometime. If—if all goes well." Her small face shadowed. "I cannot help being afraid, although I am glad too. Esmond wants a son so much. Pray for me, Kate. That this time I shall bear a healthy child."

"I am sure you will. Try not to worry, Amy. Everyone will take great care of you, especially your mother and Esmond."

"Yes." A frown puckered her smooth forehead. "Mama says it is important that I have a son, but I would dearly love a little girl. But I wish to please Esmond—he has been so strange to me at times. I expect it is all the anxiety he has lately over money you know."

I felt a pang of guilt remembering the things Esmond had said to me the night he had called at Tregedon. But I had not encouraged him that time. Indeed, I had reproached him. Yet still I could not feel at ease with Amy, and my voice was awkward as I said slowly,

"I am sorry."

Something in my tone caused her to turn her head and look at me, as if she had not seen me properly until now.

"Your affairs seem to prosper, Kate. Yet everyone thought Bryce to be a poor man."

"I do not know about that. He works hard enough."

She sighed.

"Esmond would work hard, too, if he could. But the mine is bankrupt. So Mama says. Esmond seldom talks to me of his business affairs. He says I would not understand." She hesitated, frowning again. "Sometimes I worry that he may take to gambling as his father did."

"I am sure he would not do that."

"He is always going to London. I do not know what occupies him

271

there. Well, it is no use my fretting. He would not listen to me whatever I said. Mama says I am not to worry, that everything will come right for us, and so I shall enjoy myself while I can." Her face brightened, "Do you know that twenty of us will sit down to dinner tonight? What is the color of the dress you plan to wear?"

"It is pale green."

"Green again? I can see you are not in the least superstitious."

"No, that is only foolish talk," I answered firmly as we moved back to join the others.

As Amy had said, we were twenty to dinner. The shining mahogany table in the dining room was resplendent with heavy silver and sparkling glass. A centerpiece of silver was filled with delicate blue iris, their sweet scent mingling with that of early narcissus. Laura and Paul were there, with Lady Phoebe, and all three were staying the night, as we were. The Reverend Charles Barlow and his sister were present as well as Dr. Clarkson and several other guests. It was like old times, with Borlase presiding majestically over us all. Only one thing was different. Dear Papa, who sat at the head of the table, seemed isolated in the cloudy vagueness that now dwelt in him. He spoke little and if addressed by anyone, smiled and nodded dimly but made little answer. Luckily, I was on his right hand, and I endeavored to draw him into the conversation as much as I could without distressing him. He ate and drank very little and when we stood to toast him, he glanced around in bewilderment as if wondering to whom the address was being made. Then he caught my eye and smiled tremulously but was unable to make a reply.

It was so sad I could have wept, and for a moment I wondered at my stepmother's decision to hold this birthday dinner party that could mean so little to my unfortunate father. Then I reproached myself, thinking that perhaps she hoped he might have been better able to comprehend things.

When the meal was over, and the gentlemen were left to their port, Borlase came and gently led my father away to bed, for it was obvious he was weary and past enjoying anyone's company.

At last it was time for the guests to depart, and after the local friends had gone Amy was the first to say good night and retire to bed, followed by Laura and Lady Phoebe. Esmond had gone with Paul to the smoking room. There was no sign of Bryce so I imagined he had joined them there. I was about to go upstairs myself when my stepmother, with a glance around as if to make sure the room was empty said,

"Katherine, sit down for a few moments. There is something I wish to say to you. It is about your father."

"About Papa?" I sat down in the chair she had indicated. "He—he seems well. I am sure he had enjoyed the splendid birthday party you arranged for him."

She answered gravely,

"He appears well enough, but the state of his health does not improve, and I am afraid that, from what Dr. Fullbright has told me, it is likely to deteriorate at any time in the future."

"But—but he seems no worse." I bit my lip in alarm. "I don't understand. Is it his—mental powers? He does seem at times a little more confused."

"The pressure on the brain is increasing, so Dr. Fullbright says. He called in a London specialist. Dr. Hellman has stated that at any time your father might be taken in a seizure. He thinks it unlikely he will live for another year."

A chill swept over me. I shivered in my thin silk dress.

"Oh, no! Poor dearest Papa. I cannot believe it. This man—this Dr. Hellman may be wrong—doctors cannot always be sure of such things."

"I agree." My stepmother's voice, calm and quiet, came to me as I sat cold and trembling before her. "We must indeed hope and pray that the diagnosis is incorrect. But it is my duty to prepare you, Katherine, for such an eventuality. You would reproach me if I left you in ignorance."

"Yes. Yes, of course. Thank you for—for telling me. It is right I should know." I stared down at my tightly clenched hands. "I can only pray for Papa."

"We must all do that. Perhaps you see now the reason for this birthday party—I wished us all to be together in case"—her voice

273

dropped to a knell-like note—"this time next year he should not be with us."

I sprang up abruptly.

"Oh, I do not want to think about that. It is too sad."

"I am afraid we have to face facts in this life. Heaven knows I have had enough sorrows of my own already, but I must prepare myself to bear more." She stood up, as composed as when she had sat down save for the faint puckering of lines on her white forehead. "Try not to distress yourself unduly. I will leave you now, Katherine. Good night, my dear." Her cheek, smooth and cool as a snowflake, touched my own, and she was gone from the room.

I walked slowly over to the fire and stood holding my shaking hands to the warmth of the flames, while all that my stepmother told me passed again through my mind. In a way I wished she had not told me. It was cowardly perhaps, but I would have liked to have gone on thinking of Papa being here indefinitely. Now the shadow of the coming loss would be with me all the time. But that was selfish. My stepmother had to bear the knowledge of his failing health, I must also. And yet—could she love him as I did, as I had always done?

I must have been standing there for longer than I realized. I heard someone enter the room and turning around saw Bryce coming toward me carrying a glass on a small silver tray.

He said gently,

"I have brought you a glass of wine. I understand you have heard upsetting news of your father. I am sorry, Kate. *Very* sorry. I know how greatly you care for him."

"Yes, thank you. I—it has been a shock." My voice broke off tremblingly.

"Drink this. It will steady your nerves. Perhaps things will turn out better than predicted. Doctors are not infallible."

"No, no, that is true." I was clutching at straws I knew. I sipped the wine which warmed me immediately.

"It has saddened your evening. You were happy. Unusually so."

"Yes. Stepmother was kinder to me—to us both. I wondered at it. Now I know the reason." I sighed from the depth of my being. "I

274

feel we can never be happy again at Penvarrion because of poor dear Papa. I am so sorry for him. Never to get better—only to grow worse and—and then die."

Bryce took the empty glass from my hand.

"It will do you no good, nor any good to your father to dwell on this. It would have been more considerate of your stepmother if she had not told you."

I shook my head quickly.

"No. No, I had to know. It is just selfish weakness to wish to be so shielded."

Bryce stared at me for a moment. He said abruptly, "It is time to go to bed, Kate. The wine will help you to sleep."

For a long time I lay awake. Bryce was awake for a time too. Once he put his hand on mine and said,

"Try and sleep."

"Yes, I will." I was grateful that this was the only gesture he had made toward me. Tonight I could not have borne his love making. I wanted to be left alone, to lie quietly with my sad thoughts until sleep should overtake me.

I woke suddenly, gasping and choking. I felt I could not breathe. Terrible griping pains seized me. I struggled to sit up and such a dreadful nausea overtook me that I could scarcely stagger to the basin behind the screen in the far corner of the room, where I hung retching, oblivious of everyone and everything until the spasm had passed.

When, at last, weak and trembling, I turned for support to a nearby chair I found Bryce's arm about me. He lowered me to the chair and leaned over me.

"For God's sake—Kate, what is the matter—what ails you?"

For a few moments I could not speak, only wipe my mouth and sweating forehead.

"I—I do not know. I woke suddenly—the most terrible pains. I have known nothing like it in my life before."

He chafed my fingers between his two hands.

"You must have eaten something that disagreed with you. Perhaps

275

something in the dinner. What was there? Oyster soup—fried sweet-breads? Guinea fowl?"

I stared up at him through water-filled eyes.

"You ate the same food—we all did. Is anyone else upset do you think?"

"We shall know sooner or later. Let me help you back to the bed."

I put a hand to my head against the chill of nausea that threatened once again.

"No—I will sit here for a few moments. I feel—I feel—" The knot of pain in my stomach gripped and tightened again. I was doubled up on the chair and then, when it passed the feeling of sickness came over me again. I gasped, "I am sorry—" and staggered from the chair back to the basin.

When this second attack was over Bryce carried me to the bed and laid me on it. I was almost too weak to speak but I managed to whisper,

"Fetch Carrie. I need Carrie—you cannot—"

The room seemed to recede from me—I was in a void of darkness. For a moment I felt as if I were dying. Then, after a time I heard Carrie's voice and felt her kind hands moving over me, changing my nightdress for a fresh one, wiping my hands and face with a moistened cloth.

Throughout that night the attacks continued. Carrie was there to help me, though from time to time I was aware of Bryce's presence. Gradually the spasms decreased in violence and toward dawn the miserable retching ceased and I fell into painful exhausted sleep.

When I woke my stepmother was in the room. She came to the bedside and leaned over me.

"My dear Katherine—what has happened to you? Bryce tells me you have been dreadfully ill all night through. Surely it cannot be anything you ate at dinner? You know Mrs. Hubbard is most particular over the food she prepares—she would never use anything but the freshest of lobsters for the patties."

I turned wearily on the pillow.

"No one else has suffered in this way?"

"No, my dear. And we all ate the same—at least as far as the

276

household is concerned. Whether anyone else has been upset we have yet to find out. Anyway," she added briskly, "Bryce has sent for your doctor—Dr. Laker, is it not? He will soon find the cause and, with it, the cure, for your little disorder."

"Little disorder" seemed a summary way of dismissing the ordeal I had gone through, the sensation at one moment that I was almost dying.

"Thank you," I answered feebly, and with an unexpectedly sharp glance in my direction followed by a reassuring smile, she left me.

When Dr. Laker came, he questioned me very carefully as to what I had eaten during the past twenty-four hours.

"I feel it must be something you ate for the symptoms are typical of food poisoning." He frowned. "But so far we have not tracked down the cause. And no one else has suffered such an attack, as far as we can ascertain. Mr. Dawnay has sent a messenger to enquire of the other guests who were present if any one of them has been similarly attacked." He turned to take something from his medical bag. "Meanwhile," he added, "I wish you to rest quietly in bed for another day or so and during that time take one of these powders three times a day before meals."

For two days I ate nothing whatsoever, for I could not keep any food down. I drank soda water or a little lemon barley, and as the powders took effect, I felt better and soon was able to take some thin gruel. I had never felt so weak and ill in my entire life. The surprising thing was that no one else who had attended the birthday dinner party suffered the same as myself.

So it was not the food at dinner, I thought, as I lay puzzling over the matter. Then what?

The wine? I remembered the queerly bitter taste of it and I questioned Bryce over this. Had he drunk wine from the same decanter? He shrugged, saying he would not know. The glass from which I had drunk had been handed to him by my stepmother.

My stepmother shrugged when asked a similar question. She could not remember, though she had an idea she had poured the glass from an almost empty decanter. Perhaps some dregs had been in the wine? These might have upset me.

It seemed unlikely. Dr. Laker had used the word poison. Dregs of wine were surely not in that category?

The word poison lingered in my mind. But then I dismissed it. I had been taken ill through an unlucky mishap. It could have happened to anyone.

It was almost a week before I went back to Tregedon. Bryce returned there to attend the mine and to the farm, but he drove over to fetch me from Penvarrion.

I had risen late that morning, having breakfasted in bed for the last time. Carrie was in the dressing room packing the luggage and Luke was with her—I could hear his chattering little voice and the sound of his laughter as he scrambled about Carrie's feet.

A tap came on the bedroom door and to my surprise my stepmother walked in.

"Good morning, Katherine. I hope that you are feeling fully recovered. I came to see if there was anything you needed?"

"Thank you, I am quite well again. And I think we have all that we require. But it is kind of you to come and enquire."

"It has been very unfortunate that you should be taken ill and unable to see much of your father. But you must come and see him again very soon. Come as often as you wish. Do not wait to be invited. After all, this is your old home."

I was too surprised by this turn of speech to answer, then after a moment I said,

"Thank you, Stepmother. You are very considerate. I shall be glad to visit Papa as frequently as possible. I am only sorry to have caused trouble to you and to other people on this visit."

She lifted a white hand in dismissal of my words.

"It is nothing. Do not concern yourself." Her voice sounded distrait. I glanced at her as she moved away from me toward the bed and the small table that stood beside it. Here she paused, and turned.

She moved from the bed to the dressing table and stared down at the cut glass and silver ornaments upon it. "I see that Carrie has done your packing for you. Be sure not to forget anything."

She turned to the window. There were two windows, only one of which was ajar. Between the windows and against the wall stood a mahogany chest upon which lay my velvet hat. As she came back from the window my stepmother paused beside the chest and to my surprise she picked up the hat and carefully examined it.

"What a pretty thing this is. And so becomes you, Katherine. Pray do put it on for me."

Somewhat bewildered, I obeyed her, and as I stood before the dressing table mirror adjusting the hat upon my hair she came up close behind me saying,

"Do not forget these new powders that Dr. Laker left yesterday. You will need them." She put the packet, which I had placed on the chest beside my hat, onto the dressing table, but as she did so, it seemed to slip from her hand and fall to the carpet.

I heard her give an exclamation.

"How clumsy I am. See what I have done. No, please do not stoop to pick them up—your giddiness might return. None have spilt fortunately. Keep them safe in your vanity bag or reticule, Katherine."

"Thank you, Stepmama. I will put them in here." I smiled at her as I took them from her and then I looked back to the glass to pin my hat more firmly on my hair. As I did so I caught sight of her reflection in the mirror.

Perhaps it was a trick of the light; a shadow cast by the curtains blowing in at the open window. But the expression on my stepmother's face was so strange that it could have been a stranger staring at me with such intensity and for a moment I felt fear mingle with my startlement.

Then it was gone. The curtain hung straight again, the sunlight shone into the room and when I turned around, my stepmother was smiling at me. She nodded approvingly.

"Very pretty. You must show yourself to your father. It will cheer him up to see you looking so charming."

I could scarcely say good-by to Papa without crying. All I could do was to promise that I would soon visit him again, and I was thankful that he seemed happy, although so frail.

Esmond was there to see us off, and I was conscious of Bryce's watchful glance as we said good-by to one another.

279

"I am sorry you have been so indisposed, Katy," Esmond said. "We have had little time to talk with one another."

"No. I have been a great nuisance to everyone."

He held my hand so tightly in his I could not pull it free.

"You can never be anything but a delight. To me, especially."

"Thank you." I gazed directly up at him. His face was dear and familiar as ever, and yet he was changed. He was no longer the Esmond I had loved. Or was it I who had changed? The faults of my nature, my impetuosity and reckless temper had trapped me in a prison from which there was no escape. And now I saw that Esmond, too, was his own victim. He was charming and kind but with a fateful self-indulgence, a weakness that caused him to drift with events. He did not want and would not take responsibility. He lived at Penvarrion off my father's charity. I did not condemn him for it. But I did not admire him either.

As I gently freed my hand from his clasp and turned away I knew that I had said good-by to the last of my youth.

# 21

I WAS NOT sorry to return to Tregedon. This was strange, for always Penvarrion had seemed home to me. But now it was otherwise. For the first time I began to feel that my life was there and I must make the most of it.

I looked at Bryce's dark impassive face and I felt that I was closer to him than to Esmond. We had been through so much together, shared both good and bad experiences. If the bad outweighed the good, still a bond had been forged between us. I could not fully understand my emotions, but I knew that at Tregedon I had to try and make my life with him.

Then, three days after my return, I was taken ill again.

I had all but recovered from the first violent attack, but was still taking the powders that Dr. Laker had left with me. That evening, before supper, I purposely went to my room for one of the last remaining powders and took it in a little water, as recommended by the doctor, for a faint indisposition still lingered with me.

I returned downstairs again, and succeeded in eating supper with reasonable appetite. The May evening was unexpectedly warm and pleasant. When the meal was over, with old Boris padding at my heels and Yerko, who had formed an amicable alliance with him, darting ahead among the sparse bushes and the few plants I had brought into reluctant bloom in an effort to make a garden, I walked slowly along the rough path thinking about my father and planning that I would visit him again soon.

Suddenly, without warning I was seized by the same terrible spasms of pain that had wracked me once before. For a moment I could only gasp, my hand against my side, and then, as another fierce convulsion doubled me up a dreadful nausea came over me and I fell onto my knees, retching desperately. I had no control over myself, an agony of pain had me in its grip and I could do nothing but struggle to throw off whatever evil bane caused it.

The worst of the attack receded but when I tried to rise to my feet to go indoors such a wave of giddiness swept over me that I almost fainted. I subsided onto the grass to half-sit, half-lie in the evening dusk, waiting until I had strength to return to the house.

Boris who had hovered uneasily about me, whined and then, gave his baying howl. I whispered his name, but he lifted his gray muzzle and bayed again and after a few moments I heard footsteps on the path and Bryce's voice calling,

"Boris? Here, boy. What is it—what is the—?" His voice broke off. "*Kate!* My God, you are ill again. My poor girl—my poor Kate." His arms came about me and I felt him lift me from the ground and carry me into the house, calling out for Mrs. Porritt and for Carrie as he did so.

I was barely conscious of what was happening, only of being laid on the bed, of someone bringing a basin to my hand as once more the vile and wracking sickness overcame me.

It was the night of my father's birthday party all over again. Only this time the pains were even more agonizing, the nausea more grievous. I had again the sensation of dying, of everything receding into blackness. Only Bryce's voice, constantly repeating my name, the strong clasp of his hands on mine seemed to chain me to life. I did not want him beside me, forcing me into painful awareness. His presence frightened me, I wanted him to leave me alone. I tried to protest, saying through parched and burning lips, "No. No. Go away. Go—away."

As through a cloud I saw Carrie's anxious face leaning over me, heard her saying,

"Oh, Ma'am, poor dear Miss Kate. Don't 'ee take on so. Doctor be comin'—Jem be gone after him. Do 'ee lie still, Miss Kate dear and 'ee'll soon feel better."

From time to time Mrs. Porritt was beside me too, holding the basin, wiping my face and hands with a cool lavender-scented cloth. And at last Dr. Laker came. His quiet voice soothed me, his hands were gentle as he examined me. I was given something to drink and as I swallowed it I heard myself saying,

"The wine—it was bitter." And then I slept.

It must have been hours later that I woke. Suddenly and with my brain very clear. A voice inside me seemed to say,

"You have been poisoned. *Someone is trying to poison you.*"

I lay very still. The sense of nausea was gone, if only temporarily. My only feeling was one of enormous physical lassitude, but my brain was active and alert.

Dr. Laker had spoken of food poisoning the first time I had been taken ill. Yet no one else at the dinner party had suffered in a similar way. Only I, who had drunk the bitter wine.

The wine that Bryce had brought to me. My stepmother had poured it out. Someone had added something to it.

Bryce?

I turned my head on the pillow in an agony of doubt. Not Bryce. Never Bryce. Why should *he* wish to harm me? He loved me.

No, that was not true. He no longer felt about me as he had done. He had as much as told me so. He tolerated me only as the mother of his child.

Did he then wish me gone out of his life? He would marry again, someone who would love him as he had demanded that I should.

But—to *kill* me?

It was unbelievable. I could not credit my own crazy suspicions and I fought against the black horror of it all. Not Bryce, I thought. Not *Bryce.*

But it was Bryce who had insisted I should drive the barouche when I had intended to ride Sorrel.

My thoughts kept coming back in cool and logical argument. Three times now I had been as near death as anyone could be. The broken barouche had proved no more than a bad accident, but these last two terrifying ordeals were lethal in their menace. They were weakening my entire constitution. I knew that from the digestive disturbance that lingered on after the actual pain and sickness were

283

gone. This time I would feel even weaker and recovery would take longer.

Until it happened again? I shivered, aware of a fear deep within me and as my hand moved to my throat I felt the thin gold chain of the amulet.

What was it Zena had said? "If ever you are in danger hold it between your fingers and think of the one you love."

I held it so, gazing down at the strange carving upon the green surface of the stone. Whom did I love? Luke I loved beyond anyone in the world, but I sensed that Zena meant a different love to that for one's child. Esmond? My feeling for Esmond was changed. I would always be fond of him but he was no longer the man I loved beyond all others. In my blind stupidity I had imagined myself beginning to care for Bryce. What utter folly. He was my enemy. He wished me dead.

I started up as the door opened and he came slowly into the room. I thought he must see the terror in my eyes, and I put my hand over my forehead as if to hide myself from his gaze.

"Are you feeling better, my poor Kate?"

"Yes—yes, I have slept for a long time." I hoped my voice sounded normal.

"Thank God. This has been a dreadful experience for you—for us all. I cannot imagine what can be the cause of these attacks."

"What does Dr. Laker say?" I whispered.

Bryce frowned.

"He has said very little. I think he is as baffled as we all are."

I forced myself to look at him. He seemed the same as ever; cool and polite, quietly impassive, a man in command of himself. And yet —there was another side to him. I had seen it. He could be fierce and passionate, even violent. And completely ruthless.

"You are to stay in bed for the time being. Dr. Laker is coming again tomorrow. You are to have nothing to eat—only fluids to drink. And the medicine he has left you."

I shivered. How would I know in which glass the poison might be administered?

284

"Lie back and rest," Bryce said. He turned away from the bed. "I will send Carrie up to you later."

"Thank you." I lay back on the pillow with eyes closed. Somehow I must get away from Tregedon, taking Luke with me. Could I make my father the excuse? Meanwhile I must be very careful of what I ate and drank—I would eat only the same food as the other inmates of the household ate. That would be difficult, lying up here alone in the bedroom. Somehow I must get downstairs again as soon as possible.

I felt as if I was living in a nightmare, as if everything around me was strange and unreal. I did not know what was going to happen next.

But there was no return of the sickness. For a few days I was very weak and ill and then gradually I felt stronger. I was in a state of constant vigilance, watching every mouthful I ate, being careful to only take items of food I had seen Bryce help himself to. If he was not there to do so, I left the food, pleading lack of appetite and later I would go into the kitchen and ask Mrs. Porritt to prepare some simple dish for me, saying that I fancied such and such a thing. More than once she looked surprised, but she put it down to the vagaries of my illness and willingly coddled me a fresh egg or fried me a slice of fish or made me a pasty.

Two weeks went by. Sometimes the sense of dread faded from me. Life around me seemed normal and ordinary enough. And then I would wake in the night and listen to Bryce's calm breathing at my side and the deeper murmur of the sea far below the house and I would remember. *Someone wanted me to die.* Who could that someone be but Bryce? I fought against the idea of it but the shadow of fear remained with me. I decided that the following week I would drive over with Luke to Penvarrion and make the excuse to stay there at least for a time. In July I would be twenty-one and come into my inheritance. Would it be possible for me to take Luke and go away from Cornwall, perhaps to London for surely Bryce would not follow me there?

Lying in the great four-poster bed, awake and fearful, I wondered why he should wish me dead. Because he wanted to marry again? Or because he hoped to inherit my money. But if I died before I was twenty-one, the estate went to my father. And if my father died, he would leave his money to my stepmother, perhaps something in trust for Luke. If it were true that Bryce had made these attempts upon my life, it could not be for reasons of financial gain or he would have waited until I was *over* twenty-one and had come into the Belle Tout Estate.

Such thoughts and fears churned around in my mind until sleep became impossible. Sometimes I thought I would go mad with the puzzle of it all. And in the morning I felt so weary and drained of energy that when Bryce saw my pale face and shadowed eyes he would enquire kindly after my well being and I would look at him and wonder how I came to hold such fevered imaginings. Perhaps, after all, I had simply eaten something that had upset me.

Two days before I intended to go to Penvarrion, my stepmother and Amy paid an unexpected visit to us. They came so seldom to Tregedon that when I heard the sound of a carriage in the courtyard and going to the window saw the coachman assisting them to alight, I could hardly believe my eyes.

A moment later Mrs. Porritt bustled in, bobbing and curtseying,

" 'Tis visitors, Ma'am. Mrs. Carew and Lady Borleigh to see 'ee."

I went forward to greet them and when they were seated my stepmother said,

"Amy and I were taking a drive and it was such a beautiful day we decided to come as far as Tregedon." She glanced intently at me. "Especially as we had heard from Mrs. Pleydell that you had not been well again, Katherine. I am sorry to hear that. I hope you are feeling better now."

"Thank you, Stepmother, I am quite recovered. I—I seem to be prone to these upsets. But I am well again and, indeed, was intending to come to Penvarrion and see my father. How is he?"

She shrugged and sighed.

"Much the same. Borlase brings him downstairs in this fine weather and he sits in the garden for a while, but he soon tires."

I glanced at Amy who looked surprisingly well and pretty in a dress of blue sprigged muslin with a bonnet trimmed with matching blue ribbons.

"I need not enquire after you, Amy. I am happy to see you so blooming."

Amy smiled.

"Thank you." She glanced appraisingly around the room. "You have made several improvements here, Kate. Have you furnished it afresh?"

"No, only new curtains and new rugs. Oh, and the arm chair is a recent purchase. I am sorry Bryce is not at home today. He has gone to Wadebridge market." Then I added, "Esmond did not come with you today?"

"No. Like Bryce, he had business to do. Oh." Amy broke off as Yerko suddenly appeared at the open window. For a moment he stayed there, staring around with his shining yellow eyes, then to my surprise he sprang down into the room and stalking toward me jumped onto my lap.

"Yerko!" I smoothed the gleaming black fur. "What are you doing here? He usually runs away when we have visitors," I added.

Yerko turned around on my knee and fixed me with his gaze and opening his mouth gave a harsh cry almost as if he were trying to tell me something.

"What is it, Yerko? Are you thirsty—do you want some milk?"

He cried out again in a strange way, his yellow eyes glaring at me.

Amy shuddered.

"What a fierce-looking cat—and what an extraordinary name. Yerko! I have never heard it before."

"It is Romany," I answered. "Yerko belonged to Bryce's grandmother. He came to live with us when she—died."

"Wasn't she the gypsy woman?" Amy asked. "I have heard of her."

"She was a beautiful and kind woman who was my friend," I answered stiffly. I was about the change the subject when Yerko turned and leaped from my knee. He darted in one sinuous movement across the floor and in doing so passed close to the chair in which my step-

287

mother sat. She drew in her skirts to avoid contact with him and flicked a hand at him.

"Go away—shoo—shoo!"

The sudden movement must have frightened him for he arched his back and put out a warning paw. My stepmother raised her hand as if to hit him, but before she could do so Yerko, quick as lightning, unsheathed his claws and caught the back of her thumb in a thin scratch.

"Oh. Oh, you wicked cat! Go away—go away, you spiteful thing."

But Yerko had already disappeared, a streak of black fur gone through the window the way he had come, even before I had crossed to my stepmother's side.

"I am so sorry. It is not like Yerko to scratch anyone. He must have been frightened." I bent over her, mopping at the few beads of blood. "I will ring for Minna to bring water and a cloth with which to bathe your hand."

My stepmother shook her head angrily.

"There is no need. It is only a surface mark, but you should not have such a disagreeable animal about with people. He might easily scratch Luke and hurt him—had you thought of that?"

"Oh, he would never do that," I said quickly. "He is a gentle creature in the ordinary way, for all his fierce looks."

Minna came in answer to the bell and brought warm water and a towel and the scratch which had already stopped bleeding, was wiped clean. Afterward Minna carried in a tray of tea for us and the incident was soon forgotten.

But my stepmother seemed unusually restless. From time to time she glanced at me, but when I caught her eye she looked quickly away. She stared about the room, her fingers tapping the arm of the chair. Her manner surprised me for she was invariably composed. I wondered if Yerko's misbehavior had upset her, yet there was scarcely a mark on her thumb to show damage, only a faint line where the skin had been broken.

When we had finished the tea she fanned herself with a handkerchief and said abruptly,

"How singularly warm it is today for the time of year. Do you not find it so, Katherine? You look pale and drawn. Perhaps a little walk would do us both good."

"If you would care to go into the garden," I began diffidently. "But it is a poor place—nothing much grows here—the winds are too salt laden."

"I should prefer to stroll upon the cliff—you have very fine views."

Amy stood up.

"Yes, let us go out for a walk."

My stepmother turned sharply.

"No, Amy, not you. I think you should sit quietly here. You have missed your afternoon rest today."

Amy pouted.

"Oh, Mama, I should like to come with you and Kate."

"No, dear, I do not advise it." My stepmother shook her head firmly. "You must take that little extra care now, you know, and not become overtired. And it may be windy on the cliff—you would not like that."

Amy glanced toward the window.

"No. I do not want to be blown about wearing my new bonnet."

"Of course not. Sit here for a little while with Luke for company. We shall not be long, and then you will be refreshed for the drive home."

"Will you not stay to dinner?" I asked. "We dine soon after five."

"Thank you, Katherine, but we must not stay overlong. Your dear father, you know. Now, Amy, lie back in the chair and close your eyes for a few moments. It will do you good to relax."

I was surprised to find myself walking out with my stepmother and equally surprised that she should want my company. We walked away from the house and the barns and took one of the many paths which led through the gorse toward the cliffs overlooking the cove.

It was a beautiful day, the summer world blue and gold about us. Tregedon, usually so cold and forbidding a place, for once looked almost homelike in the sunshine. The gorse smelt honey-sweet, a myriad of small brown bees hummed among its yellow blossom. Soon we were out of sight of the house and before us was the sea, a deep dark blue shot with brilliant kingfisher lights where lurked the treacherous rocks. The headland was a fresh bright green, a herd of Bryce's Frisians scattered about the steep slopes. A curious sadness came over me. Soon I should be gone from here, and as if to fill me with a regret I had never expected to feel, Tregedon showed me the only aspect of beauty I had ever known.

I glanced at my stepmother and noticed that she was in the same agitated state as earlier, her hands clasping and unclasping, a frown on her face, her under lip caught between her teeth. I wondered what she would say if I told her I planned to come and stay at Penvarrion; that I sought to run away from a husband who threatened my life. Would she be horrified, would she offer me sanctuary? But I knew I could never confide in her, or speak to her of my fears of Bryce.

I broke the silence by saying,

"I hope you feel better for the air, Stepmother."

I had to repeat the question before she turned to look at me, her eyes gleaming from under the brim of her bonnet.

"The air? Oh, yes. It has refreshed me considerably."

Her glance wandered past me, taking in the view, the steep headland encircling the cove where a fissure of cruel black rock drove into the land. She said slowly, almost thoughtfully, "This is a lonely place. There is no house here but Tregedon?"

"No—we are very remote. The village lies inland, beyond those far fields."

She nodded and walked on. I walked in silence beside her. She paused again, staring about her in the same curiously appraising way, as if she was observing something of special interest. I went to the edge of the cliff and gazed down at the sea. The tide was coming in, a strong blue swell that rolled in toward the foot on the cliffs and then fell back, breaking in white waves against the rocks. The strange pyramid shaped stones, like jagged teeth were not yet covered. Soon they would lie a hidden menace to those who were not aware of their presence.

I turned to make a comment to my stepmother and was startled to find her standing so close behind me that I fell back a step. Her voice came to me, quiet, almost whispering,

"Take care, Katherine. You are very near the edge."

"Yes." My feet slid on the grass, warm and slippery with the sun. I moved, and as I did so my stepmother caught hold of my arm. I thought she was trying to pull me to safety, away from the cliff edge, but to my amazement, when I attempted to go forward her grip prevented me. She had come so close that I felt her breath warm upon my cheek, the pressure of her body heavy against mine.

I cried in sudden alarm.

"Please let go of me. We are both dangerously near the edge of the cliff."

"Are you afraid, Katherine? See—I am holding you. Like this?" and with a sudden jerk she lifted my arm into mid-air. I was thrown off balance and would have fallen if the viselike grip on my arm had not held me fast. I thought my stepmother must have taken leave of her senses. She stared at me in so strange a way, her eyes glittering under her bonnet, her thin mouth set rigidly.

I tried to drag my arm free and for a few seconds we struggled together. I was tall and stronger than she was, and I still could not believe that she meant me serious harm but only intended to frighten me for some macabre purpose of her own.

Suddenly the fearful realization came to me that I was fighting for my life. The cliff top sloped and we were alarmingly near the edge. Although I was really taller than my stepmother, because the ground fell away I was now standing a foot or so below her and she had a leverage upon me. Slowly, inexorably, despite my desperate attempts to push her off she forced me to my knees. She had managed to twist my arm painfully behind my back so that I had only one free one with which to combat her. I struck out at her legs, at her feet, but it was useless. I fell down, my knees slipping on the treacherous grass, and the next second I felt myself go over the edge of the cliff.

With every instinct of self-preservation I clutched at the tussock grass, the clumps of gorse, the stones and rock. My fingers gripped and slid, then gripped again. I gasped a plea to my stepmother.

"What are you doing? Please—please help me. I shall fall—I shall be killed."

She bent over me. Her bonnet had fallen off in the struggle, her face was white, witchlike under the wisps of russet hair. She said in a choking voice,

"Yes—you will be killed. It is better this way—poison is too uncertain and leaves traces. I could not give you enough in the powders which I changed."

Panting with the effort of holding onto the grassy verge I stared up at her, aghast.

"You—you tried to poison me? You tried to kill me before? But *why?*" My voice broke on a sob of despair. "What have I done that you should hate me so?"

She shook her head.

"It is the money. The inheritance that will come to your father, if you die before your birthday. It is needed for Amy. I wanted Amy to be rich, but Esmond deceived her." Her voice rose scornfully. "He is poor and in debt and will remain so, like his father. Amy must be protected. I shall see to that. Your father may die any day—so you must die first."

I took a fresh grip on the grass and struggled to drag myself up and back onto the cliff.

"You are mad. They will find out—Bryce will discover that you tried to kill me—" I broke off. *Bryce,* I thought and even in the midst of my terror, relief flowed through me like a balm. Bryce had not done those dreadful things to me after all. He had never intended to harm me.

My stepmother leaned over me, hissing like a snake.

"I shall run back to the house in a little while and tell them what has happened. That you went too near the cliff edge and fell over and I tried to save you but I could not. They will believe me, for what will they find afterward but your drowned body?" She put a hand out as if to push me over but I reached up and seized her wrist.

*"No!* No, Stepmother. Help me back. Please help me. I will forget what you have done—I will keep silent—oh!" I broke off with a sharp cry as, with her free hand, my stepmother picked up a stone and crashed it down on my fingers grasping the edge of the cliff.

292

For a moment I swung in space held only by my grip on her wrist, and then, as with cruel strength she prized open my grasp I fell.

Down—down—down. Past grass and gorse and bush and rock. Catching, clutching, slithering, tumbling, I pitched past the face of the cliff and went crashing into the sea, far below.

# 22

DOWN—down—down. Gasping, choking, coughing; drowning in the deep waves that closed over my head. I could not breathe, could not see; was only aware of a nebulous darkness, of the watery grave into which I was sinking. I had heard that when people drowned their whole life flashed past them in those last moments. As I felt the life ebb out of me my last thoughts were of Luke and my undying love for him.

"Luke! God keep you, my little Luke," I cried deep within me.

The force of the fall had so stunned me that I had no strength to swim, but surfacing for the third time I made a desperate attempt to keep afloat. I was almost too weak to lift my arms. I made a weak flailing movement and for a moment was suspended on the waves. The tide, coming in faster now but still with a smooth swell lifted me gently, rocking me upon its vast bosom. Fortunately, I was wearing a dress of thin poplin and only my slippers on my feet so that I was not dragged down by the weight of heavy clothing. I felt choked and sick with sea water and I coughed to clear my lungs, lying back on the waves while I husbanded my reserves.

But the sea, rolling in with slow powerful surge, was carrying me nearer and nearer to the cliffs and the fearsome rocks. I was too faint to swim in any chosen direction and must allow myself to be taken with the tide. There was no shore as such at Tregedon cove, nothing but huge slate slabs and granite. Had I escaped drowning only to be dashed to pieces on the rocks?

I turned over and paddled feebly, like a dog. Ahead of me was the cliff, steep and black in its own shadow, impossible to climb, even if

I had found a footage upon it. I wondered if my stepmother was looking down at me, watching me drift helplessly toward the death she had planned.

I could do no more. In a moment or two I would sink under the waves or be shattered against the rocks. I closed my eyes and the swell of the sea, stronger and more powerful than ever lifted me up as if to hurl me against the cliff. As I came close to the black rocks the waves broke over my head in a rush of water that all but submerged me. Instinctively my hands clutched the air and to my amazement I felt a jagged edge of rock beneath my grasp. I held onto it. The swelling tide receded and I was left stranded upon a narrow ledge set in the face of the cliff, slimy with sea water, but for that moment a haven from the rising tide.

I lay gasping and breathless, staring around through painful salt-filled eyes. The ledge was just wide enough to hold me safe until the next wave should come and seize me in its hungry embrace. I looked around and saw behind me a slight recession in the cliff face. The opening to a cave? I pushed myself against it. The aperture was filled with rock and piled-up sand. Feverishly I dug with my hands to try to make a groove into which I could huddle, a groove deep enough to shelter from the incoming sea. But how far did the tide rise? If it came above the level of the archway in which I crouched, it would carry me off the ledge back into the waves.

I scrabbled again and some of the sand fell away and revealed a deeper fissure of space. As I scooped and dug at the rubble and sand the opening gradually widened. A rush of water behind me encircled my feet and then receded. Next time it would rise higher. And higher.

The opening widened still further—I could see a space of shadowy gloom beyond. Desperately I pushed and squeezed and by a miracle, forced an entry through a mass of wet sand and the next moment I was inside the cave.

For cave it was indeed. The roof rose above my head with the arched grandeur of a cathedral. It was too dark to see properly, but as I staggered forward across ridges of sand I felt the floor of the cave rise with every step, and for this I was thankful. If the sea came above the opening and penetrated the cave perhaps the rear of it, hidden in shadow, would still provide sanctuary?

It smelled queer and musty and unpleasant. I felt my way, stumbling over what felt like loose stones and rubble. I heard the waves thunder onto the ledge and shivered, knowing how narrowly I had escaped them. A flurry of water seeped through the opening I had made and I staggered still farther up the slope to where a patch of watery light showed. The sound of the sea rose even nearer, and to my horror I saw that the reflection of light came from a hole in the floor of the cave and that below me, foaming and boiling, was a whirlpool of water. The sea came in *under* the *cave.*

I gasped, watching spouts of foaming waves rise up into what appeared to be a narrow chimney formed in the rock. I turned terrified at an even greater noise behind me. The incoming tide, flinging itself onto the ledge as if in anger at my escape, had brought down another fall of sand and rubble. In doing so it closed the opening I had made. I was trapped inside the cave.

I sank down onto the ground, almost fainting with fear, and dropping my face into my trembling hands, I wept with despair. For a long time I lay there exhausted while my clothes dried on my stiff and aching body. I must have slept. When I woke the cave was in complete darkness except for a glimmer of light coming from the mouth of the chimney under its ledge of overhanging rock. The sea was quieter now, as if the fury of the incoming tide was spent and it was on the ebb.

I rested my back against the rock wall, lifting my loosened hair from my shoulders and suddenly I felt the chain with the talisman about my neck. As I fingered it, I thought of Bryce.

How cruelly I had misjudged him. He had never meant me harm. I knew that now. It was my stepmother who had planned the dangers that had beset me. Even the accident to the carriage must have been her doing. I frowned, remembering how, that day at Penvarrion, she had disappeared into the grounds and come in late for luncheon, how tense and nervous she had seemed on her return. She must have gone to the stables and somehow cut the leather traces.

I shivered. I would never know. I would die here in this cave from which there was no escape.

But was I certain of that? Perhaps there was some other means of exit. I had not had the strength to find out as yet.

Slowly, painfully, I dragged myself upright. Looking toward the circle of light I took a few uncertain steps and nearly fell over something that rolled away under my feet. I wondered what it might be. It was long and smooth, hard to the touch and cool. My fingers felt a curiously formed protuberance at one end.

"Oh God!" Shivering, I threw it from me for with a sense of horror I realized what the object was. It was a bone. A large bone, as if of a human limb. A leg or arm bone.

*I was in the Doom Cave.*

I should have known. The entrance blocked with sand and rock, the graveyard smell of it. What I had thought of as stones or rubble under my feet had been, in reality, *bones;* the bones of the seven men who had died here.

I could have screamed in terror, seeing in my mind's eye the gray sea-wracked corpses which had lain here and slowly crumbled into dusty skeletons. But instead of screaming I heard myself laugh aloud, a harsh unreal sound that broke the silence of the cave. What am I afraid of, I thought hysterically? I am in good company. Soon I shall join them, poor doomed fellows. Their ghosts cannot hurt me now, they may prove less dangerous to me than the living.

My overwrought nerves steadied, and I found myself praying for the poor men who had died in the cave and for myself too, that however hopeless the prospect, I might be rescued. Or if that was not to be, that God would give me strength to die alone, without fear. I prayed for little Luke, and for my father. And I prayed for Bryce. I prayed that he would forgive me in his thoughts and remember me with kindness. I knew, now it was too late, that I loved him.

Afterward I felt calmer. Stepping carefully over the scattered bones I made my way toward the patch of light. It gleamed in a curious way and when nervously I leaned over the ledge, I saw that the waves below were still now and silvered with light, as if somewhere not far distant the moon was shining.

Would someone be out at sea, I wondered? Looking for me or perhaps searching for my body? Some fisherman might be near enough to hear me if I called. Leaning over as far as I dared I shouted repeatedly,

"Help! Help! is someone there? Help me please. Help!" I cried until I was hoarse, pausing at intervals to rest my voice and listen for an answer, but none came. There was no sound save the soft ebbing of the tide through the channel under the cave.

I stared despairingly down the funnel-like opening. It was steep and narrow, and fell fifty feet or more to the sea below. The sides shone wet and slippery, there seemed no possibility of being able to climb down. And even if I had been able to, what chance would I have of reaching the open sea? The channel under the cliff was filled with water—could I swim through it? I shivered, knowing I would never dare.

Moving away from the opening I tried to explore the back of the cave, but it was too dark to see anything clearly. The cave rose steeply, I dragged myself up the slope on my hands and knees only to find an impasse, for I all but cracked my head on the roof which came down in tiers of roughly layered granite to meet the rising ground.

Breathless and panting I slid back again and keeping well away from the dangerous orifice, I lay down, abandoning all hope of escape.

I was cold and weary. Hungry, too, for it was many hours since the struggle on the cliff edge. I shuddered, remembering the fiendish look upon my stepmother's face as she slowly forced me to my knees and then, when I had tried to fight back, had crushed my fingers with a stone. The sea water had cleansed the bleeding cuts, so that although my hand felt stiff and painful, it appeared to be remarkably healed.

The fingers of my uninjured hand moved instinctively to the amulet and I thought again of Bryce, and the times we had been together came back to me. The meetings in my childhood and our encounter in the churchyard the day of my father's return from Barbados. The Midsummer Night when, so recklessly and so passionately I had given myself to him in the despairing hope of forgetting Esmond. The time he had sought me out and asked me to marry him and I had answered him with such cruel scorn. And then I had been forced to abase myself and beg that *he* would marry *me*.

Our wedding night and the shipwreck. And later the birth of Luke. Bryce had been wonderful to me then; strong yet tender, a man to lean upon. And afterward—

Tears filled my eyes as I remembered the night he had taken me by force, the shame and the humiliation of it all. And next morning he had gone away, cold and proud and uncaring.

I fell asleep thinking of Bryce's return after Zena's death. I woke with a start at the sound of my name.

"*Kate—Kate—Kate.*" A chill of fear went through me. The Doom Voice, I thought. It is the Doom Voice calling me. And then I thought "But I am in the Doom Cave. Why should the dead call me now? I am here with them."

I was cold and dazed and light-headed with hunger. My brain was not clear. But suddenly the cloud lifted and I staggered to my feet and went stumbling toward the opening above the sea. My heart was beating so fast it felt like a drum against my side. I knelt down and looked over the edge and heard the voice come again.

"Kate—Kate! Where are you, Kate?"

It wasn't possible. I must be still dreaming. The voice that called to me could not be Bryce's.

I swallowed on a dry throat and shouted back as loudly as I could,

"I am here. Bryce—*Bryce!* I am here—here in the cave."

The shadowy light of dawn showed me a figure standing waist high in water. Wet black hair framed the face gazing up at me from so far below. *It was Bryce.*

I heard myself sob his name and heard him call back,

"I am coming to rescue you, Kate. Don't be afraid. I shall get you out of there."

I could not imagine how it could be done but I believed him. I leaned dangerously over the ledge, staring down the narrow aperture. The width of the funnel could not have been much more than four feet. Like a long dark flue it fell from the floor of the cave to the sea at its base. Suddenly the circle of light was gone and I could no longer see the pool of gray water. With a shock of fear, I realized that the bulk of Bryce's body had filled up the space of the chimney. He was endeavoring to climb up to me.

I put my hand to my lips to silence the cry that rose to them. How could Bryce clamber up those steep and slippery sides where there appeared to be no possible foothold? At any moment he might fall and be injured or killed.

I leaned over as far as I dared but I could see nothing, only hear a scraping scratching sound, a sigh of effort; the grinding intake of breath when Bryce paused to rest.

During one of these pauses I ventured to call down to him, "Are you safe, Bryce? For God's sake, take care."

He answered tersely as if he husbanded every breath.

"All goes well. Do not worry, Kate. It is only a matter of time."

I sank back on my heels, my hands clasped tightly beneath my chin in prayer. "Please God, help Bryce. Save us both."

The grinding grating sound grew louder, nearer. From time to time I heard a fall of rock, the clatter of stones, then Bryce's panting gasps, the almost grunting sound of his breathing as slowly, and with tremendous exertion, he struggled up the narrow chimney.

I leaned over the ledge again and gave a cry for now I could see him. His powerful shoulders were braced against one side of the funnel while against the other were planted his feet. His arms were spread out an either side of him ready to grasp at any projection or hold they could find. Levering himself up first with his back and shoulders and next with his booted feet and all the time using his hands to maintain pressure and balance he had all but succeeded in climbing the long dark chimney.

He was nearing the ledge now which overhung the opening. I lay down on my front and reached my hands out to give him all the help I could in his last dangerous effort.

Our fingers touched. With both hands I seized his wrist and held onto it. His other hand came out to grasp the ledge. For one breathless moment he hung in space as his feet slid away from the face of the rock. Then, slowly, with every bit of help I could give him, he

300

clambered over the edge onto the floor of the cave and lay there, spent and gasping.

I put my arms about his shoulders. He turned his panting sweating face into my breast and one hand reached for mine. I did not speak, and Bryce could not. We could only stay close to one another while tears of joy and relief ran down my cheeks.

After a while he recovered. He sat up and took me into his arms.

"My dearest—my own beloved Kate, thank God you are alive. I thought I had lost you." His mouth came down on mine and he kissed me.

His lips tasted of salt, there was dust and grit on his mouth, his arms in the sodden shirt were wet about my body but I did not care. It was the sweetest most thrilling kiss of my life, the most wonderful embrace. I knew then that I loved Bryce and that he loved me. We were together. He had risked his life to find me, and if in the end we had to die here in the cave, I would not care. Except for darling Luke. For his sake we must try and escape.

Bryce kissed me as if he would never stop, but suddenly he released me and undoing a leather bag, which I now saw was strapped about his waist, he took out a whistle. He smiled as he leaned toward the rock opening and putting the whistle to his lips blew three sharp blasts and after a short pause blew three more. And faintly, from far away, came three answering pipes.

"That was to let Josh know I had found you. At the next low tide he will be waiting with the boat to take us back to the cove."

I stared.

"You—you knew I was here?"

"I *hoped* you were here," he answered gravely. "I thought I heard your voice calling. All yesterday I—we, were searching for you. I could not imagine how you might have got in here—I climbed up to the mouth of the cave, but it was blocked. Yet it looked different from when I had last seen it—there seemed to be fresh sand and I wondered if it were possible that you had been taken in there by the tide and become imprisoned."

"That is what happened," I said and began to recount all that had taken place.

301

His face darkened and his arms came tight about me when I spoke of my stepmother and her attack upon me. He interrupted to say,

"That vile woman. I returned from Wadebridge not long before she came running in from the cliff—all moans and tears and cries over what she termed 'A terrible accident.' At once we formed a search party. Jem went to fetch some fishermen to help look. Josh and I took the boat. But there was no sign of you. The tide was full —a high tide and I dreaded that you had gone down into the sea and would be carried along the coast at the turn."

I frowned.

"The tide was coming in, but it was not at full height. She—my stepmother must have waited on the cliff some while to make sure no one would rescue me."

"It was near six when I returned from Wadebridge—that was the time she came running back. I remember Amy's alarm and anxiety that her mother should be so long out walking. They left for Penvarrion straightaway for they could be of no help in the search." Bryce's jaw set grimly as he added,

"She will be brought to justice. I shall see to that. She is little less than a murderess."

"No—my father—it would kill him," I cried.

"He need never know the truth. Your stepmother will be taken away and he will forget about her. She cannot go free after such fiendish actions. Those poisonings—you might have died under them." He put his hand into the haversack and pulled out a stout rope.

"Before we can do anything we must get out of here. Rescue will not be possible before low tide when we have to pass through the gully under the cliff. It is always water-filled, but for a short while when the tide is at its lowest ebb it is possible to wade through, though the waves will be waist high. On the other side of the opening the sea is deeper but Josh will be there with the boat. We arranged this—that if I blew six blasts on the whistle he would know that I had found you."

I stared in wonderment at him.

302

"The chimney—how were you able to climb it as you did? Had you attempted this before?"

"Only once, when I was young. Another boy and I came exploring after we had heard the fishermen speak of this place. We did not get to the cave—we were frightened of what we would find here I think. People said it was haunted. But I remembered it and knew that if you were here, I would surely get to you." He paused and drew me even closer to him. "At least, I should if the weather remained calm, which thank God, it has done. If the sea had been rough, there would have been no hope at all of getting through the passage—you could have been here days, perhaps to starve and die." He shuddered. "God—when I think of it."

For a moment we clung to one another, and then I said slowly, with a glance toward the opening,

"Will we ever manage to climb down?"

He released me and started to unwind the rope he had taken out of the haversack.

"I shall fix the end of this to one of those projections over there—and lower you down tied to the rope. Then follow after you. Don't look like that, Kate. You will be safe, I promise you." He smiled reassuringly. "Do you think I have succeeded in getting this far and do not intend to complete my mission?"

I shook my head.

"No. I am safe with you, Bryce. I always have been. I realize that now."

He caught my hands in his.

"If you only knew how much I have loved you, always and always. There has never been anyone but you, Kate. Never since you were—how old? Nine—ten?"

I looked down at the hands holding mine, and then I looked up at him.

"I thought sometimes you hated me."

"It was never hate I felt for you. Anger, hurt and jealousy, yes. Those emotions burned in me like a fire, but only because I loved you desperately and could not possess you as I desired. Perhaps love

303

and hate become mixed up one with the other when people are unhappy."

"Yes." I thought of Zena's words—how the day Bryce had first taken me to meet her she had said that joy and sorrow were as a two-sided coin and one was the face of the other. So it had been with Bryce and myself, in our love.

I turned to him.

"I love you, Bryce. I think I have loved you for a long while and did not know it."

His arms came about me and through the gloom he gazed at me.

"And Esmond?"

"Esmond was my youth—part of the old life at Penvarrion. That is gone now, forever."

He kissed me slowly and tenderly and then he kissed me with a greater intensity. And as I responded to his kisses a passion of loving surged through us so that we were swept away on its tide. Far below us the sea roared in at full flood. I heard its echoing boom and then I was conscious only of Bryce, his lips on mine and his arms about me. Strangely, unbelievably, in the gloom and darkness of the Doom Cave, we came together, as once before in the moonlit woods. Among the dusty bones of the dead we found ourselves and were born again.

Afterward we lay close and peaceful, sleeping for a time and after that, eating some of the provisions Bryce had brought with him, and sharing a small flask of brandy. We talked quietly together; there was so much to say and yet, little to explain. The past was over and done with.

It did not seem long to wait for the next low tide, but it was actually noon of the following day before we could chance our escape from the cave. Bryce lowered me carefully down on the rope and followed after me, and then we had to brave the gully under the rock. I was very frightened. Bryce plunged into the tossing waves and the darkness, carrying me close in his arms, and as I clung to him I tried not to think of the great rocks above our heads. And then, miraculously, we were through and found Josh and Jem waiting in the boat to lift us to safety.

At Tregedon there were tears of rejoicing from Carrie and Mrs.

Porritt and Minna, while I hugged Luke in my arms and kissed him and hugged him again until he protested and demanded to be put down and went scampering away into the sunshine after Yerko.

The day after my ordeal and immersion in the sea I suffered a severe reaction and felt very ill. Bryce called in Dr. Laker who prescribed complete quiet and rest in bed for a few days, and at first I all but slept the clock around.

When at the end of the week I was recovered, it was to learn that my stepmother had been taken seriously ill and her life feared for. It was thought she had caught the dreaded lockjaw infection from the scratch administered by Yerko.

I felt duty bound to go over to Penvarrion to comfort my father and Amy, who of course, was entirely ignorant of her mother's attempt upon my life, but I was filled with apprehension at the thought of being taken to see my stepmother. How could I face her after all that had happened?

But my fears were needless. She was in a delirium and knew no one, and within hours of our arrival at Penvarrion, after much cruel suffering, she died. I could not help but be sorry for the unhappy woman.

We were all anxious for Amy in her pregnant state, for she had been devoted to her mother. But she rallied amazingly. Lady Borleigh and her companion came to stay at Penvarrion for a few weeks, and although Amy had not been overly attached to her mother-in-law, the old lady's kindness and gentle companionship seemed to fill the gap in her life. Esmond cherished her in every way he could, and within a few months Amy gave birth to a daughter. She was a delicate little girl, as pretty as her mother, and she grew up to resemble Amy in every respect.

Not long after this my father died and perhaps it was a merciful thing, but I was sad and grieved after him for a long time. In his will he left a sum of money to Amy, which enabled her and Esmond to go back to live at Borleigh Hall. Here she gave birth the following year to a son, which delighted Esmond. He and Amy seemed happy enough, but Esmond continued to spend a great deal of time away from his home.

Penvarrion was left to me, but much as I loved it, I did not wish to live there. It held too many shadows from the past. Eventually, Laura and Paul bought it, and that pleased me greatly. We visited them often, and our four children played with their five and grew up with them.

Yes, Bryce and I had four children. Matthew was born the following year and two daughters followed in quick succession. Isabella was tall and beautiful like my mother, but Zena was small and slim with black hair and slanting dark eyes.

When I came into my inheritance some of the money was spent on Tregedon, making many improvements so that it would be a comfortable home for our children. Money was spent on the farm too, adding to the stock and bringing everything up-to-date so that in time it became one of the best-equipped and most successfully run farms in Cornwall despite its wild and remote situation. It became a happy place, too, filled with laughter and with love. Oliver often visited us there. He became a famous naval commander and married a beautiful girl who gave him six children.

Sometimes when the winter storms rage over the old house and I hear the sea's deep roar I wake and remember the cave and for a moment am afraid again. But when Bryce draws me into his arms I forget those terrible days and am happy and secure in his love, for with every year that we live together, we grow closer to one another.

Yerko survived to be over twenty years old, a massive black statue sitting by the fireside. I would look at him and find his yellow eyes staring at me with so wise and yet inscrutable an expression in their gleaming depth that I felt he knew more than he could ever tell.

The amulet I have treasured all my life. To whom shall I leave it? I wonder. And I think, *Zena*. It shall belong to Zena, for it is in her that I see something of the strange and beautiful gypsy woman who was Bryce's grandmother and who loved him so dearly.